danger ous DNA

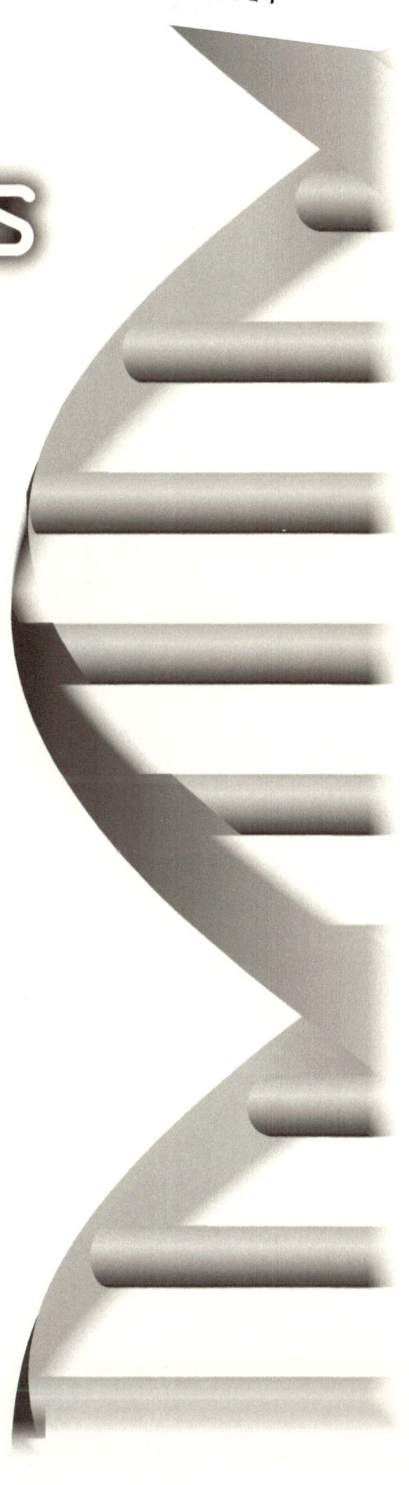

danger
ous
DNA

DAN REYNOLDS

RNR Publishing Company
Omaha, Nebraska

LCCN: 2009925443
Library of Congress Cataloging information
on file with publisher.

ISBN13: 978-0-9824125-2-7
ISBN10: 0-9824125-2-5

RNR Publishing Company
12335 Decatur Street
Omaha, NE 68154
www.RNRPublishingCo.com

Printed in the United States of America
10 9 8 7 6 5 4 3 2 1

ACKNOWLEDGMENTS

I WOULD LIKE TO THANK THE FOLLOWING PEOPLE who have helped me during the process of writing this book. For her unwavering support, I would like to thank my wife, Pat. Her encouragement has been a great blessing to me. I especially appreciate the many times she did double duty with our children, or absolved me of my chores so that I could achieve my goals.

I would also like to thank my children, who have had to share my time with a personal computer. I hope they realize that anything is possible, especially when you find something in life you are passionate about.

A special thanks to my friend Sandra Wendel, a talented editor who gave me rock solid advice, and sent me a key press release I incorporated into the story. I am lucky to have such friends.

For her expertise and keen business sense, I would like to thank Lisa Pelto, of Concierge Marketing. She knows this business like no other, and from the book cover to the interior layout, she and her team were instrumental helping me pull everything together.

Eugene (Bud) Hartlaub is an acquaintance turned friend. Without his help, this train may never have left the station.

Thank you to Mike Smart, an attorney and life-long friend, and Phil Huston, a retired cop, who advised me in the ways of courtroom practices, and police protocol.

1

STANDING AT HER TELLER WINDOW, CHRISTINE Turille saw him stride into Boatman's Bank. He was tall and blonde, wearing an expensive-looking business suit. Christine made eye contact with him, hoping this handsome man would choose her window. It worked.

She didn't notice the 9mm pistol until he stepped to the window. He raised the gun above her head in a single fluid motion and pulled the trigger. She couldn't hear her own scream over the explosion of sound echoing through the lobby. There was commotion. What exactly, she couldn't tell. Christine stood frozen, the whites of her eyes enormous as he passed a canvas bag to her. The gun was now perfectly aimed at her forehead. Somewhere in her wildly scattered thoughts, it occurred to her that the man was giving the bank's security cameras a perfect view of his face, as though he were posing. Why wasn't he wearing a mask? Did he want to be caught?

"Empty your register—NOW!" he said, his eyes on fire.

"Yes, sir," Christine obeyed without hesitation. She stuffed paper currency in the bag and tried to hand it back to him. He didn't take it.

"Have the others do the same!"

Taking a step toward the next teller, Christine almost tripped over her own feet. Recovering quickly, she assumed her position at the window. Now all she had to do was to keep her composure and wait for each of the other three tellers to comply with his demand. She realized that something else was bothering her.

This man looks more like a bank president than a thief.

Expressions of terror ravaged the faces of her fellow tellers. One by one they emptied their cash drawers. Watching their erratic movements made her realize the importance of staying calm. She drew a deep breath and hoped one of them would follow bank procedure. Christine was simply too close to the gunman to shove a dye pack in the bag or press the silent alarm. She focused on steady breathing. As she waited, her gaze shifted back to the man with the gun.

Originally preoccupied with only the cameras, the man began to alternate glances between the cameras and the main clock. Christine was young, but well trained. Even though it was easier to watch her co-workers, she decided to use the gunman's distracted condition as an opportunity to memorize his features for the police report. This meant she had to look toward the barrel of his gun, only a few feet away. Her eyes reluctantly ticked toward him like the second hand of a clock. He was long-legged, about six foot four, with platinum blonde hair and electric blue eyes. The mid-thirties figure was slender, which profoundly contrasted with his broad shoulders. His navy pinstriped suit looked expensive and impeccably tailored. His face was lean, his smooth skin deeply tanned.

He's gorgeous, she thought, almost forgetting about the gun.

The gunman shifted his eyes toward the camera once more. Christine noticed a monogram on the sleeve of his fine broadcloth shirt. Below his initials the cuff was blood stained.

Jeanine, the last teller, finished emptying her drawer. Like an anchor in a relay race, she wasted no time getting back to Christine. En route, she managed to flick her eyes to the right. Her eyes lingered on the bullet hole in the gray sky of the cheap oil painting on the back wall.

Her face filled with dread. With a pleading, almost apologetic whisper, she struggled to warn her friend. "Be careful, Christine."

Christine took the bag and set it on the counter. Her hands flanked each side of it with her palms face down and fingers spread apart in plain sight. The gunman didn't respond. Her jittery eyes moved about the lobby to catch a glimpse of the bank's customers. She could read the horror in their faces. Some of them were lying or crouching on the floor, exposed targets if things got out of hand. Others had found the shelter of a desk or structural pillar. A mother was lying on the floor, patting her little girl's back. Christine glimpsed a man peering through the doors of the vestibule with a cell phone to his ear.

The handsome gunman stood silent. He had yet to make a move for the money. His left hand was still outstretched, zeroed in on Christine's forehead. Only moments ago, Christine Turille was afraid for her life, but after studying the man's odd behavior, she had an unexplainable feeling she was not in the slightest danger. With soulful eyes, she picked up the bag and held it out, "Here's the money, sir."

The man seemed almost annoyed at her boldness. His ongoing glance at the clock made her inclined to think that he was anything but ready to leave, but why?

Shouldn't he be making his escape?

He hesitated a few more seconds, and then lowered the gun and approached the window. His left arm brushed against the counter. The monogram on his shirt; ZJW, was now close enough for Christine to make a mental note. The man tried to grasp the bag by the tie strings, but it slipped through his fingers. Christine gave him an inquisitive look. Flustered, his cheeks turned red. It appeared as though he had to concentrate to pick up the bag with his right hand. When he finally grasped it, he backed away from the counter. His monogrammed cuff had left an imprint of blood on the counter's edge.

"Everyone stay down, and you won't get hurt!" the gunman shouted. Christine believed him, and although she knew it was wrong, she found herself hoping the handsome young man would escape. He turned and moved to the exit, still grappling with the bag in his right hand. He finally slipped the gun in his pocket and carried the bag in his other hand.

Once outside, the noon sun lit the blonde man's hair to a brilliant white. Squinting, he slowly turned 360 degrees, searching for bystanders, witnesses, and signs of the police. From the crest of a hill up the street, he could see a squad car approaching. Tucking his head down, he dashed across a four-lane street with incredible speed and sprinted toward the Bannister Mall.

Officer Jacobs slowed the cruiser as he encountered a man waving him down at the curb. Pointing across the street he screamed, "The robber—he took off toward the mall! Blonde hair—navy pinstripe suit—he's running across the parking lot."

"Is anyone hurt?" the officer shouted.

"No," the bystander continued stabbing his finger in the direction of the mall, "but that guy's getting away!"

From a distance Jacobs had seen the blonde-haired man dart across the street, but his first instinct had been to secure the bank. The man in the suit simply didn't strike him as an armed robber, but spurred into action by the bystander, he made an instant U-turn and swerved to miss an oncoming car. Taking a quick right, he squealed into the mall's parking lot. He took another right turn and as he headed for the center access drive, he radioed the gunman's description and direction of travel. Once on it, he spotted the suspect quickly closing the gap to the mall's main entrance.

The cruiser's throaty engine growled, and in seconds Jacobs found himself at a four-way stop at the front end of the parking lot. Even though the cruiser's lights were flashing, shoppers in cars continued to nudge their way across the intersection.

Stupid people, he thought, *I'll have to get out here.*

The blonde gunman crossed his path about twenty-five yards ahead as the stocky officer shifted his vehicle into Park and took off on foot.

He's got too much of a head start. I'll lose him in the mall for sure.

Jacob's short legs labored as he chased the agile thief toward the entrance. He thought he heard the faint sound of sirens in the background as he pushed through the atrium's first glass door. He withdrew his .40 caliber Glock. Instinctively his thumb released the safety.

He could be halfway across the mall, he thought. Jacobs squeezed the talk button on the police radio attached at the collar of his uniform, "This is District 351—the bank robbery suspect is in the Bannister Mall on Hillcrest and Bannister Road. The suspect entered from the northwest door. He is six-foot two or three, medium build, blonde hair, and wearing a navy blue suit. Suspect is assumed to be armed."

Peering through the second glass door, the officer wiped sweat diagonally across his forehead and over his crew cut. The main corridor was crowded with shoppers. He entered cautiously, his eyes scanning the scene for signs of commotion. There was none.

Officer Jacobs was biting his cheek so hard he could already taste the blood. His heart pounded heavily, rapidly. As he made his way deeper into the mall, he shouted repeatedly to shoppers, "Have you seen a blonde man in a suit run through here?"

A smartly dressed woman came running toward him pointing a thumb over her shoulder, "He's in my store—over there!"

Jacobs motioned the woman to come to him and then turned to face the corridor. He waved his arms wildly at the gawking shoppers. "Get back—everyone! This man is armed and dangerous! Stay back! Clear the area!" He locked eyes with a middle-aged man and pointed, "Get to the other side of that store. Don't let anyone come this direction!" The man took off, stopping when he reached the far side of the store. Jacobs's tone of voice was all business. Studying the well-dressed woman who had run to him, he asked, "Who are you?"

"I'm Anna Caldwell," she replied. "I'm the store manager of Maxine's."

"Is anyone else in the store?" Jacobs's voice had begun to sound monotone, like Jack Webb, the TV actor from the '50s series, *Dragnet.*

"No," the woman said, "he screamed at us to get out. We saw his gun and ran."

Jacobs pressed the police radio talk button and updated his status. "This is District 351—the bank robbery suspect is in Maxine's Women's Wear, in the Bannister Mall—awaiting backup!" The radio squawked with a feminine, but tinny sounding voice confirming that help was already on the way.

Suddenly, he heard a shot fired. It came from within Maxine's. He quickly grabbed the store manager and pulled her to her knees behind a small jewelry kiosk in the mall's main corridor. Another shot rang out. He told the woman inside the booth to lie flat on the floor. Jacobs trained his gun on one of the store entrances and waited.

To Jacobs, the next few minutes seemed like an eternity. The man he had instructed to keep shoppers away from Maxine's was keeping them back. Most had darted away when he told them about the gunman, but a group of teens watched from a distance. Soon other officers joined Jacobs outside Maxine's. "He can't escape," Anna said. "There are two front doors but none in the rear."

Jacobs spied more officers moving along a wall, crouching as they ran. His sergeant arrived with them carrying a loudspeaker and extra protective gear. Everyone froze when they heard a third shot.

After a short briefing from Jacobs, Sergeant Morris called into the store, "This is the police. There is no way out. Put your weapon down and come out with your hands above your head." He repeated the warning a minute later and then again. "We're going to have to rush him," Sergeant Morris said. "Without a rear exit, he hasn't got a chance.

"Everyone wearing a vest?" the sergeant yelled. Satisfied that his men were all wearing protective vests, Morris gave the order.

"Jacobs—you and Miller take the lead." A team of uniformed officers stormed into Maxine's. They knocked down rows of clothes on racks as they made their way to the back of the store. When they arrived at the fitting rooms, two of the doors were closed. From beneath the eighteen-inch gap, they could see a woman's figure sprawled on the floor. The other room appeared empty. With his heart thumping, Jacobs swung the first door open. It banged against the wall and bounced back shut. Empty! With gun extended, Miller gently pushed the other door open to reveal an elderly woman unconscious on the floor. Beside her there was a canvas bag, a hand gun, and something else that confused him—a man's navy pinstriped suit.

2

DETECTIVE JOHN DIETRICH EXTENDED HIS HEAD above a ceiling panel and into the shallow space above the women's fitting rooms at Maxine's.

This is ridiculous, he thought. *This case is going to be as impossible to solve as the others. No escape route—no clues—no freaking explanation whatsoever. This guy simply disappeared.*

He looked over his shoulder and yelled to the others below, "He didn't escape through the ceiling. In fact, he never even tried." Pocketing his flashlight, he ducked, slid the ceiling panel back in place, and climbed down the ladder. "There's absolutely no room to maneuver up there. The concrete above the suspended ceiling offers nothing to hold on to, and the panels themselves wouldn't hold the weight of a small child let alone a full grown man. From the looks of it, he figured that out quickly."

"Maybe he moved that panel to throw us off, you know, delay us," a voice added.

John glanced at his new partner, Braxton Willis, "Is that what you think, Kid?"

Braxton's eyes narrowed, "I'm trying to agree with you, you ol' fart! If you'd listen long enough, you'd know it. I agree. No one could have escaped above the suspended ceiling."

John smiled at the retort. He wasn't that old. At forty-eight he had only recently discovered his first strand of gray hair. Still, there were a good twenty years between him and the young man he saw silhouetted against a backdrop of tawdry women's negligees in Maxine's.

John approached Braxton with a measured grin and rolled his eyes, "I'm sorry, Braxton, I know you don't like being referred to as *kid,* but I'm having a helluva time remembering your name—at least when I need it quickly."

"Well, perhaps calling you 'ol fart' for a while will jog your memory."

Dietrich laughed, "All right, I'll try not to call you kid any more, but I just can't get used to your name. Is there something else I can call you?"

"My friends call me Brax."

"That's no help, Dietrich teased.

Ignoring the annoyed expression on his junior partner's face, Dietrich got back to business. "All right, Braxton, let's review what we've got so far. We've got eight eyewitnesses who say the bank robber came into this store, right?"

"Right."

"We have the blue pinstripe suit, shirt, and shoes supposedly worn by the perpetrator, right?"

"Right."

"We recovered the money in a blood stained-bag, right?"

"Right."

"We've got a 9mm gun, the casings and slugs used to shoot out the video cameras, and Jaworski is dusting for prints. Seeing that our brilliant friends in blue decided it was such a good idea to knock all the clothes racks over, let's get out of here and let forensics sweep the store. Can you tell me what we are still missing?"

Braxton had just made detective, but he thought Dietrich's endless string of test questions were sometimes a little rudimentary and patronizing, not to mention monotonous. Braxton knew his answer would pacify his senior partner, at least for the moment.

"You mean besides the suspect?" He grinned. "I guess you'd be looking for the store's video surveillance tape."

"Atta' boy, Braxton. Let's go pick it up and head for the hospital."

Braxton gave John a sideways look. "What's at the hospital?"

Pulling a small spiral notepad out of his hip pocket, John raised it to eye level and read. "Let's see, an Officer Jacobs took the old lady to the hospital to have her checked out. I called ahead and asked him to detain her for questioning."

"Couldn't we just catch up with her at home?" Braxton asked.

"Maybe," John said, "but I don't want to take any chances. Jacobs said she had no identification, and the store manager doesn't remember seeing her come in. She claims everyone got out."

The video tape was waiting for them at the mall's central surveillance room. They thanked the security guard and promptly headed for North Kansas City Hospital. Twenty minutes later the detectives were asking the Emergency Room receptionist where they could find Officer Jacobs.

"He's in examination room three with Dr. Hoody," she said, looking at the clock.

The examination room door was closed. Braxton began to open it, but John caught his arm. "Knock first, Braxton." Braxton's cheeks reddened a little. In the three short weeks they had been paired together, John felt like he was teaching his young partner more than just how to be a good detective. He was coaching him on etiquette as well.

A woman's voice responded briskly to the knock, "Come in."

John immediately sensed that something was wrong. A mature female doctor was applying ointment to the top of a balding man's head. He wore a white coat identical to hers.

Is this guy a doctor? If so, I sure hope he wears pants when he sees patients, John mused. John wasn't sure, but it looked as if the balding man was naked beneath the white coat. A uniformed officer stood a few feet away holding a pen and a clipboard. He was probably filling out a report. Most police officers used every spare minute to do their paperwork.

"Officer Jacobs?" John asked. The stocky, young officer already had his eyes trained on John. He raised his eyebrows and then his chin.

"I'm Detective Dietrich; this is my partner, Detective Willis. We're here to interview the elderly woman you found unconscious at Maxine's."

Jacobs took a deep breath. Before he spoke a word his pink cheeks gave way to a complete look of embarrassment. "I'm sorry guys, the old lady's gone." He shifted his gaze to the floor, "She got away."

John's expression was one of disbelief. *You've got to be kidding,* he thought.

"How did she get away?" John asked. "And why would she want to?"

"I—I don't know, exactly," Jacobs replied. "She asked to be alone with Dr. Hoody. I didn't see it as a problem, but she clubbed him over the head and stole his clothes. The sergeant's gonna kill me when he find's out."

Braxton Willis took a step closer to Dr. Hoody. Studying the wound on top of his head, he asked, "How many stitches?"

"Seven."

"Were you unconscious?"

"Out like a light," Hoody said in disgust.

The boy has potential, John thought. He's trying to gauge the strength of the old lady, if it was even a female that hit him.

Braxton looked to John for approval.

"Keep going Kid, you're doing fine."

3

ON THE DRIVE BACK TO THE DEPARTMENT, BRAXTON noticed something unusual. Silence. John was obviously deep in thought, probably trying to make sense of this bizarre case. A sideways glance at John revealed a frown, something Braxton had never seen him wear. The image was unsettling. He almost blurted out some small talk, but something made him hesitate a few moments before breaking the silence. John seemed more troubled than Braxton deemed befitting of the situation.

John works difficult cases every day. Why is this one any more upsetting than the other cases of late? The old lady ran away? So what? She probably didn't want to be examined by some strange doctor with cold hands. What's the big deal? Why is he so concerned?

Finally, the silence was growing uncomfortable. Braxton decided to be direct.

"Something is bothering you, John. You always get quiet when something is bothering you."

John shot his partner a glance, "You know me that well in three weeks, do you?"

"I hardly know you at all, John, but I know this—you're rarely quiet. You're usually calling ahead to someone on the phone, telling them we're on the way to pick something up, or calling in a favor from someone in the department. Jesus, does everybody owe you a favor?"

John pondered a moment, "Probably—yes—I guess so." Smiling with intensity, he cocked his head and glanced in the rear view mirror.

"I know how pompous that must sound. Listen, Braxton, life as a detective isn't much different than life as a politician, or a salesman, or anything else, for that matter. You need friends, acquaintances, and strong relationships to help you get things done quickly and effectively. Yeah, I do a lot of favors for people, but I get a lot back in return."

"Is that why you burn the midnight oil every night? Doing your favors after hours?"

"Mostly—I sure as hell don't have time to do them during the day."

"It must be pretty hard on your family life."

Braxton thought he detected the faintest glint of sadness in John's expression; another first. John usually wore a perpetual smile. It was only slight, and nothing his peers would describe as deliberate. John's smile was something that you felt more than noticed and it exemplified a man of good nature and disposition. His massive six foot four frame was misleading. At first glance, John looked like he could clear a bad-tempered biker bar of its seedy clientele without breaking a sweat, but John was a teddy bear. His features weren't handsome, they hovered closer to average. His sandy brown hair was thick, and neatly combed, and his green eyes could only be described as friendly. Those eyes, warm and disarming, were his second greatest asset as a detective. His intellect was his first.

"I learned a long time ago, Kid; you can be a mediocre detective and have a great family life, or vice-versa."

"Don't get me wrong, John, but I think most people would choose the great family life. I know I would."

John nodded, "And I wouldn't think any less of you for it, Braxton. We all make our choices. But the things I do for this job, I am compelled to do. It's difficult at times, but my wife and daughter would expect no less of me. Speaking of family, aren't you proposing to your girlfriend this week?"

Braxton beamed, "Tonight's the night."

"And she'll accept?" John asked wryly.

Braxton formed a cocky smile that exposed perfect teeth. John couldn't tell if the smile was genuine or not. "Wouldn't any girl?"

John laughed a little louder than Braxton expected. It was a little grating. "I just thought of a nickname that'll help me remember your name: Brash Braxton. That's it—Brash Braxton!"

Braxton was not yet thirty. He was about six foot two, carried a medium build. The whites of his eyes and teeth contrasted sharply against his dark features and coal black hair. In their first week of working together, Braxton told John that his mother was Lebanese. His father, an alcoholic, left him and five siblings when he was only six years old. John had shared all of this with his wife, Cindy, along with his initial observations of the handsome young man. It wasn't often a detective got a new partner, and in John's twenty-two years, Braxton was his fourth. John surmised that a number of young ladies might be crushed to hear of his engagement. Despite Braxton's lack of refinement and impetuous tendencies, John liked him. Inexperience and bad habits aside, he told Cindy he believed in the kid's potential.

Braxton brushed John's ribbing aside. "You didn't answer my question, John—what's bothering you?"

John stared at the expanse of cars on the freeway. "This case is a lot like some of the others we've been working lately—lots of questions and no answers. Aren't you a little unnerved by the lack of clues at the scene?"

Braxton pondered the question, "What do you mean, lack of clues? What about the pile of clothes, the money, and the blood-stained shirt and bag?"

"Yes, John said, let's examine those for a moment. The bank teller said the perpetrator's sleeve was blood soaked, yet he didn't injure himself in the bank. That means he was already bleeding before he got there."

Braxton was trying to follow John's logic, "So?"

"Well," John continued, "we live in an age of forensic testing. He left quite a blood smear in plain view on the teller's counter. Even an uneducated thief might suspect we would collect the sample for DNA testing. They said this man appeared to be highly intelligent. He should have known better than to leave such evidence behind."

Braxton shrugged, "Who knows what goes through the criminal mind when he's in the middle of the act. Maybe he was too nervous to think clearly."

"Or maybe his thoughts were perfectly clear," John replied.

"Are you saying that this guy cut himself, that the blood smear was left behind intentionally?" Braxton asked.

"I can't say for certain, Kid, but the evidence at Maxine's seemed to have been 'neatly' laid out for us. Why didn't he try to hide the clothes and money? A ceiling tile was left ajar to delay us. If he really wanted the money, or if he really was concerned about leaving behind evidence, why didn't he hide everything above the ceiling and put the tile back in place?"

The thought had never occurred to Braxton. He was starting to feel a little like the novice detective he was.

"Other than the obvious evidence that was found next to the old lady, there are no other clues," John said. "How did this guy get away? Where did the old lady go? She must have wanted to avoid us pretty badly to hurt Dr. Hoody like that."

Braxton's teeth shone brightly, "Yeah, she really clubbed the poor guy pretty hard. You asked the doctor if he was sure she was a woman. You don't think that…"

"She was the robber?" John interrupted. "No, not at all—the witnesses all concur that the man was six feet three or four, about a foot taller than the old lady. But she may have been an accomplice."

Braxton suddenly felt uncomfortable. "What's funny is that a nurse thought she saw Dr. Hoody leave the building, yet no one noticed what happened to the little old lady."

John's voice sounded a little raw, "Now you're getting the picture, Junior."

A congested Kansas City rush hour delayed the detectives' arrival at the office by more than an hour. Willis was getting a little edgy. Every ten minutes or so, he would open a small box, study the contents for a few moments and then snap it shut.

"Still the same engagement ring in there, Brash?"

"Yup, still the same."

As they got out of the car, Braxton thought about the strange events of the day. "Tomorrow should be quite interesting," he said, matter-of-factly.

John arched his eyebrows, "What's so special about tomorrow?"

"Nothing really, it'll just be interesting to see the bank's video of the robbery, and the one from the women's clothing store."

We've got a half hour until our shift ends and in his mind, he's already clocked out, John thought. We'll have to work on that. I'll have reviewed all of the evidence before the kid even pops the question.

"The day's not over yet, Kid, we can watch a video or two before the shift ends." Braxton seemed not to hear John's comment. He continued, "You realize that video won't give you the slightest clue as to how he escaped, Brax. He shot the camera lenses out, remember?"

"Well at least we can see him enter the store, right?"

"Right," John agreed, "and just as important, we can see if the old lady entered the store." There was a big question mark on Braxton's face. It was like he didn't understand the implication of John's comment. John didn't look too surprised.

John stopped by Captain Walsh's office to drop off the videos from Maxine's and Boatman's Bank. Typically, a clip was sent to the television stations for broadcasting on the evening news. Walsh was just hanging up his phone when John stepped in the doorway brandishing his best smile. Mike Walsh was more than just John's Captain. He was one of his best friends as well. They spent more than ten years as partners before Walsh's promotion. John was considered for the promotion too, but he quickly withdrew from the competition, saying something about paperwork not being his cup of tea.

John's last partner, Rick Pettit, became a close friend too, even closer than Walsh. John suspected that Walsh's pairing him with Petit was a gift of sorts; a reward for being a loyal and supportive partner. Petit was astute, and John had learned a great deal from him, but six years was all they had together before he retired. John missed him terribly.

He wondered if he could ever teach Braxton as much as he'd learned from his old friend.

Walsh acknowledged John's entrance with a look of complete disdain. "I've already heard some of the details, John—sounds like we've got another bizarre case on our hands."

"You don't know the half of it, Mike. This guy ran into a womens' clothing store and just disappeared. There's no rear exit, no possible explanation as to how he escaped. Officers found an elderly woman unconscious in a fitting room. I went to the hospital to question her— she disappeared as well. Clubbed the doctor over the head and stole his clothes. But here's the kicker—not a single person saw her leave the hospital." Walsh's features hardened. John continued his report, "We found her dress on the exam room floor. It still has the price tag on it. It came from Maxine's."

Walsh did not take the news well. "See a pattern here, John?"

"Yeah, a pattern of insanity. I've got four cases just like this one on my desk. We haven't made the slightest bit of progress on any of them. What the hell is going on?"

"I don't know," Walsh said, "but speaking of those other four cases, why do you want them? Technically speaking, they belong to Detective Turley. You could have turned them over the minute he got back from vacation. He said you specifically asked if you could keep them. What gives? You hate petty cases like these."

John rocked back in his chair. It was true, he didn't typically work assault or rape cases, or petty theft for that matter, but then one day he found himself asking Turley to let him see these cases through to the end.

"I don't know. I suppose they all have a similarity to them. There's something whacky about the evidence. Some of it fits, and some of it doesn't. Anyway, they aren't huge cases so don't worry about them bogging me down. I just think it's weird how we got four of these in a row, five, if you count today's robbery."

"Regarding this robbery, the mayor wants to meet with me tomorrow at ten. I'd like to have you there with me." John nodded absently. Walsh decided to drop the other shoe: "I got a call from the bank's president just after the robbery. He identified the gunman as Zachary Whittman. He banks there."

"Not very smart to rob your own bank, is it?" John said with a dash of sarcasm.

"You don't understand, John. Zach Whittman is worth about thirty million—he needs the paltry few thousand dollars he stole like he needs a hole in the head."

John sat down raking his fingers through his hair. "Bizarre doesn't even begin to describe this one, Mike."

"Whittman is also the mayor's buddy."

"Figures," John replied. "How much crazier could things get?"

Walsh figured he had John sufficiently off balance. Now was the best time to blurt it out.

"I sent Moody and Connors over to Whittman's office to find out where he lives. Maybe we can pick up his trail and find him quickly." John Dietrich was pretty even tempered, but Walsh noticed his hands clench to fists and his knuckles go white.

Compelled to explain, Walsh said, "You weren't around, John—I needed to send someone quickly."

"Just promise me you'll keep those clowns off this case and out of my hair."

"I don't want them on the case any more than you do, but we're getting awfully short handed. I figured I'd have them do some of your legwork—that's all."

"If it were anyone else, I wouldn't blink an eye, but Moody and Connors?"

"Did I hear someone mention my name?"

Justin Moody stepped into Walsh's office and proceeded to the corner of his desk, "Got good news, Captain. Tom and I brought you a little gift."

John's eyes narrowed.

This ought'a be good.

"We picked up Zach Whittman. Can ya' believe it? The son of a bitch was sitting at his office desk like nothing happened. Tom's got him in detention."

John whisked himself out of Walsh's office. Moody had seen that look on his face before. He raced downstairs to tell Connors that Dietrich was on his way. John snagged Braxton from his desk. "Come on, Kid, we gotta go!"

Seeing the look on John's face, Braxton cut his phone call short.

"Gotta run, babe; see you in a little while."

Jogging to catch up with his middle-aged partner, he asked, "What's up, John?"

"The man who robbed the bank—he's a multi-millionaire, and he's waiting for us in detention."

"Holy shit—you're serious, aren't you?"

"Serious as a heart attack, lover boy. Moody and Connors picked him up at his office just minutes ago. Let's get down there before those two screw something up!"

4

TO TOM CONNORS, ZACH WHITTMAN MORE CLOSELY resembled a California surfer than the CEO of a three hundred million dollar corporation, but once the young man began to speak, his subtle intellect emerged quickly.

"Detective Connors, you rousted me from my office and prevented me from attending a meeting it took me months to procure. You have no idea what damage you've caused. Aside from the sheer embarrassment of being arrested, I left the CEO of the largest genetic research company in the world sitting alone in my conference room."

"That's unfortunate, Mr. Whittman," Connors said with a smug smile, "but I'm afraid we've got a whole lot of questions to ask you. For instance—"

A deep sober voice interrupted, "I'll take it from here, Tom."

Connors pivoted a half turn in his chair. He grimaced at the figure leaning in the doorway.

Dietrich. Shit. I knew he'd waste no time getting here.

"Look, John, it's only fair, I brought him in, so—"

"So nothing, Tom, it's my case. You and Justin please excuse yourselves from the room."

Justin didn't seem too upset. He had barely returned from Captain Walsh's office with the news that they had apprehended Whittman. He pushed his chair back, ready to leave quietly. Seething with anger, Tom Connors stood up and walked to the door, followed closely by his buffoon partner. He paused to give John a look of pure disgust.

"What—the great John Dietrich doesn't have enough high profile cases to crack?" Connors lowered his voice, "From what I hear, you ain't making much progress lately. Losing your touch?"

John looked Connors in the eyes, unshaken by the comment. "Did you advise the suspect of his rights, Tom?"

"What do ya think I am—a novice?"

"Is that a yes?" John asked with a polite smile.

Connors's eyes became slits. "Yeah, I read him his rights."

"And did you order a gunshot residue test?" Connors face lost all expression.

John raised his eyebrows, "You do know the robbery suspect fired a gun several times this afternoon, right?" Connors's ears turned two shades darker than his pink cheeks. He fidgeted with a legal pad. "I would'a got to it, John. I—I just haven't gotten to it yet."

John gave Braxton a sideways glance and then returned his attention to Connors. "Well, thanks for the assist, Tom. I'll be sure to let you in on the details as soon as the case is closed." Connors tried to remain stone faced, but Braxton could see that John's retort landed hard. Braxton snickered, something he regretted as soon as Connors eyes met his. Connors directed his attention back to John, who didn't seem overly concerned to see that he'd sucked in his gut and puffed out his chest. John seemed to hardly notice when Connors left the room.

Turning to the handsome blonde suspect, John continued. "My apologies, Mr. Whittman. I am Detective Dietrich. This is my partner, Detective Willis. We're going to do everything we can to help you, but this is a difficult situation. Do you want to call your attorney?"

Whittman appeared dumbfounded. He also seemed genuinely appalled. "I don't know—do I?"

"When you see the evidence, I think you'll want him here."

"You really are serious, aren't you? About the robbery, I mean—you really think I robbed a bank?"

John tried not to upset him. "I can't say, Mr. Whittman. I haven't had time to view the videos yet, but from what I have been told, if it wasn't you, it was certainly someone who looked a lot like you. We have a video from the bank and another from Maxine's Women's Wear. In addition, one of the bank's vice-presidents gave us a positive ID." Dietrich's voice grew soft, "I probably should mention we have gathered quite a bit of DNA evidence from the crime scene."

Whittman perked up and exhaled as if he were relieved, "Fine, gentlemen. Get your forensic people down here and swab my mouth. If the DNA doesn't match, I'm off the hook, correct?"

"There is still a matter of the videos."

"Listen here, Mr.–"

"Dietrich."

"Yes—Mr. Dietrich. I know more about DNA than any ten of your high school detectives combined. The evidence it presents is irrefutable. It is absolute, uncontestable, and unquestionable. If the DNA isn't mine—and it won't be, it belongs to a look-alike. I demand that you perform the test immediately."

As John listened to Whittman speak, he suspected that it was his intention to sound like an aristocrat. He chose his words carefully and spoke in long sentences.

Probably graduated from an Ivy-League school, John thought, turning to his partner. "Listen, Kid—run upstairs and grab Jaworski. Tell him we need a saliva swab and a gunshot residue test. If he's not back yet, get Hamiid." Braxton looked at his watch and frowned, and then started for the door. Halfway there, he stopped and turned.

"It's Braxton, John—my name is Braxton."

"Oh, right, Kid, and grab the VCR cart on your way back."

Dietrich had a few minutes to kill and thought he would make small talk. It sometimes proved a beneficial tactic to put a suspect in a false comfort zone.

"My Captain tells me you were featured in KC Magazine as the most eligible bachelor in the city. That's quite a distinction, Mr. Whittman."

"Yes, that and three dollars will get me a cup of coffee."

Dietrich chuckled, "Twenty-five years ago, I used to use that expression a lot, Mr. Whittman, but it went like this: 'That and a dime will get me a cup of coffee.'" Whittman just stared at him. John sighed and continued, "What's the name of your company?"

"Critical Strategies Genetics Research Laboratories. The name says it all."

Good God! It takes a half hour just to spit it out, John thought.

"I know little, if anything about genetics, Mr. Whittman, therefore, the meaning is not so obvious to me."

The expression on the young CEO's face clearly showed his disapproval that Detective Dietrich had never heard of his company, but then again, he was only a detective. Whittman looked determined to educate him.

"Our company is on the cusp of making great scientific discoveries. Now that the human genome has been fully mapped, startling new cures are on the way. Soon every illness the world has ever known will be a thing of the past. My company is in the business of cheating death, Detective. But disease is only half of the equation. Old age is the other foe we are battling. The human heart is only good for generating a predetermined number of heartbeats. The exact number is determined by your heredity and is ingrained in your DNA from the moment of conception—well, that and your current state of health, of course. But if we can manufacture a new heart when necessary, think about the number of lives we can save. If we can clone replacement organs using your own DNA in the recipe, the results would be astounding. Just imagine if the human body never rejected a heart, liver, or lung, or any biological tissue for that matter. Transplant surgery is about to become child's play."

Dietrich was truly impressed with Whitman's speech, although he sometimes felt these researchers were playing God. But ethics aside, how could anyone argue against saving millions of lives?

"Are you saying you can clone a single organ, Mr. Whittman?"

"Why not?" Whittman answered most seriously. "We have already cloned entire living creatures, why not just the parts we need? I know that what I am about to say will sound insane, but I believe that within the next twenty years, we will clone new organs and limbs within the host, completely eliminating the need for surgery."

"You are absolutely right, Mr. Whittman."

"About what?"

"That does sound insane."

Zachary Whittman managed a dull smile, "Consider this, Detective. Most of the medical and technological achievements made during the last two decades sounded insane, right up to the point of discovery. Advances in science have increased exponentially in the last several years, and in the field of biotechnology, things are about to explode. If all goes well, we may figure out how to clone our entire bodies every two years or so in a process called 'regeneration.' We may be able to freeze a man's aging process at the peak of his physical and mental prowess and continuously regenerate his body parts."

"Forgive me for asking, Mr. Whittman, but aren't you talking about immortality?"

"Precisely, Detective Dietrich, precisely!"

The concept was difficult to embrace, but so was putting a man on the moon. Considering that man's moon walk was over thirty-five years ago, Whittman's point was beginning to grow teeth. John was suddenly overwhelmed by a genuine sense of awe for Whittman and his research company. Although Whittman seemed to be a little pompous, he did not appear to be irrational, dishonest, or secretive. In fact, he seemed to be forthcoming in every way.

"I don't ask this next question for the sake of satisfying my own curiosity, Mr. Whittman. The answer may indeed help your case."

"Ask away," the handsome blonde man said with confidence.

"It is my understanding that you have a net worth of around thirty million. Is that true?"

Whittman nodded, "Somewhere between thirty and forty. How will that help my case, Detective?"

Somehow, John figured this man knew his net worth to the dime.

"Motive," John said. "I can't imagine anyone robbing a bank for a few thousand dollars when he has access to that kind of money."

"I already told you, I was at my office all day today. Detective Connors arrived just before an important meeting, and suddenly I was told that I am suspected of robbing a bank. I can assure you I have been in my office preparing for this meeting all day, so please be so kind as to tell me where you got your misinformation, so I can rectify the situation. I can provide witnesses."

"I'm sure you can Mr. Whittman, but so can any man of wealth. But your willingness to submit a DNA sample goes a long way with me. I hope the test comes out in your favor."

"It will, Detective, it definitely will."

5

"I'D LIKE TO CALL MY ATTORNEY NOW, DETECTIVE." Whittman stared at the table blankly. John thought his eyes had glazed over. The timbre of his voice was noticeably different.

He's lost his confidence, John thought. *Can't say I blame him.*

It was after the fourth viewing of the Boatman's Bank videos, and about twenty minutes of shifting and twisting in his chair, that Whittman's deep tan seemed to fade away. During the first few minutes, Whittman appeared to be intrigued by his likeness.

"This man is an incredibly good impostor," he said. "The resemblance is uncanny." When he saw his likeness staring into the bank's camera, he leaned in toward the monitor as though he realized that no jury on earth would doubt the likeness was him. John studied Whittman carefully. His demeanor diminished from pompous to subdued as though he was convinced that he, too was looking at himself.

Whittman recognized the pinstriped, double-breasted suit. "An excellent knockoff," he pointed out. John mentioned the small blotch on the man's left sleeve.

"Anyone can have a cuff monogrammed," he said. A few minutes later Whittman perked up and mentioned what was missing. No watch, no ring. They were still on his wrist and finger. But it was obvious that he could have put them back on after the robbery. These facts would do nothing to sway a jury.

At one point Whittman spoke up vehemently. It was when the gunman faltered when trying to pick up the money bag.

"Look, there's something wrong with him! He's having trouble taking the bag from the teller!" Then he saw the other oddity. "He's left handed! He's holding the gun in his left hand! I'm right handed!" Whittman looked at the detectives for support. John and Braxton exchanged looks, saying nothing. Whittman's eyes resumed their hollowness.

John donned a pair of cotton gloves. Reaching into a plastic bag he produced a blue pinstriped, double-breasted suit.

"Ever seen this before?"

"It looks like the suit I keep at the office—you know, for unexpected meetings. What is the brand name on the label?

"It's an Armani."

Hearing the name of the exclusive brand, Whittman's head fell to his chest. The young CEO sat motionless, waiting to call his attorney. John shoved the suit back in the bag. Taking two giant strides, he placed his hand on Whittman's shoulder. His voice was at half volume.

"Mr. Whittman, we have no choice but to book you for armed robbery. But don't worry, your attorney can probably make bail in an hour."

"What about the DNA test? How soon can I get the results?"

"It depends on our workload. It could take a day or two. Detective Willis'll get you something to drink and stay with you 'til you reach your attorney."

"John, gotta minute?" Braxton interrupted, motioning John to the door.

"Be right back, Mr. Whittman."

John followed Braxton out of the room. John's grin was playful, "What's up, Brash Brax?"

"Normally I'd have no problem working overtime, but I'm running late for dinner. Did'ja forget? I'm proposing tonight."

John's face turned sour, "I could really use you tonight, Brax—" Then he recalled the comment Willis made earlier: *"Don't get me wrong, John, but I think most people would choose the great family life. I know I would."*

"—but you're right. Go to dinner—propose to your girlfriend. I'll see you tomorrow."

A smile washed over Braxton's face. John noticed and returned the smile.

"Thanks, John. See you in the morning."

6

BRAXTON WILLIS WASN'T A DETAIL-ORIENTED PERSON, but tonight he had carefully planned everything right down to the table he'd selected in the far corner of the restaurant. Gazing across the candle's flicker, he was hypnotized by Anne Duffy's emerald green eyes. She suspected nothing—or did she? Her flowing red hair shimmered. Her black dress was stunning, especially the way she filled it. The neckline came to a V and revealed just enough cleavage to be tastefully seductive. Braxton studied her creamy white skin as it reflected the candlelight. Her soft hand disappeared when he picked it up and held it between his own. He thought about the stark contrast others must see when observing them as a couple.

I wonder what our children will look like.

Anne Duffy provided more than just a physical contrast to Willis's tawny exterior. She came from a wealthy home and was educated in the finest schools. Both of her parents were prominent figures in the community. Willis thought their differences were sometimes daunting, but Anne never gave him a moment's doubt that they were meant to be together. Over time, she'd convinced Braxton how unimportant his social status was to her. She claimed that the fact his mother worked evenings as a casino blackjack dealer, and that Braxton had loaded UPS trucks at night to work his way through college, were endearing traits. His pay-as-you-go philosophy earned him a criminal justice degree with only a small accumulation of debt by the time he had graduated. He knew that Anne admired his determination to make his own way in life. She'd mentioned it often and sometimes wondered whether she would have turned out half as well growing up in similar surroundings.

Braxton advanced quickly from uniformed officer to detective, and he could tell that Anne genuinely enjoyed talking about his work, especially the most recent cases, which seemed to defy every law of logic and reason. Braxton easily accepted the fact that not every case could be solved, but he was too inexperienced to know just how unusual these cases were.

"You look stunning tonight, Anne. Don't think you've ever looked more beautiful."

"Flattery will get you everywhere, Braxton. Keep it up, and maybe I'll go home with you."

They laughed; it was nearly six months ago they had moved in together. "So—what's the occasion? It isn't every day we eat at a place like this. Did you get a promotion?"

"Tell you in a minute. But first, I took the liberty of ordering something special." Anne's puzzled expression delighted Braxton as he waved to the maître d', who moved swiftly to the table. He placed a serving platter in front of her and removed the polished warming cover with a flourish. Her full, pouty lips formed the most beautiful smile Braxton had ever seen. "Is it—?"

Braxton's teeth appeared to fluoresce as he reached for the black velvet box. He dropped to one knee so hard, Anne looked concerned that he'd hurt himself. He opened the box and turned it so she could see the dazzling stone. "Anne, will you do me the honor?"

"The honor of what?" she replied teasingly.

"Be my wife, Anne—be Mrs. Braxton Willis."

Anne leaned back, beaming, "Of course I will," she said. "Now come here."

Anne planted her lips firmly against his. Their tongues brushed momentarily and then she looked into his eyes. "I've been waiting for you all my life, Braxton." They kissed again, and then Braxton took his chair and moved it close beside her.

"Think your parents will approve?" he asked, absently looking over Anne's shoulder.

"Of course! They love you, Braxton—they just don't like us living together out of wedlock. When we tell them the news, they'll be just as excited as we are." Braxton nodded and forced a smile. Anne admired the ring as she adjusted it on her finger. "It's just beautiful, Braxton."

∞

Jesus, the trees have gotten huge, John thought, as his car snaked through his Olathe, Kansas, neighborhood. *They're so tall and lush, or maybe I'm just not used to seeing them in the daylight.* It was only six forty-five in the evening. John was rarely home before nine, often working until ten-thirty.

Maybe Cindy and I can catch a movie or something. We haven't done that in a long time.

As he pulled into the driveway, the lawn service was just loading a commercial riding mower into a pickup. He waved at the yard crew and then opened the garage door. A growing pile of junk and trash had overtaken most of the parking space. He frowned. *I need to do something about that. Maybe next week.* The thought was getting to be a daily ritual. He left the car in the driveway and closed the garage door behind him.

"Hey, who's the quilt for?" John asked, as he kissed his wife on the cheek. Cindy Dietrich pieced a square into the intricate design that covered most of the kitchen table. "I don't know. I just keep making them. I've got three in the closet."

"Wanna take a break and catch a movie?"

"Wait a minute—it's not even seven! What are you doing home?"

"Just worked out that way. Did you say yes to the movie?"

Craning her neck to meet John's gaze she answered, "Sounds lovely, but I'd rather go for a walk. It'll give us a chance to catch up."

"Okay, hun, but let me grab a sandwich. Then I'll have something to walk off." Fifteen minutes later, John and Cindy Dietrich were walking briskly in the neighborhood, talking as they always did whenever they got the chance.

"I was noticing the trees in the neighborhood, honey. It seems like they've doubled their size overnight."

"Well, I suppose, if you consider twenty years overnight."

"Jesus," John groaned, "Has it been that long?"

"Sarah was born in this house, remember? She's only got one more year of college."

"Then we'll be empty nesters," John joked.

Cindy frowned. Her tone was flat, "That's right, John, the nest will be empty. I mean, only Sarah and I have been occupying it anyway—your side of the nest has always been empty. Are you planning on coming home to roost?"

Recalling what Braxton had said about family life, John became a little guarded.

Sounds like someone had a bad day at work.

Cindy worked for Father Harry Quinn at St. Augustine's Church. She kept house and cooked for him three days a week. The pay was fair but the hours didn't satisfy her need to keep busy, so she volunteered two days a week to help with other church activities. Before she met John, Cindy had been a court stenographer. But a dozen years as a stay at home mother had dissolved that career. Cindy began volunteering to do charitable work at church, and when Fr. Harry's housekeeper became seriously ill, he offered Cindy the job.

John thought about Cindy's sarcastic remark, "Has it been all that bad?"

Cindy looked up at her husband of twenty-two years. Seeing his grimace, she put her arm around him and pulled him close. "You needn't feel wounded, John. I've gotten quite used to your late evenings. At least you've never made me sleep alone."

John's eyebrows furrowed, "Braxton is proposing to his girl tonight. He said something that made me feel like I put my work before my family. I was hoping to hear that I haven't totally ignored you."

Cindy's tone changed, "You know better than that, John. We've had to share you more than we'd like, but Sarah and I understand—we know what you do and how important it is that you do it. It's just that you're only a few years from retirement, and I get the feeling you're not ready for that yet."

John grew solemn. Cindy had him pegged. He dreaded retirement and was eligible in only two years. But there were too many crimes to solve, too many criminals on the streets, and too few good detectives to put them away.

The Dietrichs turned the corner, walking directly into the evening sun. John hadn't responded to Cindy's last comment. She waited a minute and then pressed him on the issue. "John? You still plan to retire, don't you?"

John's voice was stoic, "I promised I would, didn't I?"

Cindy stopped dead in her tracks. John took several more steps before he realized he was walking alone. He turned around, backtracked, and sought a glimpse of Cindy's face. He already figured he'd made a mistake.

"You haven't changed your mind—have you?" she asked.

"I can't make that kind of decision on my own, honey."

"But you do want to stay with the department, don't you?"

Cindy squinted in the sunlight. John moved closer to block the sun from her face. She looked up at him, and John could see that her eyes were welling, and her chin was quivering.

"Listen, honey," John said, "it doesn't matter what I want, I made a promise—I intend to keep it."

Cindy began walking again. Her pace picked up.

So much for our leisurely walk, John mused. The couple strode quietly for a few minutes. Finally Cindy stopped and spun around, squaring off with the man who towered far above her delicate frame.

"What's wrong, John? You've been moping around the house for a week now. What's going on?"

"I didn't realize I was such an open book," he replied. "Braxton's only known me for three weeks, and already he thinks he can sense when I'm upset."

"So, there *is* something wrong!"

"No, there's nothing wrong. Everything's fine."

"It's all those strange cases, isn't it?"

John put his arm around her, "C'mon, Dr. Phil, let's go home."

"You know that I know nothing about police work, John, but you always seem to come up with your best theories when you bounce them off someone. Why don't you tell me what's happening?"

"I can't."

"Why not?"

"Cause you'll think I'm crazy for what I'm thinking."

"I doubt that, honey."

This time, John stopped walking. His teeth were clenched, which made the muscles in his jaw protrude. "I'm not kidding, Cindy. If I tell you what I'm thinking, you'll believe I have a screw loose."

"I could never think that, John. Did Braxton think you had a screw loose?"

Teeth still clenched, John looked away. "I haven't discussed it with him."

Cindy's jaw dropped to half mast. John knew damn well she was looking at him with pity.

"Don't look at me like that!" he said. Cindy shook her head.

"What?"

"I don't need to be a detective to figure this out, John. No wonder you've been out of sorts. You've got theories you haven't shared with anyone—not even your partner. You and Braxton aren't quite clicking together yet, are you?"

"Do you always have to be right, Cindy?"

Her eyes softened, "No, but I usually am."

"Why'd Rick have to retire, anyway?"

"For God sakes, John, because he could. That's what people do—they work hard all their life, and if they're lucky, they get some time to enjoy a slice of it before they die. I want you to enjoy a few years too. Contrary to your inflated opinion, Kansas City will limp along fine without you."

John saw a rock on the sidewalk. He had a strong inclination to kick it. "Are we just gonna stand here in the middle of the sidewalk, or are we gonna go home?"

Cindy was beaming.

She won again, John thought. *I can just see myself sitting in a goddamned rocking chair.* They started walking again, Cindy's arm cinching John tightly against her.

"Why don't you call Rick tomorrow and tell him about these cases?"

"Can't do it, hun. He's not my partner anymore. Gotta work this out with Braxton. He's just not ready yet."

"Well, that leaves me darlin'. Let's go home and talk. I'll fix us a stiff drink."

"How 'bout I make us a couple stiff drinks and we go upstairs?"

"Oh no you don't. We can go upstairs, we can get naked too—but we're still gonna talk. Don't want you moping around any longer than necessary."

My stomach feels empty, John thought. *What the hell happened to that sandwich I ate?* The Dietrich's started for home. Later, in bed, John and Cindy talked for an hour and a half. Cindy never once doubted John's sanity, but after they made love, she didn't fall asleep for hours.

7

JOHN ARRIVED AT HIS OFFICE EARLIER THAN USUAL
to prepare some notes and review the evidence in the Whittman
case. Now in the conference room on the seventh floor of the Federal
Building, he was adding some scribbles on his notepad when Walsh
arrived with the mayor and police chief. Captain Walsh asked John
to attend the meeting for the same reason Mayor Chase asked Police
Chief Bergman. Each wanted a trusted ally in attendance.

"You remember Detective Dietrich, don't you, Mayor?" Walsh
asked, as John stood to shake the mayor's chubby hand.

"Sure do. You were involved in the McCormick case last year."

John broke into a satisfying smile, "You have a good memory, Mayor."

"I don't need a good memory for that. McCormick was a crazy man.
If you hadn't tracked him down, there's no telling how many other
children he'd have gotten to." Jason McCormick was a child molester.
He had kidnapped two children and murdered one of them. After
McCormick's capture, John had discovered a list of other children he

had planned to kidnap. The case earned John national recognition and the ability to be selective about the cases he worked.

"Walsh here tells me you're *flat-out* his best detective; maybe the best in the city."

John caught a glint of pride in Walsh's eyes.

"John's solved some of our most difficult cases, Mayor. He's without a doubt the right man for the cases we are discussing."

Cases? John thought. He cocked an eyebrow, wondering if the mayor had an interest in some of the other screwball cases he'd been working on. Walsh had only mentioned Whittman. The mayor eased his pudgy frame into a chair at the head of the table. His pear shape all but made the chair disappear. "Good, I need our best people on this—or I should say these cases?"

Mayor Chase paused and stroked his double chin, "Do you know why I asked you here, Detective Dietrich?"

"Not exactly," John confessed, "I assumed you wanted a progress report on Zach Whittman's case, but you just said 'cases.'"

The mayor forced a brief smile and then wiped his forehead with a handkerchief.

"Exactly. But before we get started I want to ask you to keep the details of these cases confidential, until I say otherwise."

The puzzled look on John's face prompted the mayor to continue. "Zach Whittman is a personal friend of mine. He is no more capable of robbing a bank than you or I. In addition, Stuart Grady is no rapist. I've known him for years. He's got seven children—six girls, for God's sake. He's a pillar in this community. Something strange is going on here, and I need your help to clear the reputations of these men, and quickly."

John thought about Stuart Grady, a prominent businessman accused of rape. Two weeks ago, Tara Regan, a young college student, was forced into a van in the parking lot of a Wal-Mart and brutally raped. The man who had followed the girl out of the store was caught on videotape. His photograph was aired on the morning news and within hours Grady was in custody. His fingerprints were all over the van and his semen provided an exact DNA match. But there were oddities, questions that troubled both Dietrich and Grady's attorney. The girl claimed to have scratched her assailant, drawing blood. Her actions earned her a severe beating, and although the blood was Grady's, there wasn't a scratch on his entire body; no place from which the blood would have originated. Nor was there the slightest evidence of the bruising or abrasions one might expect to find on the knuckles of a man who had just pummeled someone. Although traces of his DNA were on her, there was none of her DNA on him. These inconsistencies were beginning to cause John Dietrich to lose sleep.

The mayor continued, "I'm watching these cases closely, John. I've been informed that there is substantial evidence that could be used to convict these men of crimes I'm certain they didn't commit. I need to know where you're at in the investigation. I want to know everything you know. Show me the evidence that makes them innocent or guilty."

John gathered his thoughts and opened his notebook. In a steady tone of voice, he began methodically reviewing the evidence against Grady before proceeding with Whittman's case and then three others.

"You see, Mayor, Whittman said it himself, DNA evidence is simply irrefutable. It's even more incriminating than fingerprints. Yet there are so many things that just don't add up. I've got a five-pack of crimes that should be 'open and shut' cases, but they all smell funny."

"Give me an example," the mayor prodded.

"Motive, for one. In all five of these cases I have yet to uncover a single reason that would have driven any of these men to commit the crimes they're accused of. Your friend, Whittman, for instance; he's got millions. Why would he risk everything for a few thousand dollars?"

Mayor Chase sat silently. John could sense the mayor's struggle with the evidence in what he'd just nicknamed, the "five-pack of crimes."

He's got to accept the fact that his friends are facing certain conviction.

"Irrefutable DNA evidence, huh?" the mayor said. "Well, I don't believe it. There's gotta be a way to prove their innocence."

Something told John that outside forces were responsible for the crimes, but proving it would be difficult, if not impossible.

"You say you viewed the videos of Zach at the bank and the mall?"

"Yes."

"What's your professional opinion?"

John furrowed his brow and answered slowly, "I can't be certain, Mayor. We have some convincing video of Whittman. The man on tape looks just like him, yet I believe there's a real possibility he's an impostor."

Captain Walsh inhaled rather loudly. A split-second glance was all that was necessary for John to see his eyes bulging in their sockets.

The mayor continued, "Why do you believe that?"

"It's not just the discrepancies. In each case these men have rock solid alibis—witnesses who say they were with them at the time of the crime. My interviews have turned up nothing but support for them as good citizens. I find all of the suspects completely believable, but based on the evidence, there's no question they'll be convicted."

The mayor looked even more distraught. "So at this point, you've nothing more to go on than a hunch?"

Walsh interrupted, "Mayor, I've watched John follow his hunches for over twenty years. He's usually right about them. Unfortunately, in these cases, we may never be able to prove it."

"Well, somebody'd better prove it! If these men didn't commit the crimes—who did?"

John went quiet. He had some theories, but most were half developed, and some seemed crazy beyond belief. While shaving this morning, John found himself staring at his image and questioning his mental stability, wondering how he could consider some of the outlandish thoughts he was just now beginning to embrace. But could he share them? His reputation was much too important for him to carelessly blurt them out—especially to the mayor.

He'd think I was insane, John thought.

The mayor may have noticed John's distant stare because he looked at Chief Bergman and said, "Phil, I want all the stops pulled out in all of these cases. I don't care what it costs. Do whatever is necessary to prove their innocence. You have carte blanche." John heard the comment, yet it hadn't fully registered. He was transitioning from frightened to relieved, now that he realized he didn't have to answer the mayor's question.

"And keep me in the loop every step of the way."

Bergman nodded to the mayor, and then looked to Walsh, "We will, Mayor, every step."

BACK AT THE OFFICE, JOHN FOUND BRAXTON IN the small conference room viewing the videos of Zachary Whittman. Looking despondent, John slumped into a chair beside him. "Morning, Kid."

Braxton was beaming, but John didn't notice, "Morning, you ol' fart. Why the glum look?"

"I met with the mayor this morning. He wants answers we don't have—answers we may never have."

Braxton looked confused, "What kind of answers, John? This case is open and shut."

"Things aren't always what they appear to be, Brax."

"What do you mean? Just look at the screen. That's Whittman alright. We've got him dead to rights."

John was at a loss for words. He tried not to look at the TV screen, but his eyes were slowly drawn to it. There he was, Whittman, with a gun in his hand. John had to look away. He wasn't certain he could change Braxton's perspective.

Young people, they only see with their eyes. It's too soon, he thought. *It'd be asking too much.*

"All I'm saying, Brax, is that regardless of the hard evidence, there're a lot of opposing facts that are clouding this and other cases too. The mayor thinks Whittman and Grady are innocent. He's sure of it. I can't explain why, but I agree."

With a puzzled expression, Braxton rocked his chair onto its back legs.

"You're serious, aren't you?"

"Afraid so. I've been doing this for twenty-two years, Kid. I know when things feel right and when they don't, and nothing feels right about the five-pack."

Braxton curtailed another smile.

"Five-pack?" he said. "There you go again, why do you give everything a pet name? Who the hell does that anyway?"

John didn't answer. He seemed to be deep in thought.

"So do you think some of the other cases are linked in some way?"

John gave a slight nod, "There are five cases in question, and they've all occurred within the last two weeks. All have hard evidence—DNA, fingerprints, video, or witnesses. The evidence is perfect—too perfect. Appearances would suggest that all five of these men wanted to be caught, but that goes against human nature. No one wants to be caught. And they're all fighting too hard for vindication for that to be true. There are no motives—period. And I don't think any of them are stupid enough to have been so careless in committing these crimes in the first place."

"So what are you saying, John?"

"I'm saying we have a lot of work to do, Junior."

Braxton stared at the TV monitor. "Look at Whittman—he's practically posing for the cameras."

"My point, exactly. At the bank, Whittman posed for the cameras, left fingerprints and blood smears all over the place, but when he got to Maxine's—nothing."

"What do you mean—nothing?"

John not only caught Braxton's eyes, but he got deep into them as if communicating something more than usual. "There wasn't a single fingerprint or blood mark inside Maxine's, aside from those on Whittman's gun." Braxton looked at the monitor, and then back at John. He was speechless.

"Listen, Brax, his clothes were in a neat pile waiting for us. But we didn't get to see him put them there. He shot the camera lenses out. Why? Why did this guy go from Mr. Photogenic to Mr. Shy? What didn't he want us to see?"

Braxton shrugged, "His escape?"

"No."

"WHAT then?" Braxton seemed a little annoyed. "We don't need to play twenty questions, John, what didn't he want us to see?"

John didn't mean to take Braxton this far, but he was disappointed that Braxton had not even taken a stab at the words, even if they were crazy. Braxton's mouth was agape, his eyes communicated puzzlement. John crossed his arms and waited.

Whittman took the suit off kid, what the hell did he wear out of there? C'mon, Kid, think! Something with a price tag on it, maybe?

John paused another second and decided now wasn't the right time. He sighed and answered Braxton's question, "I don't know, Kid. I have no idea." Braxton shook his head.

At eleven o'clock, the two detectives moved to John's office. John called the mayor's office and was instantly put on hold. Tired of cradling the phone to his ear, he pressed the speaker button and hung up the receiver.

"Why are you calling the mayor, John?" Braxton asked. "You were just there."

"I'm looking for a connection—a common thread in these cases."

"And the mayor can provide one?"

"He already has," John said. "He knows two of the five people we're investigating. That's a pretty good coincidence to begin with, don't you think?"

Braxton shrugged his shoulders, "I suppose so, but I doubt—"

The speaker came to life. "Hello, John. Do you have some information for me?"

"No Mayor, but I was hoping you had some for me."

44

"What can I do for you, Detective?"

"It seems like quite a coincidence that you know two of the five people we're investigating. I was hoping you could help me establish a connection between them."

"What kind of connection?"

"Any kind at all. To begin with, since you know both Whittman and Grady, can you tell me—do they know each other?"

"Absolutely," the mayor said, "we are all on the board of directors for Critical Strategies Genetics Research."

The answer brought a smile to John's face. Braxton listened in amusement. "What about the other three men?"

"I don't know any of them," the mayor replied. "I reviewed your initial reports. None of their names are familiar in the least."

Braxton began to fidget. He picked up a Guns and Ammo magazine and started to page through it. A minute later he fanned himself with it. He obviously thought John was wasting his time, but he listened anyway.

"Mayor, in my conversation with Whittman, he said his company was on the cusp of making some major biological breakthroughs. Can you confirm this?"

"I certainly can. In fact, I can tell you that if Whittman's research bears fruit, he's sure to win a Nobel prize. But for legal reasons involving confidentiality, I'm unable to say any more than that. You'll have to get the details from Zach Whittman himself. Under the circumstances, I'm sure he'll oblige."

John pressed ahead. "Is it possible, Mayor, that someone wants to sabotage these discoveries... a competitor perhaps?"

"It's possible, John. In fact, Whittman has been preoccupied with the prospect of corporate espionage since one of his scientists made a major discovery about five weeks ago."

"What discovery?"

"I can't divulge the exact nature of the discovery, only that there is another whole dimension to DNA that we were unaware of until now. It was such a stunning revelation that Whittman decided to postpone some major tests—tests he'd waited years to conduct." Braxton's fidgeting stopped abruptly.

"You still have Zach in custody, right?"

"No, Mayor, he made bail late last night, but I'll see him later today. We're going to go over the results of the DNA test. By the way, it was just as we expected—an exact match."

The mayor's voice sounded disappointed, "Well then, I wouldn't hesitate to ask him some more questions. Maybe he can furnish you with the lead you are looking for."

"I will, Mayor. Now, I need to ask for your understanding and indulgence. I want you to wear a GPS tracking device—the ankle bracelet type we use to track inmates."

The whites of Braxton's eyes got so big it left no doubt as to what he was thinking. If there had been any, his gaping jaw would have surely confirmed his disbelief.

"You can wear the ankle model completely unnoticed," John continued. "Now, let me explain why."

9

BRAXTON ESCORTED WHITTMAN TO THE INTERRO-
gation room. Deep in thought, he replayed John and the mayor's
conversation in his mind.

*John doesn't look like it, but he's a masterful interviewer. He knows more
than he's telling me. Why hasn't he told me what he's thinking? Doesn't he
trust me?*

John was standing near a frosted glass window that was brilliantly
lit by sunlight and covered by a crisscrossed pattern of metal straps.
From the doorway the intense glare washed out John's features. John
appeared as a silhouette to Whittman when he entered the room.

"Good afternoon, Mr. Whittman. I hope you were able to get some
sleep last night."

Whittman squinted against the bright light. "I suppose I did get
a few hours of sleep, Detective. But I spent most of the evening
thinking about how I would apologize for abandoning the CEO of
Bentley Genetics Limited. We had planned to have drinks and dinner
until your Detective Connors showed up and arrested me. Now I'm

not certain any amount of alcohol could make him believe my story, especially if he's seen the local news."

Whittman approached John until they were both bathed in sunlight. "We never got around to discussing the business deal that brought us together in the first place. My secretary called his room this morning to explain my situation, but he had already checked out of the hotel."

"I'm sorry to hear that, Mr. Whittman, but I do have some good news. I had a meeting with the police chief and the mayor. They are going to do everything possible to prove your innocence." Whittman nodded as if he expected nothing less.

"And what about you, Detective—do you think I'm innocent?" John handed Whittman a manila envelope.

"Here's your DNA results. Perhaps you should look at it before I answer that question." Whittman cradled the envelope in his palms.

"I thought it would take longer."

Braxton interjected, "John called in a favor, Mr. Whittman. It seems everyone in the department is beholden to him for something." John gave his partner a half smile and motioned for Whittman to sit down. Whittman plunked into a chair and paused for a moment before his shaking hands unwound the string that bound the envelope's flap. He slid the papers out and stared at the results with disbelief, "It—it's not possible!"

John studied his response. It was just as he'd expected. It was the same reaction he had witnessed by four other men in the last two weeks. Stuart Grady, David Breeling, Adam Sharp, and Tyler Werthing were also facing serious charges for crimes he believed they didn't commit. Detective Dietrich's confidence was growing in a theory that these men were indeed linked together by a common thread and a bizarre set of circumstances. He was beginning to formulate the unbelievable "how" portion of his speculation, but the "who and why" portions were so absent of facts, it made his head hurt. At any rate, his assumptions had potentially dangerous repercussions.

Moving away from the bright window, John stood before the broken man whose head hung in embarrassment and disbelief. Whittman looked much different today. His clothes were wrinkled and his swarthy cheeks were stubbled with whiskers a few shades darker than his disheveled platinum blonde hair.

"Mr. Whittman," John said, "I think you're innocent."

Zachary Whittman couldn't believe his ears. "How could you possibly believe that?" he mumbled. "The DNA—the videos—and my fingerprints—the evidence is overwhelming."

"Yes it is, but I'm investigating four other cases just like yours, and like this one, the evidence is too perfect. The crimes are all committed by model citizens who have no motives or flimsy ones at best. They all have alibis, damn good ones too. In addition, there are dozens, and I mean dozens, of conflicting tidbits of evidence. We've got to capitalize on them and look at them in a different way—until they work in our favor. Will you help me?"

Grateful to have someone on his side, Whittman answered, "I'll do anything."

John gave his partner a cheeky grin, "Brash Brax! I need the videos of Mr. Whittman. The three of us are going to scrutinize them closely." Braxton wasn't certain in which direction the investigation was headed, but he was glad to see the energy pulsing through his partner's veins again.

"Meanwhile, Mr. Whittman, I need a science lesson, and you need to tell me everything you can about your latest discovery, and why someone would ruin you to get it."

10

IT WAS TEN-THIRTY IN THE EVENING. MAYOR CHASE
had just finished his last meeting. In attendance were several members
of the City Council. It was typical of this group to have a few drinks.
It began with a bottle of Canadian Mist from the mayor's desk drawer,
but about twenty minutes into the meeting, three briefcases opened
and libations were flowing freely.

"How 'bout a game of poker?" Joe Harkin shouted.

"Naww, can't do it," the mayor said, "Gotta get up at five—'nother
goddamned breakfast meeting."

As he ushered his colleagues to the reception area, he was startled
to see his secretary, Jean Rebouche, at her desk. He swaggered toward
her and smiled, "What the devil are you doing here at this late hour,
Jeannie?"

"My home computer is on the fritz and I needed to type a school
paper for my daughter. I hope you don't mind."

"Aww, hell no. Type all the papers you want. I'm gonna straighten
up my office a bit and get home. Got an early day tomorrow."

Jean smiled at him and said, "Mayor, you look like you could use something to eat. Why don't you pick up some food on the way home, and I'll take care of straightening your office."

"You're a sweetheart, Jeannie, I'll do that, thanks."

As the mayor stumbled in the direction of the elevator, Jean entered his office and immediately found what she was looking for. Twenty minutes earlier, she had cracked his door open slightly to note his position at the table. His obese frame was easy to spot.

This is where he sat, she thought.

Wearing a latex glove on her right hand, she picked up his glass and sniffed the contents, Peach schnapps. She departed quickly, leaving the mess exactly where she'd found it.

∞

Michaela Watson was bringing a Coke to the mayor's table, but not before having a word with her manager at the Red Robin Restaurant. When she took his order, he'd made a few lewd comments and patted her on the butt. She was only seventeen and had no idea he was the mayor of Kansas City. But she knew all too well what sexual harassment was. She asked her boss to keep an eye on her, and the fat creep she was serving.

"Here is your drink, sir," she said, keeping her distance as she set the drink in front of him.

"Do you think I'm doing a good job for the city?" he asked.

Having caught her off guard, Michaela replied, "What do you mean?"

"As the mayor of this city—do you think I'm doing a good job?"

"You're the mayor?"

"Yes, I'm running for re-election. Haven't you seen my commercials?"

"Yeah, I guess so, I just didn't recognize you."

"Don't you vote?"

"No, I'm only seventeen."

Mayor Chase reached in his pocket, "Can I give you a 'Vote for Chase' sticker?"

"I suppose so," she said politely. Michaela immediately decided she wouldn't wear it. She didn't like him at all. The mayor produced a sticky political label and she moved closer to take it from him. His plump fingers peeled away its backing.

"Oh, I don't think my manager will let me wear that over my uniform," she said.

"Nonsense, this will match your outfit perfectly." He grasped her left arm near the elbow and applied the sticker just below her name tag. He used his palm to apply a firm pressure, and then his fingers wandered to her breast. He began massaging it, grinning all the while.

For a moment she was stunned, frozen in sheer disbelief that this nightmare was happening, and then her eyes hardened and focused on his.

"Stop that!" she said, jeering. "Let go of me!"

The young waitress yanked her arm free and stomped toward the kitchen. The mayor laughed, and several patrons gave him cross looks. He didn't seem to care. Within seconds an angry manager appeared with a busboy and cook.

"Just because you're the mayor doesn't mean you're above the law!"

"My good man," he said mockingly, "in this town—I am the law."

With his hands on his hips and head held high, the manager stood between the mayor and the exits. His frown disappeared and the ends of his mouth curled up, "We'll see about that, the police are on the way."

11

JOHN DIETRICH ARRIVED AT HIS OFFICE AT SEVEN A.M. Captain Walsh was waiting for him, sitting in the guest chair beside his desk. There was a look of apprehension on his face. John thought how unusual that was.

"Mornin', Mike. You're in early."

Walsh's salt and pepper eyebrows formed a V. His lips thinned before he spoke.

"Been here a while."

John paused, briefcase in hand.

"I want to talk to you before the commotion starts."

John caught the serious tone. He set his briefcase on a small table.

"What's the matter, Mike?"

"I've never known you to keep things from me, John. You've always been honest and above board."

"That's past tense, Mike. The way you said that makes me think you don't believe it now."

"Have you told me everything about the Whittman case?"

"I've shared everything I know, Mike—about all my cases. Why?"

"The Chief called me at three this morning. He says the mayor owes you a debt of gratitude."

John almost chuckled, "For what?"

"For asking him to wear a GPS tracking bracelet on his ankle. He said it proves his innocence."

John's legs felt heavy. He quickly rounded his desk and plunked into his chair.

Leaning in toward Walsh, he asked, "What happened?"

"The mayor was seen fondling a waitress at the Red Robin Restaurant last night—or at least that's the story I got. He claims he was home at the time and that the tracking device will prove it."

John let out a sigh of relief, "Then I was right."

"Right about what?"

"Someone is impersonating important people—people linked to Critical Strategies Genetics Research."

"Okay, John, maybe I should define 'honest and above board.'"

John smiled to relieve the tension. He had never in his life lied to Walsh, nor did he withhold any facts of the case, but for the first time ever he withheld an opinion, a crazy hunch. It was still too farfetched to take to its conclusion, but now it seemed appropriate to explain a portion of his theory. At least the part that wouldn't prompt anyone to require that he wear a straight jacket.

"I didn't withhold a solitary fact, Mike. You know everything I know. I just had a strange feeling that some of these cases were frauds. I thought it was possible that an impostor framed them. But with all of the physical evidence we have, you'd have thought I was insane for suggesting it."

"I still would. We've got video, fingerprints *and* DNA. It's just a bit much to suggest someone else committed these crimes, don't you think?"

Uh oh, John thought as he rocked back in his chair, *it's still too soon. I need to take this a different direction.*

"You're probably right, Mike, but you know me, I can't leave any stone unturned."

"So what's convinced you there's an impostor?"

"Hard to say. All I know is that Whittman, Grady, and the mayor all sit on the board of directors at Critical Strategies Genetics Research. That's quite a coincidence, isn't it?"

Maybe so, John, but the physical evidence against them carries a hell of a lot more weight than your hunch."

"EXACTLY! That's why I never mentioned it before. But it was just enough of a coincidence for me to ask the mayor to wear a GPS ankle bracelet for a week or so. He agreed, and now it looks like it might pay off."

Walsh looked tired. John concluded that he probably never got back to sleep after the Chief's phone call.

"Do me a favor, John. Let's shelve any talk about an impostor until we have some hard evidence to support it, okay?"

John nodded solemnly, "You got it, Captain!"

"The press is going to have a heyday with this. It'll crush any chance Chase has for re-election. But claiming there is an impostor running around the city would just make him a laughingstock. No one would ever believe it"

"Was the mayor arrested?"

"No, he walked right out of the restaurant before officers arrived. The manager threatened to stop him, but he backed down at the last minute."

"Mike, you know the mayor better than I do—he didn't do this, did he?"

Walsh stood up and stuttered on his departing comment, "I—I don't know what to think about anything, anymore. The mayor wants to see you at eight-thirty. I'm not invited to the party, so come fill me in afterwards."

12

"GOOD MORNING, MA'AM. I'M DETECTIVE DIETRICH. I have an eight-thirty appointment with the mayor."

The mayor's wiry, middle-aged secretary hesitated nervously, and opened her mouth as though she was going to say something, but stopped short. Her eyes gained intensity as she studied the mayor's door. She turned a shade of pink and composed herself, "I'll tell him you're here."

She wanted to tell me something, John thought. *Maybe she'd be more comfortable with a phone call. I need to follow up on that.* He barely took a seat before the mayor's door opened wide. "Detective Dietrich, please come in!"

The mayor's office was expansive. Finished in a rich cherry wood, one wall was completely filled with books, mementos, photos, and sports memorabilia. John slowed as he passed an end table flanked by two wing chairs. The table contained two old Polaroids in small frames. In one of them, the mayor had his arm around retired baseball player, George Brett. The other photo was a handshake pose with

President Ronald Reagan. The mayor weighed about eighty pounds less in the photos. John continued to walk the expansive room. At the rear, toward the windows, stood the mayor's desk, and just a few feet from it were two round tables surrounded by chairs. A young, well-dressed woman with long dark hair and glasses, no, the word *spectacles* seemed more appropriate, sat at the table nearer the mayor's desk.

The mayor took John's hand half shaking it, half dragging him over to meet the woman. "Detective Dietrich, let me introduce you to my attorney, Brooke Hershel." John was taken aback by the incredibly astute looking attorney. She was beautiful, but beauty wasn't what she exuded most. Her business suit looked more expensive than one of Whittman's. Her handshake was firm, her smile wasn't too ostentatious, and her hazel eyes had a confidence that John surmised would serve her well in her profession. John wondered if her slightly oversized eyeglasses weren't for effect. They gave her an added impression of intelligence and professionalism.

"It's a pleasure to meet you, Detective."

Mayor Chase and John joined Hershel at the table. The young attorney wasted no time getting to business. "Did you speak with your Captain?"

John nodded, "Quite early this morning."

"Then you are aware of the accusations that have been leveled against the mayor?"

"Yes."

"No charges have been filed, and thanks to your suggestion that the mayor wear a GPS tracking device, none will be imposed in the future. He has already been proven innocent."

John looked satisfied, "So you've already contacted the GPS Company for the data?"

"We had it within fifteen minutes of the mayor's phone call. He left the office at precisely ten-thirty-six last night. He stopped at a Wendy's drive-through window and went directly home. He was there before eleven. A technician arrived a half hour ago to check the ankle bracelet and verify its working condition and that it had not been tampered with. I have a validation certificate and a map of the mayor's whereabouts for the evening." Hershel handed John the paperwork.

"Can I keep these?" John asked.

"Those are your copies, Detective."

The mayor spoke up, "I'm indebted to you, John. You probably saved my career."

"I'm glad it worked out that way, Mayor. You should continue to wear that ankle bracelet. Whoever tried to frame you, may try again."

Hershel continued, "That brings up an important question, Detective. How did you know someone would try to frame him?"

John was mesmerized by the way Hershel's glasses magnified the specks of gold in her light brown eyes. They were so unusual. He paused, and then reached deep within himself for an appropriate answer to the question. As he thought, he began to feel the same churning pit in his stomach he got whenever this subject was approached. "I didn't know, Miss Hershel—can I call you Brooke?"

"Please."

John continued, "I was just following a hunch. You see, the mayor is on the board of directors with two other respected men accused of crimes. I'm pretty sure they are innocent too, but the perpetrator planted evidence at each crime scene, including DNA."

Hershel grew more serious. "You are talking about Whittman and Grady, correct?"

"Yes, and three others as well. I haven't established a connection to the other cases yet, but I suspect they are all connected, somehow."

"And how do you suppose the perpetrator planted this evidence?"

"I haven't the faintest clue—not yet anyway. We've still got a lot of work ahead of us."

Hershel didn't seem surprised. She showed no emotion, as she scanned her legal pad for notes.

"Tell me what you know so far."

John shared several details of the other cases, including the inconsistencies that made him suspect foul play. Had last night's incident been successful, it would have brought the total to six. There were two armed robberies, two rapes, one assault and battery, and the mayor's "near" sexual assault charge. John outlined his next steps.

"Effective immediately, I'm conducting an in-depth investigation of Critical Strategies Genetics Research. Later this afternoon, Mr. Whittman and I will discuss possible scenarios as to how DNA evidence might be obtained and planted. I know it all sounds farfetched, but it's all I've got to go on."

Hershel nodded, "What about the videos? How convincing are they?" John looked into Brook Hershel's piercing hazel eyes.

This woman could sway the mind of the typical male juror with both arms tied behind her back, probably most female jurors too, he thought.

"Damn convincing," John replied. "You're welcome to view them any time you'd like."

"Thank you Detective, I'll make arrangements to do just that."

"Please, call me John."

"Well, John," Hershel said, "looks like we'll be seeing a bit of each other. I am taking both Whittman and Grady's defense cases. If it helps our plight, I'll take the other three cases as well." Hershel slid her business card across the table. "Can you keep me in the loop as you uncover evidence that might prove helpful to these men?"

John caught a glimpse of the mayor, who was nodding his head up and down. John nodded in return, "Certainly, I'd be happy to."

"There is one more thing, John," Hershel said sternly. "We've proven the mayor is innocent, now we need to keep this from the press. If they get wind of it, they'll turn his life into a three-ring circus. For the sake of his re-election, we cannot allow that to happen. Can you talk to the victim and her manager at the Red Robin Restaurant? We need to do damage control—let them know that we intend to conduct a complete investigation, convince them that, given time, we'll find the real perpetrator."

"I need to interview them anyway, Brooke. I'll do everything I can to keep this under wraps."

"Good. You should also know—the mayor conducted a meeting here last night until ten-thirty. He and his guests had a few drinks. There were no mishaps, no misconduct, but when the mayor was leaving, he saw his secretary, Jean at her desk. She volunteered to clean off the tables and clear the glasses. When the mayor came in this morning, everything was still here except for one item—his glass.

When he asked her about it, she said she didn't know what he was talking about. She claims she was never here."

That's what Jean wanted to tell me! John thought. *She probably stopped herself because she felt it was the wrong time and place.* Hershel concluded the meeting, and John promised to keep her informed. As John walked out, Jean Rebouche slipped him a note.

13

JOHN PULLED INTO THE PARKING LOT OF THE RED
Robin Restaurant at ten o'clock. Braxton's car was already there.

Jesus, John remembered, *we were so busy yesterday, I never asked him
about his proposal to Anne. Some partner I am.*

Yesterday had been incredibly busy for John. It felt as if he and
Braxton had covered half the city interviewing witnesses, looking for
clues in what he nicknamed his five-pack of crimes. They came up
with nothing at all. However, when Whittman joined them to revisit
the videos, they noticed several things they hadn't seen during the
initial viewings.

For one thing, appearances suggested that the robber was wearing
a latex glove. It was difficult to detect at first, but Whittman was
handsome, a bit vain, and proud of the deep tan that set off his platinum
hair. When the thief struggled to grasp the money bag, Whittman
paused the video and pointed out how pale the right hand looked
compared to the left. A quick call to Jaworski in forensics confirmed
that there were no right-hand fingerprints at the scene. A second call to

Jaworski confirmed there were no right-hand fingerprints left behind at any of the five-pack crime scenes. This was the first genuine clue John had uncovered to suggest there might be a link to all five cases.

Whittman also noted the robber's posture. He claimed the man had a weak stance. John agreed that he lacked the swagger and confident nature that Whittman projected.

"This guy looks downright nervous," John said. Braxton remained quiet, but he squirmed in his chair, seemingly annoyed at the comment.

He still thinks Whittman is guilty, John thought, studying his partner. John wasted no time placing a call to a kinesics expert, someone who could testify about body language. Dr. Mary Simon had agreed to meet them in the office at three-thirty. It wasn't a lot, but John was beginning to feel as though he was making some progress.

Right now I've got to do a little PR work.

John parked next to Braxton, who was on his cell phone.

He's probably talking to his fiancée. As soon as Braxton saw John, he folded his clamshell phone and got out of his car.

"Two meetings with the mayor in two days, John? Are you taking the fast track for a promotion?"

"Very funny Brax—like I wanna be a pencil pusher. C'mon, we need to keep these guys from spouting off about the mayor's *alleged* sexual misconduct. All he needs is for this to get out to the general public." The two detectives walked to the restaurant's front door. The Red Robin was locked. Braxton pounded on the glass. A skinny pock-faced teenager pointed to the closed sign, but unlocked the door when Braxton held up his badge.

"We'd like to speak with your manager," Braxton said in a husky monotone voice. John tried to restrain his smile.

The manager, Willard Johnson, reminded John of the guy who was always picked on in high school but had somehow come into his own later in life. He commanded his teenage employees about the restaurant with aplomb. By the way they jumped when he spoke, John sensed he was a pretty tough manager.

"Mr. Johnson, we are investigating an alleged report of sexual misconduct last night. What can you tell us about the incident?"

"There is nothing alleged about it," Johnson said. "I watched the entire thing, so did my cook and one of my busboys. The mayor grabbed one of my employees by the arm and mashed one of his campaign stickers over her breast. And then he squeezed it—pretty blatantly, if you ask me. He didn't seem to try to hide it at all."

"And what were you doing while this was going on?" John asked.

Willard's cheeks reddened, and he leaned toward John.

"Well, up to that point, we were just observing, but I had the cook call the police, and then we gave that S.O.B. a piece of our minds."

"You confronted him?"

"We—I sure did, but the police took too long to get here. He'd already left. For the safety of my employees, I figured there was no need to stop him. The police could pick him up any time."

John's teeth sank into his cheek, "That was good thinking, Mr. Johnson. Now, what would you say if I told you that man wasn't the mayor?" Braxton suddenly looked away, like he was embarrassed to participate in the interview. He started shuffling his feet.

Johnson's reply was sarcastic, "I'd say that was his twin brother, or maybe an Oscar-winning makeup artist. You're not really gonna make that claim, are you? The man admitted he was the mayor. In fact, I recall him saying, 'In this town—I am the law.' What more could you want?"

John didn't flinch, but his cheek was feeling some pain. It kept him centered in the moment.

"Mr. Johnson," John said slowly, "he admitted he was the mayor, because his objective was to ruin the mayor's reputation. Why do you think he molested that girl in plain sight? He had an audience, and he was counting on everyone watching. You say he used no discretion at all—well, I think that was intentional."

Johnson's face grew sour, "I don't buy it officer. That man was the mayor, and that's that!"

"Look, Mr. Johnson, no one wants to apprehend this guy more than I do. He's been involved in other crimes as well. We're going to catch him and put him away, but I need your cooperation." John leaned in close, "We need to keep this confidential. If this story hits the newspapers, this slime ball—this impostor will ruin the mayor's reputation—he'll win and we'll lose. But if we can keep this completely quiet, he'll try again, and we'll be watching, waiting for him to make his move. Will you help us?"

"I don't think so," Johnson said. "Michaela Watson deserves to see this guy punished."

"That's what I'm trying to tell you—we want to put him behind bars." John gave him a reassuring look and then withdrew some papers from his breast pocket. "If I can prove that man wasn't the mayor, will you do what I ask?"

"How can you prove it?"

"Just answer the question, Mr. Johnson."

"Yeah, I guess so."

John spread three documents on a table. "Because of a related case, I suspected the mayor was a target for this impostor. I had him wear a GPS tracking device on his ankle. Last night, he was at his office until ten thirty-six." He pointed to a map. "This green line shows his exact whereabouts during that time. He was nowhere near this restaurant. The second sheet confirms it with a list of geocodes. Those are coordinates that are accurate within a meter of his location. The company that tracks this data inspected his ankle bracelet this morning. This certificate confirms that the bracelet was in perfect working order and that it hadn't been tampered with. You see, Mr. Johnson, we are completely convinced the mayor never entered your restaurant last night. If you want us to catch the man who did, you need to cooperate with us."

Braxton's eyebrows rose, his mouth agape. John realized his sidekick was hearing all of this for the first time.

"Okay, officer, I'll keep this quiet, for now. I'll ask my employees to do the same."

"Thank you, Mr. Johnson. Make sure they understand that this is the only way we're going to nab this guy."

John followed standard protocol and asked for a description of the man and details of what had transpired. Johnson said he thought Michaela Watson said something about him wearing a rubber glove. John got her home phone number.

The Red Robin was just opening its doors for business. "Want to stay for a cup of coffee, Brax?"

"Yeah, I guess so."

Braxton's tone was curt.

Understandable, John thought.

As uncomfortable as he felt, it was time to share all of the details of the case.

Now that the case is unfolding a bit, maybe it won't sound so crazy.

A half hour later, John was trying to read his partners thoughts. He couldn't.

"I've been doing this for almost twenty-five years, Kid, so I know damn well how crazy all this must sound, but we're living in a highly technical world. Things we thought were impossible just a few years ago are everyday technology today.

Braxton looked confused, "I still don't get what you are trying to say, John. Are you telling me there is an impostor who is an expert at disguising himself to look like anyone he wants, or are you saying there is a person who can actually change his shape?"

John clanked the salt and pepper shakers with a slow, steady cadence, "I don't know what I'm saying. I—I can't rule out either theory, Brax. Whittman and I had a long discussion about this. He says DNA is a blueprint of a person's physical makeup. He claims it's possible to recreate any part of a person from that blueprint."

"You realize your theory is way out there, don't you?"

"Indeed I do, Kid. Why do you think I waited so long to share it with you? I can't have my partner thinking I'm a flaming lunatic." John's comment brought a broad smile to Braxton's face.

"If this is true, John, how would we ever find him? If some guy can just take anyone's shape at will, he'd be nearly impossible to catch." Hearing Braxton's comment put John at ease.

He's entertaining the possibility; he doesn't think I'm crazy. Now, we can work as a team.

"We're going to have to be smarter than this guy, Brax—a lot smarter."

For the next forty minutes, John shared more details of his conversations with Whittman, as well as what he'd discovered doing his own research.

"Whittman said they recently discovered a new sub-layer in DNA. This layer contains information about our physical makeup we've never seen before, a clock that tracks our age, and possibly the genetic code responsible for evolution. Their theory is that this code has allowed man to adapt to his surroundings throughout time. It may be that this component allows a person's DNA to accept a completely new blueprint."

"So, does he think someone's using this technology to frame him?"

"I don't know. I haven't gotten that far, but we're gonna find out."

Braxton went silent. John continued to explain.

"Whittman believes this genetic clock signature could allow a person to revert to their physical age at any point in their lifetime."

Braxton straightened, "So—if I was injected with DNA that was taken when I was two…"

"You'd be a toddler again, Brax. Of course, no one understands the trigger for the metamorphosis, but Whittman suspects it's all in the code. A simple injection of DNA would not by itself begin the process, but when they discover the trigger, just think about the implications. If you could freeze and store your DNA today, it's possible that you could revert back to your current physical age and makeup every five years, or so."

Braxton looked wounded, "Why did you think I couldn't accept the fact that these things are possible? Why didn't you trust me?"

John thought for a moment, "Because it took me several days to come to grips with it myself. My reputation is important to me, Brax. I can't afford to become the laughingstock of the department. I'm sorry I didn't confide in you earlier, but we're still getting to know each other. I had no way of knowing how you'd react."

Braxton understood and became upbeat, "Don't worry, you ol' fart. Right or wrong, I'll stick by you."

"Let's be careful what we say, Kid. Connors and Moody would love to spread the rumor that we're chasing some sci-fi villain. I wish they'd spend the same energy trying to be good detectives."

"What was the pet name you gave those two?" Braxton asked with a smile.

"Buffoons, Kid—buffoons."

14

HE WAS BECOMING IRRITATED AT THE RUCKUS COMING from the table behind him.

Bunch of raucous drunken college students, he thought. The grating laughter was bad enough, but he was trying to listen to the noon news and was not catching much of it. But it really didn't matter, since there were no stories involving the mayor.

Either someone talked that girl out of reporting the incident, or the mayor had the incident squelched. If a story about sexual molestation doesn't surface by the evening news, I'll find another way to get the bastard.

Another round of laughter overpowered the TV's volume. He wondered if these kids ever studied. Were their parents paying for their drinks as well as their fancy cars and education? He slid to the corner of his booth and turned to get a better look at them. They had pushed two tables together, five boys and two girls. He caught the eye of one of the girls, a brunette. She smiled. His heart thumped and he returned the smile. He noticed her low cut top and deep cleavage before turning back to his beer. The brief glimpse brought him stiff. He began to recall the last time he was aroused. It was only a week ago.

It was in a Wal-Mart store that he had followed a busty blonde bombshell with a tiny waist and slender legs. He had waited for forty-five minutes in the parking lot for the right girl. He liked blondes. And this one reminded him of his neighbor, Brenda Langdon—only better in every way. Longer legs, tighter ass, and this one couldn't turn him down. Oh, she could try, but he wouldn't let her. She would pleasure him until he said otherwise.

He could have chosen any girl, but she had to meet three strict requirements. First, she had to be a blonde knockout—an 11 on a scale of 1 to 10. There were several beauties who qualified as he waited impatiently for his prey, but other requirements were equally important. The girl must be alone, and park in a spot where the driver's door was adjacent to an empty parking space. The blondeshell missed the third criteria. She parked next to another car. He fumed while watching his missed opportunity walk toward the store.

Fucking figures, he thought. Then he saw a woman approaching with two young boys. He grasped the steering wheel in anticipation. The woman slowed near the blonde's car. His knuckles went white as his fingers squeezed tighter.

I can't be this lucky.

But he was. The woman who was physically the opposite of the blonde he desired, grabbed the arm of her youngest boy and yanked him close to her, screaming something about watching for traffic. Then she rounded the trunk end of her car—the one by Blondeshell's and opened the rear passenger door. Instinctively, he twisted the key and looked to his right. A car was approaching. It would surely take the parking space he wanted if he didn't act quickly. He threw the shifter into D and lurched ahead making a partial swing toward the woman's car. She was strapping the younger boy in a car seat, while the other one climbed in the opposite door and sat next to him. A car honked. He didn't flinch, but focused only on guarding his parking space. The woman slammed the door, and went to the other side of the car. The car behind him honked again, but the sound barely registered in his ears.

Got it—ha! It's mine!

A moment later he was headed toward the entrance of Wal-Mart.

He found her in cosmetics. There was plenty of time to study her. The color of her hair was the same shade as Brenda Langdon's, a neighbor woman he'd lusted after for years. Her long legs were tan, and seemed to stretch forever before finally reaching the object of his affection, her perfect ass. Her breasts were well concealed behind a top that tied above her narrow waist, but he could tell they were ample. She studied lipstick color charts, held them up to the light before settling on a selection. Blondeshell noticed him staring. He smiled and she turned away. Her reaction made him frown. Within seconds, he had lost his erection. He strayed to the jewelry counter and pretended to look at watches. When she left cosmetics, he kept his distance. He let her get almost out-of-sight before following her again.

He waited for twenty minutes outside the womens fitting rooms. He imagined her trying on the tops she had selected. This was going to be good. This beautiful creature would not only provide him pleasure, but also a vengeful checkmark on the list of people who had wronged him.

Never has there been a better example of "killing two birds," he thought. *I hope he rots in jail.* He saw Stewart Grady's face. It was a kind, gentle face from what he could remember, but Grady couldn't be kind.

How could a kind man do what he did to me? How could he ruin a man's life for no reason? It didn't matter. Grady was about to pay a big price for his actions.

Blondeshell exited the fitting room carrying only half the clothes she went in with. She headed for the checkout.

Don't be nervous ol' boy. You won't get caught. No one can do what you can—no one in the world.

He found a cashier four aisles north of Blondeshell's. The line was short and as he waited his turn, he began touching everything in sight. He looked for video cameras and then alternated stares in the direction of each. He purchased nothing but a pack of gum. And then he walked toward the exit where he found a sales display and lingered behind it until Blondeshell walked by. From that moment he kept a careful distance between them. His footsteps were quiet.

He didn't want her to turn around. He reached in his pocket and withdrew a latex glove. It was lightly dusted with powder which made it glide over his right hand. The walk to her car seemed longer than he'd remembered. It was twilight, and getting difficult to see inside the vehicles. But the van he drove had dark tinted glass. As he passed the tailgate it was obvious that peering inside the van was impossible. His step hastened.

Blondeshell inserted a key in the door of her red Mazda 323. By the time she retracted it, his hand was around her throat. His left hand had a grip like a vice and he used it to his advantage. A scream was impossible. He drew her against his body and backed into the van's electric side door. A second later, he simply fell backward drawing them both inside. There was no center seat to obstruct their fall. A push of the key fob in his gloved hand and darkness closed around them.

A round of laughter erupted from the college kids. It snapped him out of his daydream. He picked up his beer, holding it at eye level. Anyone watching him would have thought he was studying the bubbles in his glass. But his eyes weren't focused. Not really. He was doing his best to remember the contours of Blondeshell's body, and the things he did to her. It was a shame to hit her. At first, it was only to threaten her—keep her quiet. But then he realized he couldn't leave her conscious. He needed time to change, time to get away from Blondeshell and the van he'd stolen.

It was the same with his neighbor Brenda Langdon. Although she wasn't as young or as perfect as Blondeshell, she had been the obsession of his life for three years. Making love to her would have been wonderful if circumstances had been different. But he had to hurt her too. He had to leave Breeling responsible for the incident. It was time for David Breeling to go to prison.

He turned around and took another look at the brunette. Her eyes were friendly.

Maybe I can coax her over to my table. Maybe I can get laid and actually enjoy it.

15

BRAXTON SAT WITH JOHN IN CAPTAIN WALSH'S office. It was three o'clock, and John was giving Walsh the details from their interview with Michaela Watson, the girl who claimed the mayor sexually molested her. John made a casual comment that the mayor's lookalike wore a latex glove. He hoped to see a reaction on Walsh's face. There was none.

"We've got another appointment in half an hour, Captain." John never addressed him as Mike in front of others.

"I won't keep you long, John. How did your meeting with the mayor go this morning?"

"He's got a high dollar attorney, Brooke Hershel—you know her?"

"Yeah, she's got a solid reputation, John. She's considered a bit of an oxymoron."

Braxton took the bait, "Oxymoron, sir?"

"Yeah, you know, things like 'jumbo shrimp,' 'deafening silence,' 'hell's angels.' In Hershel's case, she's an 'honest attorney.'"

John smirked at Braxton, "That's right, Kid—hard as it is to believe, the captain has a sense of humor."

Stretching, John fought the impulse to yawn and continued. "Hershel's decided to represent Whittman and Grady. She said she'd take more cases if we could link them to the others. She thinks it would help their overall defense. I agree. The mayor doesn't seem to need her help at the moment, but that could change quickly."

John handed Walsh the documents from the GPS tracking company and explained the results. "It wasn't the mayor, Captain. We have proof positive it wasn't him."

Walsh rocked back in his chair, staring briefly at the ceiling. When he looked back at John, his tone was serious. "Are you pursuing your 'impostor theory'?"

"It makes more sense than you realize, Captain. A lot of things are beginning to fall into place."

Walsh looked as if he was losing the battle. John recognized the trademark way he massaged his forehead. He did that whenever John became headstrong, and right now John seemed determined to stick with this theory.

"Okay, I'm listening, John. Convince me there's an impostor running loose in the city."

John recapped the facts, but first he decided to remind Walsh of their long-standing association.

"You and I were partners for ten years, Captain. We've always agreed that no crime is ever committed without a solid motive, right?"

"Right, John, but all motives aren't readily apparent at first. We may find several motives as we dig deeper into these cases."

"THAT'S the problem! The deeper I dig, the more innocent these men appear. It's almost like they have anti-motives."

Walsh looked at Braxton and motioned his head toward John "He makes this stuff up. There's no such word as anti-motive."

John smiled, "I know that, Cap', but you get the point, don't you?"

"What else have you got?"

"Five people were framed. Six, if you count the attempt on the mayor. Three of them are on the board of directors for Critical Strategies Genetics Research. The company has just made a discovery that could easily earn them a Nobel Prize and billions of dollars. There's a connection here. We need to tie the other cases to the company, and given time, we will. The young girl we just spoke with was pretty shaken up by all of this. She quit her job at the Red Robin. She also gave us this." In a cellophane bag, John held up the campaign sticker the mayor's impostor applied over the young girl's breast. "I'll bet you fifty bucks the mayor's prints are all over it."

Walsh looked puzzled, "And how does that help your case?"

"We've already proven the mayor wasn't there. Chances are just as good the others weren't at their alleged crime scenes either."

Walsh looked unconvinced. John decided it was an act. *Walsh believes me alright, he's just too stubborn to admit it.*

John placed his palms on his knees and leaning forward, continued in a soft whisper. "Didn't you just tell me the other day that there wasn't anything the mayor wouldn't do to get reelected?"

"Yeah, except go on a diet," Walsh jibed.

Braxton was enjoying the banter. He didn't realize his smile had reached the boundaries of its physical limits.

"Does molesting an underage waitress in public sound like the act of someone who is desperate to get reelected, Cap?"

Walsh let out a sigh. "What else? I need more."

"The impostor grabbed Michaela Watson below the elbow. When he did, she winced at the sensation of something pulling at the fine hair on her arm. Even before she saw it, she knew he was wearing a latex glove. It was on his right hand. In viewing the videos of Whittman at the bank, we noticed the perpetrator's right hand bore a glove. At all six crime scenes, there were no fingerprints from a right hand. And let's not forget the smudge of blood from Whittman's shirt cuff. There isn't a solitary cut on Whittman's body. Where'd the blood come from? Is all of this beginning to sound unusual?"

Walsh tried to show no emotion, but his eyes were jittery. John summed it all up.

"If you factor in the way the evidence was left for us to stumble upon, and the fact that all of the suspects vehemently deny being at the scene, then add witnesses, what have you got?"

"One hell of a mess, boys, one hell of a mess." Walsh's grimace of defeat didn't go unnoticed. "What's your next step?"

John knew he hadn't totally convinced Walsh to believe his premise, but it was clear that he opened the door to the possibility that something was wrong in all of the cases.

"We're going to spend a lot of time looking for connections and 'common threads' at CSGR." Walsh craned his head; his puzzled look said he was waiting for more.

"Abbreviation, Cap—CSGR stands for Critical Strategies Genetics Research."

Walsh nodded, "Right.".

John stood up. "Right now we have an appointment with Mary Simon. She's a kinesics expert."

Walsh scowled, "Come on, John, kinesics experts are usually brought in as a last resort in weak court cases. It's not that I don't believe in body language, but a lot of people think it's a bunch of crap. Let's not waste any time on this. Time is a valuable resource."

"I know what you're thinking, Mike, but this is no waste of time." John flinched when he realized he had let the captain's first name slip. Braxton didn't seem to notice.

"The impostor looks too much like the suspects. We need every piece of evidence in our favor."

Walsh shook his head, "Where is Zach Whittman?"

"He's out on bail, but I asked him to meet us downstairs at three-thirty."

When John and Braxton left the captain's office they headed for the conference room on the first floor.

"You were pretty convincing back there," Braxton admitted. "You persuaded me all over again."

"Thanks Brax, but the hard part is yet to come. Even if the Captain believes there's an impostor out there, how're we gonna convince him he's leaving fingerprints and DNA behind?"

"And why is he wearing a rubber glove on his right hand?" Braxton added, "What's the significance of that fucking glove?"

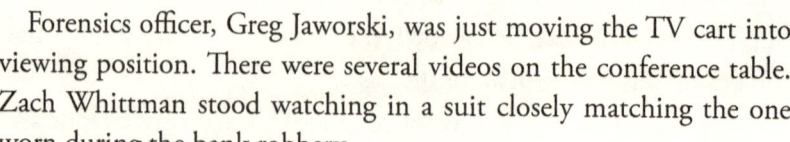

Forensics officer, Greg Jaworski, was just moving the TV cart into viewing position. There were several videos on the conference table. Zach Whittman stood watching in a suit closely matching the one worn during the bank robbery.

John piped up eagerly, "Did you get it, Greg?"

"They gave us fifteen minutes, John. The video isn't perfect, but it'll be good enough to get the job done." Jaworski was referring to the arrangements John had made with the president of Boatman's Bank to close their doors while they reenacted and recorded the robbery.

Whittman was dejected by the cold shoulder he received from the bank's president.

Obviously the old codger believed he was guilty. And none of the tellers would agree to play their original roles. Two uniformed officers provided bank security while Whittman reenacted the part of the gunman. Whittman had watched the video several times, memorizing the movements of the perpetrator. He pointed a plastic replica of a 9mm pistol at a phantom teller. Jaworski directed the reenactment, while comparing it to the original video on a miniature DVD player. When it came time for Whittman to grab the bag of money, Jaworski handed it to him, playing the part of the teller. By using the bank's video cameras, the filming angles would be identical.

"Now we have something to compare," John said. "If this kinesics expert is as good as her reputation, we may learn something valuable today." The conference table phone rang. Dr. Mary Simon had arrived.

16

DR. SIMON FAR EXCEEDED JOHN'S EXPECTATIONS. SHE began with a clear dissertation of the science of kinesics, before asking to see the tapes. It was very helpful to everyone.

"Kinesics is the science of nonverbal communication," she began. "We have all heard of body language. It is what makes us believe something contrary to what a person is telling us. It affects our 'gut' feelings, our judgment, in many ways we do not understand, and yet, we put our faith in it. We draw conclusions about a person's honesty and sincerity from little clues we pick up on but don't know how to interpret—at least on a conscious level. I am a professional interpreter in the field of non-verbal communications. I have written books about the subject, and I can help you wade through the more than 10,000 body language cues we display during every minute we interact with others. Most of us read these cues subconsciously, so I will verbalize what is happening for you."

John was sitting on the edge of his seat.

This is exactly what we need, he thought. Simon continued, "No matter how good the actor, there is no way for a person to control all of the nonverbal cues occurring in unison. There are just too many of them."

"I'll bet you enjoy watching political speeches," Braxton injected.

Simon gave him a generous smile, "Indeed I do, Detective. You probably wouldn't be surprised at my findings, but you might be intrigued by how they were derived. For instance, some body language is acceptable until it isn't."

There were puzzled looks. "What I mean is that the timing of body language is also as important, as is the number of times a cue is repeated, or what part of the body is sending the cue," she said

"The best way to avoid getting caught in a lie is to remain perfectly still—no movement, no cues. A person may rehearse keeping their upper body stiff and facial movements to a minimum. But something as little as blinking an eye, or a tongue thrust may give them away. A smile is a difficult thing to fake. It is usually used to mask displeasure or anger, but is it a genuine smile? I can tell instantly because a real smile changes the entire face. The eyes are bright, the forehead loses wrinkles, the eyebrow and cheek muscles rise, crinkles appear in the skin around the eyes and mouth. A smile is more than the curved corners of one's mouth. There are literally hundreds of components involved."

John broke in, "Dr. Simon, I'd like to introduce you to Zachary Whittman."

Simon nodded, "I recognize him from the papers, Detective Dietrich." Whittman blushed.

"We are going to show you two videos of him robbing a bank," John said. "One of them is staged. Please try not to concentrate on which robbery is real. Instead, focus on whether or not they are the same person. These two people look identical and I mean IDENTICAL. Can you tell me if they are, indeed, two different people?"

"That would be child's play for me, Detective, but I doubt that any two people could look that much alike. Even identical twins can be picked apart physically, but it's really the nonverbal cues that will distinguish one from the other."

John looked at Jaworski with incredible anticipation, "Start the first video, Greg."

Mary Simon spoke throughout the first video, noting cues they should look for in the one to follow. When the second video was played, she was completely silent until the end. John was busy trying to gauge her body language. She appeared troubled and somewhat confused, "I need to see both of these again."

John couldn't wait; he had to ask, "Are they the same person, Dr. Simon?"

"I—I don't believe so. In fact, I'm certain of it, but I cannot see a solitary physical difference between them. The likeness is uncanny!"

The second viewing was much like the first, except that Simon pointed out the difference between the two men during each clip. When they were finished, she reviewed her notes and tried her best to summarize what she had seen. "If it weren't such an impossibility, I'd say that this man was the same person, and that he was able to completely change his body language at will. But I know better. These are two very different people who share identical physical characteristics."

John nodded at Whittman and smiled, "Tell me why, Dr. Simon."

"In the first video, the man was commanding, self assured, mentally suited to his physical body. The second man was not. The second man blinked excessively, his posture was the inverse of the first man's. Their expressions, gestures, and strides were in opposition by 180 degrees. In addition, there is something seriously wrong with the second man's arm. I couldn't be certain, but was he wearing a latex glove on his right hand?"

John was euphoric. "Miss Simon, I need you to help us document what you just said. Brax, take an affidavit. I want you to list the second man's common traits and quirks, so we can look for them if he decides to impersonate someone else."

He looked at her sympathetically, I'm sorry to keep you so long, Dr. Simon, but I have three more brief videos. If you see any of the impostor's traits in the others, you'll tell us, won't you?"

Simon felt her heart pounding, "Of course I will. And don't worry about the time, Detective."

John gave her a stern glance. "No matter how crazy this might seem to you, you must tell us everything you are thinking." John headed for the door.

"Where are you going, John?" Braxton called out to him.

"I'm going to get the captain. He needs to meet Dr. Simon and hear this with his own ears."

17

JOHN DIETRICH ASKED ZACH WHITTMAN TO REMAIN behind after Mary Simon left. Captain Walsh was quiet throughout her presentation and offered to escort her to the lobby. No doubt, to ask her if she really believed that the man in the bank videos was someone other than Zach Whittman.

John shot Braxton a rehearsed glance and bobbed his head as if to tell him to follow his lead. "I appreciate you staying, Mr. Whittman, you've been very cooperative."

"What else can I do?" said Whittman. "My reputation—my entire life is on the line here."

John put on a solemn face. "Do you understand the difficulty Ms. Hershel is going to have trying to prove your innocence?"

"I think I do, Detective."

"I've believed in your innocence since the very beginning, Mr. Whittman, but we don't have nearly enough evidence to offset the videos and DNA left at the crime scene. If you don't give me more information, I'm afraid you're going to be found guilty of bank robbery."

Whittman nervously tapped his fingers on the table. John noticed immediately.

"I—I don't know what more I can tell you. You know everything I know."

John took a few steps away to put some distance between them. "I'm not accusing you of misleading us, Mr. Whittman, but somehow we've missed something important and I need to uncover it now."

"Ask me whatever you want," Whittman said. "I'll answer honestly."

John sat down across the table from Whittman. Leaning in close to him, his eyes narrowed and they locked intently with his.

"If I said this to anyone else, I'd be wearing a straightjacket within the hour, but I have a feeling you'll know exactly what I'm talking about."

Whittman's face turned pale, his uneasiness intensified as though he sensed that John was close to the truth.

"That man in the video, he's your clone, isn't he?"

Braxton's expression said he couldn't believe his ears. At the very least he seemed to forget that Whittman was in the room.

"What the hell are you saying, John?"

"It's possible," Whittman said, still tapping on the table, "in a matter of speaking."

Weak in the knees, Braxton plopped in a corner chair.

John's eyes didn't move from Whittman, "What do you mean by that?"

"Well, a clone is created from scratch, using a few cells from the host. I think the impostor is someone who was transformed into my clone by assuming my DNA blueprint."

"Then give me your best guess, Mr. Whittman. Who is that man?"

Whittman was still, "It sounds so bizarre—I've been wrestling with this for two days."

John became a little annoyed with Whittman. "Don't tell me about bizarre, Mr. Whittman. When I started this case, I couldn't even spell DNA. I had to read a boatload of crappy material—I researched my ass off, to verify the things you told me about cloning. I entertained some pretty crazy notions to get where we are today and thank God I did. You gave me very little information about your breakthrough discovery. I can't help feeling that this discovery is at the center of this whole thing, isn't it?"

"Yes."

"Who is the man in the video?"

"I can only be reasonably certain—I have no proof it's him."

"For God's sake, who, Mr. Whittman?"

"Richard Fulton."

There it was—a name. Faceless and without detail, but it was gratifying to hear. John's tongue felt the impression of teeth marks in his cheeks. He drew a relaxing breath before continuing.

"Who is he?"

"Dr. Fulton is one of my best researchers. We hired him several years ago, right out of college. He was passionate about the field of genetic research and in particular, cloning. You see, he lost his right arm in a car accident several years ago."

John's head jerked when he heard the words *right arm,* but he continued listening intently.

"His lifetime goal is to find a way to grow a new one through regeneration." Whittman paused to give an analogy. "Think of it as kind of an 'in place' cloning, where each cell in the body is replaced and cells missing from a person's DNA blueprint are created. Fulton was relentless, working day and night on a formula. He was close too, but in his hurry to reconstruct his arm, he was becoming careless. He stumbled upon an amazing discovery, a second layer in DNA, a layer containing information we have never seen before. Based on what I knew, he was ignoring dangerous facts. I couldn't let him continue without more research. The FDA is eager to shut down companies who can't prove they have taken reasonable precautions before human testing. I had no intention of being one of them."

Braxton's patience was growing thin, "So did he try it, or what?"

Whittman eluded a quick answer, as though he was determined to get to it on his own time table.

"Two years ago, Fulton had set his own deadline for human testing. We exceeded that deadline last month. He kept pressuring me to let him try it on himself, but after he discovered the second layer, I grew hesitant. I instructed some of my scientists in lab seven to review his research. While they confirmed that his theories were pure genius, they also agreed that the formula was much too dangerous to try without understanding the purpose of the second layer. After all, the formula was derived using basic DNA components. We had no idea of knowing what effect the catalyst compounds might have on bio-switches. We don't yet understand them, but we're certain their states can be altered chemically."

Whittman rubbed his eyes, he looked weary. "I was afraid Fulton wouldn't wait, so I confiscated the formula and stored it in a secure vault."

Jesus, Braxton thought, *doesn't this guy ever answer a question directly?* "Did the guy try it or not?"

John seemed satisfied with the order in which Whittman told the story, so Braxton held his tongue.

"The second layer," John asked, "that's the sub-layer of DNA you claim contains a genetic clock and possibly the components that control man's ability to evolve, is that right?"

"You remembered, Detective, I'm impressed. We know that the first layer is responsible for a person's appearance, height, hair color, and the like. But we suspect the second layer is responsible for man's adaptability to his environment and his level of susceptibility to illness. We think there are thousands of bio-switches that are set to an on or off position. Depending on the switches position, you might be allergic to penicillin or ragweed. You might be susceptible to catching colds. You may never develop lung cancer after a lifetime of smoking, where a nonsmoker could die of it at age thirty. Like I said, I believe we can turn these switches on and off chemically. I also believe this layer records man's age in a similar way that a tree grows a new ring for each season it endures. We think there is a way to reverse man's aging process. I thought we needed to understand these things fully before proceeding with Fulton's experiment. My best guess is that human testing is still three to five years away."

Son of a bitch, Braxton thought.

This time, John asked the question, "Mr. Whittman, please tell us—did he use the formula?"

"Yes."

"How can you be sure?"

"Our janitor, Wendell Peters, is friendly with Dr. Fulton. He was the last person to see him just over two weeks ago. One night Fulton came running out of his lab, delirious with joy, and for good reason. He had two arms—the formula worked."

John frowned. "How come you didn't tell us this before?"

"Would you have believed me if I had told you?"

John didn't answer. He looked at Braxton hoping to gauge his reaction. Braxton stared at Whittman sharply before he spoke.

"You can't just withhold information because it sounds crazy, Mr. Whittman. You need to tell us everything. What else did you leave out?"

Whittman studied Braxton, while he struggled for a response.

"Nothing, Detective, you know everything I know."

Somehow, I doubt that, John thought.

John raised his hand patting the air in front of him, "Wait a minute, Mr. Whittman, I thought you said you confiscated the formula and locked it up."

"That's right, but he may have had other versions of the formula tucked away in the lab or in his office. I believe he used an older version, perhaps one of those he was testing on lab mice."

John noticed Braxton raking his fingers through his hair.

"Hey Brax, would you mind getting us all a cold drink? You look like you could use a break, anyway."

Braxton nodded. When he left the room, John asked Whittman, "Where is Fulton now?"

"I don't know. I heard he was out sick for a few days, but I've been a little preoccupied preparing for an important meeting—and then there was that foolish bank robbery..." John straightened his body, his head rose high.

There's something wrong about this. If Fulton had grown an arm, Whittman would have been all over it. It's the huge success he's been waiting for.

"So all this time has gone by, and you've not been curious as to his whereabouts?"

"I was unaware of Fulton using the formula, or the fact that he was missing until two nights ago. Before then, I thought he was just avoiding me because of the memo."

"What memo?"

"I had sent him a memo a few days prior to his disappearance, halting any further testing until the board of directors gave him the green light to continue. Richard called me in a fit of rage. He said I had no right to scrub the test. He said I promised him a new arm—I owed him a new arm. I asked him to be patient, but he hung up on me. I was afraid he might try it anyway, so I confiscated the formula and stored it in one of our secure refrigerated lockers. I learned that it was that very evening that he vanished. He must have found an older formulation hidden somewhere in lab eight."

"He's got to be the impostor," John said rubbing his forehead. "Just look at the timing. The five-pack of crimes began about the same time he disappeared. You mentioned the board of directors in your memo?"

"Yes, however, I never indicated that the board made a decision to abandon testing, only that he should cease further testing until an approval by the board is given. But that's only standard protocol; the board approves all human testing."

"Now, wait a minute, Mr. Whittman, I thought the FDA approved human testing."

Whittman looked frustrated, "Of course they do. But we decide when to submit it to them. Richard may be blaming the board for lying to him or for something that may have gone wrong."

"Gone wrong?" John asked, "Like what?"

"Like an uncontrollable side effect." Whittman paused a long time before continuing. "I think Fulton is changing into other people. If one of the bio-switches did not adapt fully, he could be morphing into anyone whose DNA he comes in contact with."

"The glove!" John shouted. "His new arm! He only wears the glove on his right hand because that's the only part affected."

"I think your guess is correct, Detective. I suspect that whenever his right hand comes in contact with a source of DNA, he absorbs its blueprint, and his body rebuilds itself and becomes its clone."

John sat down, and leaned back in his chair. Five minutes ago, he had no suspect and eight tenths of a theory. But now the pieces were falling into place—except for one thing.

"Mr. Whittman, if Dr. Fulton becomes an exact clone of another person, how come his arm doesn't lose the ability to absorb a different blueprint?"

"Good question. First of all, he can't be an exact clone. My guess is that the formula wasn't ingested quickly enough, and somehow it resulted in a few bio-switches being set incorrectly. Now they're permanently stuck regardless of what form he takes."

John let out a deep breath, "I think we may have just established a motive of revenge, for three of the crimes, but I still have three more to figure out."

Whittman nodded as though knew Dietrich had his work cut out for him, "Tell me how I can help, Detective."

"Three things—first, can we dispense with the Mr. Whittman, Detective Dietrich tags? They're wearing me out." Whittman nodded. "Second, I need to start interviewing your employees right away. And third, Braxton and I need a complete tour of your facility."

Whittman's smile was barely perceptible. It was obvious he needed sleep.

"All right, John, we can go directly to our lab from here. I'll call ahead and have our VP of Research meet us. You can also interview the janitor. He works late into the evening."

Braxton returned with three Cokes. Clutched under his arm was the leather portfolio he took home with him every night. His eyes were red and his face was gaunt.

I guess it's time for people with family lives to go home, John thought. The facts and conjecture involved in John's five-pack of crimes was proving to be mentally exhausting for everyone. Even John was bushed.

John motioned his head toward Whittman. "We're headed to Critical Strategies Genetics Research. Guess I'll see you in the morning."

Braxton began to nod in agreement, and then he hesitated, "No wait, John, I'll follow you there."

I'll be damned if the kid's not hooked, John thought.

18

THERE WAS MORE ON DR. RICHARD FULTON'S MIND than getting even with the mayor. As he glimpsed at his latest reflection in one of the pub's Budweiser mirrors, he was reminded of how badly he wanted his own identity back. Although he could take any human form, assume any likeness, he longed to be himself again. He wondered if this was simply because people always want what they can't have. But no, this was different. If he were not Richard Fulton, how else would he be able to savor his technological triumph? After all, he did the impossible. He grew a new limb. Unfortunately, to return to his own body, he would need a sample of his DNA, and the only place to get it was in the high security lab at Critical Strategies Genetics Research. There he could find ample tissue and blood samples— the ones he used for the preliminary testing of his DNA for the cloning experiment. He thought that rubbing his toothbrush on his hand would change him back. The failure dumbfounded him.

Ninety seconds, he thought, broodingly, *ninety seconds in the lab and I could be myself again.* Fulton's handsome features seemed to dissipate as he thought about the experiment to clone his new arm.

Six years of research and preparation, six years of high hopes and anticipation, and for what? To see this project scrapped at the whim of the board of directors? They promised me a new arm. They broke their promise. Goddamn liars. Who the hell do they think they are?

Fulton glanced down at his hands. He had two of them now, but ten years ago, on the night of his high school graduation party, he'd lost his entire right arm. There was the typical drinking by his classmates, but he didn't participate. In fact, he and his girlfriend left the party early to drive to the lake and park under the stars. He was crazy about Amy Coder. He knew he would marry her after college. But they never arrived at their destination.

Just three blocks from the party, an eighty-one-year-old man ran a stop sign and forever ruined Fulton's carefully planned life. Both he and Amy were thrown from his Karman Ghia convertible. Fulton landed in the path of another car approaching the intersection. The oncoming car braked hard and skidded over his arm. The muscle from his shoulder to his elbow was shredded—lost forever. Even worse, Amy died at the scene from internal bleeding. Hospitalized and clinging to life, Fulton never saw Amy's body, never had a chance to say goodbye.

Throughout college and his working career, Fulton's life had become sterile, devoid of happiness. He poured himself into his studies and research. He did everything possible to avoid idle time, those little empty spaces that were once filled with Amy's laughter.

Fulton was still a young man of twenty-eight. He wasn't starkly handsome, but he wasn't unattractive either. However, since the accident, he had little self confidence with women. In fact, Fulton had few friends at all. His physical handicap robbed him of the pleasures of playing sports and diminished his relationship with male co-workers. His doctor prescribed medications for his constant depression. Sometimes, he felt almost normal, a feeling that quickly evaporated when he looked in the mirror. It wasn't his imagination that people treated him differently—they did. But Fulton's doctor insisted that his perceptions were often skewed and his feelings of ineptness amplified by the normal reactions people had to his missing limb. Often he felt rebuked in addition to feeling like an invalid.

He hated it when they stared at his shoulder where his arm once was. He loathed the pity, but even worse was the constant ridicule from people like Adam Sharp, a callous student who taunted him throughout college. The whispering behind his back, the snickering, and the wise-cracks were all at his expense, and they took their toll. Before the accident he would have bloodied Sharp's nose, but having only one arm made him feel defenseless and stripped him of his self-esteem.

Dr. Richard Fulton was a brilliant geneticist. With so limited a social life, he worked long hours and read every research study he could find on DNA and cloning. The architecture he created as a framework for cellular regeneration had instantly turned Zach Whittman into a hard core fan. Fulton claimed he could regenerate the human body and restore it to a prior state of age and health. In his own case, his DNA was unaware that he was missing a limb. His regeneration formula promised to grow him a new one. In addition, his heart, lungs, and liver, all of his organs, would be newly formed and free from pollutants and carcinogens. If scars and facial blemishes were not a part of his initial genetic blueprint, they would also disappear as new tissue replaced old. If it worked, the formula promised to put an end to disease, surgery, and old age. For mankind, it was a perfect blueprint for a genuine fountain of youth.

Two weeks ago, and without warning, the project was scrapped. At the very least, it was on permanent hold. There was little explanation from Whittman, only that the company must study his discovery of a second DNA layer for an undetermined time before proceeding.

Whittman had sent an employee to laboratory eight to pick up the formula in its final stage. It was transferred to CSGR's secure refrigerated storage locker indefinitely. As hard as Fulton tried, he could not get a straight answer from Whittman. He was ready to embark on the most important experiment in history. Why would Whittman cancel it, or even delay it?

Yes, there were risks, but those existed in any experiment involving a human specimen. The tests were completely successful in lab mice. Fulton was certain it would work on him, and on the night he received the heart wrenching news that the project was scrapped—it did.

Although Whittman confiscated the final formula, there was still a full vial of a prior version Fulton had tested on mice. It hadn't gone through the last two refinements, and for that reason, it couldn't be ingested as quickly as the final formula. But with the fleeting chance he would ever get to try it, Fulton decided it was worth the risk.

After the last of the researchers and lab technicians had left for the day, Fulton took the vial and poured the contents in a masklike device he strapped around his face. Fulton could detect the faint smell of the formula. It was a harmless, almost sweet smell, but that would change in an instant. He took a final breath and twisted a lever releasing the formula into a chamber containing a catalyst solution.

The vapor was difficult to breathe. He wanted to cough, but fought the impulse to do so. Fulton breathed deeply, taking the burning vapors into his lungs. As the room began to spin, he grasped a countertop and held on. The light began to fade, and he blacked out.

When he awoke, the mask was still intact. Fulton felt weak and barely had the strength to pull it off. He thanked God for the fresh air. His exhaustion didn't prevent his eyes from widening when he realized he was holding the mask in his right hand, a hand that hadn't existed only moments ago.

Fulton laid there, eyes closed but smiling like he hadn't smiled in years. Moments later, his eyelids opened and he focused on a sprinkler head on the ceiling. There was a tightness growing in his limbs and chest. Fulton experienced a sudden chill and a fearful thought overtook him.

Was he hallucinating or did he really have two arms, two hands? He was afraid to take another look for fear that it was all just a dream, a hallucination brought about by the formula. When he had recovered sufficient strength, Fulton rolled his head to the right and exhaled sharply.

It's there!

Getting to his feet was a struggle, and to his dismay his right arm was awkward. It didn't seem to follow his mental commands like his left arm. Fulton was prepared for that. He remembered reading how the brain often needed to be retrained for weeks, even months to get accustomed to losing an appendage. He had experienced that firsthand and assumed the opposite was true as well. Still, it was disappointing, but he would deal with that later. Suddenly infused with energy, Fulton tossed the mask in his briefcase and darted out the door.

He nearly ran over Wendell Peters, the janitor.

"Dr. Fulton, your face is sunburned," Peters said with a look of concern. Fulton felt his chin and cheeks. They were irritated and slightly sore. It was probably caused by the fumes from the formula.

"Who cares, Wendell, look at this!" Fulton raised his arms high in the air. His right arm floundered a bit.

"You have two arms, Dr. Fulton! Two hands! How did you—"

"No time to talk, Wendell—gotta go."

Fulton ran outdoors, and sprinted to his Lincoln Town Car. He squealed out of the parking lot, anxious to get home and practice using his new arm. The strangest thought occurred to him.

I could join the company golf league.

Suddenly, he laughed out loud. "What the hell do I care about the company's golf league? I can do anything—hell, I could ask Brenda Langdon for a date!" And then he realized he couldn't. It was too late. The heavenly blonde, who lived in the house behind him, the girl who never seemed to notice his physical impediment, had just become engaged to that ass-hole, Breeling. The few times they'd met, Breeling snickered at him, just like Adam Sharp had done throughout his college years. Of course, Brenda never noticed the belittling way Breeling stared at him.

Why do nice girls always fall for guys like that? Does she really know what she's getting? I doubt it.

He thought more about Brenda Langdon as he drove. He was certain she would have gone out with him if he had only found the courage to ask her. Now, maybe that could change.

With two arms, I'm as good as any man—better than most, he thought. *After tonight, I'll be famous, a celebrity. The Nobel Prize is a cinch. Maybe it's not too late at all.*

As he drove through an old section of town, he noticed the usual hookers roaming the streets. He had no desire to pleasure himself, but he desperately wanted to see how a woman would respond to him with two arms. He longed to be looked upon as an equal or, better yet, the superior man he really was. In his euphoric state, it never dawned on him how unimpressed a hooker might be to see a man with two arms. It wasn't until days later when he recalled the account, that he grasped how ridiculous he was acting. For God's sake—everyone has two arms.

He slowed the car and stopped in front of a blonde woman strutting along the sidewalk in a glittering silver skirt up to her butt cheeks. She poked her head through the Lincoln's passenger window and was immediately puzzled by the way the man was holding his hands in the air.

"Hey darlin'—look at my hands—what do you think?" he asked.

The woman took his gesture and question in stride. She probably got all sorts of crazy questions from *"Johns."* Gently stroking his arms and hands, she replied, "They look very strong," she said. "I love strong men like you." She sensuously kissed the fingers of his left hand and wet the tip of his finger in her mouth.

Her patronizing tone repulsed Fulton. "I gotta go," he said.

She clasped his hands. "Don't go, mister. I can make you feel like you've never felt before." She took his right hand and pressed it against her breast. Fulton felt an immediate reaction in his groin. And then she put his right index finger in her mouth. Two seconds later, her eyes rounded and she screamed at the top of her lungs. She spun and ran out of sight.

The hooker's scream took a moment to register in his head. It was as though he'd only half heard it. As his senses sharpened, the thought shook and confused him.

What did I do? he thought. He wasn't sure, but he knew his senses had dulled a moment ago. In fact, he felt slightly faint, and the next thing he knew she was screaming at the top of her lungs. Catching a glimpse of his once wet index finger, he realized why. The hand he was looking at was feminine. In the rear view mirror, he gawked at the reflection of the woman who had just run away screaming. Minus the heavy makeup, he was her spitting image. He felt his breasts. They were female, though smaller than hers.

Implants, he thought. He felt his crotch, *It's gone! What the hell's going on!*

Frightened, he mashed the accelerator to the floor and squealed his tires for the second time that night. It was difficult to reach the pedals, and he felt strange. His senses felt out of whack. Fulton drove furiously for fifteen minutes, but it didn't help. He readjusted the power controls on his seat. The image in the rear view mirror didn't change, and it sure as hell wasn't his. Between glances he prayed that the next reflection would be different. Maybe it was all a hallucination. Maybe he was still lying on the laboratory floor unconscious, his mind manufacturing this hideous nightmare. Confused as to his next move, he decided to go to a safe, familiar place—home.

Fulton stood naked in front of the bathroom mirror for more than an hour. He explored his new body, but took no joy in it. Fulton paid for sex twice in his life. He'd assumed that even hookers would be repulsed by a one-armed man, so he made them turn off the lights. The chance to gaze upon a female body in a well-lit room should have been a joy, but it wasn't. With empty eyes, he stood there, stroking his breasts, while his mind replayed the evening's events in a continuous loop. Suddenly, something clicked. It finally dawned on him what had happened.

My right hand! Nothing happened when she put the finger of my left hand in her mouth, it happened with my right hand.

∞

Fulton changed identities three times that night, beginning with a drunk he passed near a darkened alley. Doubling back, he found a guy tipping a bottle of Thunderbird.

"I'll give you twenty bucks for a drink from your bottle," Fulton said.

"Heyyy—you can have a drink for free, honey." Embarrassed, Fulton closed his eyes.

You wish, you fucking drunk.

Fulton's stomach was queasy. He had almost forgotten he wasn't just a woman, he was a knockout blonde. Fulton didn't like being a woman. And the thought of this guy drooling at his breasts was almost more than he could stand. Taking the bottle the man offered, Fulton didn't drink. Instead, he wiped its lip in the palm of his right hand and closed it around his fingers.

There was a flash of darkness, a moment of faint awareness, but he was still on his feet. The drunk stared at him. He rubbed his eyes and stared again, horrified by what he saw. He scrambled to his feet, and stumbled away mumbling incoherently. Holding his hands in front of him, Fulton acknowledged the masculine shape, the coarse dark hair on his arms.

It works by absorption, he thought. *Every time my right hand comes in contact with a source of DNA, my body is going to assume the host's shape. The experiment was not only a complete success, but a total failure as well. How can I live like this? How could anyone live like this?*

The bottle of Thunderbird had fallen in the grass. Fulton didn't remember dropping it, but he picked it up and took a painfully long drink.

19

JOHN LEARNED THAT WHITTMAN'S COMPANY, CSGR had tripled its size in the last four years. The decade-old company sub-contracted with some of the largest pharmaceutical companies in the world to perform biological research for new drug development. There was a lot of private genetic research occurring within their walls too. If successful, Dr. Fulton's discovery would squarely place CSGR on the map as a premier leader in genetic engineering. John estimated that the regeneration formula was worth hundreds of billions of dollars. After all, who wouldn't pay a small fortune for immortality? Secrecy, Whittman had told John, was important. They had to beat the big players to the market with a "fountain of youth" product, or all was lost. At stake were the glory, the Nobel Prize, and the name recognition that would thrust their product in the number one spot in the consumer market that would follow.

John suspected that the only reason Dr. Fulton's disappearance concerned Zach Whittman was because of the possibility of losing the race. Whittman's reputation was of secondary importance. Fulton understood the formula's infrastructure better than anyone else. But if Fulton was responsible for the crimes, he would be going away for a very long time.

Something else was bothering John. He couldn't verbalize what it was, because the thought hadn't fully developed, but another hunch, a suspicion was gestating within him. It involved Whittman. John couldn't put his finger on it, but it was gnawing at him. It started just before they left the precinct, when Whittman admitted that if he'd handled the situation better, Richard would still be here.

The VP of Research, Jim Saunders, met John and Braxton in the lobby. Whittman excused himself to check his voice and email messages.

Poor guy, John mused, *with the amount of work he's missed, he's got to be buried up to his eyeballs in unfinished business.*

"Gentlemen," Saunders began, "I understand I am to give you a full tour of our facility. Any preference as to where we start?"

"You're from England?" John asked.

Saunders raised his eyebrows. "I suppose I couldn't hide my accent if I tried. Yes, there are several of us that transferred here from our affiliate lab in London. Now, any preferences to where we start the tour?"

"None whatsoever, but we are particularly interested in labs seven and eight, and we need to fully understand your security systems."

"Well, to begin with, we have two armed security guards." John noticed a uniformed man doodling on a memo pad at the receptionist desk. It was after five, so the switchboard was closed. "The other guard is posted at the rear employee entrance."

"Any other way in or out?" John asked.

"There's a fire exit on the east side of the building, but it triggers an alarm."

Saunders cleared his throat to signal the security guard and flashed his ID card.

The guard waved and pressed a buzzer unlocking the first door. As they walked, Saunders pointed out a corridor the executive offices on the left and cafeteria on his right. They approached another locked door. There was an apparatus mounted to the wall beside it. Saunders pressed his forehead against the contour of a molded foam insert. After a barely perceptible hum, the doors unlocked.

"Retinal scanner?" John asked. Saunders nodded.

"It's the best part of our security system." They continued walking.

"We have eighteen labs, odd numbers on the left, even numbers on the right."

There were large viewing windows allowing VIPs and visitors to watch the scientists and lab technicians at work. The labs were impeccably clean and modern. On the countertops sat a multitude of analytical instruments. Saunders described them, and John recognized that several of the technologies were used by the police labs.

Saunders pointed to his right. "Over there we have UV/Visible, fluorescence, and atomic absorption spectrophotometers. On the other side, you can see rows of gas and liquid chromatographs." There were literally rows upon rows of neatly arranged instruments. John had never seen anything like it.

"Oh," Saunders added, "the instruments on the far wall—those are DNA sequencers. There's about thirty million dollars in laboratory equipment floating around these labs." Saunders's tone carried a note of pride. "We've got a couple of mass spectrometers in lab twelve." It looked like a science fiction fest to Braxton, who watched in awe as lights flashed and automated samplers rotated injecting liquids like miniature robots.

When they approached lab seven, John noted a flurry of activity. A group of excited researchers were writing gibberish on a white board. John couldn't tell whether they were mathematical or chemical formulas. An Asian woman was seated at an electron microscope. The sample on the slide was projected on a large LCD screen. "What's going on in there?" John asked.

"Big things, gentlemen. We are going to make a major contribution to the scientific world very soon."

John squinted, "What kind of contribution?"

"The kind you win a Nobel Prize for," Saunders replied.

That was rehearsed, John suspected. "Can you elaborate?"

Saunders eyes fell, "I wish I could, Detective. To be honest—even I don't know. From what Zach Whittman says, we are sitting on the biggest discovery in history."

John peered over his shoulder. "Sounds incredible. Can we look around in lab eight?"

Saunders held his ID card against lab eight's wall mounted sensor. There was a muted click as the door unlocked. Compared to the other labs, this one was stark. There were gigantic vent hoods, centrifuges, elaborate sinks, and racks of glassware, but there were only a few high-tech instruments on the countertops. "This is Dr. Fulton's lab, isn't it?"

"Yes, it serves mostly as a wet lab, but this one is off limits to the other researchers. Dr. Fulton spends most of his time in this room. That's his office over there." Saunders pointed to a closed door at the far side of the lab.

"Dr. Fulton's office is in the lab?" John asked.

"Yes, come to think of it, he's probably the only researcher in the company to have an office in a lab. Most of them have cubicles down the hall, except for a handful of window offices reserved for our Top Guns. Dr. Fulton was offered a window office, but said he'd rather be close to his work."

Our man's a loner, John thought.

John gravitated to the office door and wasn't surprised to find it locked.

"I'll need to get in here," John said.

Braxton circled the lab, scanning for anything of interest. There was a small refrigerator in the corner. He opened it and saw dozens of vials, flasks, and Petri dishes. There were a few test tubes filled with blood. The labels read "R. Fulton."

"Hey, John, look at this."

John went to the refrigerator and squatted low to view the contents. Without speaking, Braxton used his index finger to point to Fulton's name.

"Mr. Saunders?" John asked. "Has anyone catalogued the contents of this refrigerator?"

Saunders seemed puzzled by the question, "We don't make it a habit of cataloguing the contents of our researcher's refrigerators. I'm certain the last person to access it was Dr. Fulton. Is there a problem?"

"None at all," John replied." He tapped Braxton's wrist and whispered, "Call Jaworski and get him over here now. Tell him we've got Fulton's DNA." Braxton reached in his pocket and removed a tiny digital camera. He snapped half a dozen photos of the refrigerated contents and then walked to the opposite end of the lab to call Jaworski. Saunders began to fidget as John approached, but John was observing Braxton and smiled when he saw him try the door handle of Fulton's office.

"Mr. Saunders, can you unlock Dr. Fulton's office? We need to look inside." Saunders frowned in concern.

"Are you sure there's nothing wrong, Detective?"

"Not yet, we just want to see where Dr. Fulton works."

"I don't have a key. I'll need to call the janitor."

"Wendell Peters?" John asked.

"Yes, how did you know?"

"He's on the list of people I need to question. Can you have him meet us here?"

A few minutes later, Wendell Peters appeared. The janitor was small of stature, but friendly and outgoing. His southern drawl added a colorful flair to his personality. John asked him to describe his relationship with Dr. Fulton.

"He's one of the good ones, sir. A lot of the folks here have egos bigger 'n Texas—that's where I'm from—but not Dr. Fulton. He's a regular guy."

"So, you speak with him often?"

"Just chit-chat mostly, but he always treats me with respect. He's a kind one."

"What do you know about his background?"

"Not much, really. Said he lost his arm in a car crash about ten years ago. Said he'd figure out how to make a new one and I'll be damned if he didn't."

"So you saw him with two arms?"

"Yup. Must have been right after it happened too, because he was really excited. I was moppin' the hallways when he came runnin' out of this lab. I thought he was gonna whoop and holler all the way out the building. I saw it with my own eyes, cept'n' he looked like he had a little trouble usin' it."

"What do you mean?"

"When he held them up to show me, one of them wasn't in sync with the other. He probably just wasn't used to using it yet."

Pretty profound observation, John thought.

"Can you describe him for me?"

"Yeah, he's about six-foot-one, kinda' skinny. He has dark brown hair and glasses—the kind with black frames. His skin don't look like it's ever seen the sun, he'd probably burn pretty easy. He's got heavy eyebrows, you know—bushy, and brown eyes. He looks like one of them college professors."

"Any distinguishing marks?"

"Not really—well, I suppose the redness on his face is gone by now."

"What redness?"

"Well, when he came runnin' out that night, he had a red outline on his face—it only covered the area around his nose and chin, like he was wearing a mask."

John hoped like hell that CSGR had a file photo. But under the circumstances, he wondered if he'd ever see Fulton's real face.

"Can you unlock Dr. Fulton's office for me, Wendell?" When the door was unlocked, John dismissed the janitor and Saunders followed him through the doorway. John slowly wandered around its perimeter.

Stark, John thought as his eyes scanned the room. He reached into his breast pocket and withdrew a small notepad. He scribbled half a dozen notes before he began questioning Saunders.

"How well do you know Dr. Fulton?"

Saunders face had begun to swell with concern from the time Braxton began taking photos of the refrigerator's contents. By the completion of the janitor's interview, he looked mortified that something terrible had happened. Now that Wendell Peters was gone, he was anxious to speak to the detectives in private.

"Detective, exactly what is all of this about? Is Dr. Fulton in trouble?"

"I don't know yet, Mr. Saunders, but he's disappeared, and we need to ask him some questions."

"Disappeared? No, he hasn't disappeared, he's just sick. I spoke with him this morning. He said he has walking pneumonia and he'll be out for a few more days, maybe a week."

John's head jerked up. "He called in?"

"Yes, I've spoken to him three times since he got sick. I've got to tell you; there really is something wrong with him. He doesn't sound at all like himself. I didn't even recognize his voice."

Not surprising, John thought. "Did he mention if he'd seen a doctor?"

"Not specifically, but I assumed that if he had a diagnosis of walking pneumonia, he's seen a doctor."

"Does Mr. Whittman know you've talked to him?"

Saunders thought carefully. "No, I don't suppose so. We've hardly spoken since he was arrested." Suddenly his eye grew wide, "There isn't a connection—is there?"

"Please Mr. Saunders, let me ask the questions. Fulton's a loner, isn't he?"

"Yeah, I suppose he keeps pretty much to himself. How'd you know that?"

John used his arm to make a sweeping motion across the office, as if to signify that the room should speak for itself. "There's not a single personal artifact in this office. No photos, no awards—not even a comic strip on the bulletin board. Nothing here suggests your Dr. Fulton had a personal life."

Or a personality for that matter.

Both men studied the office. Except for stacks of books and research journals, the room had a bleak appearance. The desk was cluttered with reports, notes, and loose papers. The chaos carried over to the top of a four-drawer file cabinet piled high with manila folders. Two of the drawers were left open. A white board displayed remnants of a mathematical formula.

Saunders said, "Hmm, I never really noticed that before."

"Did he have any friends here, Mr. Saunders?"

"I—I guess so, I don't really know."

"What time did you speak to him?"

"Just before noon—look, Detective, I agree with the janitor. Dr. Fulton seems to be a good man. Not only is he brilliant, but I think he has high moral character. He's a little quiet and keeps a bit to himself, but there's no crime in that."

"Indeed there isn't," John agreed disarmingly. "I appreciate the tour, Mr. Saunders. Now, I need you to keep everyone out of this lab—no exceptions. Can you take us to Mr. Whittman's office?"

Ten minutes later, John had finished explaining the facts he had just learned from Saunders and Peters to Whittman, who seemed to be a little embarrassed at his incredibly poor knowledge of the situation.

Whittman shook his head. "I guess I've been so concerned about saving my own skin, I didn't bother to ask any questions."

"Did you know that Fulton spoke with Mr. Saunders this morning?"

"No, I hadn't spoken to Jim until an hour ago when I called him from the police station." John forced a small nod and smile. "Under the circumstances, Zach, that's quite understandable."

John told Whittman about the red marks that Wendell Peters described around Dr. Fulton's nose and mouth. "What do you make of them?"

Whittman's features were stoic. "There is no longer any doubt in my mind that Dr. Fulton used the formula."

"Why do you say that?"

"The red marks were left by the mask Fulton used to ingest the formula. I approved the design of that mask. The reagent we chose as a catalyst to vaporize the formula was slightly caustic. I'm reasonably sure it caused the redness Wendell described."

John's expression said he only partially understood. Whittman continued, "The mask was necessary because we needed to metabolize the compounds so they could be ingested into the body quickly. The mask was the perfect solution. It contains two chambers—one for the formula, another for the catalyst. When they mix, the formula is vaporized and ingested through the lungs. However, Dr. Fulton used an older version of the formula. It wasn't optimized for the reagent we used, and if not ingested quickly, there could have been complications—bio-switches not set properly. It could have resulted in a complete failure of the project, or in this case, complications and side effects. We won't know until we can examine him."

John nodded, "Braxton and I will try to pick him up tonight. I need his address, home and cell phone numbers, and a photo of him if you have it."

"His photo ID is on our computer system. I'll have his employee profile printed for you right away."

John continued, "Our forensics officer is on his way over. We photographed the contents of the refrigerator in lab eight. As of this moment, it is all evidence."

Whitman turned red, "I cannot allow that, John. There may be some of the formula in there!"

"I understand your predicament, Zach, but quite frankly, you have no choice in the matter. We have no intention of exposing your research, but until we determine what everything is, it's going downtown with us. There are vials of blood labeled with Fulton's name. At least we'll have his DNA, and Jaworski will dust the glassware for prints. You realize, Zach, we are only trying to prove your innocence here."

"I know, I know—it's just that I'm losing control of everything just when I need it the most."

John thought for a moment, "I'll tell you what, I'll call Jaworski. If we determine that any container in that refrigerator contains your formula, we'll leave it on the premises, but under our lock and key. Will that be acceptable?"

Whittman looked at John with grateful eyes, "You are a gentleman, John."

"Braxton, can you call the office? Tell them we need a list of phone numbers of anyone who called this facility an hour either side of noon today. Zach, I need Fulton's profile, now!"

20

FULTON DOWNED HIS FIFTH BEER. HE HADN'T BEEN to work in over two weeks. He didn't know how much longer he could claim to be ill. He had spoken with Jim Saunders, the VP of Research just this morning, alleging to have walking pneumonia.

"Your voice sounds different," Saunders said with a probing tone.

"It's the pneumonia," Fulton replied, feigning a raspy voice. "It'll be back to normal in a week or so."

"I don't suppose it really matters," Saunders explained. "We've been in a state of chaos ever since they arrested Mr. Whittman. Although some research continues, all DNA experiments have been halted. Some of my best people are sitting on their hands waiting for instructions. For some reason, there is still a lot of activity in lab seven. Rumors are flying that they've made an incredible discovery."

Incredible discovery? Fulton pondered. *Could that be my discovery?* Lab seven wasn't under Saunders's scrutiny. Neither was Fulton and lab eight for that matter. They both reported directly to Whittman. Saunders had no idea what projects lab seven was working on. Lab seven was a kind of "skunk works," providing a forum for brilliant minds to massage half-baked ideas in a think tank environment.

Whittman said my experiment was halted due to safety issues, but maybe he just shifted his priorities. Or maybe he wants all the glory for himself. Guess it doesn't really matter. Whittman lied to me and he's going to pay dearly for it. Soon he'll be in prison and I'll continue my research.

Five of Fulton's six targets had already been arrested for crimes he cleverly staged. Soon the mayor would join them. Most of them were free on bail, but sooner or later convictions would be made and lives would be ruined. Perhaps his sweetest revenge involved Adam Sharp, the antagonistic prick from New Jersey who had lived across the hall from Fulton in his college days. He was already paying for his sins against the meek.

Last week Sharp was arraigned on assault and battery charges. Witnesses told police he beat a man in a bar with a baseball bat and nearly killed him. When Sharp ran out of the bar, the owner called an ambulance and the police. No one chased him, but a few minutes later, some of the regular patrons drifted up the steps to see where he had gone. They were shocked to find him lying bruised and unconscious in the alley, just a few feet from the edge of the building. His hands and ribs were broken, and the baseball bat lay beside him. Bystanders wondered what could have happened to him. Did someone avenge the attack on the poor man in the bar? The question was posed, but never answered.

Fulton smiled at his handsome reflection as he recalled the events that had taken place earlier on that same evening. The details were much too incredible to be believed by a sane man. Fulton had followed Adam Sharp to his apartment. But thirty minutes earlier, in the very bar where the attack would occur, he had altered his form and cloned a muscle-bound biker who hung out there. It was so easy to frame his long despised antagonist. Every night the biker had two or three beers and left. That night was no exception. As soon as the biker reached the door, Fulton went to his table and poured the remaining contents of his glass into a paper cup. In the bar's restroom he removed the latex glove from his right hand and poured the dregs of beer over his fingers. Briefly, he was overcome by a mental darkness, a fuzziness that lasted only a split second, but he knew what had happened.

The transformation was miraculously quick. Each time he assumed another form, he could sense every change, every nuance of his physical being. His hearing was not as sharp as it had been only seconds ago; his height was several inches taller. He tightly filled out the baggy clothes he'd worn into the establishment. His arms felt powerful, he could sense the strength in his hands. He looked in the mirror and stared at the reflection of the stranger he saw drinking beer only moments ago. Fulton was amused to see how different the man appeared with the absence of tattoos and the long scar that no longer marred his cheek.

From the first floor hallway of Sharp's apartment, Fulton knocked on the door. Unwittingly, Adam Sharp swung the door wide open like he was expecting company. He gazed down at a baseball bat in the man's left hand. He was conscious for only seconds more. Fulton strategically worked him over, ensuring he would experience pain with the slightest movement when he awoke. Next, he draped Sharp's limp body over the railing of his apartment patio. He leaped over it and carried the body to the car. He went back to the bar and arranged Sharp's body in the alley. Using the fingers of his right hand, he swabbed Sharp's mouth and waited for the transformation to occur. In barely more than a split second, he had Sharp's face and body. Fulton mused that it took longer for his head to clear than for the metamorphosis itself. He picked up the bat.

Fulton picked a quiet man, a regular patron. The first swing of the bat broke his jaw. Two more swings and the man lie unconscious on the floor. After Fulton assaulted him, he glared at the bystanders and walked to the door. Once outside, he dropped the bat beside Sharp's body and darted past a few buildings down the street. Bracing himself against the door of a closed music shop, he smeared his right hand with the contents from a small vial. New senses came alive in him. He shed the jacket he'd grabbed from Sharp's apartment and walked with a quick step towards the bar where a crowd was gathering outside. He heard someone say that Sharp got what he deserved.

I agree, he thought, *that son of a bitch got what he deserved.*

Now Fulton sat in a booth in a different tavern brooding. Six hours had passed since he ordered his first beer, and he was beginning to get a buzz. As far as Fulton was concerned, each of the five people he'd framed got what they deserved—all but the mayor. For some reason that fat-ass escaped punishment. Fulton looked at his watch and decided to head home. He'd hatched a new plan to ruin the mayor and it was a good one. But he'd have little chance to carry it out if he were drunk.

This time I'll trash any chances he's got for reelection, he thought.

21

RICHARD FULTON OWNED A SMALL THREE-BEDROOM brick ranch that was built in the seventies. John assumed he could afford much better accommodations, but his pathetic lifestyle didn't demand it. From what John had learned so far, Fulton was a loner. He didn't entertain, nor were there acquaintances willing to show up if he did. John was trying to figure out whether this was because Fulton was a nerd, or if he just wasn't that likable. Uncertain at the moment, John was desperate to learn more about him. Parked across the street from Fulton's ranch, Braxton stared at the photo. "He doesn't look like much of a menace, does he?"

"I don't suppose so, Kid, but consider all the damage he's done. If he'd been successful framing the mayor, he'd have a six-pack of crimes under his belt."

"Jesus, John, that reminds me—why do you give all of your cases nicknames? The 'five-pack of crimes', for example."

John sniggered. "I suppose you think I'm a case study in compulsive behavior."

Braxton innocently raised his eyebrows and shrugged his shoulders.

Unfazed, John said, "It's just a simple memory technique. I started doing it about twenty years ago. It helps me remember each case, or in this instance, a group of cases. On the outside chance you haven't noticed, a shitload of information crosses our desks each day. Using these techniques, I can recall almost every case I've worked in twenty-three years."

Braxton just stared at the house.

"Let me give you an example, Brax: I was having a terrible time remembering your name until the very moment I tied the word *Brash* to Braxton. From then on, your name was solidified in my mind. I suggest you find a system of your own and soon."

"Your fancy memory technique still hasn't stopped you from calling me *kid,* has it?"

"No," John said, "you've made it much too fun for me to stop now." John watched Braxton let out a huge yawn.

"Glad you find our conversation so interesting."

"It's not you, John, it's been a long day, that's all. A lot's happened today—there's so much to think about."

"I didn't realize it until just now, but I'm a kind of tired myself. You got to admit though, we made a lot of progress today."

It was about ten after seven; the light in the sky was fading. Braxton looked at Fulton's photo again, and then he shuffled the papers to find his data profile.

"Yeah, we learned a lot, but part of me is still having trouble believing that a man can grow a new arm, or take someone else's shape."

"I know you're still struggling with this, Brax. Would you like me to explain why it's not only possible, but likely?"

"I'm not going anywhere, partner—fire away." Looking at nothing in particular, John gazed out the windshield.

"If a starfish loses an arm, it's no big deal. Starfish have natural regenerative abilities, so the starfish can grow a new one. You could cut a starfish in half, and each piece could regenerate and form two separate starfish. Salamanders can do limited regeneration, growing new tails and legs. A few years ago, scientists were not sure how salamanders were able to grow new bone, muscles, and skin all in the right order to create a new limb. But now they believe they possess a gene or a protein that sends the signals necessary to trigger and guide the growth. The process takes several months, but the salamander has a brand new leg, complete with toes and markings."

"So, John—which is Fulton, a starfish, or a salamander?" Braxton asked.

John's eyes softened and he grinned.

"Do you wanna hear this, Partner?" Braxton shrugged, but John could tell he was interested.

"This is what Whittman has been talking about all along, the genetic blueprint of DNA. Humans already do a certain type of regeneration. It's called healing. For example, if you get a scrape, or cut yourself, your skin can regenerate to heal the wound. It's not uncommon for humans to grow a new fingertip, even if it is completely severed, as long as the cut is within certain limits. It's believed that man has evolved too far to fully regenerate on his own. Maybe the gene that controls our ability to regenerate has become dormant." Braxton was now fully engaged in John's explanation. He'd lost his grin.

"Think of it this way, Brax. Our cells have become so specialized; they lack the natural ability to react in the same way as animals do in a highly predatory society. What Fulton was trying to do is find the trigger to unlock man's natural ability to heal itself on a more sophisticated level. With our highly developed brains, and advanced intelligence, it is thought that the human regeneration process could be much faster."

Braxton's jaw had dropped halfway through Dietrich's explanation.

"Jesus, John, maybe you should have been a researcher yourself. Where'd you learn all that stuff?"

"I'm not that smart, Kid, I just know where to find good information when I need it. I'll read whatever it takes to get me from one case to the next. It wasn't without a lot of digging and soul searching that I was able to accept the fact that regeneration is even possible. But since half the scientists in the country are working on it right now, I had to take a serious look at it. Everyone is convinced it will it will become a reality at any moment. That in itself was pretty damned convincing."

"Hold up, John!" Braxton leaned over to get a better look, "Someone's approaching the house!" A dark-haired, athletic looking man turned up the sidewalk. He was headed straight for Fulton's front door. "Let's go!" Braxton said, excitedly.

"Wait!" John said, grabbing his arm. "If that's him, we could never prove it. Let's see if he knocks on the door or goes right into the house." The young man withdrew a set of keys from his pocket and unlocked the door.

"Do you think it's him?" Braxton prodded.

"I don't know, Kid, but when he unlocked that door, the odds went way up."

"Should I take the back door?"

Dietrich didn't know whether to smile or frown.

Let's see what the kid has in mind. "What's your plan, Brax?"

"I thought you could knock on the front door while I make sure he doesn't escape through the back."

"And what should we arrest him for—missing work?"

Braxton suddenly realized how stupid his plan was. His eyes fell in embarrassment.

"I don't know—there sure as hell isn't anything in my training manual to cover this type of situation." John laughed.

"You've got the right idea now, Kid. We need to sit tight and watch this guy. We'll stake him out for a while and see what happens."

Frowning, Braxton let go of some frustration, "It seems to me like we're just spinning our wheels."

John grinned, "You've got the makings of a good detective, Braxton, but you're impatient as hell. Have I ever told you the story about the old bull and the young bull?"

Braxton braced himself as if he knew who would be the young bull in the story.

"No, but I have a feeling I'm going to hear it."

John didn't waste a second. His voice took on a bedtime story quality.

"From the top of a tall, steep hill, the old bull and young bull could see all of the beautiful cows in the pasture. 'Man, I'm horny,' said the young bull. 'I think I'll run down there and screw one of those heifers.' The old bull winked at him and said, 'You go right ahead sonny, I think I'll walk down there and screw them all'."

Braxton wasn't sure whether it was the way John told it, the fact that he was exhausted, or the appropriate way it fit the situation, but he laughed until there were tears in his eyes. John was glad to relieve some of the tension for him, even if for only a moment.

"I have more jokes, want to hear another?"

Braxton was holding his belly. "No, that's enough, you can stop right there."

John's eyes darted to the house. Tapping Braxton's arm, he said, "I think he's on the move; he's turning off the house lights."

Braxton leaned over to glimpse the horizon. There was only a glimmer of pink light left in the sky. Fulton's garage door opened. A gold Lincoln Town Car backed out of the driveway. John gave the man they assumed was Fulton, a comfortable lead before following him.

"We need to keep our distance, Brax. I'd bet anything Dr. Fulton's up to something."

The detectives followed Fulton's Lincoln downtown, toward Kansas City's Plaza. As they neared its edge, John marveled at its beautiful Spanish architecture. The Giralda Tower was brilliantly lit and was easily recognizable as the Plaza's tallest building, a prominent centerpiece. During the Christmas season, John and Cindy shopped in the Plaza stores they could afford. As part of a holiday tradition, the entire skyline of the Plaza is trimmed in streams of lights that neatly outline each building with colors that can be seen from miles away. But today was just a typical day in mid-September. The air was warm, but gone was the sultry humidity from the summer months. In any season, the Plaza provided a visual experience that drew countless visitors from all over the country.

At 48th and Jefferson, the Lincoln turned into the Seville Parking Garage. Empty stalls were non-existent until they reached the third level. The obese figure who got out of the driver's door was not Fulton.

"Jesus, it's the mayor, John! What do you think he's got in the duffel bag?"

Braxton was actually thinking what John had already concluded. He just couldn't say the words.

"That's not the mayor, Brax, that's Fulton! He's probably carrying a change of clothes."

This time, John was ready to move, "C'mon, let's go! Whatever you do, don't say a word. Let me do all the talking!"

They walked quickly to catch up with their prey. They were only a few feet away from the elevator door when it opened. All three men stepped in. With his right hand in his pocket, Fulton raised a black and turquoise duffel bag while pressing the ground level button with his left index finger.

John's hands were in his pockets too. Aside from making swaying body movements, he was jingling the change in one pocket rather obnoxiously. "Sayyy, aren't you the mayor?" he said with a colorful accent. It was difficult for John not to gawk at Fulton. Every detail of his appearance, no matter how minor, was identical to the mayor's.

"Yes, I am," the man said flatly.

Braxton had wrinkles at the corners of his eyes, the kind that appear with a genuine laugh or smile. John's demeanor probably reminded Braxton of a "country bumpkin," not too bright and all too talkative. "Well, it's an honor to meet you, sir." John extended his right hand, hoping to coax a handshake. Fulton didn't bite. His greeting hand remained in his pocket. "Sorry, I've had a terrible cold this week, wouldn't want to pass it on by shaking your hand."

"Well, that's very thoughtful of you, Mr. Mayor. Hey, how's the election going? What's the latest in the polls?"

"About the same," he said, a little irritated at the questions.

"Well, me an' my friend here are votin' for ya'. Yes sir, ya' got two votes right here."

The elevator descended briskly. Fulton stared intently as the backlit numerals counted down from level to level. He looked as if he was praying to reach the ground level quickly.

Is he claustrophobic, nervous, or annoyed? John wondered.

"Thank you, gentlemen—that's very kind of you."

"Don't thank us, no sir, yer doin' a good job, and that's that!"

John started to say something else, when the doors opened and Fulton bolted out to the walkway. His bulbous frame labored to reach a vigorous pace. Braxton decided the clumsy oversized duffel didn't help Fulton's efforts either. But worse were the countless elegant meals the real mayor consumed at various city functions. The mayor was notorious for his insatiable appetite for expensive cuisine. He spun right and headed for the street. John paced himself just enough to let Fulton put some distance between them.

John whispered, "How's that for getting him out ahead of us, Junior? He should be a lot easier to follow now."

Braxton grinned and whispered back, "I noticed he wasn't too willing to shake your hand, John—probably didn't wanna get ol' fart cooties."

"He didn't want to expose the glove, Kid—ten bucks says he's wearing one." Braxton kept his eyes straight ahead, his adrenaline was pumping.

This is it. Any moment now, we're going to make the arrest.

Fulton crossed Jefferson Street and headed down Nichols Road, doing his best to blend into the crowd of locals and sightseers. It didn't work. The buildings and streets were well lit. His tall, wide frame was easily spotted from a distance. "It's a busy night here," Braxton commented, "what's going on?"

"Not sure, Kid—the Plaza is usually busy, but tonight, it seems down right crowded." Just then, he saw the sign. "It's the Plaza Art Fair. I almost forgot, Cindy wanted to come tomorrow night. She's crazy about art."

As they penetrated the Plaza's depths, they could hear distant music from a live band. Vendors were selling food outdoors and the sidewalks were lined with tables, most of which prominently displayed drawings, paintings, and sculptures. They crossed Pennsylvania Street. Foot traffic was slowing as people stopped to view the exhibits, which John read had been selected from the entries of over 1,400 artists. Fulton's head bobbed up and down as he moved away from the curb side of the walk.

Body language, John mused, *I've never seen the mayor display even the slightest animation or bounce in his step.*

"Let's not fall too far behind, John. We don't want to lose him."

"Hey, Brax," John yelled.

"What?" Braxton said, giving John a sideways look.

Winking, he said, "Let's walk down the hill and screw all the heifers."

22

PEDESTRIAN CONGESTION CONTINUED TO THICKEN. The two detectives were trying to move briskly, but now they were being buffeted by oncoming shoppers. "So what's the plan, you ol' fart? Are we going to arrest him now, or wait for him to do something illegal?" The sarcasm soured Braxton's features and underlined his growing impatience.

"I thought we'd at least wait to see what he's up to, Kid. Maybe we can catch him in the act. It would make the arrest stick."

A frown was Braxton's only response.

John sensed his discontent, "Come on, Brax, aren't you curious?"

"Sure, but I'm more concerned about him getting away."

"Afraid he'll outrun you?"

"As fat as he is, John, I think even you could catch him."

They were nearing Broadway Street. There were more displays, more people stopping to admire artists' works.

John began to have second thoughts about his strategy.

If he's going to do something to damage the mayor's reputation, maybe I shouldn't let it happen. The mayor's poll numbers are fragile. It wouldn't take much to sabotage his success in the election. But catching him in the act would make the arrest stick. Aw, hell, maybe we should just pick him up now.

John gave Braxton a serious nod, "Okay, Kid, I've changed my mind—let's pick him up."

Fulton had drifted to the inside of the sidewalk and suddenly vanished around the corner of Broadway.

"Goddamit," John cursed in an edgy tone. They were still thirty feet from the end of the block. When pedestrian traffic stopped, Braxton went into a panic and began muscling his way through the crowd. A man grabbed him and slammed him against a store front.

"Watch where you're going, asshole."

Braxton was mad, but he had no time to lose. He spun away, ignoring the angry man and continued trudging forward, pushing through the crowd. John was on his tail. He threw a shoulder into the man who had grabbed Braxton.

"Police officers, asshole!" He wished his partner could have seen the man's feet leave the ground.

Not bad for an ol' fart, John thought.

Braxton disappeared at the corner, just as Fulton had done only moments ago. John was almost there. Slipping between an old couple, he turned north. About fifteen yards away, he could see Braxton standing in the street. He was twisting and turning at the torso, his eyes searching frantically for the mayor's large silhouette. Fulton was gone. John looked down to the far end of the block; there was no sign of him, nothing. As brightly as the streets were lit, there were plenty of shadows too. Fulton could be in any one of them. Was he aware that he was being followed? When he reached Braxton, John grabbed his shoulder.

Panting, he said, "Listen, Kid, he couldn't have reached the next street. He wasn't moving that fast and we weren't that far behind him. He's got to be in one of the stores in front of us, or hiding in a recessed area."

It made perfect sense to Braxton, who was still scanning the streets.

"I want you to take a careful look along the storefronts," John said. "I'll start checking the stores. Go across the street and walk along the storefronts about halfway down the block—then cross the street and come back. When you get to the corner, go into that store and work your way back to me. When we meet, we'll cross the street and do it again. If you see him, call my cell and wait for me." Braxton scowled at the comment, and then set off across the street. Keeping close to the buildings, he began checking recesses and park benches and tried to glimpse inside each doorway and window.

How could a big ape like that, just disappear?

There were so many people it was difficult to separate some of the silhouettes. Braxton concentrated on finding a single silhouette in a tall, wide pear shape. Braxton went farther than John told him to. He'd reached the end of the block. He sprinted across the street and started back toward John. When Braxton reached the street corner he looked up. Above the doors of the store he saw a sign that read "HELZBERG DIAMONDS."

He's in here, Braxton thought, shaking his head, *he's gotta be.*

John had looked at the stores in front of him: Apple Computer, Max Studio, and Enzo Angiolini.

Not very likely that Fulton was looking for a computer, women's clothes, or shoes. I'll make this brief, he thought, as he pushed through Apple's front door. He stood just inside, silently assessing the scene. His heart raced as he thought about Fulton escaping them, but something told him he was near and unaware of their presence. Apple customers were talking to salespeople. There was no tension, no hint of trouble. John realized he was biting his cheek again and anxiously moved to the next store.

∞

"Please don't shoot me," the balding man sniveled. "I've got a family."

Fulton had him positioned in a men's restroom stall, legs spread, leaning over the toilet with his palms against the wall.

"Do what you're told and you'll get through this alive. Now stay still, and shut up!" Fulton left the stall door partially open. Removing a latex glove, he went to a sink and unscrewed the cap from a brown bottle. Pouring the yellow liquid over his right hand, there was a momentary lapse in his senses. As his vision cleared, he saw the reflection of the handsome figure he favored above all the other shapes he had taken in the last two weeks. He had no idea of the man's identity. He didn't care. Fulton rinsed and dried his hands. The clothes he wore now sagged around his trim physique. He opened the duffel, placed his gun inside, and removed a pair of khakis and a polo shirt.

After Fulton slipped his foot into the second brown loafer, he pulled a latex glove over his right hand. Shooting a glance at the bathroom stall he said, "I'm going to go now. You'll wait five minutes before leaving this room—do you understand? I may be forced to come back in here, and if you've moved an inch, I'll kill you."

The jewelry salesman's nose was in the air. He did not recognize the voice he'd just heard.

Who is that? What happened to the mayor?

"I won't move a muscle," he promised.

The robbery had gone quickly and completely unnoticed. Fulton had introduced himself as the mayor to the middle-aged salesperson he'd chosen, because he looked frail and most likely to cooperate.

"I want to see your most expensive dinner rings," Fulton said, as if money were no object. "It's our twenty-fifth wedding anniversary, so I only want to see your best."

"Certainly, Mr. Mayor," the balding man replied. They moved to a different counter. Unlocking the glass door, the frail man removed a velvet-covered display case with rows of tasteless, but expensive sparkling dinner rings. Pointing to another display, Fulton said, "Bring those out too." The salesman was beaming as he contemplated the commissions he might earn on this sale. The profit margins were generous on these rings.

Fulton set his open duffel bag on the display counter. He leaned in to the salesman and whispered, "I have a gun in my pocket. If you don't do exactly as I say, I'll kill you." He raised the gun in his pocket just enough so the salesman could see its contour. The balding man went white.

"I understand," he said, "what do you want me to do?"

"Place the rings in the duffel bag and quietly escort me to the men's room."

23

BRAXTON STOOD INSIDE HELZBERG DIAMONDS. THERE were quite a few patrons in the store considering the hour.

Must be a result of the Plaza Art Fair, he thought. He could see the entire store layout from his viewpoint. The glass counters were brightly illuminated to enhance the glitter of jewelry. There was no sign of Fulton.

I was sure he'd be here. Where could he have gone? Not wanting to waste a single moment, Braxton began to drift to the entrance door.

A familiar looking young man rapidly approached from his right. He stared at Braxton as if he too looked familiar. They nodded acknowledging each other and the younger man went through the door ahead of Braxton.

Where have I seen him before? Braxton thought.

As the man was engulfed by the crowd on the sidewalk, Braxton turned to go to the next store, but thought instead of the black and turquoise duffel the young man was carrying.

That looked like the same bag Fulton was carrying. Jesus!

Braxton whirled around and began walking in the other direction. He grabbed his cell, and pressed and held the number three key. Seconds later, John answered. Braxton explained what he saw while moving through the crowd.

"He looked familiar, John, but I'd know that duffel bag anywhere. I think he's somewhere just ahead of me."

"I've got one more store to check out, Brax, but if you think that's Fulton, I'm on my way."

"No, go ahead and check it out. If this doesn't pan out, I'll just wait for Fulton to come back to his car."

"That's a good idea, Braxton. I won't be long. Be careful. And by the way—you were right."

"About what?"

"I shouldn't have waited to pick up Fulton. We should've arrested him on sight. You made the better call, kid."

"Hindsight's always twenty-twenty," Braxton said cracking a small smile. "Gotta go."

From within the shadows, behind a support column, Fulton watched Braxton pass by. He had sensed something was wrong when the man looked at him like he had seen him before. Fulton fell in behind Braxton, heading toward the parking garage.

It's him—one of the guys from the elevator! Fulton thought. *He's following me! This can't be a coincidence. Is he a cop? Where's his buddy, the obnoxious one?* He gritted his teeth when he realized the man that was following him was now between him and his car.

Son-of-a-bitch! There's no way to get there before him. If he's waiting for me I'm gonna confront him—find out who he is and what he wants. Fulton followed Braxton at a cautious distance. He patted the side of the duffel and beneath a sport coat large enough to fit the mayor, he felt the contour of his 9mm.

∞

Braxton was disappointed. He reached the gold Lincoln Town Car without seeing a trace of Fulton. At first Braxton wasn't sure about the dark-haired young man carrying the black and turquoise duffel. He kept thinking, *Maybe it wasn't him, after all. He sure looked familiar though. It could have been the guy who went into Fulton's house. But the bag—what are the chances of seeing that bag twice in a half hour?* There was one bright spot in Braxton's thoughts—*Sooner or later Fulton's gotta return to his car, and when he does, I'll be here to arrest him.*

Braxton took a small notepad from his hip pocket and scribbled down Fulton's license plate number. Cupping his hands against the driver's side window, he tried to identify several items littering the seats.

Nothing unusual. I wonder if I can read the vehicle identification number. Braxton craned his neck and squinted, trying his best to read the small numbers in the poor light. He wrote down the first four numbers and repeated the process.

"Is there something you find particularly interesting about this car?" Braxton spun around; his eyes crossed trying to focus on the 9mm the young man aimed between his eyes.

∞

Braxton moaned, unaware of his surroundings. The first thing he noticed was the searing pain in his head. The throbbing at his temples pounded loudly and matched the cadence of his pulse. The second thing he noticed was someone mumbling. It sounded like John, but he couldn't be certain. His eyes wouldn't focus, nor would his mind.

What happened? Where am I? I must be dreaming? Someone is talking to me—a woman. What does she want?

John hung up the phone with Braxton's fiancée Anne Duffy. He told her Braxton was hurt badly, and she said she would get to the hospital right away. John approached the nurse who was talking to Braxton, trying to keep him awake. It was no use. He had drifted into unconsciousness again.

∞

Anne Duffy opened the apartment door and stepped into the hallway. She was startled by what she saw. "Braxton! Oh my God! John said you were hurt badly, said you were in the hospital. What happened? Are you all right?"

Braxton's look-alike appeared shaken and scared half to death, "I—I had a scuffle with a guy we were tailing. I got a knot on my head the size of Nebraska, but as you can see, I'm not in the hospital." Anne threw her arms around him and kissed him passionately. Fulton couldn't believe the softness of her lips.

"I was so worried about you," Anne said. "Why would John say you were in critical condition?"

Critical condition? Man, I really hurt the guy, Fulton thought briefly, but the kiss was too fresh on his mind to really care. He looked at Anne with pure lust.

That red hair, those green eyes, my god, she's beautiful! He'd never been kissed so passionately. Not even by Amy Coder, the girl he'd planned to marry ten years ago, before the accident.

Is this his wife? Girlfriend? I don't know what to call her. I need her name—I knew I shouldn't have come here.

When Fulton had stripped Braxton of his gun, badge, and wallet, he noted the apartment number on Braxton's driver's license. He'd guessed the young man was single and saw the opportunity to find out more about the cops who were following him.

Bad idea. I'd better get out of here soon. But the woman was breathtaking.

"It sounds like someone was playing a bad joke on us," he said. Feigning pain, he rubbed the back of his head, "I need to lie down for a while—maybe take some aspirin."

Anne took his arm, pulled him into the apartment, and closed the door behind him.

"Pretty callous joke! You go lie on the bed, and I'll get the aspirin." Fulton stared at her ring finger.

Is that a wedding ring or engagement ring?

He started toward a hallway, but stopped short to watch her curvy figure disappear into the kitchen.

God, she's hot. Now—which bedroom? He went to the right and turned on the light.

This looks like the one.

Fulton scanned the room for a file cabinet, an address book, something to give him a clue as to what the police knew about him. He opened Braxton's top dresser drawer, but found nothing of interest.

I wonder if he has an office, a desk, something. Maybe he keeps a journal. Anne's beautiful face flashed in his mind.

She's gonna be back any second. I'd better lie down. Fulton bounced on the edge of the bed and popped his shoes off.

Who knows? I may just get laid by a willing participant. All I have to do is to say very little and play up the angle that "I'm so hurt."

Fulton took a gamble and shed his khakis and shirt and climbed under the covers. He was smiling as he smoothed the bedspread, but doused it when the incredibly stunning woman appeared with some aspirin and a glass of water.

"Here, take these," Anne said, sitting beside him. "Hopefully, you'll feel better in a little while."

Fulton wondered if she could tell he was still smiling inside. He gulped the water and swallowed the aspirin. He couldn't stop staring at Anne. His eyes fell to her breasts.

"I know what would make me feel better," he said wryly. Anne smiled at his playfulness.

"Oh, I don't think so, honey, you're hurt—sex is the last thing you need. Maybe you'll be up to it a little later. Why don't you just rest for a while?"

Fulton knew time was short. He could take her unwillingly, but why not convince her he was fine?

"I'm not dying, it's only a headache. Are you afraid I'll let you down? I haven't let you down before, have I?"

Anne thought she was seeing something new in Braxton, a different kind of humor.

"Men," she said feigning a sexist tone, "you only want one thing."

"You're wrong," Fulton said. "I want two things, and they're both under your clothes." Anne laughed.

"Well, there's one for the diary," she teased.

Anne stood up and unbuttoned her blouse. It slid down to her elbows. Then she reached around to the back of her waist and lowered a short zipper. Her blouse and skirt fell to the floor together. Fulton laced his fingers behind his head like he was preparing to watch a show. It was difficult not to stare at her tiny waist, her flat tummy. And when she unhooked her bra and slid it off, the slight jiggle of her breasts made him as hard as a rock. Her bright pink nipples provided the only contrast to her creamy white skin. No tattoos, no blemishes, she was *Playboy* perfect.

This guy has it all, he thought, *and tonight, I'll have it.*

Anne slid her fingers under the straps of her thong and lowered it enough to expose what he most wanted to see. He was almost giddy when it dropped to the floor, and he realized that she was a genuine redhead too. She giggled, and with tiny animated footsteps, ran to the bed, lifted the covers, and snuggled up to the man she thought she loved. Anne put her arm around him and began to kiss him softly. Her hand slipped below the sheets and clasped him, massaging him with anticipation. She opened her mouth to receive his tongue. Suddenly her head popped up. The puzzled look in her eyes said she was confused.

"What's the matter?" he asked.

Anne rose to her knees, studying him intently.

"I don't know," she said. "You seem different."

Fulton was growing impatient.

Maybe I should just take her.

He had never seen anything like this creature. She'd already whet his sexual appetite and now he could wait no longer. The hardness in his groin pulsed with an intensity he had never felt before. He reached up and stroked her breasts clasping her nipples between his fingers and thumb.

"If I seem different, it's because I was clubbed on the head, silly. I'm a little sore, and I've got the bump to prove it. But that doesn't mean I don't want you just the same."

Anne gave him a sympathetic look. Her pouty lips pursed, "Oh, you poor baby." She bent down, caressing his face as she let him kiss her breasts. His tongue rolled over her nipples and along soft flesh that tasted almost sweet. Her scent was delicious. He was almost delirious with joy as her fingers streamed through his hair. Her strokes were gentle, so she wouldn't hurt his injury. Lightly, caressingly, her fingers probed for the bump on the back of his head. She couldn't find it. He followed her contours with his left hand, reaching lower to massage her between her thighs and probed a recess where he found a soft nub. The velvety area was slick and inviting. His fingers probed deeper still. She quivered, ignoring the bump that wasn't there.

I must have missed it, she thought.

He drew her down and came up beside her. His fingers became rhythmic and rapid. He knew she no longer noticed the nuances between him and the man she loved. For now it was sex, a pure animalistic pleasure. The thrusting of his fingers into her made her whimper and revel in unadulterated pleasure. She drove her head back; the pouty lips were replaced by an open and wanting mouth.

More, deeper, faster—I'll bet that's what she's thinking. She'd probably be ashamed of herself if she could see how much she's enjoying it. As Fulton's fingers withdrew and found the nub, she nearly convulsed. He used long strides of his fingers to stroke it.

She is close, he thought. He raised her leg and entered her with a thrust, where his fingers had made a pathway. Anne shrieked with pleasure. His rhythm was fast and powerful. Fulton had only had sex four times in ten years, and two of those were within the last two weeks. His appetite was insatiable, his desire overpowering. He knew he wouldn't last long. But she had been primed. She was ready to come before he ever entered her.

He thought of nothing. There was only sensuous pleasure, the elation of the moment. He clenched his teeth, aware that she was convulsing uncontrollably. Now she moaned with each rhythmic stroke. He continued to thrust harder and harder, as deeply as he could. Nothing else mattered now—nothing, but reaching his own climax. He reached for her breast. The softness filled the recess of his hand and the sensation brought him rigid as he came with an incredible climax. He was finished, but the violence of ejaculation left him little solace, he wanted more. Her beauty and sexuality were too unbelievable to enjoy only once.

I will have her again, tonight. I'll try something different, anything I want. Fulton wondered how his life could have been devoid of women for so many years. They were so lovely, so gratifying. He knew the answer. But now he was whole again, any man's equal.

24

A DOCTOR APPROACHED JOHN IN THE WAITING ROOM. John hadn't been allowed to observe while the medical team examined Braxton and administered medications.

John rose from his chair, towering two heads above the man in the white coat. The doctor had thinning hair and gray stubble on his face.

"How's he doing, doctor?"

The doctor didn't smile, but John found his eyes to be compassionate. "He's a strong young man. I'm about ninety percent certain he'll pull through this just fine."

John frowned. He didn't like leaving any odds on the table, "Ninety percent?"

"He's got quite a concussion, Detective. If the swelling in his brain doesn't get any worse, he'll be okay. It's a good thing you got him here when you did." The lines in John's face deepened. The doctor looked as if he noticed, "Don't worry; we gave him something to reduce the swelling. I'm pretty sure we've got nothing to worry about. You have my word; I'll keep a close eye on him."

"Is he conscious?"

The doctor turned his gaze, focusing on a spot on the wall. "No, not yet. He probably won't regain consciousness until the swelling goes down."

"And when will that be?"

"That's something we really can't predict, but soon, I think."

John rubbed his neck, straining to think of a reasonable question to ask. "When can he come back to work?"

"He should take a few days off to rest, but he'll probably feel reasonably good in a day or two." John handed him a business card, "Will you call me if there are any complications?"

The doctor agreed, and John shook his hand and thanked him for his help.

This was too close, John thought. *If I'd arrested Fulton right away, like Braxton said, this would never have happened.* From down the hall, John could see his wife, Cindy, approaching. Her stride was quick. It was rare when a detective got hurt, and Cindy understood the crucial bond between partners. Although John and Braxton's relationship had developed slowly, it was rock solid. Cindy dropped what she was doing to be with John. As Cindy neared, John looked at his watch. It was almost ten o'clock.

Where the hell is Anne Duffy? he thought. *I called her way before Cindy, and she lives only half the distance from the hospital.* John and Cindy embraced. She held him a long time. When they sat down to talk, she took his hand and studied his face, looking for something. John noticed her stare, and looked away as he began to repeat what the doctor had told him. John knew that Cindy could see his wounds, too. Not physical wounds, but in some respects, he felt as hurt as Braxton.

∞

Anne's cell phone rang faintly in the distance. It was by her purse on the coffee table in the living room. Fulton had been petting her again, waiting for a second chance for a go at it. To Anne, he seemed a bit pushy, more demanding than he'd ever been before. It put her off.

Come to think of it, he was almost a little rough. Then she smiled and thought, *almost.*

"I need to take this call, Braxton; I've been waiting for it all evening." It was a lie, but for some reason Anne wanted a moment alone. There was something else different about Braxton, a controlling possessiveness she couldn't quite put her finger on. She didn't have time to don a robe and still catch the call, so she ran naked into the living room.

Fulton was lying in bed, nearly hard again, and disappointed that she'd left.

She's got to be one of the most beautiful women in the world, he thought. *One more romp, and I'll get the hell out of here. If I play my cards right, maybe I can come back and "do her" on a regular basis. I don't care if that cop is her husband or boyfriend. Whatever he is, she'd never know the difference.* The thought brought a smile to his face. And then Fulton looked at his right hand and frowned, *Gotta be careful. I was so crazy with passion; I never even gave a thought to which hand I was using to bang her. If it wasn't for the fact that I'm left handed, it may have been all over.* Just then, something else occurred to him. *What if the hospital calls back again? Or worse yet, this guy's partner?* Fulton drew in a short breath; *I'd better see who's on the other end of that phone.*

"I'm telling you, Anne, that man is not Braxton! He's in a hospital bed, unconscious. If you don't believe me, call the hospital and verify it—just get out of there and do it from your cell phone!"

"John, I think I know my own fiancé."

"Does Braxton have any scars, or tattoos—any identifying marks?"

"Yes, he has a little birthmark on his buttocks."

"No good, Anne, it has to be something he wasn't born with."

"Listen, John, Braxton thinks a lot of you, so I'm going to hold my temper, but this joke has gone far enough. Please don't call back tonight." She hung up the phone and turned it off.

"Who was that on the phone?"

The voice startled Anne. She whirled around and saw that Braxton was only a few feet from her. Anne felt uncomfortable at the way his eyes raked her up and down. How long had he been standing there?

"That was Trish. You remember her from our wedding, don't you?" Even as she asked the question, she wondered if she were crazy to even consider what John had said.

But John sounded so serious—and Braxton's acting so different. I need to know!

Fulton walked up to Anne and drew her against him. The action wasn't done gently. He was hard again, and ready to go.

"Yeah, I remember Trish." Anne looked at the man like a total stranger. She searched the corner of his right eye for the tiny star shaped scar Braxton had gotten in a bicycle accident as a child. It was gone.

Fulton kissed Anne on the neck. It sent a chill down her spine, and all at once she felt cold. "Braxton, I need to use the bathroom. Why don't you get back in bed and I'll be there in a minute." His hands ran down her back side from her shoulders to her waist, and then they came around and up to her breasts. He squeezed them firmly. Anne tried to push away without appearing to be indifferent to him. She forced a smile. "Go! Go get in bed! I'll be right there." Braxton gave her a quizzical look and then stared at her shapeliness before turning to go.

"Don't be long," Braxton said as he walked toward the bedroom. Anne stood naked, shaking more violently with each passing moment.

I hope he didn't notice, she thought. *Could I be wrong? What do I do?* Anne was afraid to move. She struggled for a coherent thought. *I've got to get out of here. I can't go in the bedroom, but I need something to wear. A coat!* Anne ran to the entry closet. She found a long winter coat and put it on. Looking for shoes, she dropped to her knees and snagged a pair of winter boots. She sat and leaned against the closet door and tugged them on, first the left, and then the right. When she stood up, she was startled by something moving. It was Braxton coming at her fast. Anne's eyes grew wide, and her face was infused with fear. She jumped to her feet and instinctively reached for the front door knob, but her reach wasn't long enough. She'd have made it if she had moved her feet, but it was as if they were glued to the floor. She fell and her shoulder landed hard against the door. Fulton lunged at her, and in an instant his naked body covered every inch of hers.

"Where do you think you're going?" Fulton asked, his breath warm in her ear. Anne didn't answer, and Fulton raised his head above hers. Her green eyes betrayed her as she looked again for the small star shaped scar that had disappeared. Fulton paused for a moment, and then he smiled.

"When did you know?" he asked. Again, Anne refused to answer. Fulton's hand reached for her neck, his fingers spread around her throat. He squeezed firmly.

"When?"

"There is no Trish, and we're not married." Fulton nodded, and then stood up. He grabbed Anne's arm and pulled her to her feet.

"So, was I as good in the sack as your boyfriend?"

A tear rolled down Anne's cheek. She said nothing.

He's going to kill me. Oh God, don't let him kill me!

Fulton walked Anne into the living room. He slipped her coat over her shoulders, but she clutched it at her breasts.

"No—please!"

Fulton's eyes narrowed, and he gave the coat a yank. It fell to the floor, and Anne closed her eyes so she didn't have to see their naked bodies. Then Fulton grabbed her by the neck and bent her body over the back of the sofa. She could feel his hardness as he leaned up against her.

"One scream—one word and I'll kill you, do you understand?" Anne nodded; her long red hair hid the terror on her face. "We're gonna have another go. And if you behave, you'll live to see tomorrow."

∞

John arrived at Braxton's apartment at ten thirty-five. Uniformed officers were already present. When he saw Anne's body, he felt sick. She was fully naked, bent over the couch belly down, but her head was turned backwards, looking up.

An officer looked at John and said, "What a waste, huh? Can't wait till they move her, so's I can get a look at them titties."

John put his face within an inch of the officer's. "So, you think my partner's fiancée has nice titties, eh?"

The officer's face went white, "Oh, Jesus, I'm so sorry; I didn't know—let me get her a blanket."

"Oh, that'd be great—then you can taint the evidence too!" The officer paused for a split-second, and then John could tell that he got it. Covering Anne with a blanket would transfer trace evidence to her body, a definite no-no in the book of forensic etiquette. The officer shuffled toward the front door in embarrassment.

John's head was beginning to throb. He realized he was clenching his teeth, hard. He tried to relax by slowing his breathing, but before he knew it his jaw was clamped shut like a vice. He doubted he would find much in the way of usable evidence. The semen would match Braxton's, of course. The fingerprints wouldn't matter either, and the only other evidence that would be of any help would be her time of death. After all, it would be difficult to prove that she was killed by a man who was unconscious in the hospital. Jaworski arrived with a forensics kit. John grabbed his shoulder and steered him aside.

"Greg, this is Detective Willis's fiancée. I need you to do your best work. Call Hamiid and have him meet you here. I want a report from each of you, and pay particular attention to her time of death." I need an iron clad time of death. Do you understand?"

"We'll need to do an autopsy to determine the time of death," Jaworski said.

"Then do the damn autopsy!"

Jaworski took a step backward. His mouth was ajar, and his eyes were rounded.

"S—sure, John." John clenched his teeth and looked at the officer who made the tasteless comment about Anne's breasts. "The rest of you, get the hell out of here!"

25

JOHN SLEPT UNTIL EIGHT O'CLOCK ON SATURDAY. Cindy was up at six-thirty and shut the alarm off so it wouldn't wake him. She couldn't remember when he had risen so late, but he had gone to bed with a ferocious headache. Cindy figured the smell of bacon would wake him, and it did. When she came to get him for breakfast, he was already showered and dressed. As they ate, John shared some of the details about Anne's murder, but withheld the majority of it. Cindy didn't push for more information than John volunteered to give. That was the way things were between them.

Just recently, they had discussed the likelihood that a man could take someone else's form at will. Cindy remembered the conclusion they both came to—that anything was possible. But after overhearing John's conversation with Anne last night, Cindy knew his guess was right all along. Now she understood why John had been so perplexed in recent days. But most of all, she knew that Anne's murderer posed a great danger to John and Braxton.

They know who the murderer is, she thought, *and he has already taken Braxton's identity. He could do the same to John.* The realization made her shudder. Cindy spent years worrying about John's hazardous line of work, but now she would worry more. It was almost eight-thirty.

"What are your plans today, honey?"

John gave her a stoic look and answered hesitantly, as if it were painful to speak, "I need to see Braxton. I want to be the one to tell him about Anne. I also need to call Mike Walsh and fill him in on last night's events. I know it's the weekend, Cindy, but I have some important things to do. Do you mind if I go in for a few hours?"

Cindy's blue eyes were large and her arched eyebrows gave them a look of sorrow. She said, "This is a serious case, John. Do whatever you think is necessary. I'll call Sarah and see if she wants to have lunch." John nodded.

Cindy watched John stare at his half eaten breakfast in silence. His eyes were hollow. He was so deep in thought, she wondered if an earthquake would get his attention.

He feels responsible for Anne's death. But then again, he feels responsible for everything that happens in this town. I've got to convince him to retire. No one can carry that kind of burden for long. Sooner or later it'll kill him.

"John? John? Your breakfast is getting cold."

John looked at Cindy absently. "I'm really not hungry this morning, hun. I'll get something to eat later." He stood up slowly, his chair scooting behind him.

Halfway to the door John stopped and turned, giving Cindy a somber stare. "Gone fishing."

Cindy's nose crinkled. "What? Who's gone fishing?"

John continued, "If you ever doubt whether it's me you're talking to, ask me for the password, *gone fishing.*"

Cindy returned John's serious look. "Okay, I will."

"I'll call you later."

Cindy began clearing the table. The bacon on John's plate caught her eye. Three uneaten strips remained. Tears welled in her eyes as she thought how silly it must be to gauge a man's emotional state by something so trivial.

That man would sell his soul for a single strip of bacon. In all our years of marriage, he's never left a crumb behind. Not a crumb.

∞

On the way to the hospital, John thought about what he would say to Braxton.

How do you tell someone the woman he loves is dead? His stomach churned, and the aspirin wasn't working on his headache.

Am I going to lose another partner?

John was still getting to know Braxton. They were still learning about each others quirks and habits, but they had grown close in the last few weeks. Braxton looked up to John for his experience and know-how. He had kept an open mind with respect to the incredible theories John had been hatching since the strange five-pack of crimes had begun.

I thought it might become a six-pack, but not this way. Not like this. Even if Braxton is able to work in a few days, I doubt that the captain will allow him to return to the case. It'll be too personal. The image of Anne Duffy's head twisted upward, glaring at the ceiling flashed in John's mind for the second time in five minutes. He tried to squelch it by recalling the glamour photo Braxton kept on his desk. John really didn't know Anne at all, but from what Braxton had told him, she was very sweet.

The news is going to crush him.

John flashed his badge to the uniformed officer he'd requested to stand guard outside Braxton's hospital room. There was a woman sitting in a chair, next to Braxton's bed. She was talking to him in a hushed voice.

He's conscious! John's eyes lit up, and he took a few steps toward Braxton's bed. The woman looked up at him, but didn't stop talking. Braxton's eyes were closed.

He must have fallen asleep.

John noticed a thick Lebanese accent as she spoke.

"Your brother, Faruq is coming home tomorrow. I am bringing him to see you. His company is doing very well. I still think he wants you to come to work for him, but I don't think it will happen. You never liked working inside very much. You were always my restless one. You need much room to breathe." The woman paused and looked at John. She was in her mid-fifties. Her skin was swarthy and her coal black hair was much longer than typically worn by women her age. Through the pain on her face, John could see a natural beauty, a flawless set of features she shared with the young man sleeping soundly beside her.

"Are you Mrs. Willis?" John asked quietly.

"Yes, I am Samarah Willis" she replied, with a soft, controlled voice. "And you are the man the doctor spoke about. You called twice during the night?"

"Yes, I was worried about Braxton, he was hurt pretty badly." John extended his hand. "I'm John Dietrich, Braxton's partner."

The woman gave John an almost imperceptible nod of approval as she accepted his hand. "Braxton has spoken of you." They shook hands briefly.

"Very nice to meet you, Mrs. Willis." John's head tilted toward Braxton. When did he regain consciousness?"

"He hasn't, but I talk to him anyway. Maybe he can hear me."

John's eyes softened and his head fell a few inches. He stared at Braxton for a moment, and then looked at Samarah. "I'm very sorry about your son. The doctor said he'd make a full recovery. Has he said anything more?"

Samarah nodded. "The swelling in his brain hasn't become worse, but it hasn't gotten any better either."

"Well, that's not all bad," John said. "To be honest, I was afraid the swelling might continue through the night. I guess it's just a matter of time before it recedes to normal."

In the passionate voice of a mother, she replied, "Yes, he will recover, John. He is strong of mind and body."

Samarah's speech was stiff, but her English was good. She looked at John like she expected him to say something else. He drew a deep breath and then asked, "Do you know about Anne?"

"Yes, I found out early this morning." John's expression was overwhelmed with remorse.

"Again, I'm sorry; I should have been here when they told you."

"And what difference would that have made? My son has lost his beautiful bride, and that will never change."

"I know, Mrs. Willis, but the circumstances of her death are going to be difficult to cope with for all of you. Anne was brutalized and raped by a man who looked—" John winced as he bit his cheek. "—I mean, a man who will be difficult to find."

"In that case, you had better go; you cannot waste a moment."

John leaned back on one heel. "Well, I just thought I should be here when you tell him."

"And where will Anne's killer be by the time he wakes?" John had no reply for Samara's question. But she was right. Fulton's trail was already getting cold. "No, John. This situation is better handled by family. His siblings are coming to see him. We will tell him. We will mourn together, and we will heal together." Samarah sandwiched Braxton's hand between hers. "Braxton and I have dealt with sorrow many times before. He will carry on—he will recover from this."

John didn't understand all of the implications of her statement, but he had a firm belief that Samarah knew her son to the depths of his soul. He felt a touch of comfort knowing that Braxton would soon be surrounded by family. Samarah closed her eyes and held Braxton's hand to her cheek. When she opened them, their white rims contrasted sharply against her bronze skin.

"I'm sure he will, Mrs. Willis. Braxton's an amazing young man. Will you tell him I came to see him, and that I'll understand if he wants to take a leave of absence?"

"Yes, I'll tell him, but I know my son—he won't take much time to grieve. Braxton will be back to work in a few days."

John nodded, "I appreciate that, Mrs. Willis, but he should take some time off. Our captain probably won't let him back on the case anyway."

Samarah's eyes rounded, "Why? Why would your captain keep Braxton from helping you find that man?"

"It's departmental policy, Mrs. Willis. It's rare that a cop can retain his objectivity under circumstances like this. It's just too personal."

"No! He must not! I know my son; it will do more harm than good. He must be allowed to find Anne's murderer."

John gave Samarah a sympathetic look, "It's not my decision, Mrs. Willis—it's up to the captain."

"You are Braxton's partner?"

"Yes."

"You are his friend?"

John knew where Samarah was headed with her questions.

It won't make any difference, he thought.

"Yes."

"Then change your captain's mind. Make him see what will happen to my son if he is removed from the case."

John was aware of his own body language as he averted her eyes, "I'll do what I can, Mrs. Willis."

John took a few steps in the direction of the door. Then he turned for a parting glimpse of Braxton. Samarah seemed to see right through him as she asked the next question. "Do you have clues as to where he is?"

"Not really. We have a surveillance team watching his home and the entire city is searching for his car."

"So you do know who he is?"

"Yes, we think so, but finding him is going to be nearly impossible."

"Braxton says you are a good detective."

"No better than he is."

"You find this man, John. You find this man who murdered my son's beautiful bride. You cannot rest until you find him."

John's stomach turned upside down. He could almost hear his head pounding as he looked into this mother's eyes. John was compelled to say what he knew he should not. "I'll find him, Mrs. Willis, I promise."

"Good, I'll tell Braxton you came to see him."

John opened his mouth, but before he could speak, Samarah cut him off, "I'll give him your condolences, John. His siblings are on the way. We'll take care of him, you go find Anne's murderer."

John walked to the door and opened it wide. Standing halfway inside Braxton's room and partially in the hall, John made a final comment. "Mrs. Willis, tell him he is a good partner, and that I expect him back on the job soon. Tell him I need his help." Mrs. Willis stared at her unconscious son with admiration. "I will John, I will."

26

BY TEN O'CLOCK ON SATURDAY, JOHN WAS SIPPING hot coffee with Mike Walsh in the precinct's break room. The two men were alone and both were somber. Walsh hadn't spoken in almost a minute. He was reviewing the search warrant John had prepared to get permission to search Fulton's home, but he should have finished looking it over by now. Walsh seemed distracted. He rubbed his forehead every thirty seconds or so. John guessed he was focusing more on last night's events than on the document in front of him.

John had laid out the events in great detail; He and Braxton had followed Fulton from his home to the Plaza, and that the man who got out of the car they followed was an exact double of the mayor. They lost him on Broadway, and Braxton proceeded to the parking garage to stake out his car. John heard a commotion while passing by Helzberg Diamonds. Several employees had burst out of the front door calling for help. The store had been robbed by the mayor. John ushered the employees back inside and called the forensics team. Gathering all the Helzberg employees in a small room, he explained it wasn't the mayor, but a double posing as him. He assured the manager that they would follow all required procedures for insurance purposes, but that they must keep the robbery out of the news. It might foil their attempts to catch the real thief.

John took a statement from a frail balding man who had mentioned that the last voice he heard in the men's restroom sounded totally unfamiliar to him. He deduced that there must have been an accomplice, since it was not the mayor who gave him his final orders. At that point, John knew that Braxton had been right about the young man he followed to the parking garage. A man he said looked very familiar. John called Braxton's cell, but got no answer. As soon as a uniformed officer arrived at Helzberg's, John headed for the parking garage. There he found Braxton on the concrete floor where Fulton's car had been parked. He had been hit several times over the head. Braxton's pulse was weak. John called an ambulance and followed it to the hospital. When Anne didn't show up, he searched Braxton's clothes and discovered that Fulton had taken his wallet, badge, and gun, and probably his physical likeness.

Unconsciously, Walsh was crinkling the edge of the search warrant. "Are you certain about this DNA thing, John? Are you sure?"

"Listen, Mike, you've been fighting me on this long enough. You know me better than anyone. You know I'm telling the truth!"

Walsh rubbed his forehead and then folded his hands on the table.

"I know you are, John, and I know I've been stubborn about this, but Jesus Christ, this whole thing is just too incredible!" Walsh clenched his jaw, his hands were fists. "Do you realize we may never catch this guy? What's worse is that he could wreak havoc on this city for months—or years."

"We still have a chance, Mike. I convinced the store manager to keep this quiet until he heard from you. If we can squelch the story like we did before, Fulton will probably try something else to frame the mayor, maybe something bigger."

"Yeah, but we don't know where he'll strike this time, John. You had him last night, but where will you be the next time he tries something?"

John didn't answer. He laid the store manager's business card on the table and slid it to Walsh.

"Would you call him, Mike? Better yet, can you pay him a visit? I can't tell you how important it is that we keep this under wraps."

"Okay, John, I'm on board with this." With one eye squinted, Walsh asked, "What else do you need?"

"Give me your 'okay' on that search warrant. Who's the on-duty judge this weekend?"

"Judge Heinz. He hates weekend interruptions. You'll be in and out in two minutes."

John nodded, "Good, now, all I need is some manpower. I want forensics to sweep Fulton's house this morning, and I need a couple of good officers to help me sift through evidence."

Walsh's face grew lines. John noted an uncharacteristic frown.

"Done."

"And I want Braxton back on the case as soon as he's able to work."

"That's out of the question."

"I need him, Mike."

"Forget it."

"I need him! He's the only one who understands this case like I do. By the time I get 'buy in' from another partner, it'll be too late and you know it."

"I'll assign you Connors and Moody."

"Nooo-fucking-waaay! Those two screw-ups shouldn't even be on the force! Give me someone else."

"YOU GET CONNORS AND MOODY!" Walsh shouted. There was a brief silence as Walsh and John stared each other down. Walsh's grimace slowly faded and became a look of defeat.

"ALL RIGHT!" Walsh added. "You can have Braxton. But he's got to be approved by a staff psychiatrist before he can return to duty."

John's face was red, his features ruined as he struggled for a response.

"Okay, Mike, but I want a meeting with you and those two buffoons. They take orders from me, and no one else."

"What do you mean?"

"I don't want Connors crawling back to you every time he doesn't agree with me. If he's on my team, he'd better do as he's told."

Walsh stood and smiled, "You're a tough son of a bitch, John. But you're the only chance I've got to solve this case." He headed out of the room and then paused in the doorway, "Don't let me down."

They departed from the front door of the precinct building. Walsh was on his way to Helzberg Diamonds to do damage control. John was headed to Judge Heinz's house to have his search warrant signed.

I've got some serious investigating to do.

He approached his car briskly while hundreds of details raced through his mind. He sorted them based on their importance and immediacy to the larger task at hand, finding Fulton.

Connors and Moody—I sure as hell don't need the distractions they're bound to create for us. I'd be better off without any help at all. I wonder how Braxton's doing. Gotta call Jaworski; have him meet me at Fulton's. If Fulton has Braxton's badge, he knows we're looking for him. He's probably fled the city by now.

John reached for his cell. He called Jaworski and gave him a brief explanation of the job at hand and Fulton's address.

"Meet me there in an hour, I'm headed to get a signature on my search warrant, so don't touch anything until you're sure I've got it. I'll have Connors and Moody waiting for you." There was silence on the other end of the phone.

"I know, Greg, and I'm sorry—they were all I could get."

Upon his arrival, John saw two figures waiting in a car in front of Fulton's home. His stomach made a guttural noise as he recognized them. John waved to Connors and Moody to follow him into the house.

It's gonna be a long day.

Fulton's kitchen was a mess. Connors and Moody studied the crowded countertops, as did John. "Don't touch a thing—do you two understand? Not a thing!" There were bags of clothes and labeled jars everywhere.

"Jesus, Dietrich, who died and made you captain?" John tried to hide his dislike for Tom Connors as he answered. "As of thirty minutes ago, the captain put me in charge of this entire investigation. It's linked to several other cases I'm working on. I have carte blanche to do whatever I feel is necessary. And until the captain says otherwise, you two are under my direction. Do you understand this?"

Justin Moody nodded, seemingly unaware of the tension between Connors and Dietrich.

"I suppose you requested us, right Dietrich?" Connors said. "We all know how much you value our help."

Sarcasm, what a surprise, John thought.

"I did no such thing, Tom, but if you want to remain on this case, you'll do exactly as I say and check the attitude. I'm not going to work with someone who's not focused on this case one hundred percent." Connors was seething, but he somehow restrained himself from making things worse. He and Moody were rarely assigned cases of much importance. John wondered if Connors hadn't already figured out that this case was big—really big. Connors lips were pure white slits.

I wonder if that's what swallowing your pride looks like? John thought.

Connors made his way to a kitchen countertop.

"What are all these jars for?" he asked. John thought his voice carried a "go to hell" undertone. It was amusing.

"I don't know for sure. I think they contain DNA from various people." Connors pointed, "This one looks like it's full of piss." John looked at the jar, "Could be urine, might be beer, either way, let's not touch anything. Jaworski will be here any minute. Both of you follow me." John took the detectives out to the patio and sat them down.

"I need to brief you both on five—" John corrected himself, "six cases. I'm going to give you a bird's-eye overview so you can see the connections, but I expect you to have all of the reports read by the end of the day on Monday." Connors's angry disposition seemed to be quelled, replaced by a look of sheer curiosity. After John explained everything in a logical sequence, he started giving orders.

"Justin, do you have a camera?"

He nodded, "In the car."

"I want every inch of this house photographed. Start in the kitchen. Use the highest resolution you can, so we can make enlargements. Tom, get a notepad. We are looking for clues to any place Fulton might frequent on a regular basis—clubs, organizations, etcetera. I want phone messages, yearbooks, directories, letters, and correspondence of any kind. We need to work with speed and accuracy before Fulton's trail gets cold. Don't disturb anything until it is photographed, and for God's sake wear gloves!"

Connors and Moody disappeared through the patio door into the house, anxious John suspected, to dig into the most fascinating case they had ever seen. John whispered under his breath, "Lord, give me the strength to get through this." And then he too stepped through the door, and into the kitchen where Greg Jaworski was getting ready to tag evidence. "Hold up a minute, Greg, I want to get some photos before we disturb anything."

"Already done, John, at least in the kitchen. Did you get the warrant?"

"Yeah, I did." John let out a deep breath. "Didn't mean to tell you how to do your job, Greg. I've got two others here, who aren't as savvy as you."

Jaworski smiled, "No need to explain, John, we all know about Connors and Moody."

Jaworski became serious, "I'm sorry about what happened to your partner's girlfriend, John. How's he taking it?"

"He's still unconscious. His mother's gonna break the news to him. She says he'll be okay, but I don't know if I could handle this kind of thing without going on a rampage."

"Do you think he'll be out for blood?" Jaworski asked.

John gave him a sideways glance, "Wouldn't you?"

Jaworski shrugged, "Yeah, I suppose so."

John looked in the direction of the glass jars on the counter top. They were easily identifiable as baby food jars. He recognized several names written on the jars in black marker over masking tape, Mayor Chase, Zach Whittman, Stuart Grady, David Breeling, Adam Sharp, and Tyler Werthing. Compact and portable, he thought, they could easily be transported in a small duffel bag.

"Greg?"

"Yeah, John."

"Do you know what you are looking at here?"

Jaworski cocked his head and raised an eyebrow, "What do you mean?"

John quickly explained that Fulton was a research geneticist at CSGR. He described his experiment, the miraculous new arm he'd grown, and his ability to assume the human forms of others from their DNA. Although Jaworski had been processing most of the evidence in the 'five-pack of crimes,' he had no idea as to how the cases were connected.

"I need you to know everything I know, Greg. I need you to burn the midnight oil with me for a few nights. Are you game?"

Jaworski's jaw appeared to be permanently fixed at half mast. His eyes panned the bags of clothes and the labeled jars on the counter.

"Whatever you need, John. Let's get this guy."

John patted him on the back, "Can we start tonight? I need to run back to the office and get some contact information. There are some people I need to interview right away."

"Sure, what time?"

"I'll be back at the office around six. I'll bring Chinese." John started to leave, but stopped cold.

"I hate to leave you alone with these guys, so I'll call Hamiid in—he can keep an eye on them."

27

JOHN CREPT INTO HIS BEDROOM AS QUIETLY AS HE could. He navigated around the furniture in near total darkness and began to get undressed. The clock said it was just after two-thirty.

"If that was your idea of working for a few hours, John, I'd hate to see your concept of a few days." Cindy's comment was sarcastic, but John could tell from her tone that she was glad to see him.

"I'm sorry I'm so late, honey. All of the sudden, we have mountains of evidence to analyze, and leads coming out of our ears."

"Isn't that a good thing?"

"Yes, dear, it's a wonderful thing. As of today, I've tied all six cases together. Fulton's our man."

"How will you find him?"

"That's a good question. He could be anywhere and anybody by now. We found baby food jars containing urine from the people he's framed."

"Urine? How'd he get their urine?"

"Makes it himself—after he turns into someone, he pees in a jar, so he can assume their identity again and again. The jars were all neatly labeled with their names. He had a change of clothes for each person as well."

"That's disgusting, John."

"Yeah, I know. But here's the really bad news. Now that he knows we were following him, he won't chance going home. He'll have to start from scratch, find a hotel, or apartment, a new car—his Lincoln was found abandoned downtown. He'll need to find more DNA too, but that doesn't seem to be a problem for him. The only upside to all of this is that he probably doesn't have the mayor's DNA anymore. The downside is that he may still have Braxton's."

"That's a scary thought, John. Speaking of Braxton how is he?"

"He's conscious. I tried to look in on him an hour ago, but Mrs. Willis wouldn't let me see him. At least he's surrounded by family. Mrs. Willis says they don't want to leave him alone. He's going to stay with her for a few days. He's got a pretty great family, if you ask me."

"I can't imagine how he must be feeling, losing his fiancée like that."

"Yeah, me either and I hope I never find out." John grimaced in the darkness, *Jesus, what a stupid thing to say.*

Cindy asked, "How long will it be before Braxton can return to work?"

"A few days to a few weeks, if his state of mind is okay. He's got to pass a psychiatric examination. Mike said only the doctors can make that call. Meanwhile, I'm working with a couple of morons. Jesus, I hope Braxton recovers quickly." John blindly laid his dress pants across Cindy's hope chest. He felt for the edge of the covers, raised them and slid under the sheets. His mind was still racing as he tried to put pieces of the massive puzzle together.

"John?"

"Yes, dear."

"How are you holding up through all of this?"

Cindy had just confronted John with what had been nagging at him since Anne's murder. He saw the opportunity to get it off his chest.

"It's my fault; Anne's death is my fault."

Cindy rolled on her side to face John. "What do you mean by that?"

"Just what I said, honey. Braxton wanted to arrest Fulton earlier; he asked me what we were waiting for. I thought it would be better to catch Fulton in the act of committing a crime, you know, so the arrest would stick, but Braxton was right. If we had picked up Fulton when we had the chance, Anne would still be alive."

"Oh for gosh sake, John. You can't blame yourself for Anne's death. It's not like your logic was flawed. It would have been better for everyone if you'd caught him in the act of committing a crime."

"It wasn't better for Anne."

Cindy snuggled up to John and kissed him on the cheek.

"You stop thinking like that—do you hear me? You can't control everything that happens in life. Some things just happen because they are a part of God's grand design."

Yeah, John thought, *I contributed big time to God's grand design.*

By three-fifteen, John was no closer to falling asleep than when he had climbed into bed. His mind was keyed up thinking about the new information he had gathered today. There was so much of it. He had re-interviewed three suspects who, until now, were not tied to the other cases. But Fulton's appearance changed everything. Adam Sharp hated Fulton. And now Sharp was accused of first degree assault and battery. Witnesses claim he almost killed a man in a pub with a baseball bat. Sharp swore he had never met the man who was assaulted, nor had he ever set foot in the neighborhood bar where the man was attacked. When John asked him if he knew Fulton, Sharp's expression turned ugly.

He said, "Yeah, I know him. What a freak. I went to college with that know-it-all nerd." A dry smirk spread across his face. "We used to call him 'lefty leftovers.' The little twerp *sweet talked* the university into a full scholarship and got the best job after college. No doubt people felt sorry for that one-armed bastard."

As John continued the conversation, he wondered why Sharp antagonized Fulton about his handicap. "Did he have any friends?"

"Not a single one that I know of. He was pretty much a loner, and no wonder, everyone hated the way he showed off in the classroom. He had a way of making smart people feel stupid. He wasn't much with the girls either. They practically ran from him. I'll bet the little queer never got married. He was about as smooth as chunky peanut butter."

"I assume Mr. Fulton was a pretty intelligent man. What did he ever do to you to make you hate him so much?" John inquired.

Sharp was clearly upset. "Why are you asking me all these questions about Fulton? What's that pinhead got to do with my case?"

"I never said he had anything to do with your case, Mr. Sharp. I only said he is currently under investigation."

"Good, I hope you put that twerp away forever. The world would be a better place without him."

All John could gather from Sharp's interview was that he was immensely jealous of Fulton, and did everything he could to ridicule him. Three or four years of verbal abuse and harassment might be a pretty good motive for Fulton to seek revenge against Sharp.

A more intriguing case involved David Breeling and Brenda Langdon. John had originally interviewed Langdon at the police station, but today, not only did he find out that she knew Fulton, but she lived directly behind him. Recently, she and Breeling were engaged to be married, but two weeks ago Breeling brutally beat and raped her. The incident took Langdon by surprise. She said her relationship with Breeling had been perfect. They'd not so much as had an argument, but now she was a victim of rape and determined to put Breeling behind bars.

"It's so strange that you would ask me about Richard Fulton," Langdon said. "David was talking about him the night he went crazy and raped me."

"What did he say, exactly, Miss Langdon?"

"He was telling me what a nice man Richard was, which was really odd. The few times they met, he told me he thought Richard was pretty weird. Then he asked me what I thought of him. He asked me if I found him attractive."

"And how did you answer?"

Langdon thought hard for a moment. "I think I said something like, "He's not bad looking, but he's just a little too creepy for me. I told him I did my best to avoid him. David was quiet for about ten minutes. The next thing you know, he was attacking me."

John wondered if Fulton had designs on Langdon. Maybe he was in love with her. Maybe he decided if he couldn't have her, no one could. If it was Fulton who raped her, Langdon gave him the motive on a silver platter.

John stared into the darkness of his bedroom. He fluffed his pillow and turned onto his side. Langdon never mentioned anything about Fulton in his initial questioning. Even if she had, it would have made no difference at the time. Fulton hadn't been tied to any of the cases, and his name wasn't yet a blip on John's radar. The lab identified Breeling's semen, and he was seen leaving the house after the assault. But incredibly, he was also seen with a group of friends at a local pub watching a college football game. Even the bartender swore it couldn't have been Breeling that raped Miss Langdon. He had been at the bar an hour each side of the attack.

John's eyes were still open. In the darkness he could see the faces of the people he had interviewed for the better part of the day. His head was swimming with facts. After re-examining three of the cases in the "five-pack of crimes," and inserting Fulton's name in each one, several new facts came to light.

The third case, the one involving Tyler Werthing, was perhaps one of the most perplexing to John. He liked Werthing a lot. He was a successful stockbroker with a lively and friendly disposition. In his mid-thirties, this man was happily married, raising two boys who were attending middle school. Werthing possessed only a fraction of Zach Whittman's wealth, but he was clearly financially independent. He had no reason to steal money from anyone, let alone a convenience store. But like Zach Whittman, Werthing was arrested after videos of him pointing a gun at a clerk's head were aired on the evening news. In addition to the videos, there were fingerprints and DNA left at the scene. Of course, the scenario was the same in all of the cases. But a wealthy and respected real estate broker from across town claimed he was with Werthing at the time of the robbery. Werthing's secretary confirmed his claim.

But DNA doesn't lie, or so John had always been taught. But now it looked as though it doesn't always tell the whole truth either. The implications alone could send shock waves throughout the criminal justice system.

Werthing described his association with Fulton as a "good relationship gone bad." He had been Fulton's stockbroker for three years. "Fulton was starting to accumulate some wealth of his own, until the day he'd made a poor investment choice," Werthing said. "He was bullish on pharmaceutical stocks, but a miscalculated speculation nearly wiped him out. He moved most of his money into an aggressive pharmaceutical company who only days later had a major drug recalled by the FDA. The stock plummeted instantly, and Fulton lost almost everything. I tried to get him to hold on to the stock. I told him the company would recover in six months to a year, but Richard wouldn't listen. He said I should have known about the drug recall. He said it was my business to know those kinds of things."

John asked flatly, "Did he ever make any claims of getting even with you?"

"Not that I can recall," Werthing said. "Although we did have a rather lively discussion about whose fault it was, and whether or not he could recover any of his investment."

"How much did he lose?"

"A little over two hundred thousand. I told him he had too much money in speculative stocks, but Richard was head strong. I guess he just wanted me to watch over his investments and yank them before something like this could happen. Of course, no one can see the future, especially where the FDA is concerned. Fulton should have known that better than anyone. Anyway, he withdrew his other investments and placed them with another broker. That's all I know."

John was sleepy. He tried to let go of the Fulton cases, but one more thought kept him awake. Has Fulton been watching him? Has he seen Fulton disguised in unfamiliar flesh, not knowing it was him? If not, would it happen? Could he impersonate Cindy or his daughter, Sarah? How would he know if Braxton was really his partner or Fulton?

I've got to catch him! He's a killer now; there are too many lives at stake. John pictured Anne's twisted neck, her eyes staring blankly at the ceiling while her body faced down. He saw Braxton's solemn face.

He'll never get over this, he thought as he began to drift off to sleep.

28

KEEPING A PROMISE MADE ONLY DAYS AGO, JOHN MET
with Mayor Chase and his attorney, Brooke Hershel early Monday
morning to update them on his progress. John was red-eyed and
irritable from a bad night's sleep. He carefully explained how the
cases were all tied to Dr. Richard Fulton, who just Friday evening
had made the leap from bank robber to murderer when he killed
Braxton's fiancée. Mayor Chase accepted the story without question,
making John suspect he'd talked to Whittman over the weekend about
Fulton's new abilities. John tried to reassure the mayor by adding, "I
don't think Fulton has your DNA anymore, Mayor, but until he is
found, I wouldn't stop wearing that tracking device. It has saved your
reputation twice."

"A fact for which I owe you immense gratitude," the Mayor said.
A fine bead of perspiration sparkled across his upper lip as he asked a
question that seemed to be burning deep within him. "You saw this
impostor with your own eyes, John. I've got to know—how close was
the resemblance?"

"It was you, Mayor, down to the last detail. If you were standing side-by-side, the only way I could tell you apart is by your mannerisms."

Mayor Chase shook his head; his eyes were childlike.

"What about his clothes?"

"Fulton wore a suit. I don't know what brand it was, but it seemed to fit okay, and it certainly looked like something you would wear."

The mayor turned toward his window abruptly. He spoke while looking out over the downtown area. John got the sense he was frightened and too embarrassed to admit it.

"You've made a lot of headway on this case, John. But now, we've got to find this man, and fast."

"I'm working on that, Mayor, but I haven't quite figured out how to smoke him out. We need to draw him into the open somehow."

"Carte blanche, John, anything you need—you just name it."

On his way out, John said hello to Jean Rebouche. He had called her a few days ago, after she had slipped him a note, saying they needed to talk privately. John assured Jeannie that she had nothing to worry about regarding the mayor. He told her that someone had attempted to frame him, but nothing more. Everything seemed to be back to normal between Jean and the mayor.

One less fire to contend with, John thought.

When John arrived at the office, he found a newspaper on his desk. A four paragraph article had been circled, accompanied by a yellow Post-it note that bore familiar handwriting. The note said: "Read this and come see me—Mike."

John turned on his desk lamp and began to pour through the article. It was titled: "Scientists Identify Key to Limb Regeneration."

The article was fascinating. It outlined how scientists at the Salk Institute for Biological Studies in La Jolla, California, had been able to regenerate a wing in a chick embryo—a species not known to be able to regrow limbs. It suggested that the potential for such regeneration exists instinctively in all vertebrates, including humans. John's heartbeat accelerated with each line he read. The study demonstrated that vertebrate regeneration is under the control of a powerful signaling system referred to as Wnt. Activating it, even artificially, had overcome the mysterious barrier to regeneration in animals like chicks that can't normally replace missing limbs. As further proof, scientists inactivated it in animals known to be able to regenerate their limbs, which reversed the ability of frogs, zebrafish, and salamanders to replace missing legs and tails.

A professor in the Gene Expression Laboratory was quoted as saying, "In this simple experiment, we removed part of the chick embryo's wing, activated Wnt signaling, and got the whole limb back—a beautiful and perfect wing. By changing the expression of a few genes, you can change the ability of a vertebrate to regenerate their limbs, rebuilding blood vessels, bone, muscles, and skin—everything that is needed. This new discovery opens up an entirely new area of research. Even though certain animals have lost their ability to regenerate limbs during evolution, conserved genetic machinery may still be present, and can be put to work again."

John read that previously, scientists believed that once stem cells turned into muscles, bone, or any other type of cells, that was their fate for life—and if those cells were injured, they didn't regenerate, but grew scar tissue. However, that theory had just been firmly dispelled. "Manipulating Wnt signaling in humans is, of course, not possible at this point," the professor continued in the article, "but we hope that these findings may eventually offer insights into current research examining the ability of stem cells to build new human body tissues and parts.

"For example," he said, "Wnt signaling may push mature cells to go back in time and 'dedifferentiate' into stem-like cells, in order to be able to then differentiate once more, producing all of the different tissues needed to build a limb. The possibilities are simply astounding."

The Salk Institute, John thought. *Where have I heard that name before?*

John reached for his computer's keyboard. With a burst of keystrokes, he quickly Googled "The Salk Institute for Biological Studies." In seconds he was reading background information about the independent nonprofit organization that was dedicated to fundamental discoveries in the life sciences, the improvement of human health, and the training of future generations of researchers. Jonas Salk, M.D., whose polio vaccine all but eradicated the crippling disease in 1955, opened the Institute in 1965 with a gift of land from the City of San Diego and the financial support of the March of Dimes.

I wonder how many other nonprofit organizations are working on regeneration for the betterment of mankind, instead of the almighty dollar, John thought. *The Salk Institute certainly deserves praise for its work, but I'll bet Whittman is furious that his company isn't basking in the limelight. If CSGR had beaten them to the punch, Whittman's stock would have skyrocketed in value.*

John snatched the newspaper and headed for Walsh's office. Mike was on the phone when he arrived. Hearing only one end of the conversation didn't hinder John's ability to decipher what the call was about. Walsh replied firmly, "I understand how you feel, Tom, but someone has to keep an eye on the lab. Fulton may try to reclaim his DNA or worse yet, harm Mr. Whittman. You and Justin need to be patient, and more importantly, stay sharp. Fulton can take anyone's identity—even yours! You two need to stay put until we can come up with a plan to find him." Mike smiled at John and rolled his eyes, "I need to go, Tom, don't let me down now—just hang in there and stay focused." Walsh hung up the phone.

"Let me guess," John said, "Connors and Moody are complaining about being posted at CSGR?"

"You're right on the money, John. Tom thinks that his and Justin's talents would be put to better use elsewhere. He claims you assigned them to watch Whittman's company to get them out of your hair."

John's eyes grew animated, "Well, he's half right, of course, but still, someone needs to be there."

"You did the right thing," Walsh replied. His eyes were drawn to the newspaper John held in his hands, "I see you have the morning paper. Did you read the article?"

Nodding, John said, "Twice. I also Googled the Salk Institute and found the press release. I can't tell you how timely this is. From what you just said to Connors, I assume the article has made a believer out of you?"

"Let's just say I believe that anything is possible, including nailing Fulton. Any ideas?"

"You know," John said, "I've been racking my brain and coming up empty, but after reading this article I think I may have the answer."

The corners of Walsh's mouth began to curve upward. His eyes were clear and confident in a way John realized he hadn't seen in weeks. It reminded John of the younger Walsh he had partnered with for so many years.

"We need to place a follow-up article in the newspaper," John said. "It's time to make Fulton come to us."

29

THE FAX MACHINE BEEPED AND DISPLAYED THE MESSage, "2 Pages Sent." It was after five, and John was famished, still trying to function at peak performance after barely an hour's sleep. He threw the faxed pages in his briefcase, glad to have finished writing a story for tomorrow's newspaper. It was proving helpful to have a contact at the *Kansas City Star*, someone who owed him a favor. If John's plan worked, he'd have to grant the reporter an exclusive interview. He closed the latches, grabbed his jacket and left the office deep in thought.

John drove to a middle-class neighborhood in Shawnee Mission, Kansas, and found the address he was looking for. As he approached the front door of a modest Cape Cod home, he felt apprehensive. He hadn't seen Braxton since Saturday, and even so, Mrs. Willis hadn't allowed him to visit. He'd never had the chance to express his condolences for Anne's death. What would he say? Nothing seemed quite appropriate for the situation. A moment after he knocked, the door opened wide.

"Good evening, Mrs. Willis, is Braxton home?" Braxton's mother was dressed in black dress slacks and a white blouse. Her coal black hair flowed to her shoulders, and she wore a deep shade of red lipstick. She clasped a purse in one hand and car keys in the other.

Recognizing John, Samarah smiled warmly. "John, it is good to see you. Do you have news for us?"

"We haven't found Fulton yet, but we do have a plan. I wanted to see how Braxton is doing—maybe give him an update."

"You are just in time, I am leaving for work. You can keep my son company for a while?"

"Sure, I can stay until he kicks me out," John said with a smile.

Samarah patted John's wrist and whispered, "You are a good friend. I think he misses you. I think he is ready to return to work now." John just nodded. He doubted if Braxton was in any condition to return to work. He had just been discharged from the hospital yesterday and agreed to stay with his mother for a few days. Avoiding Samarah's eyes, he glanced over her shoulder to see if Braxton was anywhere in sight.

"He's in the kitchen," she said. "I just made some kibbeh and there is plenty. Why don't you join him?"

"Thank you, Mrs. Willis, I will."

After a glance at her watch, Samarah extended her arm, inviting John inside. "I must go now. I cannot be late for work." As John watched Samarah walk to her car, he recalled that Braxton said she was a card dealer at a casino. It seemed so unlikely and John again experienced the strange feeling he was watching someone with royal blood. Perhaps it was just her mannerisms or the way she carried herself. Whatever it was, she spoke with a subdued authority in a soft, regal tone he knew he could never argue with.

What the hell is kibbeh, anyway?

Braxton sat at the kitchen table alone. A radio on the countertop played softly. When Braxton saw John's figure in the doorway, he almost smiled, but instead his eyes fell to his plate.

"Hello partner," John said in a sincere voice. "I'm sorry I haven't been to see you."

Braxton waved his arm as if to dismiss John's guilt, "Mom said you stayed with me on Friday night, and came to see me on Saturday. She said she sent you off to find Anne's killer."

John raised his eyebrows; his eyes were slightly animated. "She practically pushed me out the door."

Braxton nodded, "If you knew mom like I do, you'd understand."

"I think I'm beginning to," John replied. "She's an amazing woman."

Braxton stood up and continued speaking while he went to retrieve some dishes from a cabinet. "I couldn't have survived the past few days without her, John. She looks at things differently than most people do. She ties all of life's events together, weaves them into something that makes sense, or at least something easier to deal with."

John cocked his head slightly, and Braxton continued. "We had a lot of heartbreak as kids; she turned our pain into purpose. We weren't allowed to wallow in grief."

John stared at Braxton in disbelief. *Jesus,* he thought, *what could she possibly say to ease the pain of losing a fiancée?*

Braxton held a dinner plate in his hand and opened a drawer for silverware. He set a place for John at the table, never asking him if he wanted to eat.

That's Braxton alright, just a tad bit on the assuming side.

John suddenly grasped another similarity between Braxton and his mother. Maybe what John had been mistaking for a lack of manners were simply cultural characteristics he was unfamiliar with.

Braxton poured a dark red wine into a long stemmed glass and set it by John's empty plate. He sat down and began filling it with food. John had been so consumed by what he would say to Braxton, he didn't give much thought to the unfamiliar aroma of the food Samarah had prepared. John sat down and studied the unusual looking dish.

"That smells good… what is it?" he asked.

"It's kibbeh, a Lebanese dish."

"They're shaped like little footballs," John mused.

"Well, your eyes are still working," Braxton retorted, "try it."

John used his fork to cut through one of the egg-sized footballs and saw the stuffing inside. He could tell from the aroma he was going to like it. He took a bite.

"Wow!" John said. "It's gonna take me a while to figure out all the ingredients in this."

"It's good, isn't it?" Braxton asked.

"Delicious, "John replied. "I've never tasted anything like it."

"It takes several hours to make from scratch, but mom has been spoiling me since I came home."

John nodded, a little more serious again.

Braxton looked deep into John's eyes, "There's no doubt about it—I mean, it *was* Fulton, right?"

"Yes," John said nodding. "He assumed your identity—not only your looks, but he took your wallet, badge, and gun as well. He still has them"

There was a silence, and then John continued, "It's my fault, Braxton, if I had arrested him right away, Anne would still be alive. I made a terrible mistake, and I wouldn't blame you if you never forgive me."

Braxton shook his head, "No, John, I've had a lot of time to think about it. There is no law against looking like someone else. If we had arrested Fulton for simply resembling the mayor, how would we have kept him in custody? What law did he break? We had to wait for him to make a move."

John had the feeling that Braxton was doing for him what Samarah had done for her son all his life. Braxton was erasing his guilt, lessening his pain, and redirecting his sorrow into purpose.

"How are you feeling, Braxton?"

"Physically, I'm fine." He gave his food a blank stare. "I won't try to kid you, John, losing Anne has been more than a little difficult to deal with—but I need to get back to work—I've got to help find this guy. Can you talk to the Captain for me?"

"I already have, Brax. If you can pass a psychological exam, you can come back to work."

"I can't tomorrow," Braxton said firmly. "Anne's funeral is tomorrow." Braxton paused for a moment, and then leaned forward, "I'll do it

Wednesday. I don't want to waste any more time than necessary—not while he's impersonating me."

"I'll arrange it," John said. "It'll be good to have you back again."

John laid the Salk Institute article on the table and pushed it close to him. "Read this, Brax."

John ate while Braxton read.

"Cinnamon," John mumbled, "and do I detect mint?"

Braxton looked up and nodded. "See if you can figure out what kind of meat it is."

John cut into another fried kibbeh and studied it. There were two kinds of meat. The stuffing was a mixture of ground beef, onions, mint, and nuts of some kind. He took a bite. The shell that surrounded the stuffing was also made of meat, but it was mixed with something that made it brown in the oil when fried. It was wonderful.

"Is it lamb?" John guessed.

"You've had kibbeh before?" Braxton asked.

"Never," John replied, "just a guess. I know you don't eat many red meats, and lamb is one of the few that is popular with the Lebanese culture."

"You never cease to amaze me, John. I suppose you looked that up right after I became your partner?"

"I just thought it would be good to know something about Mediterranean food, just in case you ever had the desire to have it for lunch sometime."

Braxton used his fork to point to the shell of the popular Lebanese delicacy. "Cubed lamb we ground two or three times and mix it with bulgur wheat until it becomes a fine paste. It's stuffed with a mixture of ground beef, pine nuts, mint, cinnamon, and onion. It's a lot of work, so we usually have it only on special occasions."

"It's awesome. I guess I should expand my culinary horizons," John said, stuffing another bite in his mouth. He helped himself to more kibbeh while Braxton took a minute to finish the article.

"Interesting," Braxton laid the article down. "I wonder how many other research companies are as close to making the same discovery as Fulton."

"My guess is plenty, but it's still a race, Kid. These companies are working under incredible secrecy. The only reason that article was printed is because the research was done by a nonprofit organization. They have nothing to lose if another company leapfrogs their technology. But you can bet that because of this article, most of these companies will be stepping up their research. Whittman's company, for instance, would lose millions if another company beat them to the punch."

Braxton's jaw dropped noticibly. If it hadn't been so unlikely, John could have sworn his tawny skin had turned white.

"What's the matter, Brax?" John asked cautiously. Braxton held his hand in mid-air, motioning John to refrain from talking. He stared at the paper on the table, and then closed his eyes as if he were deep in thought. When he lifted his head he spoke confidently.

"Oh my god, John! What if Whittman discovered that another company had surpassed them—that another company was going to beat them to the punch? What if Whittman pulled the experiment from Fulton knowing damn well he'd try the formula anyway?"

At first, John didn't seem to grasp the implication of Braxton's question. But then he raised an eyebrow and leaned back in his chair while his puzzled expression slowly faded.

"CSGR wasn't ready for human testing!" John said, gazing over Braxton's head. "They probably didn't have time to complete the full regimen of FDA requirements, so they goaded Fulton into trying it. If the experiment failed, Whittman could claim his innocence. After all, he left a solid paper trail, at the very least a memo pulling the plug on the project. He confiscated the formula, but not all of it. And frankly, I don't think Whittman is that sloppy. But if the experiment was successful—"

Braxton cut John off. "He'd be a hero. He could announce his discovery to the world and his stock value would skyrocket."

"Yeah," John said. "He could probably find a quick buyer for the company and bank a few billion in the process."

The two men sat quiet for a minute, contemplating the scenario, neither man interested in finishing their meal.

John began to fidget. When he finally spoke, he sounded like he was about to explode, "You know what, Kid?"

"No, what, John?"

"I'm *never* going to call you 'kid' again."

The ends of Braxton's lips curled upward slightly. "So what are we going to do now?"

John brushed his plate aside, and scooted his chair closer to the table. "I already have a plan in place. Now—I don't know if we'll ever be able to prove that Whittman set Fulton up, but I do think we stand a damn good chance of coaxing Fulton to come to us."

Braxton inched closer, leaning his elbows on the table. Unofficially, he was back in the game.

Tapping on the newspaper, John said, "This article gave me the idea, but it's the article that will appear in *tomorrow's* paper that will smoke him out."

"What article is that?" Braxton prodded.

"I called Zach Whittman and proposed that he announce his company's success in regenerating limbs in lab mice."

"I'll bet he didn't put up any resistance to the idea, did he?" Braxton asked snidely.

"As a matter of fact, he didn't. I recommended that he declare a bogus partnership with the Salk Institute and announce that they will be moving their research to their Salk's facility sometime next week."

"I assume you cleared this with the Salk Institute?"

"You bet I did. I promised them a retraction in a week. Meanwhile, we'll get the local TV stations to carry the same story. Unless Fulton has already left town, there's no way he won't hear the news. He'll go after the formula, his DNA, or both."

If Braxton looked pale before, he certainly didn't now. His teeth nearly fluoresced in the warm setting of his handsomely dark face. His voice took on a somber note. "Do you really think it'll work, John?"

Nodding, John said, "Think about it, Brax, it's *his* formula, *his* discovery. If he let it go to California, he might never see it again. We already know he's a vindictive son of a bitch, he'd never allow it. That is—if he could help it. Whether he wants his DNA back or not, I can't say. He's a wanted man. But if he wants to take credit for his discovery, he can't pose as you, or the mayor. He's got to be Dr. Richard Fulton. Keep in mind, we have no real proof he's committed a crime. As far as the world is concerned, his only crime is that he's missed work for a couple of weeks, and he owns a collection of baby food jars full of urine."

"Baby food jars?" Braxton asked.

"Yeah, we think he keeps urine samples for the people he's planning to impersonate. The DNA in the urine allows him to assume their genetic blueprint. We've found at least one from each of the suspects in the five-pack."

Braxton squinted and leaned back in his chair. His temples bulged slightly. "It's time to put this guy away, John."

"We'll get him, ki-aah-Braxton."

"You were going to call me 'kid' weren't you?"

"Yeah," John confessed with a smile, "but I didn't."

The two men talked for another half hour, and then Braxton told John to go home to his family. When John asked what time the funeral was, Braxton told him not to come. He said he wanted John focused and working on the case. John couldn't help but draw another parallel between Braxton and his mother.

John was in an upbeat mood when he left Samara Willis's home. He had a plan to bait Fulton, and his partner was doing incredibly well. Even though it was unlikely that a man could recover from the loss of a loved one so quickly, John could only surmise that Samara had some mystical power over her son. He was in awe of Samara's ability to heal Braxton's spirit. It was one of those cultural things that he was grateful for, but would never understand.

Braxton braced his elbows on the kitchen table. He held his glass by the stem and absently swirled the wine in slow circles. He was alone now, and welcomed the silence. He'd had no time to himself, no time to think, and he needed the time desperately. Time to plan Fulton's death.

30

AT SEVEN-THIRTY ON TUESDAY MORNING, JOHN Dietrich sat in the lobby at Critical Strategies Genetics Research. He was briefing Detectives Rathbone and Kosinski on procedural pertaining to admitting employees and visitors into the building. He would repeat the briefing again shortly, when Connors and Moody came to relieve them at eight. Each team was working twelve hour shifts. Mayor Chase instructed John to minimize the number of detectives who knew anything about the case. The last thing the mayor wanted was to have rumors about a man who could morph into anyone he chooses leak into the community.

Rathbone and Kosinski were respectable detectives, but hardly a day passed when John didn't regret having Connors and Moody involved in the case. Since he really didn't have any choice in the matter, all John could do was make the best of it. Only yesterday Connors had been reprimanded for being away from his post at the rear employee entrance. He was seen in the restricted laboratory corridor flirting with a pretty lab technician. The rumor was that she hauled off and slapped him for making an unsavory comment. Normally, John would have found this to be amusing, but now he wondered when one of these buffoons would screw something up or, worse yet, get someone killed.

"Any questions?" John asked.

"Yes," Rathbone replied. "I understand our instructions just fine, but I don't understand why. How come we're lifting the security precautions we just put in place?"

John nodded, "Good question, Bones, I was about to get to that. We're expecting Fulton to try and get to the formula or his DNA. Both are locked in the secure refrigerated locker near the storeroom between labs nine and ten. We can't make it impossible for Fulton to get in the building, or he won't be able make a move for them. Whittman added some cameras in the storeroom and in lab eight. For all we know, Fulton may think his DNA is still in his lab."

Just then, Whittman pushed through the front door.

"Good morning, John," Whittman said with little expression. He didn't stop to talk, but walked down the corridor to his office. John studied his mannerisms and walk carefully; yes, it was Whittman.

Twenty minutes later, Connors and Moody arrived, and John repeated the instructions.

"Good," Connors said. "Watching employees login to their email was a pain in the ass."

Connors was referring to John's idea of placing networked computers at both entrances. In addition to using electronic passkeys and a retinal scanner, no employee was admitted through the door without producing an individualized password they received by email each day. The security guard would check it against his printed list. This and other added measures were now being dumped.

"You both understand that we expect Fulton to make a move for the formula, his DNA, and probably his research notes, right?"

Moody nodded, twiddling his car keys, and Connors made a crack, "Yeah, John, we're not stupid, we get it."

John's left eyebrow barely raised a notch. In a calm tone of voice, he continued.

"Fulton will probably read the paper or see the news by sometime midday. At least, that's the plan. But that doesn't mean he'll make a move immediately. It could happen tomorrow or maybe the next day. The front desk security guard'll keep an eye on the video monitors and radio both of you at the sign of anyone rummaging through Fulton's lab or the storeroom; both are now off limits to employees. If this happens, I don't want either of you to make a scene—just escort the suspect to the conference room and call me on my cell."

Connors rolled his eyes, and John decided to put him in check, "And I expect you to ignore the pretty girls, and stay at your position *all day.* Is that clear, Tom?"

Connors cheeks reddened, the veins in his temples showed.

John let out a deep breath, "Now Bones and Koss are going to cover your posts a few minutes longer while you two come with me. We are going to ask Mr. Whittman a few questions. I don't want either of you to say a word; you're there for the sake of intimidation. Is that understood?"

Again, Moody nodded, but John could tell Connors was choking inside, struggling to hold his tongue.

Offices lined both sides of "mahogany row," the corridor nicknamed for its lavish wood décor and ornate office furniture. Near the end of the hall, the walls opened up to an elaborate reception area, where an attractive brunette sat typing at her keyboard with blazing speed. John knew a fair amount about computers, or at least about doing online research, but he had never before heard such loud clicking, or so much of it. Trish was Whittman's gatekeeper, and she was good at it. No one got by her if she didn't want them to. Fortunately, Whittman told her to let John pass, any time, day or night.

"He's on a call, Detective Dietrich; can you wait a moment until his light goes out?"

"Sure, Trish, but can you keep an eye on his line? I don't have much time."

John walked over to the windows and plunked into a leather sofa. Connors and Moody joined him. John watched Moody twirling his keys rather clumsily.

"I wanted to mention something to you, Justin. I understand the janitor has been hanging around the lobby quite a bit." Justin dropped his keys. His eyes widened. "I'd appreciate it if you'd tell him that you aren't allowed to chat while on duty. I realize that Wendell was pretty friendly with Fulton, and he's probably just trying to keep tabs on him, but he'll only distract you."

"Jesus, John," Connors, quipped. "You got spies watching us or something?"

"No spies, Tom, let's just say that someone was concerned and mentioned it."

No one spoke again until Trish announced that Whittman was off the phone. The three men entered his office. Connors and Moody stopped by a round work table while John approached Whittman's desk. Whittman and Dietrich had graduated to a first name basis a few days ago, but John reverted to their former rapport.

"Mr. Whittman, I need to ask you some questions."

Emotionless, Whittman replied, "What can I do for you, John?"

"I've only known you for a week or so, but in that time, I've found you to be an extremely well organized man. You strike me as a stickler for details, would you say that's a fair assessment?"

"Yes, I suppose so."

"And you knew Fulton pretty well, didn't you?"

Whittman leaned back in his chair. John sensed that his guard was up. "We've worked closely for years, John; Richard was one of my most brilliant researchers. I had hopes that his work would someday earn him the Nobel Prize."

"How desperate was Fulton to try the formula on himself?"

"I told you before, Fulton had set a goal to have tried it last month. He was becoming impatient, but the FDA's procedures are riddled with red tape. We still had too many other tests to perform before clinical trials could even begin. I should have seen this coming, but I never dreamed he would try the formula at such an early stage."

"Was Fulton aware of all the FDA's protocol from the start?" Whittman was still.

"What do you mean?"

"I mean he was a scientist, not a business man. Did he fully understand how long this was going to take?"

"Well—yes, I'm certain he did."

"Then how could he have possibly been under the impression that he would be able to try the formula on himself even within the next two years?"

Whittman looked uncomfortable, his eyes grew jittery, and his hands were fidgeting. "I don't know. I guess the man was setting unrealistic expectations for himself."

"If you knew him so well, and worked with him so closely, wouldn't you have been able to manage those expectations?"

Whittman's jaw was set, his temples suddenly bulged. "You're trying to make a point here, Detective, why don't you just come out and say it!"

The way John cocked an eyebrow made Whittman turn pink.

"I'm sorry, John, I didn't mean to raise my voice."

John nodded, as if to minimize the outburst, "Isn't it true that another company is further along on regeneration research than you?"

"For God's sake," Whittman said, "where did you hear that?"

"Just answer the question—is it true?"

Whittman's body language was pegging the needle on John's bullshit meter. He was certain the next words out of his mouth would be a lie.

"We're all running neck and neck, John, but I don't know of anyone who is closer than us in this race. Now tell me, why are you asking these questions?"

"Well, I'm a little bothered by the fact that a detail oriented man like you would only confiscate some of the formula and leave several vials of it behind."

"I didn't pick it up personally, John. I sent someone else to do it."

"Oh, who?"

"I don't recall. I just remember sending Fulton a memo."

Whittman no longer looked at John. His eyes focused on the wall in the back of the room. When John didn't respond, Whittman re-engaged him again.

"When he called me, he was screaming that I owed him a new arm," Whittman said. "So I had someone pick it up and secure it."

"The mask Fulton used to ingest the formula—it wasn't confiscated either. Fulton couldn't have used the formula without it. Seems like a detail a man like you wouldn't overlook." Whittman's eyes narrowed a notch.

"What exactly are you saying, Detective, that I set him up? That I knew he would take the formula anyway?"

"I'm not accusing you of anything, but if you knew Fulton that well, you should have known how driven he was to try it on himself, you should have taken better precautions."

"Let's just call it a mistake, John, an oversight. I had no reason to put Dr. Fulton in that kind of danger."

"There's only one motive I can think of, Mr. Whittman—stock value."

John lost Whittman's eye contact again. He stared off to one side of his desk.

John continued, "If Fulton took the formula and it worked, your company would be the darling of Wall Street. You'd be courted by every major biotech company. Your stock value would soar through the roof, and you'd probably wind up a billionaire."

"I would never take such a chance, John; it's ridiculous to even entertain such an idea."

"I don't know," John said, trying to maintain an even tone. "If the project failed, you could claim that you did everything you could to stop it. You could insist that Fulton was insane and forged ahead without your approval. You'd probably get hit with some fines, but all in all, I'd say it'd be a pretty good gamble. You set him up, didn't you? You led him to believe that the board of directors was concerned about his safety. All because he discovered a second layer in DNA that no one understands yet. This so-called second layer has never been the cause of a delay before. You didn't even have to report it. No wonder Fulton was so upset."

A loud crinkling of paper made John turn around. Everyone stared at Justin Moody. He was pale and sweating. He clenched a handful of crumpled documents from Whittman's work table.

"Justin, what's the matter?"

When he realized all eyes were on him, Moody swallowed hard and wiped his wrist across his forehead, "Sorry—I don't feel too well. I'd better get to the restroom before I get sick."

Moody release the papers and left in a hurry.

"Jesus, he don't look so good," Connors said. "Maybe I ought'a go make sure he's all right."

John nodded, "Good idea. Let me know if he needs to go home. We'll need a replacement for him." Turning back to Whittman, John tried to pick up from where he'd left off. "I can't say you've broken any laws, Zach, but I think you may be guilty of unethical behavior. Unfortunately, it probably wouldn't affect your success in building your fortune."

Whittman was stone faced. "I'm disappointed in your lack of trust in me, John. I have done nothing but cooperate with your investigation."

"True, but you had no choice; your plan backfired when Fulton decided to frame you. If he discovers what you've done, he'll be vindictive; your life could be in danger."

Almost reflexively, John's eyes widened and he inhaled a deep, sharp breath. He spun toward the door and darted out of the room. Whittman was left alone, nervous and confused.

31

JOHN CAUGHT UP WITH CONNORS AT THE LOBBY restroom, but there was no sign of Justin Moody. Connors ignored John, crossing his path like he was a total stranger. Then a thought hit him and he tore through the lobby and ran outside.

He knows. I'll bet he went to see if Moody's car is still in the parking lot. John walked toward the front guard and waved Rathbone and Kosinski over to join them.

"Did you guy's see Moody leave?"

"Yeah, I saw him." Kosinski said. "What was his hurry?"

Rathbone added, "Yeah, He bolted through the front door and just kept running."

"Kept running—where?"

"I don't know… North. I watched him until he was out of sight."

"You didn't think that was a little odd?"

"Yeah, I suppose. But we're talking about Moody here, and quite frankly—he's a little odd."

Kosinski cut in, "What's all the worry about Moody, John—what's up?"

John took a deep breath. "That wasn't Moody, boys."

Rathbone's eyes widened, "Are you saying that was our impostor? Are you sure? Because I thought you said Fulton wouldn't come 'till later—after he'd read the article in the paper."

John's expression soured, "Maybe he gets the early edition. Hell, I don't know, but I'm telling you that was Fulton."

The front guard was shaking his head and decided to throw his two cents in. "I think you guys are a little confused. Dr. Fulton doesn't look anything like the fella that ran out of here."

John bit his cheek and then raised his eyebrows at the detectives before answering. "You're right. That man didn't look anything like Dr. Fulton. C'mon boys, let's go have a seat in the lobby."

They moved to a grouping of lobby furniture and sat down, and then John explained what happened in Whittman's office. When he was nearly finished, he eyed Connors sprinting back to the building from the North parking lot.

Tom can really move when he wants to, John thought.

Connors pushed through the front door like he meant business and joined the others.

John looked at Rathbone, "Bones, I want you and Koss to concentrate on a fourteen block perimeter of this building. Keep an eye on bus stops, and look for someone wearing a white shirt and brown herringbone sport coat. Remember, Fulton may not look anything like Moody anymore. Ask for identification from anyone you find suspicious, and if he can't provide it, he goes downtown, understand?"

"Got it," Rathbone said. The men stood, and then he and Kosinski left. As Connors waited for his instructions, he resembled a little boy who was squirming because he had to go to the bathroom.

John wished he could tell Connors to go home—permanently. He knew he was about to piss him off. "So Justin's car was still in the lot, right, Tom?"

"How'd you know?" Connors features tightened.

"It's a little trick I use. I call it 'asking questions'. Just about everyone in the lobby saw him bolt out of here. He ran north until he was out of sight." Connors face turned pink.

"Well, I'm not doing us a lot of good standing here talking to you."

"You're absolutely right, Tom. I need you to stay with Whittman. I don't want you to let him out of your sight."

"No way, Dietrich! I'm gonna go look for Justin."

John shook his head, "Sorry, no can do. Besides, you know that wasn't Justin, don't you? You know that was Fulton who ran out of here, right?"

"Maybe, and maybe not. I'm not convinced of anything yet."

"Well, I am," John snapped. "And I need you here, protecting Whittman."

"What's the matter, Dietrich; afraid I'll find him and rob you of all the glory?"

"Jesus, Tom, is that what you think? You think this is all about glory? Did it ever occur to you that cops take orders and do what they're told because it's the right thing to do?" We haven't even caught Fulton and you're worried about getting credit for the collar."

John studied Connors. He was pretty sure that not a single word he was saying was registering in Connors's head. John looked out the windows. Fulton was out there. And every minute that passed made the odds of catching him that much greater. The more feet on the street right now, the better. Even the feet of an oaf like Connors might help.

"Tell you what, Tom; I'm calling the captain to get more resources on this. I'll give you twenty minutes. By that time we'll have plenty of officers out there looking for him. Start ten blocks north and work your way back here. There's a residential area down the street. Make a note of anything that looks suspicious. Fulton could easily break into someone's home and wait until dark to disappear."

"I know the drill, Dietrich, I'll find the bastard."

"Good, Tom, I'll call the captain, and tell him you'll be bringing Fulton in."

"Mind if I go now?" Connors said.

"Twenty minutes, Tom, then I want you with Whittman!"

John turned away and dialed Captain Walsh's number and pressed his cell to his ear. He could feel his heart pound as he waited for Mike to pick up on the other end. There was a click when Mike picked up the receiver, and John cut in and began speaking quickly.

"Listen, Mike, we need a dozen cruisers searching a twenty block area north of Whittman's lab. I also need a couple more men down here."

Walsh could sense the urgency in John's voice, "Tell me what's going on, John, what wrong?"

"Fulton was here, I'm sure of it!"

"What? Already?" Mike said, "It's only eight-fifteen!"

"Yeah, he jumped the gun on us."

"He must have seen the newspaper. What happened?"

"He may or may not have seen the paper. I think he was already planning to come, Mike. He was posing as Moody. He was in Whittman's office when I questioned him about Fulton."

"Christ, John, what did he hear?"

"Everything!" John paused long enough to swallow. "I was drilling Whittman about how I think he set Fulton up to inflate his stock value. If I were Fulton, I'd be looking for a way to get even. I think Whittman's in danger."

"How do you know it was really Fulton?"

"When I met with Connors and Moody this morning, Moody never said a word. Come to think of it, I don't think he ever looked me in the eye. I didn't really think much about it until we were asking Whittman some questions. When I mentioned that I thought he set Fulton up, Moody crushed a handful of papers from a worktable, and then he said he felt sick and had to get to the restroom. You should have seen him, Mike. For a split second, he didn't look like Moody at all. Connors went after him, but he wasn't in the restroom."

"I'm still not convinced it was Fulton. How can you be sure it was really him?"

"Besides the fact that he took off like a bat out of hell?"

"Yeah."

"Remember what Mary Simon said?" John asked.

"The kinesics expert?"

"Right. She said, 'The best way to avoid getting caught in a lie is to remain perfectly still—no movement, no cues.' Justin never said a word this morning; he nodded a few times, but avoided my eyes. The son of a bitch was in Whittman's office with us, I know it! By now, he probably knows he can't get to his DNA or the formula."

"What happens when he reads the paper?" Mike asked. "Will he believe the story, or suspect he's been duped?"

"I don't know—I think I mentioned the story to him. I can't remember."

"Listen, John, I want someone to be with Whittman around the clock. We can't take any chances."

"I agree," John said. "I need two men to cover the entrances. Connors can shadow Whittman."

There was a brief silence on Mike's end, "You *want* Connors to cover Whittman?"

"They deserve each other," John said sarcastically. "Anyway, I need those men. I also need someone from forensics to come down here and check out Moody's car. It's still in the parking lot."

"You think Moody's okay, John?"

"I don't know anything at this point, Mike."

There was a short pause, and then Walsh continued, "Jaworski's gone today. I'll send Hamiid. Are you all right, John? You sound a little shaken."

"I guess I am, Mike. This is scary… in fact, it's goddamn frightening. For all I know, Fulton might be in the building again. He could've already come back under another identity."

"I'm sending four men, John—two uniforms and two detectives. Use them any way you see fit."

"Thanks, Mike, and don't forget the cruisers. His trail's getting cold." There was a note of uncertainty in John's tone. Mike wasn't sure he had ever heard anything like it in his old partner's voice. John turned and began walking in the direction of Whittman's office.

Walsh's voice became subdued and calming. "Keep your head on straight, John. You'll get this guy, I know it."

John hoped it was true, but Fulton was right in front of his nose, and he never knew it. He had sensed something was wrong, but by the time he was fully aware of it, it was too late.

John reached Whittman's office and walked right past his secretary. Whittman's face was a combination of fear and puzzlement. He knew something was wrong, but what? John wasted no time telling Whittman that he thought Fulton had been impersonating Justin Moody.

"I think you're in danger, Mr. Whittman. I'm going to have someone accompany you twenty-four hours a day. Detective Connors will take the day shift and I'll find someone else to take the evening shift. I imagine you value your privacy, but you're going to have little of it 'til we find Fulton."

Whittman plopped into his burgundy leather chair. He ran his fingers through his platinum blonde hair. His eyes scanned his desk, but John was certain he wasn't really looking at anything.

John placed his palms on Whittman's desk, and leaned in. "I'll have Connors stick to you like glue, Zach. If you go to the restroom, he'll go to the restroom, if you go home, he'll go with you, and so on. He'll need to search any premises you enter, okay?" Whittman nodded and gave John a weak smile.

"Zach," John said in a calming tone, "I'm sorry this is happening, but we'll get Fulton. Our presence is going to be a little intrusive, but you've gotta be willing to put up with the inconvenience. We're only looking out for your safety." Whittman continued staring blankly across his desk.

"Detective Connors will be back in about a half hour. I'd appreciate a call whenever the two of you are on the move." With that, John headed for the lobby.

I wish Braxton were here, John thought. He remembered how little he trusted Braxton when he first became his partner. Now, there was no one he trusted more.

If I could just bounce some ideas off him.

Staring out the front doors, John decided he could use some fresh air. He pushed through both sets of glass and stood for a moment in the warm morning sun. It felt glorious. Even better, it felt safe. There were calming sounds of chirping birds, and the buzz of a mammoth dragon fly that zigzagged around the bushes that flanked the sidewalk.

How many more times will Fulton be within my grasp without my knowing it? John pondered. *How can anyone possibly outsmart a criminal they can't recognize? All I'm doing now is cleaning up messes. It's going to get worse. God, it's going to get a lot worse. I've got to protect Whittman—he's the key now. He's the bait, the only way we'll ever get Fulton.* John thought about Justin Moody. *I wonder if he's alive.* Then he thought about Wendell Peters, the janitor who had been seen hanging around the front lobby, talking to Moody for hours. John turned and headed for the front desk.

John asked the security guard, "Have you seen Wendell Peters, the janitor?"

"No sir, officer, he usually doesn't come in 'til around ten." John started to amble back toward the door, but the guard's comment stopped him. "Come to think of it, there were a lot of people looking for Wendell yesterday afternoon. I guess he must have left early."

"What time was that?" John asked.

"Around four-thirty. There was a real mess in lab four. One of the chemists broke a bunch of glassware. I thought it was kind of funny they had to clean it up themselves for a change."

"Do you remember him leaving the building?"

The guard paused for a minute and then shook his head, "No, I don't. But he might have left using the rear door."

"What exit does he usually leave from?"

Pointing over John's shoulder, the guard replied, "The front, but that's because he likes to park his car under the lights. You know—in case he has to work late."

"Where?" John asked, "Where does Wendell park his car?"

The guard walked toward the front door and pointed, "Right over there. Well, waddya know, there's his car right there."

"Which car?"

"That gray primered '66 Corvair. It's his pride and joy."

John gestured toward the switchboard system, "Page Wendell. If he doesn't answer, call him at home. If he's not there, I want you to page your maintenance technician and have him meet me here."

John paced the lobby. A few minutes later, he watched the security guard as he was being pointed out to a tall, wiry young man in his early twenties.

"You wanted to see me, officer?" he asked as he approached.

"Yes, I'm Detective Dietrich. Are you the maintenance technician?"

"Yeah, I'm Paul Bjelica," he said nervously.

"When did you last see Wendell Peters?" John asked.

"I don't know, I suppose around noon yesterday."

"Well", John said, "he's not at home and nobody saw him leave. So you and I are going to search every inch of this building until we find him."

About a half hour into the search, John's phone rang. It was Hamiid Hamoodi.

"Hey, John. It's Hamiid. I'm at Moody's car in the parking lot." Hamiid's voice was hushed. "I think you'd better come out here." John stiffened at Hamiid's serious tone. He didn't ask any questions, but told him he'd be right out. The parking lot was only a two-minute walk. The outdoors would be a good break from the tight quarters he and the maintenance tech had just finished searching. The narrow corridor containing the company's phone system wiring was making John a little claustrophobic.

John turned to Bjelica, "I need to run up front for a few minutes. Do you want to take a break until I get back?"

"Sure," Bjelica replied. "D-do you really think we're going to find Wendell around here somewhere?"

John studied the young man carefully. "I wouldn't count on it. Tell you what, Paul, why don't you take about twenty minutes. I'll meet you back here then." The young man managed to force a half smile. John led the way as the maintenance technician followed, weaving through another narrow area. Nervous, Bjelica slipped a screwdriver from his tool belt and tapped the handle along the walls, on boxes, and even windows. Passing a row of mobile trash containers, he used the screwdriver to flip the hinged lids up, one at a time, like it was a game. They had been emptied, which was why Paul hesitated at the third container. Something was slightly protruding at the top. When he inched closer, he recognized the tip of a shoe, just before Wendell's entire body came into view.

"Holy shit!" Paul reeled away and tripped, falling on his backside. "Son of a bitch!"

On the floor, Paul kicked his feet wildly until he had scooted himself up against the hallway wall. His eyes were large and filled with fear. Even though he could go no further, his feet continued to push and kick. John spun and ran to his side. Paul didn't take John's extended hand. He was still kicking his feet, keeping his back pinned against the wall.

"What is it, what's wrong?" John asked, studying the horrified look on the young man's face.

Bjelica's arm raised slightly, his finger pointed, "Look in there!" John approached the trash bin and looked down. He closed his eyes for a moment to compose himself. He slid his hand under Wendell's pants leg, just above his sock. His skin was cold. He wondered why he even bothered. From the shade of blue on Wendell's face, it was obvious he had been dead for a long time. John picked up his cell and began to dial Walsh's number, but then he noticed the hysterical expression on Bjelica's face. He put the phone in his pocket.

A few more minutes won't hurt. I need to manage this before it gets out of hand.

John kept a hand on the maintenance man's shoulder as he escorted him to the break room and got him a cup of coffee.

"Sit here for a few minutes, Paul. I'll send an officer back to stay with you. Meanwhile, I don't want you to speak to anyone about this, okay? I'm going to shut this place down for the day, but I'll need some time to do that. Do you understand?"

Bjelica was visibly shaking; he clasped the coffee cup like it was a valuable source of heat. He shook his head, yes.

On his way to the front of the building, John called Walsh and told him about finding Wendell Peters' dead body. He requested more men and said he was going to shut the lab down. At the front door John noticed two uniformed officers who must have arrived with Rathbone and Kosinski's replacements. He told them what he had just found, and sent the officers to the exits. He instructed one of the detectives to go to the break room and keep Bjelica company. The other detective accompanied John to Moody's car.

The trunk lid of a black, late model Pontiac Grand Prix was raised, and John went right to it. Hamiid was bent over, head in the trunk, and when he straightened, John could see he was holding an evidence bag in one hand and tweezers in the other. Glancing down, John noticed Justin Moody's body. It resembled a roped calf from a rodeo. But Fulton hadn't used rope. Moody's hands and feet had been bound behind him with gray duct tape.

"Is he alive?" John asked without the slightest hope of a positive response.

"I'm sorry, John," Hamiid said, shaking his head. John didn't like Moody much, but he really didn't hate him either. Most of the time he was simply offended at the way he idolized his partner, Tom Connors. Moody followed Connors's lead without hesitation. He was like a mindless robot, giving little thought to the ramifications of his partner's instructions, no matter how ridiculous they were. John knew that Moody would never be a great detective, but he often thought he could have been a better one had he been paired with a different partner.

Connors will be crushed when he hears the news. And why not? How could he possibly find someone else who would look up him the way Moody did?

"There's no doubt Fulton did this," John said confidently. "Find anything else interesting?"

Hamiid reached into his kit and removed a bag containing a latex glove, "Will this do?"

John nodded, "How did he die?"

"Blow to the head. His skull was crushed with something narrow, like a crowbar or tire iron." John stooped over the trunk and noted that what was once a pool of blood had darkened in color after soaking into the trunk's carpet.

John had little to say. "When you're finished here, there's another body inside, Hamiid. But take your time with this. The captain is sending more help. I'm going to evacuate the premises."

John turned and started to walk around the car. He stopped short at the sight of a black and turquoise duffel bag on the passenger seat.

"Hamiid!"

The forensic officer's head shot up, his eyes peered over the raised trunk lid.

"Have you checked inside yet?"

Hamiid shook his head, "I started with the trunk." John went to the passenger door.

"I need to see what's in this bag."

Hamiid stooped over his tool case and removed a wedge followed by a strap tool from the same compartment. Like a seasoned locksmith, Hamiid inserted the tools between the passenger glass and the window sash. After a few slight maneuvers, he tugged the tools upward and the door unlocked.

"You're wearing gloves," John said. "You want to do the honors?"

Hamiid unzipped the duffle. He removed a pair of blue jeans, shoes, and a polo shirt. What John saw next took his breath away. A wallet, ID badge, and two handguns were surrounded by several small vials of urine.

Gotta be Braxton's things, John thought.

"Open the wallet."

There it was. Braxton's mug shot stared at him from the plastic of his driver's license.

"Get someone down here to pick this up right away. Have them check the contents for prints. He'll probably find several sets including the mayor's."

John turned and continued his trek back to the building. The detective trailed him in silence all the way to Whittman's office. John didn't acknowledge Trish, but walked straight into the office. There, he found Whittman slumped in his leather chair, nearly asleep, his head resting on his propped up fist. Connors was back, watching in complete boredom. John was surprised to see Connors after their last conversation. He'd almost expected him to disobey his orders and continue looking for Moody. In this instance, he'd have let it slide.

"Tom, did you find Fulton?"

Connors shook his head.

"That's okay," John said, "I forgot to tell the captain you were bringing him in, so you're off the hook." Connors eyes narrowed.

"Mr. Whittman!" John said firmly to get his attention. "We need to talk." Whittman opened his eyes slowly; there was no life in them.

"Zach, I want you to dismiss your employees." Whittman straightened himself in his chair. It took a moment to absorb what John had said.

"Why? What's going on?"

John lowered his voice, "There have been two murders, Zach. I think we need to close your facility for a few days."

Whittman looked like he was having trouble catching his breath. Even though John suspected he had made some bad choices, he felt sorry for him.

"Who—who was murdered?"

"Your janitor, Wendell Peters, and one of our detectives." Connors ears perked up when he heard the word, "detectives."

"Hey, Dietrich, who was the detective?"

"In a minute, Tom!"

"Listen, Zach, why don't you have Trish get on the PA system and announce that everyone is dismissed for today and tomorrow, and that work will resume on Thursday. Have her tell them you want everyone out of the building in fifteen minutes."

"How will I explain?" Whittman began, and then he realized it really didn't matter.

"Lives are at stake, Zach; we need to close the doors."

Whittman reached for a legal pad, and began scribbling a message. He wrote three succinct lines, then read them over, scratched out one word and inserted another.

"I'll give this to Trish." Whittman said, and stepped out of his office. John looked at Connors who was glaring at him.

"It was Justin," John said, "we found him in his trunk. The man who was here with us earlier was definitely Fulton." John watched Connors's glare turn to hatred.

"This is your fault, Dietrich; you've run this entire investigation like a Girl Scout meeting."

"Is that so? Well, he's your partner! I don't recall you telling me that he seemed any different this morning. Every time I tried to talk to him, you interrupted me. If you'd let him talk for himself, maybe he would have said something to give himself away."

"Yeah, right! We all know your superior intellect would have spotted something only a fine detective like yourself could see."

"I don't care what you think, Tom, and I don't have time for this conversation. There's a murderer out there who can assume anyone's identity, and he's running loose in our city. If you have a plan to capture him, let's hear it, otherwise, shut the hell up!"

Connors fists were clenched. John could tell he wanted to take a swing at him. Every muscle in his body seemed to be flexed, and the veins in his neck looked like strips of red licorice. John couldn't figure out what was holding him back. At the very least, Connors seemed ready to explode.

The PA system crackled, and Trish's voice began to announce that employees were dismissed until eight o'clock Thursday morning. Connors stared John down during the entire message. John didn't budge.

"If you want to take a moment to see Justin, you'd better do it now," John said. "Otherwise, you'll have to see him at the morgue, and I still need you to stay with Whittman." Connors's narrowed eyes resumed a rounder shape, but the hatred remained. He straightened a little and then stormed out of Whittman's office.

32

BY SIX P.M., JOHN HAD CHALKED THE DAY UP AS A complete loss, a train wreck, an unexplainable tragedy. After Whittman sent his employees home, a team of detectives scoured CSGR's facilities from top to bottom. Captain Walsh showed up, and he and John joined the search, looking for clues in the back rooms and corridors. Four uniformed officers patrolled the perimeter and kept watch over the exits. The police were no closer to finding Fulton than they were this morning. Only now, it seemed less likely.

An hour ago John had received an unpleasant call from the mayor. It seemed as if the mayor had forgotten all about the progress John had made earlier in the case, or that he had saved his precious political career more than once. City Hall could only focus on one thing: two more murders.

How was I supposed to know that Justin Moody was really Fulton? All John could think of were the words Mayor Chase used to describe the murders, "a tragic blunder."

John understood the mayor's panic because word had somehow leaked to the press that a police officer and one of Whittman's employees had been killed within the walls of CSGR. Rumors were flying that the murders had something to do with the miraculous discovery mentioned earlier in the Kansas City Star. Now it was national news.

When John was convinced that there was nothing more to do at CSGR, he went home. Now he stood at the kitchen stove, turning strips of bacon and flattening a mound of hash browns like it was a delicate operation. A pat of butter melted in a small frying pan awaiting the eggs. He concentrated so intently on the simple task, he didn't hear his daughter ask him if she could finish making his dinner. Cindy was massaging the small of John's back, trying to loosen the tightness her fingers felt in his muscles, and the tension she sensed in him.

"I don't think your father heard you, Sarah."

Sarah, who often found ways to baby her father despite being a full-time college student, scooted her chair back and walked to the stove, relieving John of the spatula.

"Here, gimme that before you hurt someone," she teased. "You and mom sit—I'll finish this." John smiled and kissed Sarah on the forehead, "Thanks, little girl, I'd probably just burn it anyway." John and Cindy sat down at the kitchen table. No sooner had John's backside met the chair than he was once again in deep thought. Cindy watched him with concern.

John wondered what he would do first thing in the morning. He knew that Fulton wanted revenge. He'd already proven he was vindictive and would use any means to settle the score with Whittman. It was ingrained in his character, his sense of justice. Fulton had made more than just physical transformations during the last few weeks. He had changed from a law-abiding citizen, a respected research scientist, into a full-fledged killer. John concluded that each murder became easier for Fulton than the last. That horrible realization frightened John to the depths of his soul. How would John know when he saw Fulton? How could he protect Whittman, the mayor, or anyone else Fulton decided to go after? Of course, the mayor was probably off the hook now that Fulton realized Whittman acted alone in setting him up.

One thing bothered John terribly. It gnawed at him from the moment the maintenance man discovered the body. Wendell Peters had befriended Fulton and possibly looked up to him. What could have happened to make him murder a friend? Was the formula affecting his mental faculties, or did a lifetime of ridicule and harassment from people like Adam Sharp finally make him snap? Was Fulton losing his mind, or does power really corrupt?

John thought about the delicate balance between a man's physical and spiritual health. Maybe Fulton could no longer tell the difference between a friend and foe. Maybe some event tipped the balance of Fulton's perspective, making him see things off kilter. Unfortunately, when it came to Fulton's state of mind, John could do little else but speculate.

John tried to take a logical approach to wrap up the days events. He had a team of uniformed officers comb the outside parking lot, check every remaining car, every dumpster, every nook and cranny. Now that CSGR was secure, no one would be admitted in or out until the police department could put a better plan in place. Detective Rathbone had been reassigned to spend the evenings with Whittman. John felt much better having a top-notch detective stay with him. Now he hoped that he wouldn't be accused of bias when he pulled Connors off the case tomorrow.

Connors had already complained to Captain Walsh that John was doing a lousy job with the investigation. Walsh dismissed the comment, confident it was motivated by jealousy, spite, or possibly anger over Moody's death. When Walsh told John what Connors had said, John took the opportunity to express his concern that Moody's death might have had a terrible impact on Connors. There was no way he could concentrate on protecting Whittman in his current state of mind. Even at his best, Connors wasn't a very good detective.

Forensics was still gathering evidence from Moody's car. Captain Walsh had it towed to the police garage. Before today, there wasn't much physical evidence to go on, and why would there be? With regard to Fulton, they usually found only one thing—the suspect's

DNA. John was right about the glass vials and Braxton's gun. They were peppered with fingerprints. For the very first time they discovered right-handed fingerprints, and Braxton's and the mayor's were among them. They couldn't count the right hand fingerprints found in Braxton's apartment, because they may have been left by Braxton before Anne's murder.

Then there was the other unexpected find—a latex glove. The police had seen videos of Fulton wearing a glove while impersonating Whittman. Now they had some hard evidence supporting John's theory as to why until now they had yet to find a single right-hand fingerprint at a crime scene.

He couldn't wear it while impersonating Justin Moody, John reasoned. *It would have given him away.* John thought back to an earlier conversation with Whittman, when he'd suggested that CSGR employees should dip their hands into a bowl of someone's DNA before they enter the building. John immediately retracted the comment, saying, "What a stupid idea, that's absolutely ridiculous."

Now, he thought, *Maybe that wasn't so ridiculous at all.*

Cindy was still watching her husband. She saw him frowning at the kitchen table, and decided to bring him back to the conscious world.

"John? What's so upsetting?"

"Oh," John's eyes focused on her, "nothing, I just had a silly thought, that's all."

I need time to figure this out, John thought. *Whittman is the right lure; I just need to figure out how to set the bait on the hook. I need some time to unwind and think!*

While eating his dinner, John confided a few details of the day's events to Cindy and Sarah. It was a little more information than they'd heard on the news, but he trusted them not to discuss active cases with anyone else. He told them that most of the detective work was over, and that the only challenge that remained was to find and arrest Fulton. The arresting part was easy, but finding him nearly was impossible.

33

DR. RICHARD FULTON HAD A PASSION FOR WALKING, but today he'd overdone it. Perhaps if he hadn't waited so long to stuff napkins in Detective Moody's shoes, the blisters wouldn't have gotten so bad. In his current body, Fulton's feet were a size ten. The shoes he'd changed into early this morning were at least two sizes bigger. But he was forced to flee CSGR and left his duffel bag in Moody's car. Without a change of clothes, he had no choice but to continue walking in oversized shoes.

Things hadn't gone as planned. Posing as Detective Moody only got Fulton inside CSGR's main building, but he never reached his goal. Fulton had intended to visit Jim Saunders, the VP of Research, and snag his coffee cup. Once he took Saunders's physical shape, he would have killed him, a simple task in his private office, and taken his security badge. That was all Fulton would need to make his way to the small refrigerator in his lab. There he would confiscate the vial of blood containing his DNA, and his research notes, so he could re-create the formula. But that detective, Dietrich, explained that everything had been moved to the secure refrigerated locker.

They were expecting me to come for it.

Fulton ran out the front door after hearing Whittman's conversation with Dietrich. Fulton wondered if those detectives knew it was him when he ran out of the building. If they didn't know it then, they surely know it by now. He had planned to take Moody's car, but somehow he had lost the keys. He wasn't sure where, but he thought he dropped them when Detective Dietrich asked him to refrain from talking to Wendell Peters. The comment took him by surprise. Stunned as he was, he must have forgotten to pick them up. The mistake wasn't fatal. It only forced him to depart on foot.

By now, they've discovered the car and the body of that idiot detective.

He also realized how vital it was to keep a vial of urine in his pocket. He'd transitioned from baby food jars to small polypropylene vials only days ago. It saved him from being captured. When he realized he'd lost the car keys, he transformed himself into his current shape, an unknown man with dark chiseled features, and a taut, strong body. With arms swinging back and forth in opposing cadence, he'd begun his exhilarating walk across town. Physically, he felt just like a kid again.

It's amazing the balance a second arm provides.

Fulton walked in the direction of the downtown area. He'd immediately shed the sport coat and tie and stuffed them in a neighborhood garbage can. The slacks weren't really a problem. He just cinched his belt a little tighter. After the first two miles, he'd unconsciously begun to favor one foot over the other.

Fulton's heart was beating fast, somewhat because of the day-long walk across town, and partly because he was approaching the spot where he'd met the hooker, the one who screamed the night he'd discovered his ability to assume the genetic blueprint of another human being. He didn't know whether to laugh or cry as he replayed that night's events in his mind.

Almost there, just another half mile.

The steady rhythm of his stride was exhilarating on this cool autumn evening. The light breeze evaporated Fulton's perspiration as fast as his body could produce it. He was tiring, but continued walking at a brisk pace. Hours ago, he had rested while eating in a café. It was also a chance to grab a stack of napkins to stuff in his shoes. He stopped again to enjoy the warmth of the fading sun from a park bench. He thought about stealing a car, but he was in no hurry. When he began walking, he had no place to go, no particular destination in mind, but he couldn't help feeling there was a reason he had finally sought out this place.

Throughout his college years, Fulton had abandoned most forms of sports and exercise, but walking afforded him the luxury to think and study at the same time. When weather permitted, he would take his lecture notes with him, peering at blocks of shorthand, and memorizing every word. His single-mindedness for his studies was another excuse for his classmates to pick on him. As if anyone needed a reason beyond his handicap. David Sharp and his cronies sometimes followed him and often got ahead of him just so they could block his path.

That twisted son of a bitch got his kicks by making me step off the sidewalk and go around him. Blips of those images flashed in his mind several times today.

But I'll be damned if I'll ever budge from a sidewalk again. I'll be goddamned. Fulton took a deep breath and unclenched his fists. *Jesus, why did I come here?*

Fulton's home was only a few miles further, but he couldn't go there. The police might be watching. Hotels were out of the question. The street was littered and dark. The light in the street lamp where he'd met the hooker was burned out, but that didn't deter the scantily clad women from working their posts. With the handsome young face he currently wore, Fulton was sure he'd be propositioned quickly. The same question continued to echo over and over in his mind.

Of all the places I could lose myself tonight, why here?

Maybe it's because this was the last place I was me. Fulton realized he was feeling sorry for himself and re-answered his question; *You need a place to sleep tonight.*

He stopped and looked at his reflection in a pawn shop window. The man staring back at him was much better looking than Richard

Fulton could ever hope to be. Tall and dark; his body had a lean firm shape. And he felt good in this body. Better than he'd felt in his lifetime. So why did he long to be Richard Fulton again? Although brilliant, Fulton was considered a nerd, and to some a loser.

A woman approached from his left.

"Hey darlin'—lookin' for some company?" He stared only at his reflection, and his eyes twinkled sadly like those of a basset hound.

"I'm not looking for company," Fulton said dryly. The woman moved closer, her image joined his in the glass.

"You look down, honey, why don't you come with me. I can make you feel better."

"I doubt that."

"Really," the woman said, "I can take the edge off."

Fulton placed his palms on the glass, amidst the dimly lit secondhand jewelry. He rested his forehead between them.

"Do you have a place where we can go?" he asked.

"Down the street. C'mon, I'll take you there."

He bought her for the night. She lay asleep, the blinds casting striped shadows across her naked body. Fulton had intercourse with her never knowing her name. She began to tell him, but he stopped her. Names, like his physical appearance, were no longer significant.

What the hell am I doing here? He knew the answer. She was shapely, she smelled good, and her apartment was a safe haven. The alarm clock had been jostled in the heat of passion. Its display was out of view, but it emitted an intense blue glow against the wall. Fulton laid in bed wondering what time it was.

Three, maybe four?

The words spoken earlier by Detective Dietrich had rung in his ears the entire day. He still heard them.

"There's only one motive I can think of, Mr. Whittman—stock value."

Fulton imagined his hands around Whittman's neck, his eyes bulging, begging for mercy. Dietrich's voice continued to play in his head.

"If Fulton took the formula and it worked, your company would be the darling of Wall Street. You'd be courted by every major biotech company. Your stock value would soar through the roof, and you'd probably wind up a billionaire. If the project failed, you could claim that you did everything you could to stop it. You could insist that Fulton was insane, and forged ahead without your approval. You set him up. You led him to believe that the board of directors was only concerned for his safety."

What a fool I've been. I trusted that bastard. Here I thought I was through being ridiculed, but Whittman treated me worse than all the others. He gambled with my life just to line his greedy pockets. He saw Whittman's blue eyes as he responded to Dietrich's accusations.

"I would never take such a chance, John; it's ridiculous to even entertain such an idea."

LIAR! Fucking Liar! Fulton clenched his teeth.

Fulton sat up, draping his legs over the edge of the bed. The woman next to him stirred and pulled the sheet over her.

Jail's not good enough for him. I'll kill him.

It was the twentieth time today the thought ran through his mind.

Maybe I can get some of his money, transfer it to a Swiss bank account and leave the country. But how? I can impersonate him, but I don't know anything about his finances, but I've got to get some money. I've got to be ready to get out of here.

The day's long walk hadn't provided any answers for Fulton. Along the way, he'd obtained another cash advance with his credit card. With each advance he wondered how long it would be before the police or the FBI would freeze his assets. He assumed the reason his credit cards were still working was so the police could track him down if he used them to get a hotel room, but ATMs were safe. They couldn't watch all of them. He considered other scenarios for getting cash. He even considered assuming the identity of an armored truck guard, but robbery was too risky. His thoughts turned to Whittman.

What if I kidnap him? I could force him to open a Swiss bank account for me—a numbered account. I could make him transfer millions into it—then I'll kill him and get out of the country!

Fulton liked the idea. It was a sweet combination of revenge and irony.

I'll let Whittman set it all up. Use his money to get me a new identity, a passport, airline tickets. It's perfect.

I'd have to impersonate another police detective to get to him. But which one? Tomorrow, I'll get close, like I did with that idiot Moody. I'll figure it out.

Fulton felt a small tinge of guilt as Wendell Peters's image flashed in his mind. He had killed the poor janitor just to get close to Moody.

A casualty of war—too bad there'll be more.

34

SCOOP STARVED REPORTERS HUDDLED AT CSGR'S front doors, in hopes that Whittman would appear. John Dietrich sat in his car fifty yards away. He watched a reporter run along the roof while others tried unsuccessfully to peer in the front mirrored windows.

What's that guy think he's going to do, go down the chimney? John shook his head in disgust as he cradled his cell to his ear.

"Bones? Have you left yet? Good, don't bother. The lab is swarming with reporters. Keep Whittman at home. I'll have someone relieve you in about an hour." Detective Rathbone asked how Connors was doing.

"Not too well, Bones. I'm having someone take his place. Don't know who, yet, but I'll call you back and let you know. Whoever it is, ask to see a badge and ID. We can't be too careful."

The morning news was awash with conjecture about Critical Strategies Genetics Research and its founder, Zachary Whittman. The Kansas City Star revealed that yesterday's story announcing a partnership between CSGR and the Salk Institute was a hoax. A

TV anchorwoman surmised it was a stunt to inflate stock prices, while others suggested it was a ploy to divert attention away from Whittman's alleged robbery of Boatman's Bank.

John stared at the ever growing circus of reporters at the north end of the building. He considered telling them that Whittman wouldn't be in today, and then he smiled and drove away.

Why ruin a good thing. This will keep those blood suckers busy and out of my way.

On the way to the office, John called Walsh and arranged to have Detective Kosinski relieve Rathbone. Aside from Rathbone, John felt Koss was one of the best detectives on the force. A tad bit young perhaps, but responsible, and smart as a whip. *Braxton's going to be just as good a detective—better, if I can help it.*

When John arrived at the precinct, he found plenty of reporters lurking in the hallways. No doubt they were looking to fill in the blanks in the Whittman case. John took a few detours and reached the coffee pot unscathed. With a hot cup of coffee in hand, he headed for Walsh's office.

It wasn't the first time John witnessed Walsh get his butt chewed. John listened as Walsh held the telephone at arm's length. He could hear the mayor's voice ranting relentlessly. John turned pink and started to retreat, but Walsh smiled and motioned him to sit. John was squirming uncomfortably, and his eyes began to wander somewhat nervously. He caught a glimpse of Walsh's secretary, Sue Strattman. She was watching Walsh intently through the glass.

No, John thought, *she's watching me.*

The moment their eyes met, she turned around and began to shuffle papers.

Strange, I can't remember when Sue didn't give me a smile or just a nod of acknowledgement. She looks upset about something. John wondered if something had happened, if there was some bad news he wasn't aware of. Concerned, he began to scan the office, looking for telltale signs of a problem. When he looked her way again, Sue spun in her chair and began to type on her computer. John started to stand, but he heard Walsh hang up the phone. Rubbing his forehead, Walsh looked ragged.

"About the mayor," John said contritely, "I'm really sorry, Mike." Walsh couldn't help but muster a bit of sympathy for him.

"Not your fault, John, don't sweat it. The mayor's just running a little scared, that's all. He's wondering when he'll be implicated in this mess."

"I guess he's got a right to be worried," John said. "The election's not far off, and it won't take long for those nosey reporters to discover he's on Whittman's board of directors. Next thing you know, they'll find out about that waitress at the Red Robin and the robbery at Helzberg's."

"Yeah, we gotta move on this, but fast. How's Whittman doing?"

"Don't know—just spoke to Rathbone, but didn't think to ask." John rested his arms on Walsh's desk, and leaned in closely. "Whittman's our only chance of nailing Fulton—you know that don't you?" Walsh blinked repeatedly at his desk as though it would help him figure out a solution. Then he stopped.

"I know. But I can't help thinking we're playing with fire here. I know you think Fulton will make a move on him—"

"He will, Mike."

"But what if he succeeds? What if he kills Whittman? What then?"

"Well, right now Whittman's facing jail time. He knows as well as we do the only way to prove his innocence is for us to arrest Fulton. If we can prove Fulton impersonated him and the others, we're home free." John studied Walsh's eyes. There was no emotion, no confidence in them.

"And how do you plan to protect him?"

John pushed away from Walsh's desk. "I don't know. I thought we could camp out at his place—keep him under watch every minute of the day. I'm going to go home and get some clothes. Don't worry, we'll keep him safe." Walsh stood up and turned toward the window.

"Well, you'd better figure it out, John, you'd goddamned better know, cause they'll be no more chances. If Fulton gets Whittman, there's nothing left for him here. We'll lose him for good."

"Gimme a couple of hours to put a plan together, Mike. I can do it from Whittman's house. I know what we've gotta do, I just need to lay it out."

"Why don't you hash it out with your partner?"

John's voice was distant, "Yeah, I guess I could give Braxton a call."

Walsh continued staring through the blinds.

"He's in his office, John. He passed his psychological exam yesterday."

"No shit?" There was a musical quality in John's voice. "I'll get back to you, Mike." John flew out the door. Walsh never saw the smile on his face.

Braxton's desk was cluttered with file folders and newspapers. John stepped into his office beaming, but his smile evaporated as soon as he saw the photos of Anne Duffy's mangled body spread across his desk.

"I'm so sorry, Braxton."

With a nod, Braxton swallowed hard. John noticed how carefully he controlled his response. He may have passed a psychiatric exam, but there was no doubt that his partner was fragile.

"I had to see them sooner or later." Braxton slid the photos in a manila envelope, and then into a file folder and brushed it aside.

"I know you passed your psychological interview, Brax, but are you sure you're okay to work on this case? I mean—it can't be easy."

Braxton took a deep breath and looked up at John. "I heard about Moody and the janitor—how are you holding up, John?"

Way to turn the tables, Kid.

"I'm fine—there's a lot of pressure to find this guy, but that's no big surprise."

"Tell me what happened yesterday," Braxton said leaning back in his chair. He motioned to an empty chair and John scooted it beside his desk and sat down. John explained the details of yesterday's events, doing his best to leave nothing out. Finally he said, "We only have one more chance, Brax. It's like the captain said, if we don't get Fulton before he finds Whittman, there'll be nothing left to keep him here." Braxton's stony face said he understood the stakes were high. The situation couldn't be grimmer than it already was.

"If he overheard you blaming Whittman for setting him up, he's not going to rest until he gets revenge."

"You know it, Kid, so we've got to be ready for him, and like it or not, Whittman's the bait."

"What are you thinking, John."

"I've been hatching a plan since yesterday, but it won't work unless we can let Fulton in on it."

"What do you mean?"

"I need to let him know where Whittman is, but we have to make him work for the information, or he'll sense it's a trap."

John laid out the details. The further he delved into the plan, the more excited Braxton became.

Walsh appeared in the doorway. "C'mon you two! Sue says there's someone downstairs with information about Fulton's whereabouts."

Three minutes later, the detectives rushed back up the stairs. Braxton took the steps two at a time, leaving Walsh and John behind. There was no one waiting for them at the front desk. Rick, the desk sergeant, claimed that no one had even asked to see them.

"You never called my secretary?" Walsh asked.

Rick shook his head, "Never talked to her. What's this all about?" Walsh and Dietrich stared at each other, briefly. Rick never got an answer.

When they arrived upstairs, Walsh and Dietrich joined Braxton, who was asking Sue Strattman's co-workers where she had gone. Gwen said she thought she'd gone to the bathroom. Braxton left to check it out.

"Why would she fabricate such a story?" Walsh asked.

John turned away from the others and lowered his voice, "Because that wasn't Sue—it was Fulton."

Walsh dashed into his office and called the desk sergeant.

"Rick, we're looking for Sue Strattman. If she tries to leave the building, detain her, and give me a call." Rick must have repeated his earlier question, asking what this was all about, because Walsh turned red and said, "You wouldn't believe me if I told you—just do it, okay?"

Within minutes, Walsh and John had questioned the others in the office. Kathy said she thought Sue was acting strange. Gwen agreed.

"I asked her about her daughter's wedding plans, and all she said was that everything was going as planned. Tell me *that's not weird.*"

Hearing that, Walsh became pale. Sue never missed an opportunity to talk about her daughter's wedding. "What did she do after we left?"

"She went in your office for a minute, then she went to the bathroom—I think."

"Was she carrying anything?" John asked.

"Sorry, John, I didn't notice."

John followed Walsh back to his office and watched as he sank in his chair and ran his fingers through his gray streaked hair.

Three... two... one..., John counted to himself. Walsh began massaging his forehead.

We have liftoff, John thought.

Walsh spoke to the center of the room, "Right under my nose, Jesus, he was right under my nose!"

A line formed between John's eyebrows. "Makes you feel downright violated, doesn't it?"

Walsh didn't answer. His eyes searched aimlessly for something to hold his gaze. Finally, he raised them to John. It wasn't difficult for John to sense the hopelessness Walsh felt. He'd been wrestling with the same feelings all week.

"Look, Mike, I was just explaining my plan to Braxton. Now seems like a good time to explain it to you." John sat down, and began to reach for his coffee cup.

Oh crap, what the hell did I do with that thing? Probably left it on Braxton's desk. He continued, "I think Fulton either bugged your office or, at the very least, used a mini-recorder to tape our conversation and picked it up when we went downstairs. Either way, he probably knows we plan to stay with Whittman."

"Well, that's just great, John! Whaddaya suppose we should do now?"

"Stick with the plan, Mike." Walsh cocked his head, questioning the logic in John's statement.

"I wanted him to know, Mike. I need him to know what we're up to. How else could I get him to come to us? In fact, just in case he didn't get the message, I think you should hold a press conference and announce it again."

"Yeah, the mayor'd love that."

"The mayor doesn't have to nail this guy, Mike—we do!"

"You said you were going to explain your plan."

"Yeah, I did. I'll need to borrow a couple of police officers, Nick Ford and Larry Granewski."

"Granewski?" The mention of the officer's name made Walsh's head jerk. "Jesus, this is getting interesting."

"Wait'll you hear what I want him for," John said.

35

NICK FORD WASN'T VERY TALKATIVE FOR A POLICE officer. At least that's what Braxton was thinking during the drive to Whittman's house in Lee's Summit, a small town on the outskirts of Kansas City. Ford's police dog, Dozer, was a constant distraction, panting heavily in Braxton's ear from the back seat. The canine's warm sour breath and the occasional nudge from his wet nose were starting to grate on Braxton's nerves.

I'm glad we don't have much farther to go, he thought, checking his rear view mirror. *I don't know which of them would make a worse traveling companion.*

Another wet bump from Dozer's cold nose made Braxton frown and wipe his ear. He was about to ask Nick to make him lie down, but the sign up ahead caught his attention.

There's my exit.

Braxton took the ramp from I-470 South onto NE Bowlin Road. He'd driven this stretch of highway a hundred times and never taken this exit. He took a right and then a quick left on NE Anderson Lane, and he saw the sign: Lakewood Oaks Country Club. It looked like a small, but meticulously manicured golf course.

"I wonder if Whittman's home is on the lake or the golf course," Braxton said out loud.

"Guess we'll see, soon enough," Nick said, staring out the window. Braxton glanced at his scribbled directions, trying to find the name of the next street. "NE Fairway Homes Drive. Who do you think comes up with these crazy street names?"

"Dunno," Nick responded.

Braxton was smiling now. The sharp contrast between John and Nick was laughable. John was outgoing and often humorous, while Ford was a man of few words. Braxton found his turn, and then the next. He followed NE La Costa Street as far as it went. The street ended where two homes evenly split the rounded end of a cul-de-sac. The home on the right was Whittman's. Braxton pulled into the driveway. Nick grabbed his duffle bag and let Dozer out the rear door. Dozer was a young and lively German Shepherd with a smooth coat of fur. He trotted to Nick's side and sat at attention, still panting furiously.

"Let me introduce him to Mr. Whittman," Nick said, stooping to pet Dozer, "then we'll tour the grounds to get him acquainted."

"Sounds like a plan," Braxton said. He knocked on the door and it was immediately answered by Detective Kosinski.

"Hey, Koss, we're here to join the party," Braxton said.

"Hey, Brax, good to see you. I can sure use the company. Mr. Whittman's been on the phone all day."

Nick and Braxton began to enter the house, but Kosinski blocked their way, "Sorry to do this Brax, but Dietrich insists that I check badges and IDs."

Nodding, Braxton said "Way to go, John, take no chances."

Kosinski checked Braxton's ID first, and then Nick's.

"Okay, guys, come on in."

Nick and Braxton craned their heads in all directions to take in the lavish surroundings. Kosinski smiled as if he knew what they were thinking.

"Not a bad a place to hang out, eh? Wait'll you see the view." Kosinski led the way to the rear of the house.

"This place looks like a museum," Braxton said. "Some designer must have made a fortune here." About mid-hallway, Braxton passed an office on his left. Whittman was slouched in a chair, talking on the phone.

Stepping through the sliding door to the deck, Braxton caught his breath, "You weren't kiddin'— this is some view." There was a distinct division down the center of Whittman's property. To Braxton's left, Whittman's home shared the lake shore with another home at the end of the cul-de-sac. But most of Whittman's back yard butted up to the putting green of a short par 3 hole. A soft breeze brushed against Braxton's cheeks, complementing the warm sun that bathed the rear of the house. Braxton tried to take it all in at once. The lake water was slightly rippled in spots, and smooth as glass in others. Trees lined a ridge here and there, but it was the lush greens of the fairway contrasting against a cool blue sky that sent chills down Braxton's spine.

It's gorgeous. Anne would've loved this.

Down the slope, near the water, he saw a combined boat house and covered deck.

I wonder how often Whittman takes the time to appreciate the view from here, Braxton thought. Considering what he knew of Whittman, Braxton figured it was a rare occasion.

Dozer seemed to enjoy being outdoors. He ran from one corner of the deck to the next, sniffing until he had covered all sides. It appeared as if he were trained to do so. Nick looked like he was already sweating in his navy blue uniform.

"I guess Whittman's going to be on the phone for a while," Nick said. "I think I'll take Dozer for a walk around the property."

Braxton extended his arm in a wave across the expansive grounds that sloped steeply toward the boathouse, "From the looks of it, you'll be walking for a while."

"Yeah, this place is huge. Guess we'd better get to it."

"You can always take one of the golf carts," Kosinski said. "He's got two of them parked under the deck."

"That's okay, we'll walk."

Nick and Dozer took the stairs from the deck to the yard. Kosinski went back inside and glanced through the glass doors to check on Whittman. He was still on the phone and hadn't moved an inch. Kosinski strode back to the deck's railing, propped his foot on redwood board, and watched Braxton as he admired the landscape.

"Heard about your fiancée, Brax. I'm really sorry."

"Thanks, Koss," Braxton replied with a nod. "I'm hell bent on catching this guy. There's no telling how many people he's going to hurt."

"Your partner seems to think Fulton'll make a move on Whittman. What do you think?"

"John's a smart man. In fact, most of the time he's pretty damn brilliant. Yeah, Fulton'll show up. He wants Whittman in the worst way. If it'd been you Whittman set up, wouldn't you be looking to get even?"

"Yeah, I suppose so, but not by killing him."

Braxton closed his eyes and tilted his head toward the sun. His own thoughts of killing Fulton had come and gone while under his mother's care, but they were back again. No amount of 'talking it out' would change his mind. This place was perfect. When Fulton made his move, he would simply pull the trigger and claim he was protecting Whittman, or that it was self defense. He just had to make sure he was the first one to get to him. He'd be vigilant, stay awake all night if that's what it took, but one way or another, he'd see Fulton dead.

Braxton continued, "Well, that's you talking, not Fulton. I have no doubt he'd kill again in a minute. Put yourself in his shoes. He lived through ten years of ridicule, ten years of anticipating the day he'd be normal again, and now he's a freak—not to mention he's never gonna get the credit for making the discovery of a lifetime. Yup, he's already killed. Why shouldn't he kill again?"

"Why didn't he just go to the police in the first place?"

"Who knows?" Braxton said. "Every man has his breaking point. Maybe his was losing his identity. It was all he had left."

Koss gave Braxton a sideways look, "You sound like you feel sorry for him. Jesus, this guy killed your fiancée."

"I suppose I do, a little." Braxton paused for effect. "Did you know he didn't use the right version of the formula? It may have worked, but Whittman confiscated the good stuff and left an old version behind. It wasn't matched to the reagent they were using. Maybe that's why it didn't work right."

Kosinski's jaw dropped a bit. "Why the hell would he do that? That's ridiculous."

"Whittman had to confiscate the current version to make it look good," Braxton replied. "To make Fulton desperate enough to try it—to show him he meant business. Maybe he thought Fulton still had a newer version of the formula hidden somewhere, but as it turns out; the most recent formula was five versions old."

Kosinski shrugged, "Sorry Brax, but I have no idea what you're talking about. You've been hanging around Dietrich too long."

Braxton smiled, "I'll take that as a compliment, Koss."

The two men laughed.

"Did Whittman hear the captain's press conference?"

"Yeah, we both heard it. He told me to let him know when it came on. I hope it's enough to get Fulton here."

"I'm not a gambling man, Koss, but if I were, I'd bet Fulton shows up tonight."

Braxton didn't tell Kosinski about Fulton's appearance at the precinct, but after Walsh's press conference, he was twice as certain Fulton would show.

The press conference had been held just before noon. In a shocking statement, Walsh said that the police department didn't believe that Whittman had anything to do with the robbery of Boatman's Bank. He also said they suspected that Whittman's life was in danger by the same person responsible for the deaths of two men at CSGR yesterday. Walsh concluded by announcing that CSGR would be closed until further notice, and that the police were posting "a couple of officers" at Whittman's home for protection.

"Yeah, he's coming all right, he's coming tonight," Braxton uttered.

Kosinski watched two tiny specs headed for the lakeshore. "Why the K-9, Brax?"

"John thinks he may come in handy if we have to chase this guy half way across the golf course. Like I said, John's a smart guy."

John Dietrich pulled into his driveway at two-thirty. He'd planned to join Braxton and Kosinski at noon, but was delayed when he joined the precinct's search for Sue Strattman. John liked her and was worried that she'd been hurt. Sue was a kind, bubbly woman, and John wished there were more people like her at the office. Everyone was relieved to find her unharmed in a storage room in the basement. John felt sorry for her. She was clothed in only her undergarments, and her hands and feet had been bound with duct tape. What they didn't expect to find was Steve Grossman, the shipping clerk, lying beside her. He was in his underwear too. His wrists were duct taped to a water pipe.

Captain Walsh pulled them aside and told them they could go home after they answered a few questions. Both Steve and Sue were now wearing navy blue police raincoats. Sue Strattman was nervously fidgeting and tugging at hers, so Walsh began with Grossman.

"Tell me what happened, Steve." Grossman was short in stature and his clothes usually hung on his boney frame. He was in his late fifties. A grey mustache ran down the sides of his mouth to his chin. It made him look less frail. He stroked it as he answered the question.

"I was sorting the mail when this guy came in through the overhead door. I should've had it closed, but it was really hot in here. He looked like a nice young man, late twenties, coal black hair. But when I noticed him scanning the layout of the shipping room, I became suspicious, so I asked him if there was something I could do for him. He said he needed directions to the Federal Building." John was listening to Grossman speak, but he kept glancing at poor Sue. She was shaking as Grossman told his story. John felt a little foolish. He remembered how strange Sue had been acting toward him when he was in Walsh's office. When was he going to stop trusting his eyes and rely on his instincts?

"I started giving him directions," Grossman said, "but the guy looked confused. He didn't seem to be too familiar with the downtown streets, so I went to the overhead door to point him in the right direction. I must have walked ahead of him, because that's the last thing I remember until I woke up in a dark closet, taped to a water pipe."

Sue was next. Walsh must have figured that she would want some privacy because he nodded, patted Steve on the back and then waved to a junior officer to join them.

"I want you to take Steve to see a doctor," Walsh told him. "Then take him home." Walsh looked calm. His voice was firm and low, almost soothing. John watched him turn to Sue.

"What can you tell me, Sue?"

Sue Strattman's recollection was a bit more embarrassing. It was difficult to tell the captain, but Walsh did his best to coach her through it.

"Steve Grossman called my desk." Sue stopped and looked at Grossman. "At least I thought it was him. Anyway, he said a large package had arrived for me. He asked me to come down and take a look at it, so I did. I thought it might have been a wedding gift for my daughter. Anyway, he pulled a gun on me, and told me to go into the storage room. I couldn't believe my eyes—there was Steve, another Steve, lying half naked on the floor. His hands were wrapped in duct tape, and he was attached to a water pipe."

"What happened next, Sue?" Walsh's voice was soft and calming.

"He made me take off my clothes." Strattman's eyes affixed themselves to a spot on the floor.

"For a minute I thought he was going to rape me, but he just tied me up like Steve. He turned me on my side and faced me toward the wall. Then he did the strangest thing—he put his finger in my mouth!"

John couldn't help interrupting, "Which hand, Sue?"

Strattman gave John a sideways look, "I don't know—right, I think. Then I could hear him. It sounded like he was getting dressed. I tried to look over my shoulder, but I couldn't see anything, and Steve was unconscious. Before I knew it he turned out the light and closed the door. I just closed my eyes and rested until you guys found us."

"Anything else, Sue, any detail at all?" Walsh asked.

Strattman pulled the lapels of the raincoat tightly around her, "No, that's all."

"Are you sure about which hand he put in your mouth?" John stood perfectly still, awaiting an answer, but there was a long pause. Strattman stared at him like he was crazy to care about such ridiculous details.

"It was the right hand, John."

The two men exchanged sideways glances, and then Walsh looked as if he was forcing his calm demeanor.

"Let's get you home, Sue. I'll have one of the girls upstairs take you." Walsh plucked his cell from his hip as if he were going to call upstairs. Then he grasped John's elbow and steered him away from the others and said, "Get this son-of-a-bitch, John—pull out the stops and just get him!"

John was doing his best to think of any stops he hadn't already pulled out as he packed two days of clothes and his shaving kit in a leather shoulder bag. Minutes later, he was en route to Whittman's house when his cell rang.

"Daaad?"

It was Sarah, but her voice sounded troubled.

"Hey, little girl, everything all right?"

"No—I've been kidnapped. I'm sorry dad, I thought he was you." John stepped on the brakes harder than he'd intended. The car behind him honked. He pulled to the shoulder of the interstate and screeched to a stop.

"Sarah! Are you okay? Did he hurt you?"

The next voice John heard made him stiffen and brought bile to the back of his throat. It was like a recording of his own voice. "Your daughter's fine, Detective, and will remain so—as long as you do what I say."

36

"PRESS 35589 AND THEN THE ENTER BUTTON."

John reached out of his car window and pressed the key code in the sequence Fulton had given him. A rickety chain link gate on wheels slowly rattled its way to his left. John pulled ahead of the gate and put the phone back to his ear.

"What now?"

"Drive straight ahead," Fulton said. "When you reach aisle H turn left. You'll see me standing in front of unit 28."

This place was old. Mature trees concealed the entire storage locker facility from the street. The lockers varied in size. The corrugated metal roofs were rusting, and the buildings had been painted dozens of times. Thick curls of the most current yellow paint were peeling from rotting boards. Garbage and car parts littered every nook. There was a hodgepodge of musty odors, but most were overpowered by the smell of mold and motor oil.

As his tires crunched along pieces of trash and glass, John strained to think of a way to wrest Sarah away from Fulton without getting her injured. His mind was a complete blank. There was only fear for his daughter's safety. John drove slowly through the storage locker facility. He was terribly distracted. Every time Fulton spoke, John's mind fought the impulse that what he was hearing was his own voice. When he'd first heard it, there was the smallest amount of novelty mixed with the repulsion he felt over the experience. The novelty quotient quickly dissipated, and it became a hard core nightmare. John couldn't call Captain Walsh or Braxton during the drive because Fulton had insisted that John keep talking all the way to the storage locker facility. John kept asking about his daughter, Sarah, but Fulton skirted his questions. Instead he diverted the conversation to Whittman. John didn't give up much information, and finally refused to talk at all until Fulton told him his daughter was unharmed and in a safe place. The ball in the pit of John's stomach doubled in size when Fulton said she was tied to a chair to which he'd affixed a bomb. From that moment, John couldn't concentrate on anything else.

Fulton's killed several times now, John thought. *I've got to take him seriously.*

"Plastic explosives," Fulton said coolly, "enough to rearrange your daughter's every molecule. Unfortunately, she can't rearrange them— put 'em back together like I can."

"What do you want from me?" John asked.

"I'll tell you when you get here," Fulton said. "And just in case you have any idea of surprising me, keep this in mind—the detonator in my hand is the type that engages if I let go of the button."

"I won't try anything, Fulton; I just want my daughter back, safe and sound."

"Spoken like a true father."

"What about you, Fulton, do you have any family?"

"Why no, Detective, I'm all alone. So you see—I've got nothing to lose in this endeavor."

"Look," John said, "I know what Whittman did to you. Surely there are plenty of laws he broke. Why don't you turn yourself in and I'll testify as to what he did."

"It's a little late for that, don't you think?" said Fulton. "But I do have to thank you, Detective; I wouldn't have known my good friend Zach set me up if it weren't for you."

"You can thank me by letting my daughter go. She's done nothing to deserve this. Just turn her loose, and I'll help you any way I can."

"Your daughter will be fine. All you have to do is follow my instructions to the letter."

So far, John had done everything Fulton instructed him to do. He turned off his police radio, talked to Fulton nonstop, and followed his directions to the storage facility. Now he was turning onto aisle H. The locker numbers incremented slowly. John was still trying to devise a plan. He saw a figure standing in front of an old powder blue pickup truck about twenty-five yards ahead.

Will he kill us? John wondered. *I can't just give him what he wants. I've got to do something. But what?* John couldn't take his eyes off the man who had deceived Sarah so easily. Had she been too trusting? No, she simply believed her eyes. She could never look at her father and think bad thoughts. It just wasn't possible. John knew Fulton would be his exact duplicate, and as he neared locker 28, he was mesmerized by what he saw.

No wonder Sarah was fooled so easily. For Christ's sake, it's really me!

"Put the car in 'Park,' Detective. Then get out slowly." Fulton waived the detonator in front of him as he spoke. John was still holding his phone. He closed it, slipped it in his pocket, and then opened the door. He was trying to assess the layout of his surroundings, but he couldn't pry his eyes off of Fulton.

The likeness, it's perfect. John raised his hands in defeat.

"Okay, Fulton, I'm here. What now?"

John watched the corners of Fulton's mouth turn up and hoped to God his smile wasn't as ugly.

"I want you to move slowly, detective, very slowly. Place your gun, wallet, and badge on the hood of the car."

I knew it! John thought. *He's going to go after Whittman disguised as me. Whittman's as good as dead.*

John went for his wallet first. He moved slowly so he wouldn't spook Fulton. His badge was next. After opening his jacket, John released the snap on his shoulder holster and grasped his gun. He wondered if he could get a shot into Fulton and somehow keep the detonator's button depressed. It was a desperate, futile thought. As he withdrew his gun, Fulton held out the detonator at chest height, as if to say "Don't even think about it." John placed the gun on the hood of the car with the other items.

"Now, back away," Fulton said, with a threatening voice.

John obeyed and Fulton picked up the gun. Then he let a huge sigh dissipate in the air.

"Here, you might want this." He tossed the detonator to John, but the throw was short. It hit the ground with a hollow clink.

"You bluffed me," John said in a gruff voice. His eyes glowered at Fulton.

"And you fell for it, Detective. I suppose I might have too if someone had my daughter."

"Forget it," John said. "You've got what you came for. Now keep your word and release her."

Fulton shook his head slowly, "I never said I'd release her. I only said I wouldn't harm her, and only then if you cooperate." John stood there motionless. His heart pounded with a merciless rhythm. He felt ashamed that he'd been tricked so easily and even now his thoughts were shallow. He could only focus on getting his daughter out of harm's way.

Where the hell is she, in one of these? John eyed the lockers. *Is she okay? You'd better hope so, ass-hole.*

Fulton held the cards, and it seemed he was going to play every last one.

"Where's my daughter?" John asked, bracing his shaking hands against his sides.

Fulton motioned behind him, "Open that door." John turned around and faced an old metal overhead door. Hoping to see Sarah on the other side, he lifted, grunting under its weight. The door opened like the tambour door of a roll top desk and coiled into the rafters above.

Seeing Sarah was like catching the first breath after several minutes without air. She was sitting on a tool chest. Her eyes squinted against the sunlight. Her wrists and ankles were bound with duct tape, a treatment John suspected he might receive soon. Even though her mouth was taped shut, he asked, "Are you all right, little girl?" She nodded, and her eyes welled up with tears.

"I need your clothes, Detective."

John turned to Fulton and pleaded, "There's no need to take this any further. I told you I'd testify against Whittman. Let's talk about it before someone else gets hurt."

"No can do, Detective. Too much has happened, but thanks for the offer. Now, out of those clothes."

"There's a good chance my men will kill you."

Fulton's eyes narrowed, and he cocked the gun. "There's a good chance *I'll kill you,* if you don't get out of those clothes!"

John disrobed down to his boxers and socks. As he did so, he memorized the layout of the room. A light switch was nailed to a stud left of the door. John hadn't noticed before, but the room was full of tools and boxes of ceramic tiles. Several broken pieces lay sprawled across the floor. Stacked boxes formed an aisle leading to the rear of the room. Five gallon buckets and bags of tile grout were heaped thee high.

"Sit here." Fulton pointed to a row of boxes, stacked only two-feet high. John felt as naked as he was. As he sat, his backside felt the sensation of cool hard ceramic through the cardboard. Fulton went around behind him.

"Hands behind your back."

John complied, and Fulton went to work. He arranged John's arms so they were crisscrossed. With the first layer of tape, John knew he could no longer escape. He'd lost his chance.

"How do you do it?" John asked.

"Do what?"

"Turn into other people."

Fulton applied several windings around John's wrists. He knelt to tape his ankles.

"DNA," Fulton said, "it doesn't take very much."

"About what you'd get from a used drinking glass or a coffee cup, right?"

Fulton smiled. It was unsettling for John to watch.

"You're a pretty good detective."

Then Fulton scooted a large bag of sand or tile grout behind John and looped a long piece of tape around it and between his wrists.

With raised eyebrows and an annoying smirk, Fulton said, "Can't have you walking around just yet." John's features tightened.

This is just fucking great. That bag must weigh fifty pounds. Think, John, think! We're almost out of time.

"It's not too late, Dr. Fulton. We can still press charges against Whittman. Maybe you can say that the formula caused you to do these things."

Fulton didn't respond, but instead ripped a piece of tape to cover John's mouth. John's eyes darted to Sarah as he spurted a final comment, "Don't worry, little girl, everything's going to be all right."

John and Sarah watched Fulton change clothes. It took him a minute to figure out how to wear John's shoulder holster. Fulton picked up the clothes John hoped he'd leave behind, and removed three labeled vials from his pants pocket. They were nearly full of a clear yellow liquid.

Urine, John thought. Fulton slipped the vials into the side pocket of John's sport coat. Fulton took a last look around and snatched the roll of duct tape. John felt his stomach sink. The remaining tinges of hope were gone.

"Good luck to you, Detective. We won't be seeing each other again. I hope someone finds you alive and well." Fulton flicked off the light and tugged a rope and the garage door closed.

The rattling of a padlock was shortly followed by the fading sound of John's car leaving the premises.

I should have called Mike. What was I thinking? At least someone would have known where I was. Then John realized that was the reason Fulton had kept him on the phone all the way to the storage facility.

Sarah must be scared to death. I wish I could at least talk to her.

John's thoughts were interrupted by a sound inside the room. It startled him. It didn't come from the vicinity where Sarah was sitting. It came from the back of the room. The sound was clearly that of something grating against sand or gravel. John turned his ear toward the noise. It was quiet again.

What the hell was that? John resisted any conjecture. Instead, he sat motionless, praying it was a one time occurrence. A minute later, his instincts gripped him. He began to twist his wrists in an effort to free himself. It was no use. The tape was thickly wrapped and too tight to afford him much movement.

The only way to get these off is to cut them.

John began to review the image of the room's layout he'd committed to memory. Perhaps he could back up against something sharp, something that could cut or puncture the tape.

I feel like I'm in a damned MacGyver movie.

Another scraping noise invaded the silence.

Jesus—that sounded like an animal! Heart pounding, he sat still, waiting for the next sound.

There it is again! His mind went wild with the notion of a raccoon or a possum in the room. Whatever it was, it was far too big to be a rat.

Did Fulton leave something poisonous behind? The noise soon became rhythmic, a scrape, then a pause, a scrape then a pause. John tried again to free himself. The duct tape may as well as been handcuffs. He'd have to find a way to tear it. He tried to stand, but sitting so low to the ground made it difficult to find the leverage he needed to get to his feet with what seemed like a fifty-pound bag taped to his wrists. As he tried, the bag moved, scraping the floor as he tugged. It made the same sound as the creature behind him.

It's the sand from the grout. That's what's making the scraping noise. It's all over the floor. So what the hell is coming toward us?

The scraping of sand grew more consistent, and the sound was moving closer.

Whatever it is, I've got to get between it and Sarah.

John's eyes were growing accustomed to the darkness. Although it provided no usable illumination to the room, he could see a hairline border of light around the overhead door.

If I get turned around, I can use that to get my bearings, he thought. John spun on the box and fell to the floor. Pushing with his feet, he dragged the bag of grout along with him. The sand stung with each push as it ground itself into the skin of his arm and shoulder.

Got to get to the aisle—keep that thing from reaching Sarah! John pushed until his head hit something.

A box! I'm in the aisle, and just in time! Whatever was moving was almost upon him. The small amount of light from the door's edges provided no illumination in the direction John's eyes were scanning. He was frantic. He didn't even have clothing as a barrier between him and the creature. He pictured sharp teeth and claws. His head was tilted in the trajectory he estimated the creature was coming from.

Maybe I can head butt it, he thought, scare it back where it came from. Another scraping sound and John felt something nudge his chest. He went ballistic. He began thrashing wildly. He brought his knees up as far as the tape would allow and drove them in the direction of the oncoming creature. He stopped abruptly when he heard a familiar sound—a human sound. Someone was trying to scream, but the sound was muffled.

Duct tape! Whoever it is can't talk through the duct tape. The muffle was definitely a man's low voice. John mimicked the noise to let him know he understood.

God, I hope I didn't hurt him. He knew he'd landed at least one good kick in the right direction. John rolled on his back and let out a deep breath through his nose.

The first thing we need to do is communicate. I've gotta get this tape off my mouth.

John scooted to the corner of the aisle. A stack of boxes would provide exactly what he needed. He drove his cheek against the corner of a box and began swiping his face, rotating from cheek to mouth. On the third try, he felt the tape's edge stick to the box and fold over slightly. With each swipe the fold became a little larger and finally stuck to the box. He pulled his face away slowly. The tape stuck to the cardboard and peeled away from his lips.

"Got it!" he yelled. "Sarah! There's someone in here with us—a man, I think. He's bound and gagged, just like us, so don't be afraid. We're going to get out of here."

John pushed with his feet to get back to where the man's head had butted his chest.

"Listen, whoever you are, I need you to get your face to my hands so I can pull the tape off your mouth. Do you understand?"

"Mmm hmmm." It sounded like a muffled "uh huh," so John took that as a yes. Rolling over, John positioned his hands to face the stranger. There was another scraping noise, and then John felt the man's hair.

"Closer," John said, "and tilt your head up as far as you can." The man pushed again. John scooted slightly to align himself properly. He could feel a growth of whiskers on the man's face, maybe a week's worth, maybe more. His reach was severely hampered, but he didn't need much. He found the corner of the duct tape and began pulling. The man drew his head back to help, and jerked. The man blurted:

"Son-of-a-bitch—that hurt!"

John laughed out of sheer tension. "Lose a few of those whiskers, didja?"

"Yeah, almost lost a few of my teeth too. Whoever you are, you kick pretty hard."

"I'm sorry about that. I thought you were some kind of animal."

"Oh? Tell me you haven't been talking to my ex-wife—have you?" John laughed again.

"John Dietrich, Detective—Kansas City Police Department."

"Really? Well, who says there's never a cop around when ya need one— Dave Casper, Custom Tile Setters, Incorporated."

"I'd like to shake your hand, but I'm a little tied up at the moment," John said.

"Mmmm, mmmm." The muffled voice was feminine.

"That's my daughter, Dave. She's either telling me that was a bad joke, or I should hurry up and get us out of here. I couldn't agree more. How tightly are you taped?"

"Yer daughter? What's she doin' here?"

"Long story—how tightly are you taped?"

"Pretty damn tight. I'm also dragging a bag behind me. I'm pretty sure it's tile grout."

"Yeah, me too," John said. "You know, duct tape tears easily once you get a cut started. If I could just stand up, I could probably find something sharp to rub up against."

"No need, John. There's sharp pieces of broken tile all over the floor. If you can snag one, I can cut the tape."

"Okay," John said, "I'll see what I can find."

"There should be some broken pieces in the aisle, just ahead of you," Dave said. "I dropped a whole box of floor tile last week. Never got around to cleaning it up." There was a clink of ceramic pieces as John scooted into them. He maneuvered until he found a small sharp piece. John and Dave positioned themselves back to back, and Dave began making small careful rips in the tape. John kept tension on the tape by pulling his arms apart. It made his muscles cramp. Finally, they cut through the last winding of tape.

"We're through," Dave said, "now cut mine."

"Gimme a minute," John said, "the damn tape is still stuck to my wrists. I can't pull them apart." John twisted his wrists to separate the duct tape from his skin. The cramping now extended from his neck and shoulders to the muscles in his arms. He moaned as he fought the pain.

One more time, he thought.

Ahhhhhhhhhhhh! John's silent scream rang in his ears. The painful maneuver demanded a scream of some kind, even if it was confined to his thoughts. But his effort was successful. His hands were free. He brought one arm in front of him, then rolled on his back and raised the other.

"For crying out loud," he said, "I'm getting too damn old for this." His entire body felt like a lead weight. He rubbed his arms to ease the cramps.

"Okay, Dave, hand me that sharp piece of tile." John reached out in the dark and felt for Dave's hand. He took the ceramic shard from him and cut the tape around his ankles. Then he stood up and carefully made his way to the overhead door. Feeling for the light switch, John found it in the exact spot he had committed to memory. He flicked it on and saw Sarah squinting from the sudden gush of light. Behind her, on the floor, a man was craning his neck to see him. The man who said his name was Dave had a puzzled expression on his face. It took only a second to figure out why.

"You're wondering why I'm in my underwear, aren't you?"

"The thought did cross my mind."

"I won't go into a lot of detail. Let me just say that someone stole my clothes at gunpoint."

Dave nodded, "Fair 'nuff."

John walked to Sarah and carefully peeled the tape from her mouth.

"You all right little girl?"

"Yeah, I'm okay. But I've never been more scared in my life. That man looked just like you, Dad. You can't believe how much he looked like you." John struggled with the tape around her wrists.

"I know, I saw him too, Kiddo. It was about the most unnerving thing I've ever seen."

"Well how will I ever know it's really you again, Dad? When you come home from work, when we meet for lunch, how will I know?" John put his hands on her shoulders and looked her in the eyes.

"You'll know. You saw the differences, didn't you? You're a smart girl; I know you saw the differences." Sarah nodded, "Yeah, his smile was eerie, but it was too late, Dad, by the time I noticed anything different, it was too late."

"Right, but you'll never forget it; he'll never be able to fool you again." John knelt down and cut the bindings on her ankles.

"Besides that, Kiddo" John said, "I plan to have him in custody by the end of the day."

"There," John said as he tossed the tape aside. "Now, give me a minute to take care of Dave." John lifted Dave off the floor, and sat him on a box, and then went to work on his bindings.

"What did your daughter say about that man looking just like you? What was he a makeup artist or something?"

"Yeah, something like that." John noticed the gray stubble on Dave's face was discolored by a long streak of dried brownish blood. It trailed down from his head. "You're hurt. How'd it happen?"

"Don't know for sure," Dave said. "Never even saw what he looked like. Must'a snuck up 'n hit me with something. I was just picking up some tools for a tile job."

John studied Dave's face. He was a rugged looking man in his mid-fifties. His black eyebrows contrasted sharply with his gray hair, and he had the broad nose of a prize fighter.

"There," John said, as he pulled the remaining tape from around Dave's ankles, "now let's get out of here." All three of them rubbed their wrists as they studied the overhead door. John felt uncomfortable in his boxers.

"You don't have any clothes in here, do you?" John asked.

"Not in here, but I've got a change of clothes in my truck. You can use 'em, if you promise to get 'em back to me."

"Deal," John said. "Now, how do we get to your truck?"

"I got just the thing," Dave said. He ran to a cabinet in the back of the room and reappeared with a large black molded case. He laid it across two tile boxes and opened it. "No outlets in this room," Dave said, "but with these, guess we won't need them." The case held a matching set of Craftsman cordless power tools. Dave grabbed the small circular saw and went to the door.

"This ought to do it." He squeezed the trigger, and the saw wailed. He eased the blade against the metal. Sparks showered his arm. It took nearly a minute to pierce the door. When it did, the blade jammed.

"Shit!" Dave turned around and looked at Sarah, "Scuse the French, young lady."

Sarah's tone was serious, "Use all the French you want, Dave—just get us the hell out of here!" Dave eyed John and smiled.

"Don't think this blade will take much more abuse," Dave said. "These doors aren't made of the cheap aluminum crap they use today—these are steel doors." He yanked on the saw to pull it out of the slit he'd created. "Yup," he said, studying the blade's edge, "It's already shot."

37

FULTON TRIED HARD TO REMAIN CALM. DEEP BREATH-
ing helped a little. His eyes constantly flickered between the road,
speedometer, and the radio's clock. He exhaled sharply.

*Watch your speed. No need to push it, everything's going exactly as planned.
All I've gotta do now is to keep my head when I pick Whittman up.*

He strained to stay focused, but there were many issues chipping
away at his concentration. He fidgeted at the wheel, and his speed
began to wander above the speed limit as he thought of what he must
do next.

His scheme had worked flawlessly so far, but there were gaping holes
in the final phase of his plan. He knew Detective Willis would be at
Whittman's home. At least that's what he assumed based on the recorded
conversation he'd retrieved from Walsh's office. The micro recorder was
a good idea, but it gave him less information than he'd hoped. All he
knew was that Whittman would be guarded at his home.

How many other officers will be there?

How well do they know this Dietrich guy?

Will they know I'm not him?

How am I gonna get Whittman out of his house and downtown to that hooker's place?

Fulton thought about the woman he'd spent the night with. She wasn't too bright. It was incredibly easy to gain her trust and convince her to give him a key to her apartment. It didn't hurt that he had paid her in advance for a second night's favors. It was the last of his cash, but it didn't matter. Once he got Whittman there, he planned to force him open a Swiss numbered account and transfer millions into it. Surely one of Whittman's hot shot money managers could make it happen with a simple phone call. Then he could kill Whittman and leave the country. The bigger problem was getting in and out of Whittman's house without his identity being discovered. He imagined himself strolling into Whittman's home, pulling the trigger on his body guards, and calmly walking out with a gun to the back of the man he hated above all others. It seemed so easy in his thoughts, but nothing he had done so far was easy. Fulton almost came unraveled when the office girls at the precinct asked him how his daughter's wedding plans were coming. He had no background on the woman whose identity he'd taken, and no idea what they were talking about. Fulton only knew her name was Susan, and that she called Mike Walsh "Captain." That was enough to get him through a brief charade as his secretary, but just barely. The entire charade was foolish, and he might not be as lucky again. Fulton needed to get in and out of Whittman's home quickly, with no questions asked.

It's a big place. What part of the house are they keeping him in? His office? Fulton thought about it hard. *Yeah, his office— Whittman's probably on the phone trying to keep the company together. He'll be glued to that telephone.*

Fulton was only a few minutes from Whittman's home. He gnawed on his lower lip as he tried to recall the floor plan of the house. He'd been there three times, including last year's executive Christmas party, and most of the layout was still vivid in his mind. Whittman only invited the top brass and a select few researchers. Fulton was one of them, but he hated going. Conversation didn't flow easily between him and others, and when he discussed his research, he could see their eyes glaze over with obvious tedium. Fulton spent most of his time away from the guests. He found that Whittman's kitchen provided him with a little solitude, and a way to avoid awkward conversation.

Fulton liked to cook, and Whittman had a true chef's kitchen. There was a double wide stainless steel refrigerator, and a monstrous six burner stove. A separate refrigerator with a glass door displayed about fifty bottles of wine and champagne. Beyond the unused pots and pans hanging on display from the ceiling, Fulton could glimpse the beautiful scenery of the lake and golf course. One year there was an early snowfall, and he had a breathtaking view of the sloping backyard with the moon glistening across a shimmering lake. It was that picture postcard view that solidified the image of Whittman's property in his mind.

Fulton envied Whittman. It wasn't because of his wealth; it was because he demanded and received respect, something Fulton had never experienced. But with each passing Christmas party, Fulton knew his time was growing closer to that elusive feeling of satisfaction. It wouldn't be long now, and the whole world would have to pay him his due. His name would be revered like that of Albert Einstein.

Those thoughts were gone now. That was before he used the formula, before he had killed, and long before Whittman had set him up. Fulton had forgotten he was driving. The speedometer had crept twenty miles an hour over the speed limit. He eased up on the throttle. His slitted eyes returned to normal, and focused on the road. He tried to relax his grip on the steering wheel. Then he realized he was holding his breath. He exhaled.

That son-of-a-bitch. He ruined me, just when my life was about to turn around—just when things were getting good—he betrayed me. A tear jetted straight down his cheek, and onto the lapel of Detective Dietrich's sport coat.

∞

John dangled his feet over the edge of a makeshift chair he'd stacked together from boxes of tile. Sarah was using her feet to sweep the shards of tile out of the aisles. John had stepped on a piece which went right into his foot. He'd managed to get it out quickly, but now he was leaving bloody heel prints on the floor. Dave was still studying the overhead door.

"There's no way, John, no freaking way we're gonna cut through this front door." John wasn't the handy one in the group, but he'd already figured that out. He was staring at the rafters above.

"What about the roof, Dave? I know its corrugated metal, but isn't it thinner? Couldn't we cut through it?"

"Got no ladder, an even if I did, I'm not sure I'd wanna try it. It's a long way down from there."

"Well, we've got to figure something out. It's been another hour. I'd be surprised if Fulton hasn't already gotten to Whittman by now."

It can't be that hard to get out of here, John thought. *We've got tools. We're missing something. If only someone would come by, we could yell, or bang on the door.*

Sarah waved at her father, "You can walk around now, Dad. I think the floor's pretty clear."

"Thanks, Sarah. How are you holding up?"

"Well, I'm not tied up in the dark, and that lunatic is gone, so I guess I'm okay."

John gave her a reassuring smile, "I promise I'll get us out of here soon, Sarah. There's a way out, I know it."

Thirty minutes later, John was waiting in anticipation. The answer was so simple. He wondered why it had taken him so long to figure it out. Dave was embarrassed too. John tried to minimize their inability to plot an earlier escape by suggesting that their circumstances had simply made it too difficult to think clearly.

"Do you have everything you need to do this?" John asked.

Dave smiled as he rummaged through a cardboard box, but when he glanced up at John, it was as though he could read the underlying concern in his blue-grey eyes. They were rounded, child-like, almost pleading.

"Got plenty of battery power, John. Pretty darned sure this'll work." He popped a battery in the butt end of his drill and raised it to the back wall and began boring a hole.

Dave had failed on two attempts to cut through the overhead door. The circular saw was no match for its thick gauge steel. The blade was mangled, and Dave didn't have a spare. The three captives had sulked for a while, occasionally exploring another possible way out, but none of them seemed plausible. It was Dave's comment that finally jarred John's memory and spurred the solution they were looking for.

"Too bad we can't just cut through the wall," Dave had said. "The wood is soft pine, but then we'd just wind up in someone else's locker." It was true. John remembered seeing lockers on either side of number 28, but he also recalled how narrow the buildings were. Then it came to him.

"Dave!" John had said, "We're going the wrong direction! I don't think there's anything on the back side of the wall! Am I right?"

Dave's eyebrows arched like steeples as he thought about the question John had posed. "I'll be goddamned, John, there sure as hell ain't. We're workin' on the wrong side of this room." Dave had run back to the molded case and grabbed his jig saw, and started counting blades.

"Six. Fan-fucking-tastic." Dave turned red and avoided Sarah's eyes so he could pretend he was unaware of his profanity.

Now John and Sarah watched hopefully, and when suddenly the drilling stopped, Dave withdrew the drill bit, and sunlight poured through the hole.

"YES!" John shouted.

Dave drilled three more holes. Each of them marked a corner of the rectangle he intended to cut out of the wall.

"That was good thinking, Dad," Sarah said. "Not bad for a man who doesn't even own a power tool." Dave gave John a sideways look. John just shrugged.

Dave ejected the battery from the drill, and snapped it into the jig saw. He inserted the blade through the hole he'd just drilled, and began sawing in an upward direction.

Over the drone of the saw, Dave yelled, "Look, John! It's cuttin' through this old wood just like butter." It took only a minute for the blade to travel upwards from the first hole and connect to the second. While Dave made the next three cuts, John grabbed Sarah's arm and moved her away from the noise.

"Listen, Sarah, I'm going to drop you and Dave off at a gas station down the road. I want you to call your mother and have her come pick you up. Tell her to take Dave wherever he wants to go. And get his phone number, so I can get his truck back to him."

"You're taking his truck?"

John nodded, "Got no choice. Fulton's going after Whittman—I can't let that happen."

38

FULTON WAS PARKED TWO DOORS EAST OF WHITT-man's house. There was no sign of police fortifying Whittman's home, but there were automobiles in the driveway. Fulton's hands firmly gripped the steering wheel. His face lacked the slightest tinge of emotion as he stared out the windshield of John's car.

Only two cars; a good sign. It shouldn't be too difficult to shoot a couple of police officers, especially when I can get within arms reach of them. Fulton looked on the seat beside him, thinking how glad he was that he'd remembered to bring the roll of duct tape. *It'd be better to just bind them, and lock them up—avoid the noise of gunshots. I'll find out where they're keeping Whittman, and then play it by ear. But if that red head's boyfriend is here, he might get out of control. Hmm—can't say as I blame him. What a knockout she was. Still, if he gets out of hand, I'll kill him with his own partner's gun. Before I'm done, Detective Dietrich may wish I'd killed him too.* A disgruntled look appeared on Fulton's face. *Too bad, I kind of like the guy. Without him, I'd never've known that Whittman'd set me up. Oh well, life's a bitch. At this point, what's a few more casualties?*

Waiting for the sun to set was painful for Fulton, who was growing ever anxious, but the cover of darkness would give him much better odds of escaping. Fulton paused and thought about the cars in the driveway. He remembered how he'd been forced to leave CSGR on foot.

I need some insurance. Maybe I'd better park this car on the next street. He patted John's holster and grinned, *I'm sure I can convince one of the officers's to give me their car keys, and if something goes wrong, I'll have a backup vehicle waiting.*

Fulton backed the car up a few feet, turned around in a neighboring driveway, and drove off in the opposite direction.

About forty minutes after Fulton drove away, Ford and Dozer appeared in the front yard. It was the narrow end of Whittman's pie-shaped lot. Ford studied the yard layout for the fourth time today, while Dozer zigzagged between shrubs sniffing every scent. Ford tossed a hard black ball toward the mailbox.

"Fetch!"

Dozer exploded toward the ball. Like a heat seeking missile he found the target, leaped, and caught the ball in mid-air of the third bounce. He trotted back to Ford, holding the ball loosely in his teeth.

"Good boy, Dozer." Ford took the ball and scratched him under the collar. The air was losing its autumn warmth. Ford looked at the sky. It was a beautiful shade of pink. With each minute it was getting noticeably darker.

"I just knew it, Dozer," he said scratching his partner's ear, "that son of a bitch is gonna wait until dark to show up. We haven't heard from John, either. He said he'd be here around noon, and then he changed it to three o'clock—well where the hell is he?" Ford threw the ball for Dozer a few more times, praising him each time he returned with it. Then he stood up straight and took a deep breath.

"C'mon boy, let's go checkout the boathouse."

∞

John was cruising at ninety on I-470. Dave's vintage Chevy pickup shimmied and shook, making it difficult for John to concentrate. In fact, he'd just come to realize he was driving without headlights. He searched for the headlight switch, and pulled the old chrome knob out until it clicked twice. Fulton hadn't shown up yet at Whittman's house. John called Braxton while squirming into Dave's change of clothes. A pair of too small shoes sat amidst the clutter on the front seat where Dave had left his cell phone. John told Braxton that his next call would be to Captain Walsh, though it didn't make much difference now that Braxton had been warned. After all, he claimed that Fulton would make a move on Whittman today, and he was right. But why hadn't he shown up yet? What the hell was Fulton waiting for?

John told Braxton to warn Kosinski and Ford that Fulton had his wallet, ID and gun. At first, Braxton was a little suspicious of John's claim, but he played along.

"I'll tell Koss right away, but Ford just left with Dozer. They've done little else but patrol the grounds."

"Good," John said, "they're doing their job." Something was troubling Braxton, there was a note of uncertainty in his voice.

"It's hard to believe that Fulton did the same thing to you that he did to me, John."

"Yeah, the only difference is that he didn't club me over the head. I got a good look at him, Brax. He's the spittin' image of me. If our movements hadn't been out of synch, I'd swear I was looking in a mirror."

"So what am I supposed to do, John? You tell me you're coming here with no ID. How do I know you aren't really Fulton setting me up to arrest John Dietrich?"

John's voice took on a familiar joking quality, "Well, I don't think Fulton's ever had the pleasure of eating your mother's kibbeh."

There was a slight pause, and Braxton replied in a low voice, "Thanks, John, a little reassurance doesn't hurt, right?"

"That's why you're going to be a good detective, Kid. Now be careful, Fulton's wearing my clothes, so he'll look conservatively boring, just like I usually do. I'll be wearing an orange T-shirt and blue jeans that are way too tight. But you know me, Brax, no matter what I'm wearing you can tell us apart, but only by talking to us. If you're ever in doubt, ask me a question no one else could answer. Tell the others the same. The three of you need to be ready for anything."

"How far away are you, John?"

"About twenty minutes. I had hoped Fulton would make his move before dark, but now I'm glad he waited."

"Nick would disagree with you. I don't think he's too comfortable patrolling the grounds in the dark."

"That's where his dog comes in, Brax. Dogs aren't afraid of the dark. And if we need to chase Fulton, that dog will have him on the ground before he can get a hundred feet away."

"The dog was a good move, John."

"Hey, Brax—do you have a spare gun?"

"Yeah, got one in the trunk. I suppose you'll need to borrow it?"

"Yes, get it in the house right away. I don't want anyone going outside after dark, except for Nick and his dog." Before ending the phone call, John reassured Braxton that everything would be fine. He hoped he was right. Then he began to dial Captain Walsh's number. Before John pressed the last digit the battery died. John tossed the phone on the seat and wondered what else could possibly go wrong, but overall, he felt fortunate. After all, he could still be bound and lying on the cold concrete of Dave's storage shed.

Poor Sarah, this whole thing must have scared her to death. She's never had to deal with anything like this before. She sure was brave though. Then John pictured Cindy. He didn't wait for her to arrive at the gas station, but he could see her expression anyway. She'd be wearing a face that said "I'm scared as hell for you, but go ahead and go."

Maybe I should retire; it's been a pretty rough ride for her.

John glanced in the rear view mirror. He didn't just see his reflection any more; now he saw Fulton's reflection as well. John wondered if he'd hesitate if he had to kill a man who looked just like him. But the slightest hesitation could get him killed instead.

I really don't wanna hurt you, Fulton, but so help me, I'll kill you if I have to.

A blinking road construction sign brought John back to the moment. It was now dark, and he was only a few minutes away from Whittman's home.

No one's been killed so far today. I hope I can keep it that way. Fulton could have killed us. It would have been easier and faster, but he didn't.

John was confused. Fulton had become unpredictable. It didn't seem that there was any rhyme or reason to when he might kill.

Nick Ford had been a K-9 officer for six years. His first dog, Jackson, had been killed by an experienced thief who burglarized wealthy homes. Because of the ever present danger of coming face-to-face with a guard dog, the thief always wore protective padding around both of his arms. Ford had arrived at the scene with two other officers while a burglary was in progress. During a foot chase, Jackson had attacked the thief just as Ford had commanded, and had taken the burglar's left arm. Jackson wrestled the man to the ground, but the padding had been too firm to allow the dog's teeth to sink into his flesh, and the man stabbed the dog repeatedly with his free hand. Even after being stabbed eight times, Jackson wouldn't release his assailant's arm until Nick arrived. Jackson's death had been a terrible blow to Ford, who had grown quite attached to the dog in the year they had partnered together.

Ford continued to work with other dogs, but he handpicked Dozer at only six weeks old. He named Dozer after the mammoth yellow clad earth movers after watching him bulldoze his siblings aside at feeding time. The pup didn't appear to be mean, but he was strong and aggressive. Ford did only light training with him during the first eight months, allowing Dozer to be a pup and enjoy his childhood. But after that, he trained Dozer relentlessly. John and Ford met on a case they worked together and became fast friends. John was fascinated by the way Ford read Dozer's every move. It was as though they communicated through telepathy.

Behind Whittman's house, Dozer led the way down a gradual embankment to the lake. A light breeze filled the air with the smell of burning wood, probably from a neighbor's patio. The sky was dark, and a quarter moon reflected off the lake accompanied by dozens of lights from homes bordering the other side. As they approached the boathouse, Dozer broke his stride and took off at full speed. Ford didn't call Dozer to come back, but tore off after him. About fifteen yards from his destination, Ford reached to his side and drew his Glock. A look of shock hung on his face when he rounded the edge of the boathouse.

"John! Jesus, what are you doing down here?" Dozer's tail was wagging. He must have picked up John's scent fifty yards back.

John looked frightened. He had backed himself against the boathouse, stiff as a board.

"We didn't scare you, did we?"

John tried to relax a little, but his voice was shaky, "Just took me by surprise, that's all."

"I was beginning to think you weren't going to show. You said you'd be here around three."

John was calming down, "Yeah, I just had to finish up a few things at the office. Where's Whittman?"

"Upstairs—right where he's supposed to be. Braxton and Kosinski are taking turns watching him. I finally got a chance to introduce Dozer to him. I don't think Dozer was too impressed." At this, John's look-alike smiled.

"No, I don't suppose he was." Fulton read Ford's name tag while Ford holstered his gun.

"Oh, you told me to check IDs John, even yours. I suppose we should get that out of the way."

"Right, Nick," Fulton said. He was relieved that producing Dietrich's ID wouldn't be a stumbling block. He handed his ID wallet to Ford.

Nodding, Ford said, "Well, now that 'that's' out of the way, you wanna walk with me or go back to the house?"

"Both," Fulton said. Let me tour the grounds with you to get the layout, and then I'll head up to the house." Fulton was feeling comfortable that Ford didn't notice any difference between him and the man he was impersonating. A little more confident, Fulton extended his hand to scratch Dozer behind the ear. It was a mistake. Dozer whined and took a step back.

Uh oh, better do this quickly.

Fulton shrugged and raised his eyebrows, "Is he okay, Nick?"

Ford studied Dozer carefully.

"Dozer, COME!" Dozer went straight to Ford, ignoring everything else. Ford ruffled his coat, and scratched him beneath the collar.

"Yeah, he's fine."

Fulton didn't hesitate to speak, "So, what is this place?"

"Kinda neat, isn't it? It's a boathouse with a deck on top. Whittman's got two boats inside, along with a refrigerator and a Port-a-Pot."

"The guy's got too much money," Fulton said quickly. "Can you have the dog check it out for us?"

"Sure thing." Ford opened the door and gave a hand signal. Dozer assumed a different personality and began to search every nook and cranny in the boathouse, sniffing all the while. Ford studied Dozer's movements carefully. The dog disappeared around the far side of Whittman's pontoon boat. Fulton clumsily reached for his gun. The holster was made for a right-handed person. Releasing the snap took an extra second, which seemed like an eternity to him.

"Backup, Nick!"

Ford turned around and his eyes grew wide. He saw John motioning him aside with his gun. He moved back and to his right, and he watched John close the door, trapping Dozer inside.

"I'm going to need your uniform."

"What are you doing, John?"

"Don't patronize me, Nick. It's kind of obvious who I am by now, isn't it?" Nick didn't answer, but stared at Fulton in disbelief. "Now, take your clothes off!"

As Ford undressed, Fulton reached around to the small of his back and retrieved a roll of duct tape. Dozer appeared at the door, barking through the glass.

"Son of a bitch," Ford said, "Dozer knew something was different about you. I should have seen it too."

Fifteen minutes later, Fulton walked up the embankment toward Whittman's house, dressed in police officer's blues. Ford's body felt stronger and more agile than most he had sampled in recent weeks.

This was a stroke of luck, Fulton thought, *I got another officer out of the way, this uniform will make my identity more convincing, and with this body, I'm in much better shape to defend myself.* Dietrich was tall and strong, but at forty-seven, he had begun to develop a paunch that would have slowed him down.

At least I know I can run a good distance if I have to.

Fulton stopped walking and craned his head, listening carefully. Having traveled a third of the way to the house, he could no longer detect the K-9's barking.

Counting the dog, that's three down. I wonder how many more police officers are inside. Fulton continued walking. The closer he got to the house, the more he wondered if he could get away with kidnapping Whittman.

This is crazy. These guys are trained officers—I'm a goddamned geneticist. But then he thought about the element of surprise.

I can get away with almost anything when people don't suspect who I am. If I can take them on one at a time, I can beat them all.

39

BRAXTON SAT AT WHITTMAN'S KITCHEN TABLE staring at the spare gun he agreed to loan to John only fifteen minutes ago. He had partially disassembled it and wiped it down with a soft cloth. It helped pass the time as he waited for his partner to arrive. Braxton held his hand out. It hovered over the table without as much as a quiver.

I should be nervous. The man who killed my fiancée is coming here in my partner's skin. I should be climbing the walls. But he wasn't. Braxton recalled how impatient he had been to arrest Fulton when he had impersonated the mayor at the Plaza. He remembered the knot in his stomach, the anxious feeling.

And yet, here I sit calmly waiting to kill him. Where's the adrenaline? What's wrong with me? Maybe I'm just walking down the hill so I can screw all the heifers. The image brought a smile to his face. And then he realized it wasn't lethargy or a misplaced feeling of confidence that quelled his nerves. It was yoga.

His mother had mastered yoga as a young woman and insisted that Braxton meditate several times a day since Anne's death. Their long talks did nothing to help Braxton heal his spiritual wounds, but the yoga exercises did manage to keep him calm. The technique was instrumental in helping him pass his psychological exam. As a child, he and his siblings practiced yoga daily. Samarah said it gave them an edge that other children didn't have. Braxton had all but lost his appreciation of yoga and meditation during college. It simply didn't fit his lifestyle, and how could he pick up chicks if they thought he was a freaky Maharishi type? One of his college friends used to tease him relentlessly, asking him if he could levitate his body while meditating. Braxton's answer was always the same; "No, but I'll levitate your face if you don't shut up."

Braxton had never calculated the calming effects of yoga. It was so integral to his daily life he had no basis for comparison—until now. As a child growing up without a father, and living far below the poverty level, Braxton was well aware of the social and economic differences between his and other families. He lived in a predominately white neighborhood, but the homes were old and most were in disrepair. The neighbor kids would ask him if he was Mexican. His swarthy skin confused them. For a while, he said he was, rather than admit he was Lebanese. He was proud of his heritage, but the word sounded too much like Chinese, which for some reason sounded funny to many children. Braxton never liked being the brunt of jokes, and soon learned how to deal with childhood politics. A good punch in the nose took care of whatever yoga didn't. But for the most part, Braxton was a level-headed boy. He was sometimes impatient, but as he reached adolescence, he had adopted his mother's tranquil temperament. By Braxton's sophomore year in high school, he had become very popular, as he was handsome, smart, and athletic. He now boasted of his Lebanese birthright, and no one dared make fun of it.

Braxton picked up the Glock, pulled the slide back, and squeezed the trigger. Hearing a solid thunk, he used his palm to shove the 9mm magazine in place.

John should be here any second now.

During the last two hours, Braxton had plenty of time to contemplate how he would kill Fulton. John Dietrich was his only obstacle, but John was more than a partner to Braxton, he was his friend and mentor, and Braxton trusted and respected him. Since Braxton was younger and faster than John, his best bet was to manipulate Fulton into a predicament where he'd have to run. Then he could chase him to a distant spot where there would be no witnesses. He could claim self defense.

The sliding door opened, and Ford stepped in from the deck—alone.

"Hey, Nick, where's Dozer?" Ford scanned the kitchen, then down the hall, and finally looked at Braxton.

"I tied him to a railing on the patio. Don't worry; he'll bark if he sees anything."

"You wanna take him some water? You guys have been at it for hours."

Ford nodded, "Yeah, maybe in a little while."

Braxton's face changed expression, and then he shrugged.

"Hey, I've got bad news and good news, Nick—Fulton kidnapped John and his daughter—locked them both in a storage shed, but they escaped."

Shit! Fulton thought.

"John said that Fulton took his clothes—got his gun and badge too. Say's he's the spitting image of him. Scary stuff, huh?"

Ford's facial expression was exactly what Braxton expected. His eyebrows formed a frown with pronounced vertical lines that separated them. Ford's intense eyes wandered around the room, leading Braxton to assume he was thinking about how dangerous Fulton was, and the implications of John's identity theft.

"You talked with him?" Ford asked.

"Yeah, about fifteen minutes ago. He should be here any second."

"Jesus." Ford said. Braxton thought he was going to say something else, but he didn't. He was motionless, as if contemplating something important. His frown slowly melted away, replaced by a look that anyone would read as nervous.

"Hey, its okay, Nick," Braxton said in a calm voice. "Like I said, John will be here any time now." Ford stared at the gun Braxton was holding.

"Mind if I go upstairs and check on Whittman?"

"No need. Koss checked in with me just before you came in. Everything's fine."

"I just thought…"

Ford was interrupted by a knock at the front door. Braxton jumped to his feet.

"That's got to be John." Braxton walked down the hallway at a brisk pace. Ford followed him part way down the hall and watched as Braxton disappeared toward the front door. Fulton stopped abruptly.

So let's see—there's an officer upstairs, plus the redhead's boyfriend, and that Detective Dietrich. I've got to keep a distance from these guys, especially Dietrich. I have no idea how well they know each other—how well they know this K-9 officer. Fulton stood motionless, unsure of his next move. His eyes wandered to the door a few feet ahead of him and to his left.

Whittman's office.

He took a few more steps forward and peered into the room. Fulton's eyes lit up. There was Whittman, seated behind his desk, facing the computer on his credenza.

I thought he was upstairs.

Fulton placed his hand on the gun at his hip and walked into the room. Whittman didn't budge. Fulton pressed on until he was at his side. By then he noticed it wasn't Whittman sitting there. It was a man about the same age, with the same build and hair, but his facial features were completely different.

A decoy? You gotta be shitt'n me!

The man rolled his head to the right.

"Hi Nick. Wanna take a turn in the chair? My neck is killing me."

So Whittman is upstairs—just like the redhead's boyfriend said, but I can't just waltz in and get him—too many people here. I need to get these guys alone, one at a time.

"Sorry," Fulton said, "I'm afraid they'd have a hard time pawning me off as Whittman."

"Yeah, but Larry sure does a helluva job, doesn't he?"

Fulton pivoted to see John and Braxton in the doorway. Both men appeared to be in good spirits.

Damn. How the hell did he get out? Fulton wondered.

"Larry, how long have you been in that chair?" John asked.

"I dunno, five, maybe six hours."

John shook his head, "Why don't you take a break and stretch? Let's get something to eat."

"I'm all over that," Larry said.

Larry Granewski was a desk clerk. His gentle disposition suggested that's where he belonged. Although he usually wore the standard issue blues of a Kansas City police officer, he didn't wear a side arm, nor did he feel the need to flaunt one. On multiple occasions, John had noticed how much Granewski looked like Whittman from his back side. He was tall and had the same unusual platinum colored hair. When John asked him to be a decoy for Whittman, Granewski jumped at the chance to get out of the office.

"Tell you what, Larry," John said, "you scour the refrigerator for food. Pull out anything that looks good. We're going to go upstairs and have a five-minute meeting, okay?"

"There may not be any food left when you get back, John."

John laughed, "I'm afraid I'll have to take that chance, Larry." The three men started down the hallway, and John yelled over his shoulder, "Larry, lock the back door!"

Braxton assured John there was plenty of food.

"Whittman had the delicatessen deliver two massive meat and cheese platters with all the fixings."

"Great, Cindy'll be glad to know I'm not going to starve. Remind me to call her in a little while, would you, Brax? She's probably going nuts about now."

Kosinski heard the commotion on the first floor and was waiting outside Whittman's bedroom when John and the others reached the top of the stairs.

"Welcome back, John."

"Thanks, Koss. You have no idea how good it feels to be back."

Whittman's bedroom was larger than most living rooms. When John entered, he walked to a grouping of furniture where Whittman was consumed by a book he was reading. John noted two words from the book's long title, "Amassing Wealth." When Whittman noticed John staring, he smiled, laid the book on a table, and stood to greet him.

"I heard what happened, John. I'm very sorry." John gave Whittman half a nod, and the two men shook hands. When the others reached them, John asked them all to be seated.

What the hell have I gotten myself into, Fulton thought.

John slipped the shoes he was wearing off his feet.

"Aaaaah, that's better," John said, "these shoes are fucking killing me. Now we can talk. If you haven't already noticed, Fulton took my clothes." John's features contorted as if to say he was frustrated and embarrassed at wearing the tight orange T-shirt and the carpenter jeans that were up to his ankles. "My shoes too."

"I can give you something that will fit you better, John."

"Thanks, Zach, the sooner, the better." John's voice took on a commanding tone "Okay, folks, let's get to it. We need a plan, and not just any plan. Our Dr. Fulton is smart—slippery too. We need to have a series of passwords or hand signals we can rely on to help identify each other."

Braxton agreed, "That's a good idea, John. We need to be able to trust that Fulton's not among us, and that's probably the best way to do it."

John continued, "Every half hour, I want to hear everyone spout off a password, in alphabetical order. If you're alone, your password is 'Adam'. If you're in a group, the next person will take the next word in the alphabet—Boy, Charlie, David, Edward, and Frank. That's enough to get through the six of us. Memorize them. If anyone misses a word, they will be suspected of being Fulton and will be relieved of their weapons and handcuffed, until we are convinced he is not. Is that clear?"

There were nods from everyone.

Ha! Another stroke of luck, Fulton thought. *If I had missed this meeting, I'd have been discovered in no time.*

"Next, I want Brax and Koss to pee in a jar." Heads shot up in response to John's statement. Fulton went rigid.

"Fulton assumes a person's shape when his right hand comes in contact with another person's DNA. Since we know he's been using urine to trigger the transformation, we'll do the same. All we need is DNA from two people to cover the bases. Every hour, we will dip our fingers into one urine jar, and then the other. This will ensure Fulton hasn't infiltrated our ranks."

Koss made a face, "That's gross, John."

"Yeah, I know. But better gross, than dead, right?"

Fulton wasn't listening. He was numb and hundreds of fragmented thoughts now raced through his mind.

Urine? No! I'm finished! Caught! Kill! Escape!

Fulton glanced up at Braxton.

He's staring at me. HE KNOWS!

Fulton shifted his eyes to Whittman. He tried to relax his features to maintain facial calmness that would convince everyone he was composed and didn't have a care in the world.

If I can look at this asshole like he means nothing to me, it'll convince him I'm Ford. Fulton tapped his hand on his knee like he was keeping the beat of a tune in his head. He strained to think of other things a calm or disinterested person might do. But nothing came to mind. Instead, he began to sweat. Unwanted thoughts seeped deep into his psyche, *Whittman, you son-of-a-bitch—you're dead! Wait a minute! That gorgeous redhead! If Braxton knows who I am—I'm dead too. I gotta get out of here!*

"Let's eat first, John," Braxton said. "I'm gonna need something to drink if I'm gonna fill a cup." John opened his mouth to disagree, but Braxton's eyes were large, intense. His gaze lingered with John's.

Ford stood up, ready to go downstairs. His knees nearly buckled under him. John noticed. Ford's breathing seemed strained. Glancing at Braxton, John gave a barely perceptible nod.

"Come on, let's eat," John said calmly. "Mr. Whittman will continue to have his meals up here. Koss, can you fix him a plate?"

"No problem." John and Braxton watched Ford amble toward the door. John touched Kosinski's shoulder and whispered, "Keep an eye on Ford," then he turned away, not giving Kosinski a chance to react or respond.

Kosinski caught up with Ford, and they exited the room together. John looked at Whittman, "I need those clothes right now, Zach—tennis shoes, if you got them."

"Be right back, John." Whittman went to his closet.

John stepped within two inches of Braxton, "You know something, partner, spill it!"

Braxton was ready. He'd been waiting for a moment alone with John. He spoke quickly, but rationally.

"When Ford came in the house about fifteen minutes ago, he didn't bring his dog in with him. He said he tied him to a railing on the patio. I thought that was kind of odd."

John nodded, "It is."

"Then I asked him if he wanted some water for him. They'd been out in the heat for hours. He said maybe later."

"Not like Nick at all," John said. "He caters to Dozer, feeds him before he feeds himself."

"I don't know him very well, John, but from what I've observed so far today, I'd say that's an understatement. And you should have seen his face when you said we were gonna dip our fingers in urine. He turned white as a ghost, started fidgeting like crazy. He saw me staring at him. I think he knows I'm suspicious"

"Damn!" John said. "I was too busy flapping my gums to notice, but I did see him stumble. And when I looked at him, he seemed awful nervous." John looked down at his stocking feet and frowned. Braxton looked too, but only for a second.

"That dog's never even taken a piss alone, Brax. Nick would never leave him outside."

"What do you wanna do, John?"

"Well, it's him, Brax! Goddamit, it's him! Get down there! Don't let on that we know anything. Just keep him in your sights. Let me get some shoes on, and I'll be down in a couple of minutes."

"Oh shit!" Braxton said. "I left my spare gun on the kitchen table." John waved his hand through the air, dismissing the comment completely.

"He's already got a gun in his holster, Brax. I doubt he'd be much more dangerous with two." Braxton shrugged, "Yeah, I suppose."

"By the way Brax, I read you loud and clear." Braxton looked
puzzled.

"A few minutes ago, something in your eyes said, 'shut up, and follow my lead.' I wasn't a hundred percent sure, but I sensed something. It reminds me of the way Ford reads Dozer."

"Are you saying I'm your dog, John?" John smiled broadly.

"I think you know what I'm saying, partner."

Braxton returned John's smile and headed to the door.

"Wait!" John called. Braxton turned around.

"There's a glass on the table, Kid. Fill it up and take it with you." Braxton scrunched his nose, and then nodded.

"Pissing in a glass—the things I do for this job."

John ran to the closet. Whittman had a pair of khakis and a polo shirt draped over his arm. He was looking for shoes.

"What size shoe do you wear, John?"

"Doesn't matter, Zach, these look plenty big for my feet." John grabbed a pair of Nikes and ran back to a chair. Whittman followed quickly.

"What's the matter, John? Don't you want the clothes?" John was already tying the first shoelace.

"I think Fulton's downstairs. He's the one in the blue uniform."

"The K-9 officer?" Whittman asked. John tugged at the shoelace of the second shoe and began tying.

"Yeah. Now I want you to stay here, got it?" John didn't hear an answer, but if Whittman responded, he'd have missed it anyway. He was already halfway across the room.

Downstairs, John appeared from the end of the hallway into the kitchen.

"What'll it be, John? Pastrami, roast beef, ham, turkey?"

"Larry—where'd everybody go?"

"They're eating out on the deck. All except Braxton. If I can find the knife, I'll cut his sandwich in half and take it to him. Where the hell did that knife go?"

Jesus! John thought.

John slid the back door open and disappeared into the darkness.

40

JOHN FOUND OUT WHAT HAPPENED TO LARRY Granewski's missing knife. It was used to pierce several holes in Kosinski's chest. But the knife itself was gone. Kosinski's dinner plate was on the deck surrounded by potato chips and roast beef. John shuddered.

Where's Braxton? Did he go after Fulton? John scanned the deck and then the back yard. There was no sign of anyone. Then he dropped to one knee and placed two fingers across Kosinski's jugular vein. No pulse. He didn't expect one. Kosinski's eyes were closed and his face retained no remnants of expression, no sign that he'd been in pain. John bowed his head.

Sorry, Koss—I'm so sorry.

Biting his cheek, John stood up and squinted in the direction of the moonlit yard and golf course. With only a quarter moon, it was difficult to see anything in the distance.

I can't just stand here. I need to go after him. But how can I leave Whittman alone? John started to run back inside and almost collided with Larry

Granewski who was standing at the sliding door. The appearance of panic overwhelmed Granewski as he looked down at Kosinski's body.

"Oh God! Is he—alive?"

"No," John said. He placed his hands on Granewski's shoulders and firmly moved his mortified body to his left. He picked up the Glock on the table and started to shove it in the waistband of his pants, and then he stopped cold.

"Here," John said, handing the gun to Granewski, "take this. Lock all the doors and stay with Whittman until I get back. I need you to call for backup and an ambulance. Then, get hold of Captain Walsh and tell him to get down here—fast! Can you do that?"

"S—sure, John. You're going out there?"

"Got no choice, Larry—now, be careful!"

John darted out the door, and Granewski locked it behind him. John opened Kosinski's jacket and reached for his holster. His gun was gone.

Son-of-a-bitch!

There was a loud thudding of footsteps descending the redwood stairs. The man in Granewski's clothes stood at the door, peering through the glass. A moment later, he glimpsed a shadowy figure he assumed was John, driving off in a golf cart. He slid the door open and stepped out to the deck. From Kosinski's right pocket he withdrew a set of car keys.

Under his breath he said, "It's time to make my getaway."

Still in his bedroom, Whittman waited patiently for dinner. He sat holding a book, but he wasn't reading. He was preoccupied—troubled by the thought that Fulton had entered his house undetected. He tried to remember what officer Ford looked like when they were introduced earlier that afternoon. There didn't appear to be any notable differences between him and the man he'd seen a short while ago. Fulton had been in Whittman's presence twice in the last two days and had gone unrecognized both times. It was both amazing and unsettling.

Whittman knew all his money couldn't protect Fulton if he was caught by the police. And if he was caught, the formula would go with him. Whittman had entertained thoughts of making him a deal. If Fulton would agree to continue to work on the formula, he could assume a new identity and work in CSGR's affiliate lab in England. In exchange, Whittman would give him his DNA back and help him find a solution to the problem of involuntary physical adaptation. But could it be stopped? Whittman believed that with more research into bio-switches, they could figure out how to turn them on and off at will. Of course, the police could never know about the arrangement. But how in the world would he ever get Fulton alone? He's probably in custody by now.

"Mr. Whittman?"

The voice startled, Whittman. Reflexively, he snapped his book closed. Whittman looked up and exhaled slowly. Relieved at seeing Officer Granewski, he closed his eyes briefly.

"It's Larry, right?" Granewski nodded. "Yes, sir."

"I apologize for reacting like that, Larry, I guess you spooked me."

"Sorry Mr. Whittman—didn't mean to. I came up here to protect you. You need to know something—Fulton was here. He killed Detective Kosinski. The others have gone after him."

Whittman's eyes fell to his lap. "This nightmare's never going to end, is it?"

"Don't worry, Mr. Whittman, I called the police. They're on their way, and I'll keep you safe until they get here.

John's golf cart was incredibly fast. It was obviously not a stock unit from the golf course. With the wind in his hair, John wondered if it were fast enough to catch up with Fulton. But which way did he go? John passed the tee for the 16th hole. It butted up to the back yard of Whittman's northeast neighbor. The green was just an easy seven iron shot across the lake. John was having trouble seeing in the dark. He could make out the lake on his left, because lights reflected on its surface, but everything else was black. The choppy ride seemed to hinder John's thinking.

This is bizarre. How did Fulton ever get this far? He may be a brilliant geneticist, but he's just not the criminal type. He doesn't interface well with people, but he's never been a physical person until now. He's probably made several slip ups, but we just didn't notice because we trusted our eyes and not our instincts. I can't blame anyone for that—not even myself.

In the distance John could see a curving line of faint lights from homes that bordered the golf course. They were coming up fast.

The lake is tapering off—there must be a cart path up ahead. The cart took a jolt from a deep rut. It jarred John so hard he felt a sharp pain shoot up his back. He wanted to slow down, but he kept the pedal to the floor. He felt another thud, but not as jolting.

There it is! John caught a glimpse of the cart path he had just driven over. He slowed and made a wide arc. Finally on the path, he concentrated to stay on it. John began to round the edge of the lake. The string of houses on his right provided almost no additional light. But there was enough light to see an oncoming cart speeding toward him.

Jesus, now who's that?

Reflexively, John reached for a gun that wasn't there. And then he realized where it was.

Aww shit! I gave it to Larry! Nothing to do but wait and see who it is.

John's eyes were adjusting to the darkness. The moonlight cast his features in a dismal blue light, but the canopy of the approaching cart shadowed the driver. The cart slowed and stopped about ten feet from him.

"Is that you, John?"

It's Brax, thank God!

"Did you see anything?"

John stepped on the pedal and came up beside him.

"Nothing, Brax—how 'bout you?"

"I went all the way to the end of the cart path. It crosses a street up ahead. Didn't see a thing."

"I wish I'd known you'd come this way, Brax, I'd have taken a different direction."

"There wasn't any time to lose, John. Who's watching Whittman?"

"Larry's with him. I gave him your gun."

"So you're running around out here without a gun? You got balls, John."

"Yeah, I know, as big as your mother's kibbeh."

Braxton chuckled as he pictured the lamb-covered footballs. "What'll we do now?"

"I had Granewski call for backup and told him to get Walsh down here. If the Captain hasn't already thought of it, we'll get a chopper too. That'll give us infrared and a spotlight. Let's get back and check out the perimeter of the house. Then we can head in. Why don't you take the front, Brax, and then drive down the street a block or two. I hate to play cowboy, but if you see anything, fire a shot. I'm going to take the lakeshore back."

Braxton said, "I'm on it." His cart lunged forward and the whir of its motor faded into the darkness.

John yelled. "Don't trust your eyes!" as Braxton took off on the cart path. John veered west, toward the lake.

What a comedy of errors, John thought. *Connors was right. I've run this operation like a Girl Scout meeting. I've got no gun, no radio, no phone, nothing. I let Fulton strip me of everything. But worst of all, we lost Nick and Koss. How could I let that happen? It could have just as easily been Braxton.*

John's cart hugged the lake's rugged edge all the way to the boathouse. As he approached it, he noticed the American flag atop a twenty-foot flagpole. It wasn't difficult to see with a floodlight directed upward to illuminate the colors. What John saw next surprised him. A man was strapped to the flagpole. He was stripped down to his underwear, twisting and wrenching to get free.

That's got to be him! Please God, let it be him! As John drew near, he could make out more details.

Yes! John screamed in his mind, *it's Nick.*

John could tell that Ford heard the hum of his cart as he approached. Ford pivoted around the pole and then stood motionless. John rushed to him and pulled the duct tape from his mouth.

"John?" Nick spoke uncertainly.

"Yeah, Nick, it's me." John studied Ford's bindings, and then his thoughts turned to Fulton.

This guy must own stock in a duct tape company.

"Fulton did this, John. I couldn't believe my eyes—he looked just like you."

"I know, Nick. And as soon as all of us stop trusting our eyes, we'll catch him."

"What took you so long to find me?"

"We didn't know Fulton had taken your identity until just a little while ago." John hesitated, "He killed Kosinski." Ford's head began to sink to his chest, but then he jerked it upright.

"Is Brax all right?"

"Yeah, he's headed up to the house. What about Dozer?"

"He's in the boat house. Can you let him out?"

"Not 'till you're free, Nick. I'd prefer not to have Dozer rip my arm off." Ford's hands were behind the flagpole. The duct tape was matted and looked like a silver rope. Ford's feet were wrapped as well, but it was the strands around his chest that caught John's attention. John tapped his index finger on Ford's hairy chest.

"This is gonna hurt, my friend."

"I don't care about the pain, John; I just want to get free."

"Fair enough, Nick."

John had no knife, but the keys to Dave's pickup truck were plenty sharp.

"Keep the tape taut, Nick." John made several sawing motions across the top of a section of tape that wasn't as badly snarled as the rest until he'd cut a quarter inch gash in it. John pocketed the keys, and placed his fingers on each side of the cut and yanked. The tape ripped clean. As soon as John yanked it off, Nick extended his arms in the air like they were wings.

"Oh man, does that feel good." John knelt and repeated the procedure on Fords ankles. When John cut the strands behind Ford's chest, he grabbed one end of the tape, and paused while he looked Ford in the eyes.

"Do it!" Ford said.

John yanked, and created a swath of smooth hairless real estate across Ford's chest.

Ford dropped to one knee.

"Shit! Fuck! Son-of-a-bitch!"

"Well, that covers a shit-load of expletives," John said, smiling.

Ford didn't respond. With watery eyes, he got to his feet and ran to the boat house, opened the door, and went inside. John spied a pile of clothes on the ground. They were his.

My holster, my gun! John couldn't believe it, but there they were. He removed the Glock from the holster.

Feels light. John turned the bottom side up. *No wonder, he ejected the magazine. Probably threw it in the lake.* John checked his ammo pouch.

Well, well, I guess Dr. Fulton can make mistakes after all. Good! At least now I know how much he knows about guns and holsters. He missed both spare magazines. John slammed one in the Glock's handle and chambered a round. John knew Ford would be a few minutes. He stripped off his shoes, shirt, and pants, and put his own back on. As he was tying his shoes, Ford and Dozer emerged. Ford had found a bowl and a bottle of Perrier water in the fridge. He poured the water, and Dozer waited patiently for approval.

"Okay, boy!"

Dozer lapped at the water like he hadn't had a drop in weeks. Ford approached John with a serious look on his face.

"Who was he last, John? Me?"

"Yeah, Nick, he was you."

"Aww Fuck! That's just great!"

"What's the matter, Nick?"

"Dozer can't track him. It would be like tracking me, and we've been over every inch of these grounds. Everything's tainted with my scent, it just won't work."

"Well, there goes our last best chance of getting him," John lamented. "Wait a minute, the chopper! C'mon, Nick, put your pants on. You can put the shoes on in the cart. We've gotta get to the house—now!"

By the time John and Ford reached the house, Braxton was stooping over Kosinski's body.

"Where's Whittman?" John asked.

"He's gone," Braxton replied.

"That's not funny, Brax!"

"No one's joking, John. Whittman and Granewski are both gone."

Dozer was sniffing and whining at a redwood chest near the door. Ford went over to him.

John's eyes grew large, "You don't think that…"

"Fulton is Granewski?" Braxton interrupted. "Yeah, I do. I called the captain, John. Granewski never phoned him, never called for backup, or an ambulance. I found these out front." Braxton handed John a set of keys.

"They belonged to Koss. Looks like Fulton was going to steal Koss's car, but fortunately, you parked behind him. You blocked him in."

"Jesus, the one thing I did right all day, and it was completely by accident."

"HEY GUYS! You need to see this!"

Nick was kneeling at the base of a large redwood chest. There were patio chair cushions scattered all around it.

Uh oh, those cushions belong in the chest, John thought.

Dozer was dancing skittishly. Ford held up a navy blue police officer's uniform. It was his, but his eyes remained fixed on something else in the box. John crouched to get a good look. Officer Granewski had been stuffed in the box. He was naked, down to his underwear. It wasn't the stab wounds, but Granewski's mangled position that made John feel queasy. A bloody kitchen knife lay on top of him.

Nick shook his head, "I'd say Brax is right on the money, John."

"He's taking us down one by one—this inexperienced geek is kicking our asses!" John's outburst was uncharacteristic of him. Braxton tried to calm him down.

"He fooled all of us, John, not just you. We're on to him now, we know how he operates."

"Tell that to Larry and Koss—tell that to Justin Moody and Wendell Peters. Sorry you guys didn't make it, but we're on to him now."

Braxton frowned, "Yeah, I could tell it to Anne too, but it wouldn't do me any good now, would it?"

John turned his head away, "I'm sorry, Brax."

"Don't be sorry, John, let's just get him. The captain is sending backup, lots of it. When he gets here we'll regroup."

"No time Brax."

"But, John…"

"Don't you get it, Brax? Fulton has what he came for! We only have a small window of opportunity to catch this guy, or we'll never see him again. He's wasted some time trying to find a getaway car. As far as we know he's on foot. Nick! Do you think Dozer can find him?"

"That depends, John. Do you think he's still impersonating Larry?"

"Doesn't matter," John spouted quickly, "we're gonna look for his travel partner. Brax—go in the house and find me some of Whittman's dirty laundry. And hurry!"

41

FULTON STOPPED TO REST. HIS SIDE WAS ACHING, AND he was out of breath. Whittman was panting too, but he didn't look nearly as exhausted.

"At least it's not uphill," Whittman said. Fulton could only nod.

I came this way. It didn't seem so far, Fulton thought. *All that running, and we haven't even gone a third of the way. Hell, it's no wonder I'm so exhausted; I'm in the body of a police clerk.*

Fulton planned to make his escape in Ford's athletic body, but his plan changed abruptly. It changed the moment Dietrich announced that he would test everyone by dipping their fingers in urine. Fulton panicked. When he and Kosinski left Whittman's bedroom, he knew he had only seconds to act, not minutes, or he'd be discovered. When they entered the kitchen, Larry Granewski was making sandwiches. He was cutting a six-inch roast beef sub in half with a large chef's knife.

I need that knife, Fulton thought.

"What'll it be, gents? Pastrami, roast beef, ham, or turkey?"

"What you've got right there looks good to me," Fulton said. He picked up half a sandwich, set it on a plate, and headed out the door.

"Where are you going, Nick?" Fulton looked back at Kosinski, "I'm going to sit on the deck. Why don't you join me?" Kosinski picked up the other half of the sandwich and threw a handful of chips on his plate. Then he stepped out to the deck.

Fulton stared at Kosinski's plate.

Perfect, he thought.

"Where'd you get those chips?" Fulton asked.

"They were right there on the counter," Kosinski said, "in a big white bowl."

"Let me grab a handful—be right back." Fulton slid the door open, walked to the counter and took a large handful of chips. He looked at Granewski, "Hey, does Whittman have anything to drink?"

"Let me check," Granewski said. He opened the refrigerator door and stooped over to look inside. "Yeah, we got diet Coke, and some bottled tea and water. What'll it be? Nick? Nick?" Granewski retracted his head from behind the door, but Nick was gone, and the door to the deck was closed.

Fulton's plate was heaped with potato chips. He hoped Kosinski noticed.

Got seconds not minutes, he thought. *Willis and Dietrich will be down any minute.* Now he was ready. Kosinski stood at the railing, his plate straddling a redwood two by six. He had one foot propped against a redwood rail. He crunched on a chip as Fulton began his trek from the back door to take a place beside him. When Fulton was directly behind Kosinski, he exploded into action. He grabbed the knife handle from beneath his plate. His first thrust landed squarely in the middle of Kosinski's shoulder blades. Fulton took his other hand and bent Kosinski over the railing just in time for the next thrust of the knife. It pierced deep into Kosinski's flesh. The stabbing became wild and fast and Kosinski had no chance to react, no chance to call for help. Fulton's eyes were wide when he let go of him. Kosinski grasped at his plate as if it would hold him up. He collapsed to the deck, pulling his plate over the top of him.

The back door slid open.

"Hey, you guys want a drink? What the hell…" Fulton fumbled, but managed to draw his gun, and point it at Granewski.

"Get out here, and close the door!" Fulton ordered. Granewski obeyed, not saying a word.

"Out of your clothes, FAST!" Fulton shook the gun in his hand as he said it. Granewski slipped his shoes off, staring all the while at Kosinski's body. A quick tug of his belt, and his pants dropped to the deck. He unbuttoned his shirt, and threw it on top of the pile.

"Open the trunk." Fulton waved his gun at a redwood trunk, just a few feet from Granewski. It was full of chair cushions. Granewski didn't even ask, but began to empty them onto the deck.

"Look," Granewski said, "I'll get in, and I won't yell or scream, but there's no need to kill me. Just tell me how long you want me to be still."

Fulton took a step closer, "Ten minutes," he said. "Now get in!"

Granewski steadied himself by grabbing the lid and placed one foot inside the box. It was when he dropped to one knee that the knife's blade pierced his back. Over and over, faster and faster the blood-stained blade hit its mark. Granewski slumped and blood oozed from his wounds and dripped down his sides to his chest. Fulton threw Granewski's arms in the box and used his foot to cram him in. Fulton raced to change into Granewski's clothes. They did not fit as Granewski was lanky and tall. Fulton reached into the trunk to touch the blood on Granewski's back with his right index finger. The mind numbing transformation was swift. When Fulton's head cleared, he was three inches taller. He found himself staring at Granewski's resting position, which was so twisted that Fulton couldn't tell what parts should be face up. The image brought him back to the moment.

Jesus, gotta hurry!

Fulton slipped the shirt on and buttoned only the bottom two buttons. He pulled Granewski's pants up and jammed his feet into the shoes. Throwing the knife in the chest, followed by Ford's uniform, Fulton slammed the lid and darted back into the kitchen. He was buttoning the top button of his shirt when Braxton arrived.

"Hey Larry, where's Nick?" he asked. Fulton never looked at Braxton, but went to the refrigerator and opened it, "The boys decided to eat on the deck. Are you hungry?"

"I'm starved, but don't fix me anything, yet."

Braxton slid the door to one side, but never closed it. His words were easily heard in the kitchen.

"No—Jesus, not again!"

Fulton ran to the door and saw Braxton staring at Kosinski's body.

"Oh my God!" he said, convincingly.

"How long were they out here, Larry?"

"Just a minute or two. They grabbed a roast beef sandwich and stepped outside. I never even heard a scuffle."

"Then Fulton couldn't have gone far. I'm going after him. I want you to run upstairs and get John." Fulton turned and ran down the hallway. He stopped at the stairs and waited. Less than a minute later, Fulton heard muffled footsteps from the upstairs hallway. He quietly rushed back into the kitchen, and piled some ham and cheese on a hoagie bun. John was in a hurry, but Fulton was certain it was for some other reason. After Fulton's comment about the missing knife, John ran outside and discovered Kosinski's body. Moments later, he too was gone.

What irony, Fulton remembered thinking. *The last two police officers not only leave me with Whittman, but give me a gun and put me in charge. This is too much.* Fulton looked over his shoulder and glimpsed the cedar box containing Granewski's body. His remorse for killing Granewski lasted perhaps a millisecond. Fulton had run out of duct tape, and there was no way he could trust that Granewski would stay in the box. Granewski was after all, a police officer. Fulton dropped to one knee, and fished the car keys from Kosinski's pocket. Minutes later, still in Granewski's skin, he was leading Whittman down the stairs. He'd explained that John wanted them to head to the precinct station. It was the safest place for them. Whittman said he felt like a sitting duck, and was more than willing to go downtown.

When they reached the driveway, Fulton recognized the truck from the storage shed.

"Son-of-a-bitch, that asshole parked behind me." Whittman shot a look at Granewski, focusing on his eyes. The quiet man who served as Whittman's decoy appeared to be coming unglued. Granewski had been very quiet, almost timid until now. But now his eyes had swollen with anger. Was it just nerves, or was it something else?

"Come on, Mr. Whittman. I know where we can find another car, but we'll need to cut across the golf course."

"Wait a minute," said Whittman, "isn't Fulton out there?"

"He's probably long gone by now," Fulton said.

"Well, if that's the case, I think we should just stay here. We've got a gun; let's go inside and wait for the police."

Fulton looked at Whittman with disgust.

"The police aren't coming; old friend—you and I are leaving here, and we're going to find a place where we can talk. Understand?"

"Richard?"

Fulton smiled, "In the flesh—well, not exactly my flesh, but you get the point."

"Richard! I was hoping I could talk to you alone. I was worried about you."

"Yeah, your concern for me has been overwhelming. Like when you let me take the formula—one that was five versions old! You set me up!"

"I only let you do what you'd have done on your own, Richard. You were chomping at the bit to try it. And you had success with that version. It should have worked."

"Yeah, it worked, all right, you son-of-a-bitch. IT'S STILL WORKING!"

"Listen, Richard, I can get you out of this. We have a facility in London. We can use the corporate jet, you'll be safe there."

"And why would I want to go there?"

"To continue your research, we'll find a way to fix this."

Fulton paused. He looked at Whittman with hatred and disgust, but his angry features began to fade as he considered the idea. The lines on his face softened.

This could be my ticket out of here. A new identity, a passport—and he'll cough up the money too. I can kill him later.

"I want two million in a numbered account—tonight!"

"I can get you half that tonight. It will take me a day or two to convert some assets, but I'll get the rest."

"You know how to set up a Swiss account?"

Whittman sounded convincing, "I have two numbered accounts already. I'll call my broker tonight—let's just get out of here!"

"Okay, Zach, I'll do it. But if I catch you straying from the plan, even a little, I'll kill you—understand?"

Whittman nodded, "I understand."

Fulton motioned with the gun. "Let's go. I've got a car parked on the other side of the lake."

The two men ran around the east side of the house, farthest from the lake. They sprinted fifty yards to the only tree that stood between the 16th tee and their destination.

"I hear something," Whittman whispered. It was the hum of one of Whittman's golf carts, approaching from the direction of the golf course. The two men kept out of sight, behind the trunk of the massive oak tree. The cart whizzed by, and Fulton could make out the silhouette of the man driving. It was Detective Willis. They watched quietly. The cart slowed a little as it labored up the incline on the side of Whittman's house and disappeared out front. Fulton moved to the front of the tree. Whittman leaned against it. In the distance, Fulton saw the other golf cart. From his vantage point, it appeared as only a speck as it approached the boat house.

"That must be Dietrich. C'mon! We're clear all the way to the car!" They tore off at full speed, keeping on the grass along the cart path.

42

HUNCHED OVER, HIS HANDS BRACED ON HIS KNEES, Fulton panted hard. It was their second stop to catch their breath. Fulton looked up at Whittman, who was only panting half as much. Fulton straightened, and turned around to see how far they'd traveled.

Another eighty yards. We've gotta do better than this.

"Come here!" Fulton barked. Whittman raised his eyebrows, and approached him cautiously.

"Open your mouth."

Whittman took a step back, "What are you going to do?"

"Just open it!"

Whittman's mouth inched open. His eyes widened, and he watched as his suspicions were confirmed. Fulton used his right index finger to swab Whittman's mouth. In the dim moonlight, Whittman could only see a little of the metamorphosis. It took only seconds. Granewski was tall and blonde like Whittman, but he was a lanky man. In the first instant, it was as if someone used an air compressor to inflate

Granewski's body. It simply took another shape. Fulton tried to keep his balance, but stumbled and fell to his knees. When he looked up, Whittman gasped.

"My God—it's me!" The transition should've taken months, not seconds. Fulton remained on his knees. He didn't appear to hear the comment. It was as though he needed some time to clear his head. When Fulton stood, he looked into Whittman's eyes.

"You're fascinated by all this, aren't you?"

Whittman's likeness even sounded like him. He was no longer panting. He stood still, waiting for an answer.

"It—it's amazing!" Whittman said, "A miracle."

"To hell with the miracle; it's a curse, Goddamit! I never wanted any of this. I just wanted my arm—"

Fulton closed his eyes.

"—and the respect I earned for this discovery. Can you understand that?"

Fulton's fists were clenched. His tone was desperate, and pitiful.

Whittman looked down at the dark grass.

"I didn't know it would work out this way, Richard. But I promise you, I'll get your DNA back. No one can prove it was you who did those things. They can suspect you, but they can't prove a thing."

"You're wrong! If they catch me, they'll prove it. All they need to do is dip my fingers into someone's DNA and watch me change. I had jars of it all over the house, including yours and the mayor's."

"Then we won't let them catch you. From London we can work on a cure. We'll find the bio-switch responsible for these involuntary changes and reverse its state. Then you can come back."

I'm not coming back, asshole. Once I have my passport and money—once the jet is waiting for me—you're dead. I'll make damn sure of it.

"We're wasting time," Fulton said. "I've got a fresh body, so we're gonna run like hell. And you'd better keep up." Fulton began to jog. As Whittman caught up, Fulton continued to accelerate until they were at a full sprint.

John and Braxton sat ready behind the steering wheels of their golf carts. Ford had just given Dozer the scent of Whittman's clothes and the command to hunt him down. The dog was restless. Dozer began sniffing and moving in different directions, and then he settled on a path moving north from Whittman's back yard, toward the golf course. Ford jumped into the seat next to John.

"He's got it, let's go."

John stomped on the pedal and veered to the right, in the direction of the cart path.

"I don't get it—Fulton's going the same direction Braxton and I just came from. Why did he go this way?"

"Maybe he knows you've already searched the course—maybe he thinks you won't backtrack," Ford replied. "There's no doubt we're going the right way, Dozer's got the scent."

Watching the K-9's silhouette intrigued John. Dozer no longer had his nose to the ground.

The scent must be fresh. Maybe we're not too late.

They approached a mammoth oak tree, and Dozer circled it before darting away. Dozer was running hard now. Whenever John got too close to Dozer, he'd ease up on the pedal and coast for a second, and then mash it to the floor again. Braxton kept to John's left, but this time, he'd taken the faster cart. He didn't wait for John or Dozer and was already ten yards ahead of them.

John hit a rut. It jarred his teeth into the flesh of the cheek he'd been biting all afternoon. Wincing, he ran his tongue along the deep cut. It hadn't healed from the half dozen times he'd drawn blood this week. He gnashed his teeth to avoid another injury.

The moon had risen higher in the sky, but it didn't help visibility. The cart path was only a few shades lighter than the dark grass. In the far distance, John saw a familiar sight, a curved landscape dotted with the faint lights of homes backing up to the golf course. A thought overtook him.

My car! It wasn't in the driveway. It wasn't on the street either. Fulton parked it on the other side of the lake—that's what took him so long to get here—that's where he's going! God if we miss him we'll have no more chances—and Whittman's good as dead.

John called to Braxton, but he couldn't hear him. He'd gained another five yards.

Maybe he'll get there first. Go get'em, Kid!

The carts sliced through a pocket of cool air. It was almost chilling against John's sweat covered face. His cheek hurt, but the pain kept him focused. John leaned over to Ford, "I think Fulton has a car waiting on the other side of the lake."

"We're making good time," Ford said, "I think we're gonna catch him."

John gazed in the distance, "It would sure make up for all the blunders of the day."

Fulton glanced to his right. Whittman was not beside him. He stopped and turned around to see a dim silhouette of Whittman walking with his hands on his hips. He ran back to him.

"I thought I told you to keep up."

"I'm trying—Richard—I just need—a minute."

"We don't have a minute, Zach. In a minute, this place will be crawling with cops. We're just about out of time." Whittman was shaking violently. His eyes were dancing in their sockets. He was near exhaustion. Fulton tried to gauge their final distance. They were just rounding the lake.

"It's not that much farther, you can make it, Zach."

"I don't know—my side—it's going to burst." Fulton gritted his teeth. During their last rest, he felt the same way. He wasn't sure he could have run any farther if someone had held a gun to his head. He was already panting again too.

Christ! What am I supposed to do?

"All right, Zach, you've got one minute to rest. Take deep breaths."

Whittman dropped to his knees, and then fell to his side. He laid in the grass desperately filling his lungs with air. Fulton stared down the cart path.

What is that? Is that someone coming?

He froze for a moment, not breathing, even though his body clamored for oxygen.

It is! It's someone on a golf cart!

The image was small, a faint gray smudge. He could not yet hear the electric motor, but it was approaching fast. Fulton patted his pocket and felt the hard edges of a gun.

It's dark. I could lie down, wait for him to get close, and put a bullet in him. We could use the cart to get to the car. But what if I miss? Fulton looked to his right.

We could hide in one of these homes—we can take someone's car.

"C'mon, Zach. Someone's coming. We gotta go—NOW!"

Fulton grabbed Whittman's arm and tugged, but Whittman was all dead weight.

"Help me, you fool, someone's coming. Getcher ass in gear!" Whittman pulled himself up by grappling at Fulton's clothes.

Look at him. He might as well be drunk—he can't even stand. Fulton pushed Whittman back at arm's length, and reached into his pocket, withdrawing the gun.

So much for well laid plans.

Whittman's eyes bulged. He stammered, "N—no, Richard—Nooooo!"

The gun exploded from Fulton's hip, illuminating the terror in Whittman's face. The crack of the shot rang through the course, and a sharp echo bounced back. Whittman dropped like a heavy sandbag. When Fulton looked up he was shocked at how far the cart had traveled.

Shit!

He spun and ran up a steep grade toward the closest house.

Braxton wasn't sure what it was he'd heard over the sound of his golf cart, but he was certain he'd seen a flash of light ahead. It was just a blip, but it seemed to correspond with the sound.

Might have been my imagination, but I don't think so. Braxton kept his eyes focused on the exact spot where the flash occurred. He concentrated on nothing else. As he approached the vicinity, his eyes scanned wildly until he pinpointed something in the grass.

A body!

A heavy foot locked the brakes on Braxton's cart, and he skidded to a stop. He leaped out of the cart and ran to the sprawled body of a man whose face was buried in coarse grass. Braxton knelt beside him and turned him over. Whittman opened his eyes slowly. There was no emotion in them.

"My God!" Braxton exclaimed. "Mr. Whittman, an ambulance is already on the way. I'll get them down here to take care of you—do you understand?" Whittman's eyes ticked a millimeter closer to Braxton's face.

He's trying to look at me.

Braxton looked at Whittman's blood-soaked shirt. The dark stain was now seeping down his sides.

He's not gonna make it. He's losing too much blood.

Braxton grasped the ends of Whittman's shirt and ripped it open. The bullet hole was near the heart, and blood oozed from it. With one hand on top of the other, Braxton formed a compress against the wound. He wondered if he could keep Whittman alive. A faint heartbeat was present, but its rhythm was irregular.

Son-of-a-bitch! I was way ahead of John. If Fulton hadn't done this, I'd have had a bullet in him by now. I can't leave now. Gotta keep Whittman alive.

A nudge behind Braxton's ear made him start. Dozer pranced skittishly beside him. Ford ran to Dozer and tried to calm him with an embrace. It didn't work. John approached apprehensively, as if he already knew the extent of Whittman's condition. He stood over

Braxton and Whittman looking down at them. His expression said what was on his mind.

"I'm sorry this happened, Zach. We're gonna do our best to get you outta here, and to safety, but you've gotta hang on—do ya hear?" There was no response.

"I—I think his heart stopped, John."

John dropped to his knees, "Move over, Brax, I'll give him CPR." Braxton raised his arm to stop him.

"You can give him CPR for a month, John, it won't help. He lost too much blood—he's gone." A long look into Whittman's eyes made John shudder. They were fixed in a permanent stare. Pinpoints of moonlight reflected from their glossy surface. John stood and looked around him, while Braxton wiped his bloody hands in the grass. There was no sign of Fulton in any direction. John's voice was sharp.

"I think Fulton went in the direction of this hill." John looked up the steep bank. At its top were a row of homes.

"I'm going this way."

John climbed the hill as quickly as he could. Braxton and Ford followed, but Dozer overtook them all.

John stumbled on the uneven terrain. He swore under his breath, and dug in harder, faster.

No more killing, Fulton—no fucking more!

At the top of the hill, John faced the back of a two-story home. No lights were on. He ran between two houses in search of Dozer.

Maybe he still has Fulton's scent.

Streetlights cast the exclusive neighborhood in an amber glow. Mature trees blocked much of the light from the houses. In the stillness, John heard Dozer whining at the stoop of the brick two-story next door. Braxton and Ford appeared.

"Never seen you move so fast, you ol' fart."

John ignored Braxton's crack, "What do you think, Nick? Did Dozer track him?"

"I'd stake my life on it, John. He's been acting crazy ever since we found Whittman. There must have been two scents, and the second one probably ended here."

"All right," John said, "no one gets hurt. Do you understand? Three of us go in this house, and four of us come out. Trust no one. If you need to confirm an identity, use this password—ol' fart."

Braxton smiled.

"Okay, Nick, take Dozer around the back of the house. One of us will let you in from the deck when we get there. Brax, come with me."

"Dozer, come!" The K-9 ran to Ford like his job was finished. He wagged his tail and awaited praise. Ford gave him a quick embrace and then took off.

Braxton had his gun drawn and at arm's length when John knocked at the front door. No one answered, but the lights were on. John opened the glass storm door and then the oak entry door behind it. With a gentle push, he let it swing open. He could hear a television playing loud in another room. Reaching for his holster, John drew his gun and double-checked the safety. They entered the house.

John looked up at the open staircase. There were plenty of lights on upstairs. He motioned to Braxton to move through the living room. They would converge around the corner. John walked down a hallway. He could see a kitchen floor ahead. He gently elbowed a door on his right. The bathroom was empty. A door on his left yielded an empty coat closet. The television grew louder with each step.

John reached the end of the hallway. He could see Ford and Dozer through the kitchen's sliding door and Braxton, who had circled through the dining room and was positioned behind a countertop island. John gave a sharp nod of his head, signaling for Braxton to cover him. Braxton came around the counter and unlocked the kitchen door for Ford. Then he took a stance with his gun extended. John rounded the corner and took three large steps toward the family room. Then he quickly backed away and holstered his gun.

John signaled to Braxton and Ford for a conference.

"There are three little boys watching TV in there," John whispered. "Braxton, I want you to stay here and keep an eye on them."

Braxton frowned.

"Sorry, partner," John said, "but I need Dozer to finish the job and take me to Fulton."

Ford attached a short chain to Dozer's collar and headed to the staircase. Braxton was still frowning.

How am I gonna get this bastard now? He re-staked his position on the other side of the kitchen island.

"Be careful, John."

John nodded. "Don't come up unless you hear a shot fired."

John turned and met Ford at the stairs. A little part of Braxton wished to hear a shot.

43

JOHN SQUEEZED PAST DOZER AND FORD AND ENTER-
ed the master bedroom. The room was empty, but John could hear the
shower running. Ford held on to Dozer's collar, but Dozer dragged
him to the bathroom door and whined. John placed his hand on the
doorknob and whispered.

"If we're wrong about this, Nick, the department's gonna get hit
with a helluva lawsuit. You know that, don'tcha."

Ford nodded, "Dozer's never been wrong, John."

"Let's hope he's not this time." John inhaled deeply, turned the door
handle and darted in, gun held outright.

"POLICE! Put your hands in the air!"

"WHO IS THAT? WHAT DO YOU WANT?" a female voice
screamed.

John saw a fleshy image through the steamed shower door.

"Police officers, Ma'am," John said, "I'm sorry, but you need to put
your hands in the air and come out of there."

"I'm naked," the voice said.

"I realize that, Ma'am, but you need to do what you are told. Put your hands above the glass and come out."

"How do I know you are police?"

"If I was here to molest you, I'd have just opened the door and grabbed you, now come out!"

A pair of feminine hands appeared above the glass door. The woman pushed the shower door open with her shoulder, and her hands quickly moved to cover her breasts. The woman was a brunette of about thirty. John's eyes never left her face, and his heart sank as he noticed her expression. She was obviously embarrassed. He began to lower his gun, but changed his mind.

Is she really embarrassed or just acting? Something's not right here. Don't trust your eyes.

John reached in his breast pocket and held out his ID wallet. "Detective John Dietrich, I'm sorry I have to do this, Ma'am." The woman nodded.

"At least let me put on a robe," she pleaded.

There was a towel and a robe draped over a chair by a dressing table. John motioned for her to get it.

"Slowly, please."

John held the gun on the woman and watched her dry her arms so she could slip them into the sleeves of her robe. She seemed genuinely frightened as she cinched her belt tight, but wouldn't Fulton be frightened if he were cornered?

Trust no one.

Dozer was trying to get into the bathroom, but Ford had a firm grasp of his collar preventing it. John waved his gun.

"Let's go in the other room and talk. Steam continued to rise from the empty shower stall. The woman walked through the doorway, almost coming to a complete halt, when she saw the K-9. John waved the gun and the woman picked a spot and stood in the middle of the room. John kept a distance, and composed himself for questioning. Ford and Dozer went into the bathroom.

"What is your name, Ma'am?"

"Kristine—Kristine Hoffmann." The woman's eyes were round and jittery. She repeatedly raised her eyebrows and motioned her head toward the bathroom as she talked.

She wants me to look at the bathroom. I don't trust her. Ford's got it covered.

"Where's your husband?"

"He was out-of-town this week. He should be home any minute." The woman finally pointed to the bathroom and mouthed the words, "He's—in—there."

Oh my God! John thought. *Is he? Or is this a diversion, a trap?*

John motioned to the woman to come toward him as he inched closer to the door. He kept her in sight, and then he began to back into the bathroom, but it was too late.

A gun exploded. A door flew open and slammed against the wall. Someone ran from the closet and collided with John before he could turn and take aim at the assailant. They tumbled to the ground, the man landing on top of John.

Whittman—NO, FULTON!

Each man clawed at the other's gun. John grasped Fulton's gun hand, but their arms were tangled, crisscrossed. Fulton was left handed, while John used his right.

He's got Whittman's body, that's how Dozer tracked him.

John struggled with the awkwardness of their position, as did his opponent. He looked into Fulton's eyes. They were dark, ugly. And yet his own eyes told him he was fighting Whittman, not Fulton.

Dozer leaped into the room and began barking at them. The K-9 had been trained to use his powerful jaws to take a gunman down, but both men were already on the ground.

Dozer took hold of the arm holding the closest gun. John felt Dozer's teeth close like a vise. His tweed jacket provided some protection, but it wouldn't last long.

Gotta get rid of my gun.

Dozer was using leverage to take John's arm down. John summoned all his strength and flung the Glock behind him. It traveled about two feet.

Now there's only one gun to go.

Preoccupied with Dozer, John had allowed Fulton to gain an advantage. The tip of Fulton's gun was now pointed down, and only inches from John's chest. John had watched Ford train Dozer. There were specific commands for everything, and John wanted Dozer to take Fulton's gun arm. But the command eluded him. There was only one word he could think of.

Dozer—ATTACK!

Dozer recognized John's voice. He obeyed the command, letting go of John's arm and attacking the arm with the remaining gun. Fulton wore a short-sleeved shirt. Without any barrier between his arm and Dozer's teeth, the dog drew blood immediately.

John's euphoria turned to fear as he realized that by taking Fulton's gun arm, Dozer had wrenched it directly over his shoulder. The further he drove it down, the closer it came to his chest. Fulton smiled, and for the first time, John thought he looked like anyone but Whittman.

"I always liked you, Detective—it's a shame you have to die."

There was a muffled noise, and suddenly all the weight was lifted off John's body. Braxton jumped on top of the man he had just kicked squarely in the jaw. He landed two punches before realizing Fulton lay unconscious. Amazingly, Dozer still had Fulton's arm in his mouth.

"Dozer—COME!"

John rolled to his side and watched Dozer go to Ford, who crouched in the bathroom doorway.

"Good boy, Dozer, good boy!"

Ford ran his fingers through the fur around Dozer's neck and scratched him vigorously, but he only used one hand. He'd been shot in the shoulder. John slumped to the floor and closed his eyes.

"I've never been so glad to see anyone in my life, Brax."

"You didn't think I was gonna let an ol' fart do the work of a *real police detective,* did you?"

Eyes still closed, and with a broad smile, John replied, "No, I suppose not, Kid."

Braxton retrieved the guns on the floor while John got to his feet. Braxton looked at the unconscious man on the floor and moved to his far side. Braxton's hand was slick with blood. It took about three seconds for his grip on the Glock to change position, and his finger to slide into place along the trigger. Braxton's legs were shaking almost as much as his arm as he raised the gun and pointed it to Fulton's head.

"Brax!" John said, "What are you doing?"

"I'm trying to decide whether prison is worth avenging Anne's murder. No, let me correct that statement—her *rape* and murder."

"Brax… don't! That would bring you down to his level. You're far too good for that."

"Am I, John? I've already killed this bastard fifty times in my head. I've beaten him, broken his bones, and even castrated the son-of-a-bitch. Am I still far too good for this?"

"But that was in your head, Brax. Any man can have those thoughts. How could you avoid them? But acting on them is different. It's certainly not you. You're the best detective I know, Braxton. I shudder to think how good you'll be some day—but not if you do this."

The burning sensation in Braxton's hand broke his concentration. He looked up and saw the woman in the robe. Fear filled her face. Braxton was still shaking. It made it difficult to holster his gun.

"I'm very sorry, Ma'am. This man is a killer. He raped and murdered my fiancé. I apologize for the invasion of privacy."

John added, "I know it sounds crazy, but this man can take any human's shape. I thought you were him in the shower."

The woman nodded her head in acknowledgement, but her eyes said John's story was a little hard to swallow.

John spotted a phone on the nightstand near her bed. He pointed to it, and spoke softly, "Ma'am, I'd like you to use that phone to call 911. Tell them Detective Dietrich says to send several squad cars and an ambulance." She nodded and went to the phone. She kept her eye on all four men as she dialed for help. John turned to Ford.

"Are you okay, Nick?"

"Yeah, I'm fine, John. Funny thing, I can hardly feel the gunshot, but my head is killing me. Fulton slammed me hard against a tile wall. I hit my head and was woozy for a while."

John looked at Braxton's hand and asked, "What about you, Kid? Is that Fulton's blood or yours?"

"A little of both, I think. I caught his teeth on my knuckles. Don't know why, but it burns like hell."

"Why don't you go wash your hands Mr. 'real police detective,' then you can pat this guy down for me."

"Good idea," Braxton said, handing John his gun. "Jesus, it burns."

Braxton rinsed his hands in the bathroom sink while John stood over Fulton.

He's out like a light. I can't believe it; this fucking nightmare is finally over.

John stood over the body, staring at the man who looked like Whittman, sleeping.

"You have no idea how close you came to making us buy these nice people new carpet."

It was so strange looking at the image of the man he saw die only minutes ago.

I promised Zach he'd be okay. Didn't exactly keep that promise, did I? How many people has Fulton killed? John was too exhausted to figure it out.

Braxton reappeared wiping his hands on his pants. His bleeding knuckles left red stripes on his khakis. Then he knelt down beside Fulton and began patting him down. He gave John a sideways look and a grin.

"Ol' fart!"

"Dumb kid!"

Ford walked toward Fulton and looked down at him.

"What this guy does, should be impossible. How does he do it?"

"Careful, Nick—John'll give you an hour-long answer, if you don't watch it."

"I'll save that for the pub, and the well deserved beer I'm gonna buy the two of you."

"The beer?" Braxton asked. "We catch the most elusive criminal in history, and you're gonna buy us a beer?"

John took in a deep breath. His leg was shaking slightly too. He smoothed his slacks with his hands and exhaled.

"All right, how about a steak dinner and all the beer you can drink?"

"As long as I can bring Dozer," Ford said coolly.

"Not only can you bring him," John said, "we'll make him the guest of honor."

Braxton gave John a look of admiration, "Bringing Dozer was brilliant, John. We couldn't have done this without him."

"Yeah," John said, smiling, "Nick has only one more trick to teach him—"

"What's that?" Ford asked.

"—never to bite the arm of a police officer."

The tension in the room was melting. The joking remarks and quips helped them feel a sense of normalcy again.

"C'mon Brax, we'd better get some cuffs on Fulton, before he wakes up."

"Let's do it, old man."

They rolled Fulton on his side and brought his hands behind him. Dozer watched like a curious pup. Braxton got the first handcuff on and brought the other hand close enough for the second cuff. Dozer sniffed Fulton's hands and licked one repeatedly. Before Braxton could shoo him away, he was jolted with fear. Things were shifting. Fulton's body was shifting! Braxton let go of him. His eyes grew as big as half dollars, and he scuffled back several feet.

"Something's wrong!" Braxton yelled. "He's collapsing!" Dozer showed his teeth and growled. All eyes were on Fulton, and within seconds, a new tension filled the room.

"Oh my God!"

John heard a female voice, it was the woman from the shower, but he didn't look at her. He couldn't take his eyes off Fulton. The entire room was staring at a perfect clone of Dozer. He was half buried in Whittman's clothes. The dog's eyes were open, but he didn't move. He just looked ahead in a daze.

"Jesus Christ," John said in amazement, "we've lost our suspect."

There was a long moment of silence. Braxton got to his feet like he felt safer to be off the floor.

"Can we change him back?" Braxton asked.

"I don't know," John replied, "but if we can't, I guess we'll be sending him to the pound instead of prison."

Braxton caught John's eye. "Maybe it'll be less paperwork," Braxton added.

Ford walked to the canine and knelt over its body. He ran his hand up and down its side, and then scratched the dog behind his ears.

"It's incredible," Ford said. "The things I have seen today are impossible."

Braxton smirked, "I know I shouldn't find any humor in this…"

John returned the smile, "I know, Kid, I know."

44

THE COURTROOM WAS WIRED WITH EIGHT CAMERAS.
Three of them belonged to the Kansas City Police Department. John
and Braxton paused at the courtroom doors, on their way to meet
with Brooke Hershel and her legal team.

"That's the one, right there." John pointed to the largest of the
cameras. "It's a high speed camera, like the one National Geographic
uses to film nature specials. Its takes so many frames per second
that when the film is played back at normal speed, the wings of a
hummingbird appear to move in slow motion."

"Can't think of a better application for it than this," Braxton said.

"Yeah, the mayor even hired a production company to film it. They
aren't taking any chances."

Braxton took a few steps forward, and craned his neck to see the
sides of the room. People were jammed into every alcove. He turned
to John.

"I thought the general public wasn't allowed at this hearing."

"They aren't."

Braxton furrowed his eyebrows, "Then who the hell are all these people?"

"Lawyers—half the damn lawyers in town, from the looks of it. Hershel warned me the word would get out, but I never thought it would be this bad." Braxton still looked puzzled.

"Think about it, Brax; they're here to witness a case that could change the course of criminal forensics forever. Nothing's going to be the same. How can we get a solid conviction on someone if there's a chance the DNA was manufactured and planted? How do we know who committed a crime, even in cases where there was an eyewitness? We had lots of eyewitnesses, but in every case, Fulton was the guilty party—not the person accused of the crime."

"Jesus, John, we won't be able to arrest anyone unless we catch him in the middle of the act. Once he's out of sight, he can claim it was someone else."

"It sure seems that way partner, but I think that might be a few years off. I think we still have time to come up with new ways to identify criminals—I hope. C'mon, we're due in conference room C."

Braxton trailed John into a large conference room bustling with activity. The talking and clatter was almost deafening. Brook Hershel spotted John from across the room and waved him over. John zigzagged through the masses, nodding and shaking hands with acquaintances, a few of whom were defendants in the five-pack of crimes. Plastic crates of depositions and courtroom documents were stacked by the wall where Hershel stood.

"Morning, Brooke. I thought you were going to avoid the circus atmosphere."

Hershel pursed her lips, "We did our best, John, but in order to prepare for this in three days, we had to let a lot of people in on our secret. Are you ready?"

"As ready as I'll ever be."

"Good. Let's move over to the corner, I need to brief you on a few issues."

Braxton was left alone, but only for a minute. As he stood there rubbing his bandaged knuckles, forensics officer, Greg Jaworski approached. Jaworski looked as though he were irritated by the size of the crowd. He slipped into the spot John vacated.

"Hey, Brax, can you believe this mess?"

"After last week, I'd believe that pigs can fly. You here to testify?"

"Yeah, today I'm one of the DNA experts," Jaworski said. "But tomorrow I'll be back to head gopher."

Braxton restrained his smile. "Is someone having a pity party?"

Jaworski's face relaxed and the lines between his eyebrows disappeared. "Aww, there's some 'high brow' DNA expert who's scheduled to testify today. He won't be on the stand half as long as me, but he'll make twenty times more money. Does that seem fair?"

"Maybe not fair," Braxton replied, "but that's life. The better known you are, the more money you make."

"I hear John is scheduled to testify four times. Does that mean he gets four fees?"

"It doesn't work that way, Greg, but you know John—the man loves to talk. I'm surprised he's not paying the court to tell his story."

Jaworski laughed. "Miss Hershel claims there shouldn't be any cross-examinations. She says this hearing will be over in three hours."

Braxton's expression was half grin, half frown, "You believe her?"

"Normally, I'd say its pretty wishful thinking," Jaworski admitted, "but this is a hearing, not a trial. Apparently, Miss Hershel worked it out so the prosecutor won't intervene until all the witnesses have been questioned. She says he'll never get the chance to recall a witness because the evidence will be overwhelming."

Braxton knew what Jaworski was hinting at. Everyone was counting on Hershel being right. Although John had told Braxton it was unlikely that the prosecutor would actually sit quietly through three hours of testimony, he did agree to it. All it took was a little prodding from Judge Palmer.

Braxton shrugged and said, "Well, three hours isn't much time, Greg, but even if it takes twice that long, it'll be well worth it."

Jaworski smiled, "It doesn't hurt that Miss Hershel had everything scripted. I know every question she'll be asking, and the answer to each. If everything goes as planned, we'll be out of here by lunch time."

"When did you begin to think that the cases in your 'five-pack of crimes' were related, Detective?" Brooke Hershel asked John the question in a tone of voice that made her sound sincere, as if she really wanted to know. John had been on the stand for ten minutes. In her opening statement Hershel had already laid out a strong foundation for the testimony that would follow. She declared that all five of her clients were framed for crimes they did not commit, and that during John's investigation, five more people were murdered, including one of the defendants, Zachary Whittman. Hershel went on to state that she could prove there was only one man responsible for it all. John had already given an overview of the alleged crimes. Now he was answering the questions Hershel fired at him, one at a time. Hershel held a legal pad. She also wore the oversized glasses that gave her an added air of intelligence and sophistication. Her questions were succinct and orderly, and John had no difficulty following her lead. John looked out at hundreds of faces as he answered the current question.

"Even before the fifth crime had been committed," John said, "I knew something was terribly wrong. They had all occurred within a short time frame, and they all had the same MO."

"But each crime was different, Detective Dietrich. What do you mean by 'the same MO'?"

John leaned forward, his voice crystal clear. "As much as there were eyewitnesses that saw the crimes occur, there were also eyewitnesses who could vouch for the whereabouts of each of the defendants at the time of the crimes. In many instances, the defendant's eyewitnesses were more credible, but I also had to factor in the evidence. There were fingerprints, DNA smudges, and videos involved in most of the crimes, but it was 'easy evidence.' We're convinced that it was intentionally left for us to find. In the case of robbery at Boatman's Bank, our kinesics expert concluded that Zach Whittman's look-alike intentionally swiped his bloody cuff on the teller counter. What kind of criminal goes through so much trouble to get caught, and then denies the crime?"

Hershel's face was stoic. She looked in the direction of the State Prosecutor, Charles Drummond. He was grinning as if to say, *You don't have a chance in hell.*

Hershel continued, "Tell me about the evidence involved in Stuart Grady's case."

John could swear that his perfect recall and clarity came from the confidence he felt looking into Hershel's hazel eyes. This woman led him precisely where she wanted him to go. She knew exactly what to do, and conveyed it in her questions.

"Stewart Grady is accused of raping a young woman. We arrested him just hours after the crime, and yet there was no DNA evidence on him. She had his semen in her, but there was no residue from either of them on him. The young woman had been beaten, supposedly with his fists, and she claims she drew blood when she scratched him. We did find traces of Grady's blood under her fingernails, but there were no claw marks on him, no abrasions on his fists. With all the evidence we have against Mr. Grady, we have an equal amount proving he has never as much as shaken this young woman's hand. By the time the fifth crime occurred, I knew for sure these cases were connected somehow."

"How did you know this, Detective?"

"To begin with, Stuart Grady, Zach Whittman, and Mayor Chase are all on the board of directors at CSGR—that's short for Critical Strategies Genetics Research. It's a mouthful. You can understand why we use the acronym."

"You mentioned Mayor Chase. Was he kept informed on your progress?" John looked at the obese figure in the second row to his right. The mayor was squirming in his chair.

"Yes, and thank God for him," John said. "The mayor gave me the first clue that a common thread existed. I thought the odds were far too great that he would know two of the five people involved in these cases. So I decided the link must have something to do with CSGR, and if so, the mayor might be a target as well. The mayor humored me when I requested that he wear a GPS ankle bracelet. The same kind convicts wear when on house arrest."

Hershel's jaw was set, but her eyes were smiling, "What happened next?"

"Someone impersonated the mayor at a Red Robin restaurant. The man molested a waitress in plain view of the customers."

"When you say 'impersonated,' do you mean this man looked like Mayor Chase?"

"Yes, several witnesses still insist it was the mayor."

"Then how can you be certain it wasn't him?"

"The GPS Company was contacted immediately following the incident. They obtained the mayor's coordinates for the evening. The following day we had the device certified, and not only was it working perfectly, but it hadn't been removed or tampered with. I also had them do something unusual, Miss Hershel. When they installed the bracelet, I had them fingerprint the mayor. We both kept a copy. He was fingerprinted again when they returned to certify the device. We matched his fingerprints at the Red Robin, but the mayor never set foot in there that night."

"Thank you Detective Dietrich, that will be all for now."

Before John reached his chair, Hershel had already called the first of the four remaining defendants. She spent about five minutes with each, having coached them prior about answering her questions without giving additional information. The final question she asked each of them was whether they knew a man named Richard Fulton. They simply answered yes, with no elaboration on the matter. Then she called the witnesses for the defendants, who gave convincing alibis as to where they were during the times in question.

Captain Walsh was on the stand for ten minutes. He testified to John Dietrich's experience and qualifications. He said that John was the finest detective in the city, and that he had watched Dietrich unravel these cases from the beginning. He admitted that at times he didn't like the direction John was going with his theories and that the implications were just too unbelievable to accept as true.

"What theory was so unbelievable, Captain Walsh?"

Walsh hesitated. John wondered if Hershel had instructed him to do so for effect.

"That a man could change his DNA blueprint at will."

There were murmurs from the spectators. Judge Palme brought his gavel down and ordered silence.

"What does that mean, 'that a man could change his DNA blueprint at will,' Captain Walsh?"

"It means that he could change his physical form from his own to someone else's. It means that every hair on his head, every freckle on his body, and every fingerprint would match the host person's." There were more murmurs in the courtroom.

"Yes, I can see why you would find such a theory difficult to believe, Captain Walsh. But as you've said, you've watched this case unfold, and you've seen all the evidence. Do you believe there is such a man? Someone who is responsible for all of these crimes?"

"I do."

"And what is this person's name, Captain Walsh?"

"Dr. Richard Fulton."

Hershel made a long stride toward the stenographer. "Let the record show that Dr. Fulton was an employee of CSGR and that all of the defendants have admitted to knowing him.

Hershel called Dr. Dino Patell. He was a well-known research specialist in the field of genetic engineering. Hershel asked him to read two paragraphs from a recent press release from the Salk Institute. With a thick Indian accent, Patel read the excerpt. When he was finished, Hershel asked, "Dr. Patell, do chickens have the ability to regenerate missing limbs?"

"No, they do not."

"And yet, this press release from the Salk Institute claims they cut of the wing off a chicken and it grew back. Do you believe this?"

"Yes, I do."

"But you just told me they do not have this ability—please explain."

"Not on their own, no, but this experiment was done under controlled conditions using a chicken's embryo. The Salk Institute found the exact gene responsible for enabling the embryo to regenerate its wing. They further proved its existence by disabling this gene in a salamander, so it could not regenerate a leg."

"The press release indicated that regeneration may be possible in humans. Do you believe this?"

"Absolutely, we will see limb and even organ regeneration in our lifetimes."

"What about changing a human's DNA from one genetic blueprint to another? Is this possible?"

"I have never seen this, but I cannot discount the possibility of it happening. In the last five years, I have seen many impossible things happen."

The prosecutor was squirming in his chair. John noticed him shaking his head, but so far, he was quiet.

CSGR's VP of Research, Jim Saunders, was the next witness. He testified that he had known Richard Fulton for eight years and that he was a hard-working researcher in the area of genetics. He said it was common knowledge among the employees that Fulton had lost his right arm in a car accident the night of his high school graduation.

"But other than that, no one knew much about him," Saunders said. "I think the accident kind of crippled him socially, too. He pretty much kept to himself. But he was brilliant, and by that I mean he was intellectually gifted. He was researching regeneration, but I had no idea how close he was to making a discovery. I guess there were clues, but Richard didn't report to me. I just supplied him with chemicals and test equipment when he needed them."

"Mr. Saunders, did you know a man named Wendell Peters?"

"Yes, Wendell was our janitor. He was murdered last week."

"About four weeks ago, Dr. Fulton stopped coming to work, is that correct?"

"Yes."

"But he kept in touch with you. Did he tell you why he couldn't come to work?"

"Yes, he said he had walking pneumonia and that he might be out for a few weeks."

"And a few days later, you had a conversation with Wendell Peters. Can you tell me about that conversation?"

"Well, Wendell told me that Richard came running out of his lab one night. Said he held up two hands."

"But you just told me that Dr. Fulton only had one arm—one hand."

"That's right, but what I didn't know was that the formula Richard was working on was to regenerate his own arm. Apparently, the experiment worked."

"Before his death, Zach Whittman suspected that something went wrong with Dr. Fulton's experiment. What did he think went wrong?" the attorney asked.

"The formula was ingested into Fulton's lungs. We suspect the catalyst didn't metabolize the formula fast enough for all the bio-switches to set properly."

"Can you tell us what bio-switches are, Mr. Saunders?"

"Yes. They are similar to the gene the Salk Institute isolated in the chicken embryo. They can be turned on and off. Richard discovered an entirely new sub-layer of DNA that contains hundreds of bio-switches. While Richard did grow a new arm, whenever it came in contact with another source of DNA, he took the hosts blueprint."

"In layman's terms, Mr. Saunders?"

"Dr. Fulton involuntarily changed into anyone whose DNA he came into contact with."

No one could hear Hershel dismiss Jim Saunders over the uproar.

John nudged Braxton, "All this circus needs now is a trapeze act."

"Well, you've got to admit, John, this was pretty hard for us to grasp—just think about how hard this must be for these attorneys."

John laughed so hard, tears formed in the corners of his eyes. Judge Palmer was calm as he banged his gavel repeatedly. It was as though he understood that no audience could hear such testimony without reacting that way. John stole another look at the prosecutor, Charles Drummond. He was laughing out loud, and the shaking of his head had grown exaggerated. It sobered John from his own laughter. It took nearly a minute for the chatter to subside.

"This is not a circus," the judge reminded the courtroom. John looked at Braxton and bit his cheek.

Palmer continued. "If you can't constrain yourselves, I'll be forced to clear the courtroom. Is that understood?" Silence ensued.

"You may continue, Miss Hershel."

Mayor Chase took the stand, squeezing his large frame into the witness seat. Hershel asked him only one question.

"Where were you on the night Helzberg Diamonds was robbed?"

"I was at home with my family," Chase replied, "and Reverend Pritchard joined us for dinner."

"Well, there went a complete side of beef," Braxton whispered. Reverend Pritchard was even bigger than the mayor. John turned red and bit hard.

My poor cheek is never gonna heal, John thought.

Hershel called on John again. He flashed Braxton a grin from the stand and thought it best to avoid looking at him completely. The two men had been joking with each other like high school kids for three days. After what they had been through, it was good therapy. John was still under oath, and Hershel wasted no time getting back to business.

"Detective Dietrich, I hold here a police report in which Mayor Chase is named a suspect in the jewelry robbery at Helzberg Diamonds. What can you tell me about this?"

"My partner, Braxton Willis, and I were keeping a watch on Dr. Fulton's home that night. We watched him back out of the driveway and followed his car to the Plaza. When Fulton got out of the car, Detective Willis and I were shocked."

"And why was that, Detective."

"The man didn't look anything like Fulton. In fact, he looked exactly like Mayor Chase."

"Again, I need to ask, Detective, how do you know it wasn't the mayor?"

"At the time, we didn't, which is why I insisted on speaking with him. The three of us took the garage elevator to the street level. I asked him some questions about his reelection campaign in the elevator. He gave me vague answers and did his best to avoid speaking completely. The real mayor knows me, but this man had no clue as to who I was. I'm certain he had never seen me before that night. The next day we got statements from the mayor's family and Reverend Pritchard, and we confirmed the GPS data which again verified that he was at home during the Helzberg robbery."

"And the man who looked like the mayor, who do you think it was?"

"It was Dr. Fulton. We followed him through the crowded streets of the Plaza, but lost him right in front of Helzberg Diamonds. Of course, we didn't know he had gone into the store until later, but the jewelry salesman said that the last thing the mayor told him was not to leave the restroom for ten minutes. He also claimed that the mayor's final words didn't sound like the mayor at all—that his voice had changed. I believe that Dr. Fulton had already assumed another identity before heading back outside."

"And the jewelry salesman—did he see him change?"

"No, he was in a bathroom stall with his hands against the wall. Detective Willis and I couldn't find any sign of Fulton outside, so we began searching the stores for him. Detective Willis had gone into Helzberg's to look around. He saw a mid-twenties man leaving with a black and turquoise duffel bag, just like the one the mayor's impostor carried. By the time Detective Willis made the connection, the man had disappeared into the crowd. Detective Willis decided to go to Dr. Fulton's car and wait for him. When Fulton got back to the parking garage, he took Detective Willis by surprise. He struck him repeatedly with the butt of his gun. Detective Willis was critically wounded and Dr. Fulton stole his identity. Later that evening, Fulton raped and killed Detective Willis's fiancée."

The courtroom was still.

They either believe me, or think I'm nuts, John thought.

The Vice President of the GPS company testified as to the validity of the reports involving the mayor's whereabouts, and the accuracy of the data.

When Hershel called the kinesics expert, Mary Simon, to the stand, Simon repeated the same rehearsed definition of the science of body language that she had given to John, Braxton, and Whittman when they met. John could tell that she made the same profound impression on the courtroom that she had made on him. He noticed Judge Palmer nodding in agreement several times. She then described the two very different videos of Whittman and Fulton at the bank. It was Simon's expert opinion that these were two completely different people and that Fulton lingered at the bank in order to provide as much video evidence as possible. The bloody smudge from his cuff, she insisted, was left intentionally.

Forensic expert Greg Jaworski's testimony was perhaps the most interesting of all. He had accumulated and logged all of the evidence to date. He described the labeled jars of urine confiscated from Fulton's home. There were clothes and shoes in sizes to fit each of the defendants, and Mayor Chase as well. Jaworski found the black and turquoise bag which still held the jewelry from Helzberg's Diamonds and a latex glove in Justin Moody's car the morning he was killed.

Jaworski explained the pattern of left-hand only fingerprints at all the crime scenes and presented a photograph captured from the bank videos of Whittman's look-alike wearing a latex glove on his right hand. The semen in Anne Duffy's body belonged to Detective Willis, but her rape and death had occurred while he was unconscious in the hospital. The evidence all pointed to an impostor, but there were still no witnesses that could identify Fulton from his photograph at even one of the crime scenes.

On John's third trip to the stand, he was asked to describe the day's events that finally led to Fulton's capture. John began with the abduction of Susan, Mike Walsh's secretary, and the bogus phone call that was responsible for allowing Fulton access to Walsh's office, presumably to retrieve a recording device.

The next topic was the kidnapping of John's daughter, Sarah. It was at the storage facility that Fulton admitted that he could use another person's DNA to change his own veneer. John described what it was like to look at Fulton as an exact clone of himself. He said he couldn't find even one physical difference in the two of them, but that their movements and expressions were completely dissimilar.

John went on to give the details of his escape, and Fulton's later appearances as Officer Ford and Officer Granewski at Whittman's home. The final scenes that John described were of his scuffle with Fulton, and his metamorphosis from Whittman's likeness to Dozer's four-legged body. Kristine Hoffman, the woman from the shower witnessed that transformation as well, and John read her deposition testifying to it.

Hershel requested a fifteen-minute break in which John and Braxton used the bathroom, and then hit the hallway in search of a coffee machine. So did half the courtroom. The detectives settled into about twenty-fifth place in line.

"We'll never get to that coffee, Brax."

"You're right, John. Hey—wasn't there a coffee pot in the conference room?"

"I don't recall, Kid, but our chances are a helluva lot better there than out here." No sooner had they stepped out of the line, than John's eyes were assaulted by the unexpected sight of Detective Connors.

"How's it going in there, Dietrich?" John thought that Connors's voice was too cordial. There wasn't enough hate in it.

"Going pretty much as planned, Tom, we're almost finished."

"I heard a rumor." Connors glared at John like he expected him to fill in the blanks for him. John had a pretty good idea of which blanks he was looking for.

"Lot's of 'em flying around this morning. Are you planning to stick around for the grand finale? You'll have a tight squeeze if you can get in. Half the lawyers in town are in that courtroom." Connors knew John wasn't going to answer his question. He switched modes.

"Well, either you're gonna hang this Fulton creep, or you're gonna make a fool of yourself. Either way, I'm happy." John looked into Connors's eyes and felt a tinge of pity for him. John knew Connors's new partner, Roger Madsen, and from what he'd heard, the relationship was antagonistic. Madsen hated Connors and took every opportunity to make him look foolish. Connors had been reduced in stature by orders of magnitude. There was no one who looked up to him anymore. No one to sing his praises. John figured Connors would either put in for a transfer or quit the force.

"Well, I don't plan to make a fool of myself, Tom. Guess that leaves hanging this Fulton creep."

"Well, don't blow it, Dietrich. Justin deserves to see this guy behind bars." John didn't acknowledge Connors, but stepped around him.

"Excuse me, Tom. Braxton and I have some important business to tend to." John and Braxton walked in the direction of the conference room.

"What do you suppose that was all about, John?"

"Dunno, a last ditch effort for Tom to feel like his old self again, I suppose—who knows."

In the conference room, Braxton poured the dregs of the coffee pot into two Styrofoam cups.

"Here, it may not taste great, but it'll be good and crunchy."

"No gripes here," John said.

Braxton took a sip of coffee and then stared inside the cup, frowning. "I never said thanks, John."

"Thanks? Thanks for what?"

"For stopping me—when we caught Fulton."

"That's ridiculous, Kid. You weren't going to do anything."

Braxton shook his head, "I wanted to kill him. If you hadn't been there, I might have pulled the trigger."

"You know, Brax, I've given this a lot of thought over the weekend. I do think you wanted to kill him, but you looked for every excuse not to go through with it. I didn't stop you—you stopped yourself."

"Guess I'll never really know, will I?"

"Maybe you'll have a doubt or two in your life, Kid, but not me. You're a good detective, and a great partner. I'd trust you with my life."

Braxton's eyes welled a little, but no tears ran down his face. He changed the subject.

"The experiment, do you think it'll work?"

"I don't know. I give it a fifty-fifty chance."

"But it's always worked before."

"I know, but things are completely different now. We'll know in a little while."

"What about Saunders? Do you think we'll get him?"

"Yeah," John said with a sigh, "Saunders is going away for a long time."

John looked at his watch.

"C'mon, Kid, let's go finish this."

45

JUDGE PALMER APPEARED FROM BEHIND THE BENCH and climbed to his chair overlooking the courtroom. Brooke Hershel entered the courtroom from a side door. The judge sounded the gavel, and the instant silence seemed unnatural. The bailiff announced that the court was now in session.

"Miss Hershel," Judge Palmer asked, "are you ready to continue with the case?"

"Yes, I am, Your Honor."

"You may proceed."

"I'd like to recall Detective John Dietrich to the stand." The judge nodded, "I'll allow it, Miss Hershel." John turned to make a comment to Braxton, but froze when he saw him rubbing his bandaged hand. John wasn't certain, but it seemed as if he were still in pain.

Does it still burn?

Braxton's eyes met John's, and he stopped abruptly. John walked to the witness stand, gathering his thoughts for the upcoming questions. Hershel put her glasses back on. She looked at John and gave him an outright smile that said the day had gone well. John gave her a single nod.

"Detective Dietrich, you obtained a search warrant this weekend, didn't you?"

"Yes," John said, "after Zach Whittman's death Friday night, we had many questions that could only be answered by searching his records. We had planned to question Mr. Whittman within the next few weeks, but his death and the capture of Dr. Fulton changed our timing."

"I object!"

John looked in the direction of the voice. He saw the prosecutor, Charles Drummond, standing with his fists clenched. His cheeks were red and his eyes were round. He pointed at John and began to rant.

"Detective Dietrich is claiming to have captured Richard Fulton. From what I was told, they arrested a German Shepherd. I cannot allow him to tell the courtroom this cockamamie story. It's ridiculous!"

Judge Palmer didn't look at all surprised. His voice was calm when he addressed the prosecutor. "Mr. Drummond, would you approach the bench, please?"

Drummond took a few long strides and reached the bench with his fists still clenched. John was smiling as though he were amused.

Judge Palmer crouched down so his head was closer to Drummond's. John could hear the whispering that the rest of the courtroom could not.

"We had an agreement, Charlie."

"I know Judge, Drummond replied, trying to stifle his voice, but this is ridiculous, and you know it!"

"I know no such thing. What I do know is that this hearing has been very carefully planned, and you are either going to win or lose this case based on what we see in the next hour or so, and you don't have much to say about it. Now go sit down and hold your tongue."

Drummond lowered his head, and realizing what he was doing jerked it up high again.

"I'll hold my tongue, Judge, but I hope we don't come out of this looking stupid."

Drummond returned to his chair, and Judge Palmer nodded at Hershel.

"You may proceed."

Hershel didn't miss a beat. She picked right up where she had left off.

"Detective Dietrich, you were saying that your timing had changed?"

"Yes. We couldn't take a chance that something would happen to Mr. Whittman's computer, and the evidence we needed. So we got a search warrant and spent the weekend pouring through his files and personal computer."

"What kinds of questions did you have for Zach Whittman?" Hershel asked.

"I wanted to know why it was so important for him to drive his stock prices up. I wanted to know the name of the company that agreed to buy him out if he could prove Fulton's regeneration formula worked. Up until now, I was pretty certain that Richard Fulton was just a pawn in a scheme to raise CSGR's stock value. But now that we've examined the documents from Mr. Whittman's computer, I'm sure of it. I believe that Dr. Fulton was goaded into using his formula because of the deceptive tactics of Zach Whittman and Jim Saunders."

John had his eye on Saunders as he finished his sentence. Saunders stiffened.

"You can't be serious!" Saunders said in a cynical English accent.

"You will have your chance to address the court, Mr. Saunders," Judge Palmer said sternly, "until then; I suggest you wait until I give you permission to speak." Saunders leaned back in his chair, doing his best to look offended at the accusation John had just leveled against him.

"You say you found several documents, Detective—tell us what you found."

"For starters, Miss Hershel, CSGR was in deep financial trouble. Not the kind of trouble that would put them out of business in a year, or even two, but without question, the company could not have survived for three years."

"Why is that, Detective?"

"Well, it takes eleven to twelve years to take a drug from concept to market. During that time, it's all costs and no profits. Once a drug is available on the market, its prices are usually steep enough to help the pharmaceutical company recover their investment in a relatively short period of time. Well, CSGR had two drugs that went bust after ten years in development. They were completely scrapped because of dangerous side effects. The company laid out a tremendous amount of cash to get them approved by the FDA, but for these two drugs there will never be a payback. Few companies the size of CSGR could take that kind of financial hit and survive. Whittman desperately needed Fulton's discovery, but he didn't have the resources to fund another five to six years of testing. They needed to raise capital by either selling stock, or selling the formula itself."

"How does Mr. Saunders fit into the picture?"

"Jim Saunders is from England. He originally worked for a U.K.-based bio-tech company that CSGR bought out three years ago. It turns out that he was brokering the sale of stock to a competing U.K. company. We found a letter from Jim Saunders to this company claiming that CSGR had discovered the secret to regenerating organs and limbs, and that they needed a partner to complete their research. The company responded with a commitment to make a sizable stock purchase, if CSGR could provide concrete evidence that Dr. Fulton's formula worked."

"Saunders flew the buyers in posing as CSGR employees from the office in England. Whittman and Saunders got Fulton talking about his formula, which wasn't too difficult seeing it was his life's passion. They saw the results of the tests on lab mice, and they got to see for themselves that Fulton had only one arm. Now all they had to do was to come back and revisit Fulton after the experiment. If he was able to grow a new arm, they'd have a deal."

"And you can prove this, Detective Dietrich."

"Oh yes, we have more than enough documentation to prove this and more."

"Such as?"

"I have the memo Whittman sent Dr. Fulton claiming that he needed to cancel the regeneration project because of Dr. Fulton's discovery of a second layer in DNA. He said that until they understood it, his research would have to wait. Fulton swore the second layer just contained bio-switch attributes, but nothing dangerous—nothing that should delay the project for even a day. He said that the discovery posed no threats whatsoever.

For years, Whittman allowed Fulton to believe that human testing was much closer than it actually was. I found an old email from Zach Whittman on Fulton's computer. They had clearly agreed that Fulton would be able to try the formula before the end of the year. Whittman knew how badly Fulton wanted his arm, not to mention the fame for making the greatest scientific discovery of our time. When the project was halted, Fulton suspected something else was wrong and made the decision to try the formula, even though it wasn't finalized."

"Mr. Whittman told me that he'd sent someone to pick up the formula in Fulton's lab. I asked him who it was, but he claimed he couldn't remember. I didn't buy that, and decided to see who had access to Fulton's lab. Mr. Whittman's secretary has an elaborate scheme of assigning access keys to employees. Every key is numbered and coded. Other than Dr. Fulton, Jim Saunders and Wendell Peters were the only employees with a key to Fulton's lab and office. Saunders claimed that Fulton didn't work for him, and that he had no idea what he was working on. But the correspondence on his computer says otherwise. He was reporting Dr. Fulton's every move to Zach Whittman. Saunders kept tabs on Dr. Fulton, read his notes, and documented his progress with lab mice. He knew exactly which version of the formula was most likely to work successfully, or at least he thought he did. He left an older version of the formula for Dr. Fulton to try—one that had been stable and successful in regenerating limbs in lab mice."

"But things didn't go the way he planned. Dr. Fulton grew a new arm all right, but whenever that arm came in contact with another person's DNA, he'd turn into their exact clone. It was an involuntary physical response. He couldn't help it, and he resented it. I'm not defending Dr. Fulton. His actions were abhorrent. But the fact is none of this would have happened if it hadn't been for Saunders and Whittman."

Hershel turned to glimpse at the prosecutor, and then at Judge Palmer, "I would like to place the aforementioned documents into evidence, Your Honor."

"You may do so," Palmer said. Hershel waved to the back of the room, and the doors opened wide. Her staff carried six plastic crates of documents into the courtroom. They stacked them to one side of the judge's bench. John glanced across the room at Saunders. He was staring at the floor. John looked to his left. The prosecutor was drumming his fingers on the table. John sat upright and waited to be dismissed.

Hershel walked to the stand. "Thank you for your testimony, Detective Dietrich, you may step down." John returned to his seat, and Hershel signaled a group of engineers standing by the entrance. Then she went to her table and picked up a different legal pad.

John spoke in a low voice, "Whaddaya thinking, Kid?"

"Just thinking about Anne. She was so interested in these cases. I wish she could have been here to see this." John didn't know what to say. He made a fist and tapped Braxton on the arm.

The courtroom had twice the circus atmosphere that it did just a moment ago. All eight cameras were now manned, and technicians were testing microphones. The anticipation of something big was mounting. There was an open area in the middle of the courtroom which was marked with a red "X" taped to the floor. John watched the commotion and felt the familiar tinge of pain in his right cheek. He relaxed his jaw and turned to Braxton.

"This is it, Kid—keep your fingers crossed." Hershel addressed the judge.

"Your Honor, thus far, Dr. Fulton has only been a suspect for the crimes my clients have been charged with, and the murders of five people. I believe the evidence we have compiled is compelling and is more than sufficient to prove my clients' innocence. And yet, we have been unable to produce the guilty party, Dr. Fulton. You have heard testimony stating that Dr. Fulton was transformed from his last host, Zachary Whittman, to the body of a German Shepherd. We are going to try an experiment that may work or fail. We estimate our chances of success at fifty percent. But even if this experiment fails, I will move that all charges against my clients be dropped."

Judge Palmer granted Hershel permission to proceed, and the people in the courtroom were stirring. The rumors they'd heard were true. Hershel motioned to the guards at the courtroom's entrance. They opened the doors and two men wheeled a gurney to the spot marked with an "X" on the floor.

I've never seen such showmanship, John thought. *This woman is amazing.*

The men who wheeled in the gurney wore white lab coats, as if to give them an air of scientific knowledge and authority. There was something on the gurney, something covered with a blanket. The two men went right to work. They removed the blanket to a wave of gasps and murmurs. There on the gurney was the canine John Dietrich had testified was once Dr. Fulton. Attorneys from around the room began to jostle each other for a better view.

Judge Palmer brought the gavel down hard, "The next person who moves without permission will be removed from this courtroom." Again, there was silence. The courtroom cameras began to hum.

Hershel moved to the best vantage point to address the room.

"If you've guessed that this is the dog that was once Dr. Fulton, you are correct," she said precisely. "The police had confiscated several vials of Dr. Fulton's blood from a secure refrigerated locker at CSGR. But it is questionable as to whether we can restore him back to a human form again. He now has the brain, the body, and the central nervous system of a canine. Since his transformation, Dr. Fulton has been in a vegetative state. He has been unable to eat or drink, or even blink his eyes. He has been kept alive with feeding tubes. If the experiment works, it is doubtful that Dr. Fulton will ever be able to think again as a human being. His memories are most likely gone forever."

Hershel removed her glasses. She looked nervous for the first time today.

"Gentlemen, you may proceed." One of the men opened a small kit. Both men slipped latex gloves over their hands. The other man loosened the straps restraining the listless dog to the gurney. The first man picked up a small clear vial. The contents were dark red. He popped the lid off the vial and inserted what looked like a children's watercolor paintbrush. He began to paint the canine's right front foot with blood from the vial. John noticed that the dog's fur had been shaved up to what would have been a human's elbow. The only sound in the courtroom came from the cameras. The high-speed camera made a shrill whine.

The transformation began, first, with a convulsing jerk from the dog's chest and then with a kick from his hind leg. It took nearly two seconds for John to notice how much bigger the dog had become. And then, within the space of another two seconds, everything happened at once. The fur disappeared, hands sprouted, and a human form took shape. A man's legs grew until they extended over the edge of the gurney. John didn't blink as he reached in his pocket and withdrew Fulton's corporate photograph.

"It's him, Brax. It's him!" No amount of banging from Judge Palmer's gavel was going to quiet this crowd. The noise was deafening. There was pushing and shoving. Flashes began to go off from cameras smuggled into the room. The judge waved his hand and nodded. The guards in the front of the courtroom started driving the crowd back. Four more guards came in from the main doors. The witnesses and experts seated in the front two rows turned to watch the courtroom slowly clear. One of the men in white jackets threw the blanket over Fulton's mid-section. John stood and waved at Judge Palmer. The judge motioned John to come forward.

"C'mon, Brax!"

The two men approached the bench, and Judge Palmer leaned over to hear them.

"Sorry about the circus, Your Honor."

"I believe you warned me about this, John. We were ready for it."

"Yes, your men were right on top of it, Judge."

"You know," Judge Palmer said, smiling. "I just saw one of our own attorneys jump over the bar and take a picture. Got himself cracked over the head with a police baton too. He's gonna have a hell of a headache."

Guess there were no ambulances to chase, John thought, but he nodded and smiled. "You never know what gets into people at times like this, Judge."

"Oh, I don't blame 'em," Palmer said. "That display was absolutely amazing."

"Yes it was, Your Honor. Now, if it's okay with you, I'd like to take a quick look at Fulton. I need to know whether he's dangerous, or if he's still in a vegetative state—may I?"

"Can't think of anyone I'd trust more, John, but please be careful. Wouldn't want to ruin my perfect safety record." Judge Palmer rolled his eyes with the comment, and John laughed.

As he and Braxton approached the gurney, the last thirty or so people were literally being pushed out of the courtroom. John could see men and women in the hallway craning their necks to see what was going on. The first thing that John noticed about Fulton was his eyes. They were glossy, emotionless, and still. John stared at them waiting for Fulton to blink. He did not. Nor did they follow John's finger as he moved it to each side of Fulton's face. Next, John blew a puff of air in his eyes. There was not as much as a tick of movement from them.

"Well, I'm convinced," John said. "I've never seen anyone fake that."

Braxton raised his eyebrows and looked at John intently, "Fake what?"

John explained, "Your eyes are too sensitive not to twitch when hit with a sharp puff of air. We'll have the doctors do more tests later, but I don't think we'll be having any conversations with Fulton soon."

Convinced that Fulton was unable to move, John got closer to Fulton's right arm. He scanned it intently, and then moved to his left arm. He was looking for any discernable difference between their physical appearances.

"It's amazing, isn't it Brax?" John said softly. "One arm absorbs DNA, the other doesn't. Yet, there's no telltale sign that one is different from the other."

Braxton didn't respond. He just stared blankly at the man who killed his fiancée.

John looked at the front of the room. Brooke Hershel was watching him by the judge's bench. John addressed one of the men in the lab coats, "Make sure those straps are snug—just in case. C'mon, Brax, let's let Brooke wrap this up, and then we can get out of here." John waved to the judge, and he and Braxton sat down.

Hershel continued, "Your Honor, in lieu of all the evidence, I would ask that the charges against my clients be dropped immediately."

Judge Palmer looked in the direction of Charles Drummond. "Based on what I have seen and heard today, I would say that's a reasonable assumption. Mr. Prosecutor, how does the government respond?"

Drummond had just finished wiping his forehead with a handkerchief. "The State is in full agreement, Your Honor. I move that the charges against the defendants be dropped, and that we detain Mr. Saunders until I can have a warrant issued for his arrest."

Jim Saunders jumped to his feet and his mouth opened, but he didn't say a word. John assumed he was speechless.

"Granted!" Palmer said forcefully. And then Judge Palmer picked up a roster and found the list of defendant names.

"The State hereby drops all charges against the defendants Zachary Whittman, Stuart Grady, David Breeling, Adam Sharp, and Tyler Werthing. This case is dismissed." And with that, Judge Palmer brought the gavel down one last time.

Officers, you will take Mr. Saunders into custody."

Jim Saunders backed away from the court officers as they approached him. He shot a look at Judge Palmer and spoke as though he was terrified. "Judge Palmer. You—you said I would have an opportunity to speak."

"And so you shall, sir. It looks like you are going to have a trial of your very own."

Way to go, Judge, Braxton thought. He gave John a "thumbs up." John smiled.

There were cheers from the row behind John and Braxton. The defendants ran over to thank Brooke Hershel. Braxton looked on with satisfaction, and then he frowned.

"So why is it that the attorneys get all the thanks?" Braxton asked. "All she did was ask the questions. We dug up the evidence, chased down the bad guy, and your testimony was flawless. Where's our thanks?"

John patted Braxton on the back.

"I appreciate you, Brax."

"Very funny, you ol' fart."

"You know," John said, "there isn't a cop in this city that doesn't feel slighted at one time or another, but we're not in this line of work for the glory—are we?"

Braxton's shoulders slumped. His lips thinned as he pressed them together.

"You sound like my mother."

John said, "I'll take that as a compliment." The comment brought a smile to Braxton's face.

"You know that steak dinner, and my promise of all the beer you can drink?"

"Yeah, I'd hardly forget that."

"Well, I talked Hershel into buying. Actually, she offered. So I guess she's grateful for the job we did. I told her Ford and Dozer need to be there, and she agreed." Braxton was still smiling, but he was unconsciously rubbing his bandaged hand.

"How are the knuckles?" John asked. "You've been rubbing them a lot." Braxton held his hand out and opened and closed it twice.

"Oh, they're all right."

"Do they still burn?"

"Naw, they just itch a little. It's the bandage."

"Don't let them get infected, Kid. And keep that bandage clean."

"Okay, Mom. Now, if you don't mind, I'm hungry. Can we go get a burger, or do you need Hershel to buy that too?"

"Sounds good to me. Let me say congrats and goodbye to Brooke." John waited in line to say goodbye to the victorious lawyer. Braxton watched the courtroom empty.

I doubt I'll ever work another case this exciting. Don't know if I want to. What a horrific ride it's been.

Braxton drifted out to the hallway in search of a well-lit window where he unraveled the bandage around his knuckles.

Only a slight change, he thought. Braxton held his fist against the window. There were no cuts, no abrasions, and most unusual, no scabs. The deep gash caused by Fulton's teeth across his knuckles was gone, but then again, it was gone an hour after he punched Fulton Friday night. The troubling change was in his tawny skin. From his fingertips to his wrist, Braxton's hand was white. He wondered about his fingerprints.

Are they still mine? Should I tell John? No, he thought. *I don't want to end up being studied by a bunch of researchers like a lab rat.* Braxton rewrapped his hand up to his wrist, and then rubbed it gently, while he waited for John.

Damn, he thought, *it still burns.*

ABOUT THE AUTHOR

DAN REYNOLDS HAS SPENT MORE THAN THIRTY years in cutting-edge industries including scientific laboratory equipment and computer software. He was born and raised in Omaha, Nebraska, where he currently lives with his wife and children.

www.ingramcontent.com/pod-product-compliance
Lightning Source LLC
Chambersburg PA
CBHW020437270626
47155CB00022B/502